The
Happy
Family
Murders

Special thanks to Leo Tolstoy, who said that *happy families are all alike*.

Special thanks to Mikita Brottman, whose delightful book titled *The Solitary Vice: Against Reading* introduced me to the idea that a *grimoire* must be read backward if you wish to erase its spell.

The Happy Family Murders

Third book in the series titled
Grimoire - the Bros Grim Breakfast Serial - a story in pieces

By Jon Rieley-Goddard

BaldyBooks
Buffalo, New York

Photo of the author by Cathy Rieley-Goddard

Cover photo and all drawings by the author

First Edition December 2013

1 2 3 4 5 6 7 8 9 10

ISBN-10: 0982937857
ISBN-13: 978-0-9829378-5-3

To Tom Oh
-- for his support

To Roger
-- for his encouragement

To Cathy
-- for her love

My Spy Boy and your Spy Boy
 sittin' by the fire,
My Spy Boy told your Spy Boy
 gonna set your house on fire.
  -- traditional song

Prologue

Ma's Day and the return of April Fools
|09May10|

First, a few relatively punless definitions --

Prologue.

1) Expert or favorably disposed tree for milling, such as yew, which has been felled, bucked into eight-foot lengths, and limbed.

2) An expert-level, or professional, blog (qv) var. sp. **prolog**.

3) Worn, if not archaic, sp. for a ref. to front matter such as in a book or novel.

Expert.

1) Former drip under pressure (with thanks to some unknown comic spirit).

Like that. Relatively punless. Here's another.

Grimoire.

1) Poorly constructed furniture imported from Eastern Bloc, found in the bedroom, cf **clothes closet**, **chest of drawers, wardrobe, armoire**.

2) Book of spells meant to be read forward or backward.

3) Series title of books by **Goose Grim** (qv) of which this is the third.

≈ ≈ ≈

Hi, it's me.

Friends call me **OhJim**, Pop called me **OtherJim**, and you can call me when I get back to Buffalonya, which may be a while, and since we left on April Fool's Day, you might just take anything I tell you with a grain of salt or a bag of peanuts.

The bald bobblehead next to me is Jim, who is the less elder of my two brothers (the other, and eldest, being **Goose**).

The two guys in the front seat of this cavernous Crown Vic, heading south?

Later for them, and that.

Jim, Goose, and I share a history and the same father, and his last name, which was **Grim**.

We three call ourselves the **Bros Grim**, and we run an eponymous Private Investigations company, based in the capacious backroom of a dusty, dear used bookshop, **Caspar's Books and That**, in the northern reaches of Our Town, Buffalonya, New York, on the extreme and the eastern edge of Lake Eerie.

Caspar's Books and That (as in **Yeah, we got *that***) exists on several levels. We sell used books, we gather in the backroom to ply our trade, and we maintain cover for a group of over-the-hill ex-spooks who exist on even more levels than our beloved bookshop does.

Am I going too fast for you?

Didn't think so.

≈ ≈ ≈

As my brother Jim and I head south, hunched down in the back of this tank on tires, of a sort that screams ***POLICE DETECTIVE***, I muse on the assignment that we have from the Tribe.

The Tribe.

That would be the collection of ex-spooks, spooks in training, and various hangers-on that forms a quasi-criminal enterprise that operates in Robin Hood fashion at the sufferance of a collection of **Three Letter Agencies**, or TLAs, of more variants and permutations than Mother Goose has tail feathers, or tales, let alone letters.

As the Psalmist says, **You are grass**, and as the Africans say, **When the elephants fight, the grass suffers**, though we have not withered yet, or gotten trampled by the TLAs.

When we gather to do business, as **the Tribe**, we call ourselves the **F-Troop**, which is a quasi-Robert's Rules corporation that has no status, 501(c)(3) or otherwise, but is the figment of imagination of three little boys who were raised by a wonderful post-war refugee from the Eastern Bloc and one-time spook named Missus McFeather (**Ma** to us) whom our Pop hired as housekeeper, reality principle, and all-in female presence for his three motherless little sons. Or as Pop would say, **You three little bastards**.

The story of Pop's three concurrent sex affairs that issued in us, in a matter of days, forms the core of our family identity and makes the celebration of Mother's Day a mockery.

Ma's Day, alternatively, is a yearly jubilation on the 4th of July.

Ma came back into our lives a year ago and has died by violence since that time and been resurrected in the media, having never left our midst, as the prime consequence of a hoax dreamed up and laid down by the Tribe and certain of our three-letter partners.

Said hoax is generally known in Buffalonya as the **Double Daily Double Murders**, which weren't, but this was not general knowledge until we decided to make it so.

In other words, Ma and three others of our Tribe were murdered but only in the media, for reasons strategic to our efforts to protect our way of life, which up until two years ago was hidden in plain sight, in **Caspar's Books and That**, in the frosty northern reaches of Buffalonya, on Delaware at Junker.

More on all that in a moment.

≈ ≈ ≈

The F-Troop had its genesis in a comment that Pop made about my brothers and I when we were little guys. Waving his middle finger in the air, Pop said that **this is the sum total of your collective I.Q., you little bastards**.

Pop was **joking.** We have understood the banana peel aspect of what is loosely called **humor**, from that day. The F-Troop grew out of Pop's one-finger salute.

Pop was, himself, something of an S.O.B., by choice and by nature/nurture. One might **love** Pop, especially if one were his son, but one did not really **like** Pop, any more than one would want to hug a porcupine.

At least the three of us didn't.

Rather than being raised by wolves, S.O.B.s, or foster families, we grew strong and healthy, at least in body, through the work of our dear Ma. The one positive thing that Pop taught us, other than the truth about I.Q. and humor, was to see ourselves as a **tribe** rather than a **family**. I remember the lecture that Pop gave us, when we were still learning how to read, about the tribe mentality of the Apaches, who led one another by example and inclination.

For example, Pop said, **one Apache might say, I am going to raid the fort; anyone who wants can come with me. Or not.**

Pop, as you can see, was not politically correct, nor am I, I suppose, for perpetuating Pop's piggy words and concepts. My brothers and I value political correctness about as much as we value right-wing talk radio.

Or left-wing talk radio.

But I digress … and will continue to do, like a herky-jerky pitcher who throws change-ups inside change-ups until you wind up striking out, gladly.

However, digressive or not, of the three sons who could by right expect to receive the gift, I am the one who received **Pop's watch** after he died.

And boy is that another story.

≈ ≈ ≈

Notice that the two men sitting on the front seat of the Crown Vic are taller than we are, here in the back, and where we barely clear the back of the mouse grey bench seat upon which they sit, at the corners, and where we only show our bald heads out the side windows, which are, I admit, tinted to a degree that flouts the relevant state law, the two giants up front display large heads and wide shoulders out windows with less tint than ours.

As targets go, their heads would be hard to miss.

The upshot is that Jim and I are, in this dim light of late afternoon, probably only dimly visible to those who encounter this regulation unmarked **_COP DETECTIVE_** Crown Vic of a certain age and character.

Driving our tank is Agent Luke Parmgartner, whom you can call **Agent** if it is your misfortune to meet him professionally rather than socially.

Sitting beside Luke, at the far end of the car couch that is the front seat of your elderly Crown Vic, is **Mister Ed** AKA **Mr. Blue**, one of the retired but still trusty spooks from **Caspar's Books and That**.

This writing of mine is starting to sound juvenile in my own ears, which makes me wonder why Goose has passed to me the baton of narration. By the time I am done telling you about our trip to Pittsburgh, and all the adventures that we are sure to have, I will be more than glad to hand back to Goose the baton. I imagine that I will invite him to stick it where the sun don't shine, but we shall see.

After all, we return to Buffalonya with some rather startling facts, and we arrive just ahead of some gruesome developments.

But I digress into the future, which I am prone to do.

Blame it on Pop's watch.

≈ ≈ ≈

Luke looks like a spook, which he is, and he acts like a spook, which he does without strain or effort, and he drives like a crash dummy or a statue such as **The Thinker** would.

Upright, minimalist, competent, lights out/no one home.

Like a cop.

That's our cover, and we are, thanks to Tommy, (about whom **much** more is to come) calling ourselves **Operation Next-of-Kin**, a cross-platform effort of the Tribe and its murky TLA sponsors, who have given us Luke for muscle and Mister Ed for brains. Why Jim and I are along for the ride is anyone's guess.

My mind is a blank.

Maybe we are the **huevos**, but somehow that seems unlikely.

Even though we are a couple of good eggs with shiny heads to match.

Mister Ed, broad of shoulder and loud of voice, is our resident expert on journalistic ops of the covert sort. Thus the nickname that comes from that old television show about the talking horse, with a long-necked nod to Mister Ed's covert time as an **editor** on several metro newspapers that will remain blissfully ignorant of his true nature. Which is why we also call him, once in a while, **Mr. Blue** -- in honor of the non-repo pen with blue ink that no editor feeding info to an offset press would ever be without.

When the Tribe, meeting as the F-Troop, breaks into parliamentary mode, Mister Ed is our parliamentarian. A more gloriously pedantic parliamentarian you are not likely to meet, on either side of the **Great Divide of Life**. In the life to come, Mister

Ed will be parsing the heavenly discourse for the angels when they let down their wings and do their tribal business.

As is the case with any human endeavor, there is a story, and a long one, about why the four of us are aping a contingent of public servants, of the sort who swear to serve and defend, on an official trip in a loudly unmarked Crown Vic with the tiny, shiny hub caps and the understated but always present plaque on the back, just above the bumper, on the right side and over near the tail light, that says, in letters cast in 36 pt. type --

Police Interceptor

What do we infer from this mix of covert intentions and overt trappings?

Disinformation.

The disinformation coming to your eyes, that you are seeing a boatload of police types on a long trip for some official reason, is balanced nicely by the reality that an agent on loan from a TLA, a spook long in the tooth but still capable of recently proven violence, and two bald retired guys in casual clothes are making a big show of traveling to Pittsburgh.

We have specific tasks that flow from that long story that I still have not told you.

≈ ≈ ≈

Two years ago, Jim and I had only just arrived in Buffalonya to reunite with our long-lost brother Goose, who was living with a lovely woman named Eve, who owned a swell used bookshop that she had recently purchased from her friend, mentor, and one-time handler, a white-maned and -bearded veteran of covert wars named **Caspar**. After a while, in the dark, being fed manure by Goose about his past and our future, and having settled on the **Bros Grim, Private Investigations** as an amusing way to spend our time and earn our living, certain events occurred that forced Goose to tell us of his past as a longtime and now-retired spook who had been recruited by Pop.

Big surprise, that. Who knew?

We didn't.

We thought that Goose was a fugitive from fairy tales just like we were.

Turns out, he was a fugitive from ghost stories.

And recruited by Pop?

We thought that Pop was a traveling salesman like Willy Loman, but it turns out that Pop was a lot more like George Smiley.

Our first case was to investigate the death of a man whom Goose, and Eve, assumed was a missing member of the Tribe named **Mr. Black**. After three deaths widely known as the **Mystery Man Murders** and after we dug until we found the dirt that had accumulated in some very public places, such as the Buffalonya Police Department and the Eerie County Coroner's Office, the Tribe detected in the shadows the presence of a serious, semi-focused, and somewhat bumbling enemy who had engineered the **Mystery Man** business to embarrass us and force our quasi-criminal enterprise into the light of community scrutiny.

And that is what happened, as testified to by a three-part series in the **Daily Afterblatt, Lake Effect edition**, by Jane Carlotto, their senior crime writer (and a friend and associate, under it all, of the Tribe via Tommy).

A year ago, we went on the offensive, with the able assistance of our sponsors, creating four bogus deaths -- Ma, Nancy Chino, Goose, and Eve -- that the press called the **Double Daily Double Murders**. Our efforts at counter-covert activity aimed at flushing out our foe had a murderous conclusion, right in our own sandbox.

No hoax, that.

Three thugs, bent on killing Ma and anyone else in their way, burst into the bookshop, from both ends. When the book dust settled, two or them were dead, including one who died from a spike high heel stomped deep into the right eye, followed by a steel pipe blow to the head. The leader of the thugs, one Peter Principe, was critically injured in close quarters by Goose.

Principe continues in a coma in an undisclosed location, in a Buffalonya hospital. We figure that he is a dead man, if the code be followed that such pukes live by. Someone will whack him, of that we are certain. Only God knows the time and day, but we know the rest.

Our view.

Operation Next-of-Kin is a follow-up to leads generated from the aftermath of the so-called **Big Bloody Battle Among the**

Books. The three thugs were based in Pittsburgh. We know their names and former addresses, and those of their families. We intend to interview these folk to find out what we can about just who it is who wants us all dead. A fistful of bogus badges and papers and the Crown Vic should carry the day, with some help from Agent Luke and Mister Ed, who look like cops and carry themselves so, when they want to. Jim and I look like a couple of bobble heads, but we'll put on our black suits and overcoats, and should slide right on by.

Since it was Ma's name that the thugs were shouting when they attacked us, it is very, very personal for all of us.

That is no way to treat a guy's mother.

Someone is to blame.

They will pay.

≈ ≈ ≈

The **Big Bloody Battle Among the Books** happened on March 15 -- yet another reason to beware of the **Ideas of March**. On April 1, we were, and are, on the road to Pittsburgh, we four, and you just might keep that date -- April 1st -- in mind since I or Goose, and anyone else who holds the narrative baton, will insert lies, and damned lies, among the facts and fictions that form the stories that we offer for your instruction and delight in this book form.

Honestly.

Goose values **trust** over **truth**, and he will not willingly tell the truth if he does not have to. As you can see, he is his father's son. Add to this what we call the **Requirements of the Service**, and you can see that what we post to our private, secure blog, and what Goose redacts into books of fiction, like an Old Testament scribe stealing and stitching together any written accounts that he can lay hands upon, are as close to the truth as the sun is to the moon in comparison to the distance to the stars. Mind you, the alignment of planets can be confusing. Things are closer than they appear, at times, and further apart than they seem, at others. You have been, yet again, warned.

What is true is that what you see is what you get.

What you make of what we make of this material is your choice.

My view?

We tell stories that could be true.

We do so without malice toward anyone and for reasons that we ourselves do not always understand.

This may seem cynical on our part, but it is also the way that we act toward one another, which probably makes things seem more confusing and more cynical-seeming, to you, than ever. This is because the way the Tribe acts toward one another works well, on all level, and because the Tribe is capable of good work that focuses a collection of strong and crazy personalities like a broken bit of carnival glass can focus the sun's rays.

Trust me.

We are hot.

Smokin'.

≈ ≈ ≈

When we got our marching orders, it was in the backroom at **Caspar's Books and That**.

Early on April Fool's Day.

"The F-Troop will be in order," Goose said.

"What a fine piece of foppery, Mister Chair Sir," Jim said.

"Yeah," I said. "Next you will have us wearing Jeanne's cast off kitten heels and coming to order as an **Order of Garters**."

Jeanne, light of my life, and my brother's as well, smiled sideways at me in a manner suggestive of lemons and sugar, bitter and sweet.

"You may be able to fit into the shoes," Jeanne said, "but you will not pass the physical."

"Yes, Oh-Dear," Eve said. "You would totter and fall like a tart after a night of drinking and vice."

Eve gave me her Buddha Girl smile, the one that gladdens all hearts.

"Be that as it may," Goose said, "we have work to do."

"Work makes me break out," Jim said.

"Yeah" I said, "but not into song. More like a prisoner with pimples."

"Bingo," Tommy said. "You two Jims have just taken two steps forward, to join Luke and Mister Ed in volunteering for a rotation of detection in Pittsburgh. I move it, Mister Chair Sir."

"And I second it," Jim said, "though more from habit than conviction."

"Yeah," I said, "but as the nuns say -- **don't get in the habit**."

"Like that old story about the **Sister** and the **Brother**," David said.

David gave us his bug-eyed smile full of good will from behind his round glasses.

Jeanne leaned over and speared David's ear, moving her lips from side to center, to make room for her clever tongue to dart between her red lips and return, in an eye blink.

"That is of the spiritness, my beautiness," Ma said. "Your bucko is getting all the good licks in, ain't he now and soon, my gypsy love. I am of making the third a second later, Goosy."

Ma gave Jeanne and her young consort a rogue's smile of toothless joy.

As you can see, Ma has only a nodding acquaintance with the idioms of English. However, do not assume that this means that Ma is not smart, wise, and penetrating.

"I accept your call, Tommy," Luke said, "because my master said I would."

"And I," Mister Ed said, rising, "accept en route to making a few comments and observations ala **Robert's Rules of Order**, if I may, Mister Chair Sir."

"Be of personal privilege," Goose said, "and let it fly, my friend of the many and fine distinctions."

Ed bowed, like a Great White Crane landing on a pile of girders in garters.

"I notice, in the first case, Mister Chair Sir," Mister Ed said, "that there is a motion on the table, which was made, in order, by Tommy, affiliate member of Tribe and Troop, with voice and vote in his portfolio and police work on his mind, if one can credit his words, and I do believe, based on past performance, that one indeed can do such, until such time that Tommy signals otherwise, by subsequent words or deeds. We received a second from one of the principals of the motion, to wit, Jim Grim, and although this is somewhat irregular, I will recommend that you, Mister Chair Sir, allow it. However, the **third** offered by Ma (Mister Ed bowed from the waist like a respectful crane to Ma, who gave him her rogue's smile) is both fanciful and egregious. To keep such utterances in these proceedings from becoming also ubiquitous, I would urge you, Mister Chair Sir, to silently and resolutely ignore the suggestion and to simply call the vote but not the question. That, I believe, is all, I believe."

We hooted, whistled, and clapped.

"That is a lot, you believe," Jim said.

"Yeah," I said. "I believe it."

≈ ≈ ≈

Jeanne came to us two years ago, early on in the **Mystery Man** phase of our recent history. David, whom she has cleaved to like a pretty book jacket clings to good young adult fiction, was already one of us when Jeanne appeared.

Jeanne, who is very much a Punk Princess with Goth overtones, has matured. Maybe it is the bookshop influence, but there is now an additional overlay that speaks of the Librarian. She still favors heels (thank you, Jesus) and narrow, snug black dresses, with burgundy accents at lips and toes, but she has taken to wearing glasses, for reading, which to my body and mind boosts her to a new level of all-consuming interest.

David is David, and that is a good thing. He is young and fearless, with a deceptive build. He and Jeanne make a cute couple. They are the future, and we are their past, and we continue to meet in the one place -- **now** -- where past and future reside, collide, and collude in tribal fashion.

The traces of the cute couple's murderous response to the attack on Ma (guess who wielded that spike heel and who wielded that length of pipe) are evident around their eyes and in the untimely furrows on their handsome foreheads. It will be a while yet before the memories of that day take their places at the back of the class rather than in the front row, hands up, and giving pert answers to all the teacher's questions, to the point where none of the other students can get in a good or kind word.

And I digress, again.

Pop's watch.

≈ ≈ ≈

Absent from this meeting of the F-Troop, complete with the **F-Troop salute** when Goose called the vote (two thumbs up, with two middle fingers touching at the tips), were the once missing and thought dead Mr. Black and his succulent main squeeze, celebrated local actress Nancy Chino. While the Tribe met, they were at the **Roll In and Crawl Out** in their usual places on adjoining barstools. Mr. Black calls the **Roll In** our forward position, and he will not lightly leave his post, even for a called meeting of the F-Troop.

Two of our more covert associates were also missing from the meeting, mostly because the work they do for a living is vital to our interests. Police Commissioner Meme Shiva and Jane Carlotto, senior crime reporter of the **Daily Afterblatt, Lake Effect edition**, joined our quasi-criminal enterprise through the offices of Tommy, and Tommy has more offices than the House and Senate combined and more sources than any one agent, from any TLA, has any right to have. But Tommy does, and we have become addicted to his effortless production of the needed fact at the pregnant moment.

Brother Tommy, like a slightly older version of David, and a slightly younger version of Mr. Black, is lean and capable. The word **lethal** leaps to mind. Tommy wears black wide-sided glasses and has a head of vaguely punkish hair that goes this way and that in a seemingly disordered fashion that only hours in the chair can produce, at the hand of a gifted cosmetologist named (oh, I don't know) Madge or Millie.

Three others round out the roster of our Tribe.

In descending order of likely appearance, they are **Wild Billy**, **Mr. Red**, and **Det. William "Joe Bob" Schmidt**, who works for Meme (and Tommy) and is the partner of an old foe -- (or a big fat fop, more like) -- Det. Joe Blucote.

And still yet another person remains, and is a presence, in our memories, and who is large despite his diminutive stature -- Pop. Our Pop is as big a presence in death as he was in life, and a paragraph will not suffice to describe him. I leave it to Goose to add to Pop's profile. I will confine myself to the final three that I have mentioned.

Wild Billy patrols the lower levels of the bookshop (outside the strike zone and below the knees) and jumps on the backs of unwary patrons who bend down to look at titles. As a bookshop cat, Wild Billy has no equal. Some of our patrons come more for the cat than they do for the books. Gen. William Donovan, a Buffalonya boy who went on to do great things, overt and covert, earning the nickname of **Wild Bill** along the way, is Wild Billy's namesake and was Pop's mentor.

Mr. Red, who is as bald as the next guy, if that guy is Grim, sits, by his own choice, at the front desk of the bookshop, at all times and even when the F-Troop meets. His reasons are equal parts of loathing for the antics that go on in the backroom and his zeal in being the first line of defense for the Tribe in general and Eve, whom he calls **Eveie**, in particular. Mr. Red, ably seconded by Mister Ed, stopped one of the thugs who broke into the shop from the front. Misters Red and Ed credit their elderly appearance with giving them the split second that they needed to administer critical blows to the windpipe and temples of the attacker whom they stopped with extreme prejudice.

Det. William "Joe Bob" Schmidt has a day job as partner of Det. Blucote, but his covert role has something to do with Tommy that we do not, Tommy assures us, **need to know** the details of. Joe Bob, a quiet man of great intelligence, wit, and kindness, is the first Native American detective on the Buffalonya force, and he has been the target of racist jesting, including the Tribe's bestowing upon him his nickname, which bespeaks an extreme contrast of man and moniker. Before we knew the inner man, we had mocked the outer one, not knowing that it was his cover that we were mocking.

≈ ≈ ≈

"Jim," I said, because I am always talking, "the darkness surrounds us. Why don't we, and why not, get a bleeping big car …".

"Drive!" Jim said, "for crissake watch out where you're going!"

From the back bench seat, the sounds of brotherly levity.

From the front, no change in the Mount Rushmore pair, whom we took for granite. Jim and I are used to being ignored, and taken for granted, when we crack wise. We thrive on it.

"Look," Jim said, "two pees in a pod."

"Yeah," I said. "I could use a rest stop myself."

After heading west and south from Buffalonya for an hour and more, we entered Pennsylvania. Luke pulled over at the **welcome-to-PA** rest area.

We walked in, two rows of two, with the beef in front and the jokers in tow.

There was no way that the four of us could avoid being noticed, so we didn't try. After all, what Tommy had described as a fact-finding mission of police work was also a coat-dragging exercise in **Let's Grow a Tail**. We were the tethered goats, and the big guys were our guarantee of continued life and abundance. On balance, we wanted to be noticed and by as many people, especially other players, as we could rope in.

In Pittsburgh, the strategy was the same, and I am here to tell you, when I bleeping-well please, what the results were. Too bad for you that I am striving to equal, nay exceed, my brother Goose's successes as a storyteller, and that I am poaching on his patch the way he does when he floats a puny pun that goes down like a soggy cardboard hamburger from a fast food palace.

The freeway's edges were kissed with the green of new grass, and the snow of winter was gone, even from the dark places under trees and bushes and grape vines.

The big guys were noticing other things such as lines of sight and possible threats, as was their nature, and Jim and I were looking around in the darting way one does when one scents the possibility of pretty woman in public places. Row one was doing slow swivels of negation, and row two was miming the rapid no-no of random focus. We might have needed a choreographer, but in terms of covert goals we were sticking out and making ourselves noticeable. However, the collection of truck drivers, soccer moms, and old folks populating the rest stop didn't seem to care one way or the other, beyond an occasional stare that lingered for an extra count of one or two.

"Take me to your leader," Jim said.

"Yeah," I said, "or to the piss tube, and I hope it comes up first."

≈ ≈ ≈

Now that you have a working knowledge of who we are, here is a repeat of a blog post that I made just before leaving to the Tribe's secure blog over our Virtual Private Network, which is a **tunneling technology**, which amuses me. I expect to see Bilbo or Frodo, in the company of a band of dwarves, pop out of the computer screen and beat me about the head and shoulders with axes and heavy hammers.

Four April Fools in a Vic, *steeling* away

For reasons that will become clear in a few weeks, Jim and I -- in the back seat of an elderly, well-maintained Crown Vic, police blue in color, driven by Agent Luke Parmgartner, with Mister Ed riding shotgun --are leaving Buffalonya (**steeling** away, as it were) under cover of darkness for a top secret, hush-hush trip to Pittsburgh, as in PA.

Our task is to follow up on leads concerning the three attackers, particularly the two dead ones, but also Peter Principe. It was this last-mentioned hunk of burning love and hate that got us a driver and a bodyguard.

Not too shabby, eh?

You could say, ala Tommy, **Bingo**.

Since we will be busy as a rabbit pulling fur, I will write the story of it all in a single post after we return.

Why me?

The answer to that begins with Jim's indifference to a writing assignment (did you know that he is illiterate and that we have to witness his X with our initials and a notation of **Jim Grim, his mark**?), my secret life that you do not know about, and things like that. Truth is (and I am no better at the **truth thang** than Brother Goose is, to be completely honest), I have not made up that story yet. I am still working on the scenarios and back-stories that Jim and I will spin in Pgh.

We are hoping for a legend in our own time.

We tried to get Jeanne as our driver, but she refused to be away from her boy toy David for that long a time.

Can you believe it?

She did give us a well-worn black peep-toe pump apiece to remember her by (I got the left one).

As it is, we have about a ton of protection, with the down side being that we cannot see over their huge, square heads. Up side is that we can hide in the back without doing more than slump down.

That may prove handy.

The windows are tinted and blast-resistant. There are steel plates in the doors. If we drop down and turn around, we can pull the center cushion out to gain access to the arsenal in the trunk. Everyone has a Dick Tracy for secure communications. Jim and I have Kevlar vests on, steel-toe brogans, handguns under our hairy armpits, and a few toys that no one but us and our muscle shoal, up front, needs to know about.

The True Blue detective special Crown Vic is meant to announce, to friend and foe alike, that we are on an official (quasi-official anyway) junket. In our pockets and wallets are enough bogus papers, laminated photo id badges, and shiny shields such that we will be able to open any door that we want opened.

You might want to memorize the case name -- **Operation Next-of-Kin** -- and our case names, **Agents James Baker** and **Jim O. Tinker** (me).

If you see us, our challenge question is -- **Do you know the way to the Frick?** Your answer is -- **No, but I can find out; I have a map**.

After you have that committed to memory, eat your hard drive and mums the word, Bob's your uncle, and we are outa here.

-- OhJim

≈ ≈ ≈

Email from: Mister Ed
To Goose Grim

Subject: House of Verbs. Open again.

Mister Chair Sir,
I rise in virtual indignation, sir, to offer an antidote to the pervasive poison of ignorance that surrounds us re: grammar and usage.

I realize, sir, that many if not most, or even all of our associates including you but not me, would tell me to shut up and go away about a subject so boring. Not to me, though, sir, is this topic, and judging from the general tone of posts, replete with typos and worse, I offer this and other occasional essays to come, in general and in specific, on this topic so important to me. In this, be you ruled by me, sir.

Never mind, sir, that we communicate on a virtual private network. We still owe the words our best for their highest.

Your servant,
Ed

House of Verbs

Grammar, Style, and Usage for Writers

Part One: General

'House of Verbs, Don speaking,' he said ...

"House of Verbs, Don speaking," he said to the backshop guy on the internal line. "We have a special tonight on adjectives ... three for a dollar."

Don was one of the more playful News Editors that I answered to in many, many years of copy editor work on daily newspapers.

House of Verbs.

I was looking right at Don when he picked up the phone.

Two things were apparent.

One. He had an odds-on chance that any caller on that line would be not only a member of the International Typographical Union but also a backshop printer who knew Don.

Don liked to laugh.

Two. Don made up his patter on the spot. I could see it in his eyes. House of Verbs was a one-time inspiration.

But here it is, and here he is. And here I am. And you, the most important person of all.

The reader. The reader, also, who is or will be a writer.

House of Verbs. Open again, under new management.

What does that mean '... for writers ...'?

A book *for writers* would look like *this*, I suppose.

Or maybe a book for writers would resemble a book for readers who have written and who will write again.

Repeat offenders.

So far, in addressing this question -- for writers -- I have told the truth, but that makes little or no difference, to me or to you, in my view.

Okay, then, let us go at the question this way --
> **What does a writer seek?**
> **What does a writer seek to avoid?**

That gets us closer to the point.

Short of my slipping your computer a clever cookie and monitoring your digital life, I am guessing here. Even if our keywords match and our libraries have significant overlap, and my wife and your girlfriend get together once a week for coffee (with an executive summary of topics covered, from my wife, on my desk by close of business), and I somehow can inhabit your skin and can jack into your brain, I'm still guessing.

I'm guessing at what matters to you, a writer who is just like or sorta like or not at all like me.

∎ ∎ ∎

Given the challenges of sentience and the unreliable, unruly nature of letters and words, to say nothing of sentences and paragraphs, I resolve to write about **my** hopes, **my** dreams, **my** fears, and **my** experience as a writer, editor, and publisher.

House of Verbs. Open again, under new management.

OhJim continues --

It may seem like an obvious thing to you, but it is true that one can only look out a car window for so long, especially when getting there is not half the fun. As the sun went down, and the shadows grew to black universes, in our sight, Jim and I looked and looked, and neither of us had the courage to ask the big guys up front the universal question.

Are we there yet?

And I don't mean **where you go, there you are**. I mean the kid question, borne of boredom and fatigue.

Being in Pittsburgh was slightly better than being on the way there, in the dark. However, being in Pittsburgh, as the days piled up, was like being in the military -- long periods of boredom broken up by moments of pure terror, only in our case the contrast was between long periods of aimless activity broken up by moments of deep insight followed by a patter of puns.

"Jim," I said, "I believe that we are here for our sins."

"I hear you." Jim said. "I can see that we must have had a really good time."

"Yeah," I said, "but I don't remember a thing, only sometimes I can hear the click of Jeanne's heels, like Pop's watch under my pillow."

"You put Pop's watch under your pillow?" Jim said. "That is just whack."

"Yeah," I said, "and Jeanne snuck into my sleeping bag the night before we left."

"You wish," Jim said.

"Yeah," I said, "and I alone lie."

We were hanging out in the safe house (Luke's term) that we were staying in while in Pittsburgh. It was a small brick Victorian wedged between two taller Tudors, on a middling hill in the Highland Park section of the city. Like so many parts of Pgh, Highland Park is a crazy quilt of architectures, sited on seesaw streets that find their level at any buildable angle.

Some days, Luke would disappear, not to return until the small hours, and we never knew what he was doing or where he had been. As he told us, the first time we asked, we did not need to know yet.

Luke said he was laying groundwork, but we figured that he was laying pipe and told him so. Which got us that Mounty Rushmore reaction.

When Luke would wander in, we would tell him where he had been -- pole-climbing in his low-rise briefs and a crooked smile at this little strip club in the Hill ... **woking his dog**, just ahead of the animal-hugger cops from the SPCA ... peddling his narrow patoot way down on Fifth Avenue where things definitely get interesting in the hours with single digits ... throwing his mama, whom he kept in a pumpkin shell, under a cross-town bus at rush hour.

Luke is a grim and humorless man, y'all.

I mean ... **y'uns**.

After all, this is Pittsburgh, home of the **gummy band** and the practice of duct-taping a lawn chair or two to the street to mark one's parking place in front of one's house.

Notice, I pray you, the tense change of tenses, from present to past, and back again. In other words, we ain't there anymore, Toto, and I for one am happy as a clam and back in my own bed with Pop's watch under my pillow (I lied to Jim).

≈ ≈ ≈

I do love to tell a good story without too many references to fact, and I guess that I am distorting things a bit. There were some good moments in Pgh that yielded some solid leads.

I got to accompany Mister Ed when he and I, flashing our bogus badges, walked up to the house where the sister of victim No. Two, Gary Clyde Grant, lived with her drug-dealing and ever absent biker man. While we were interviewing sister Carla Jane Jimmersoll, Jim and Luke were out in Kittanning, interviewing the parents of Gary Clyde Grant, whom Jeanne and David killed with a heel and a pipe.

I was excited. The sister, we knew, from Tommy's brief on the two dead men, was furious about her brother's death and had been muttering threats of revenge into her cell phone, which were picked up by persons and toys in Tommy's TLA outfit.

We all agreed that we would split up in pairs to interview the parents and sister of victim Gary Clyde Grant and the parents of the other victim, Eric X. Royce. This was our common thinking despite the fact that Royce was the pukier of the two dead guys by far. Thing was, his parents had cut him off from any contact years ago and were not furious, but mortified, that their son had died the way that he did while trying to do what he was stopped from doing.

The big prize, however, we were saving for last and had not yet drawn straws to see which of our two teams would interview Gary Clyde's ex-girlfriend, a punk-look dancer with the stage name **Kiki Tiki Toye**. Luke was still waiting on a current address for her.

Carla Jane was home alone, which was the way that we planned it, with the help of some information from Luke. She and her biker man lived in a brick building divided into four large and old apartments, perched on a hill in the Hill District. She answered the door, in an old sweatshirt and torn jeans, no shoes or socks despite the cool weather.

"Yeah?" Carla Jane said. "You look like cops."

"Agents Blue and Tinker, Miss," Mister Ed said, flashing his badge and jabbing his huge index finger at my head when he said **Tinker**. "We want to talk with you about your brother, Gary Clyde Grant."

"Gary Clyde is dead, you bleep," Carla Jane said. "There is nothing to talk about."

"Not in our view, Miss," Mister Ed said. "For starters, we would like to discuss your plans for revenge."

"I have no idea what you are talking about," Carla Jane said.

Her face had turned as red as her dye-tortured hair.

"Look," I said. "Why not have us in for a few moments. We can sit and chat about your brother. There are many questions that we still have about the way that he died. That case is far from closed, I assure you, Miss."

I smiled my best good-cop bobblehead smile and shrugged my shoulders.

"My brother should not be dead," Carla Jane said. "If you agree with that, I guess I can talk to you for a while."

Carla Jane opened the door wider and let us in. She led us to a room off the foyer of the apartment and indicated chairs that looked like fugitives from a cushion-testing lab.

The apartment had high ceilings covered with embossed tin painted white. The floors were paint-flecked natural wood. The windows were double-hung and rattled like a dying corpse when someone drove by with the bass cranked on the car stereo. Being the Hill, and being an urban situation, that was a frequent occurrence.

Biker boy was doing a brisk business at the factory where he worked as cover for his drug sales. The apartment was in the thousand-per-month rental range, easily, and Carla Jane looked like a cross between a coke whore and a retired exotic dancer with the emphasis on **dancer**.

"What can you tell us about your brother's relationship with a man named Peter Principe?" Mister Ed said, referring to a notebook pinned down by a poised pen.

"Principe?" Carla Jane said. "**P.P.** is the bad news behind the bad news."

"And," Mister Ed said, "what was your brother?"

"Gary Clyde was a choir boy by comparison," Carla Jane said. "A bleeping choir boy who did not have a clue. Principe played him like a cheap harmonica and Gary Clyde danced to his tune."

"Small time?" Mister Ed said. "Big man with small brain?"

"Bleep you," Carla Jane said. "The truth hurts. Gary Clyde was out of his league with even a small-time bleep like Principe. And as for his friend, Eric X., I would kill the bleep if someone else hadn't. He was to blame for my brother's bad choices."

"How so?" Mister Ed said.

"Gary Clyde was like a little boy when it came to Royce. Royce got him into all the trouble that Gary Clyde ever got into. When I got a call from Gary Clyde's probation officer, asking where in the bleep Gary Clyde was, I knew that it was going to turn out bad. Gary Clyde had not had a clear thought since his girlfriend threw him out for not contributing. Maybe that's why he went back in with those two. The money was good."

"How good?" Mister Ed said.

"Good enough to have Kiki twitching her padded patoot and inviting **Gar-Gar** to come home again when he got back from his business trip. Kiki ain't the brightest spotlight in the strip club, but she is nasty and is nicely focused on Kiki."

"So the girlfriend, one Kiki, was under the impression that her **Gar-Gar** was on a business trip. What was **your** understanding?" Mister Ed said.

"Gary Clyde called and told me that he and the other two were taking an overnight trip to Buffalonya to do a bit of hunting for a rich bitch client of Principe's."

"Name?" I said.

"Gary Clyde never said and I never wanted to know. Just **Rich Bitch**. That's all he ever said."

"Meaning, I take it," Mister Ed said, "that your brother and his associates had done other jobs for this woman. A woman, right?"

"Yeah," Carla Jane said. "Always Principe and Royce and always for the **Rich Bitch**."

"How often?" I said.

"Only now and again or every once in a while, going back a couple of years. Before that, it was the **Hoarse Horse**, and don't ask me who that was, 'cause I doesn't know, does I?"

"I'm sure you have no idea," I said, "but to return to the Rich Bitch."

"You can set her on a pencil and spin her, Baldy, for all I care," Carla Jane said. "It don't make me no never-mind. I said I don't know anything about her."

"Who might?" I said.

"Kiki. Ask the whore, and frame your question with a twenty or two and you just might get lucky. You will get lucky, sure, but she also may have some information, too, if you know what I mean, and from the looks of you, I'm not at all sure. Especially you, Baldy."

"I'll take that as a ringing endorsement," I said. "Do you have an address for the alluring Miss Kiki?"

"Kiki Tiki Toye can be found on any weekend night or any weekday night, except for Mondays, at a place down in the Strip District called the **Cat's Pause**. It's in the Yellow Pages, Sport."

We made our excuses and walked to the door.

Only later did I find out what the **Strip District** really was.

"You never told me why the case is still open about my brother's death," Carla Jane said.

"We want to get at whoever was paying the bills and setting the agenda," Mister Ed said. "You've been of assistance."

"That warms my cold heart, Fat Boy," Carla Jane said, shaking her red head. "Warms my cold bleeping heart."

≈ ≈ ≈

"The parents were heart-breaking," Jim said. "Tiny house, tiny street, small dreams turned into nightmares. They couldn't tell us anything about their son, they said, because they had told him to stay away a long time ago. Their only information came from their daughter, whom they called **Miss Carla**."

Mister Ed and I had gone first, in describing our visit with sister Carla Jane.

"We didn't know about this Rich Bitch going in," Luke said, "but it would not have made any difference."

"Only glimmer was from a letter that they gave us from their son," Jim said. "They had not even opened it."

Jim held up a small envelope.

"Listen to this," Jim said, taking out a single sheet of wide-ruled paper torn from a child's school tablet.

Dear mom and dad,

Let me comes home and sees you. Please. I have a bad feeling about all these years and I do miss you. Miss Carla tells me about you ever time I sees her, and she say she tri to get you to let me come sees you but you always changes the subject. What I done she hasn't done twice? I'm going away for a few days. Lets me come and sees you when I gets back. I'll been having $$$ then and I can gives you some. Please.

**Your loving son,
Gary Clyde**

"Wow," I said. "I'd like some bitters and gall with my irony, please."

"Yes," Jim said. "These parents were stone-faced about the man who once was their son. They called him **him**. Never by his name. Only **him**. When Luke asked them what the son had done that had angered them, they said it was when he began hanging around with Eric Royce. They said that Royce was evil and violent but that there was no talking to **him** about it. After the two got into trouble and there was some jail time, they told **him** to stay away or they would call the cops, which they did until there were no more visits from **him**."

Jim raised his eyebrows.

"It was spooky," Jim said. "If they couldn't call him **him**, they would say **he** or **his** or something equally vague like **that one**. When it would get confusing and we would ask who **he** was, they would say, with heat and venom, **him!** And glare."

"Sad and depressing," Luke said.

"The wife was this mouse of a woman," Jim said, "with thin bleached blond hair that looked like a wig made from floor sweepings at a low-end beauty parlor. She might have been a pleasant person at one time, but only if that time had been on some other planet. The husband was a mismatched bookend to her. Same sad story. Beer gut, comb-over, brown canvas tennis shoes like mental patients wear. They tried to be gracious, but their depression and rage was too much for all of us."

Luke smiled a rueful smile worthy of Jeanne.

"Jim, here," Luke said, "has clearly never been to Kittanning, never gotten up close to a steel worker who hasn't worked since the 80s. Buffalonya has its moments, sure, but you haven't been depressed until you've been to the steel-bound parts of Pittsburgh. It's like the Rust Belt finishing school for the terminally depressed. You haven't really lived until you sit in a house on the Grant's street and gotten some of that good old northern hostility with that overlay of instant coffee made with tap water that passes for hospitality."

We all looked at Luke with thoughtfulness.

"Well," Jim said, "who wants to take in the Tiki show down at the **Cat's Pause**? Some tits for your tats?"

≈ ≈ ≈

Luke's sources came through with a current address for Miss Toye, which was her real name and a fortuitous match for the assumed stage name of **Kiki Tiki**. After drawing straws, and doing a little happy dance on Jim's and Luke's heads, Mister Ed and I headed for the Hill while Jim and Luke headed for Dormont, to have a pro-forma interview with Royce's parents, who had taken a page from the Grants' playbook and had cut off all contact with their son Eric.

Luke and Jim saw it as the equivalent of giving a batter a walk, but they were willing to play catch and follow through with the Royces. Good thing that they did, but there I am running ahead again like Pop's watch.

Mister Ed and I, old hands at visiting the Hill, found Kiki's apartment without incident and got buzzed in. It was early afternoon, and a tousled bottle blond with big everything was waiting at the door of Kiki's apartment when we walked up.

"Miss Toye?" Mister Ed said. "May we come in? We're here to talk with you about your ex-boyfriend Gary Clyde Grant."

"Are you from the police?" Tiki said.

"We're with a federal concern," Mister Ed said, showing Tiki a badge. "That is Agent Tinker and I am, as you can see, Agent Blue." Ed pointed an index finger at me and a thumb at himself.

Yawning, Tiki led us into her apartment, which was small. As soon as we stepped over the sill, we were in the living room, and after Tiki put the daybed in shape, we had our choice of seats. I chose the other end of the daybed and crane-like Mister Ed folded himself, carefully, into an old chesterfield-style overstuffed chair with a suspiciously lumpy cushion.

Tiki was a curvy girl in her mid-20s, dressed in a ratty housecoat that once might have covered enough of her to avoid embarrassment. The girl, clearly, was still growing. Her face, which once might have been pretty, showed the effects of last night's heavy makeup. In keeping with the general punk theme, her hair was a shade of pink reminiscent of poster paint. The studs and various pierces in her nose and cheeks were a contrast to an angry margin of red with slight swelling.

Pierces and pancake makeup don't mix.

"I'm happy to help," Tiki said. "Gary Clyde was a sweet man and although we had our differences, he was going to move back in after he got back from a business trip to Buffalonya."

"Ah," Mister Ed said. "A business trip. Did he say what the business was?"

"Something about plumbing supplies, Gary told me," Tiki said, "but the policemen who came to see me with the bad news said that Gary Clyde had broken his probation and was killed in self-defense by someone in a bookstore. That don't make no sense to me, no way, at all. Gary Clyde didn't read any too much. Why would he be in a bookstore?"

Mister Ed nodded, sagely.

"People do things that surprise us, sometimes," Mister Ed said, "even ones we think we know."

Tiki's generous face was as blank as a lawn ornament as she heard Ed out.

"Did Gary Clyde ever talk to you about a man named Peter Principe?" I said.

"I guess he did," Tiki said. "That jerk is my boss. We haven't been paid in weeks. I'm down to my tips and gifts from the patrons."

I looked at Mister Ed, who was looking at Tiki.

"Did either your boss or your boyfriend," I said, "ever talk about working for a rich women?"

"The **Rich Bitch**," Tiki said. "I didn't like the name, but I sure heard it often enough. She is Peter's girlfriend in a way of speaking, in the past, anyway."

"Does she have a name that you can give us?" I said.

"I don't have a name, but I do have an address," Tiki said. "The Rich Bitch lives at Peter's house. That hasn't changed."

"I show an address on Murray in Shadyside," Mister Ed said. "Is that the one?"

"The very same," Tiki said, "but don't bother calling before dinner. The woman is a vampire, I swear."

≈ ≈ ≈

Email from: Mister Ed
To Goose Grim

Subject: House of Verbs. Open again.

Hello, Mister Chair Sir, from Grammar and Usage, a small but accurate planet at the edge of the known universe.

Judging from the favorable reception that I have had from others (a special thanks and a hug for Jeanne, a fellow traveler, who sent encouragement and concise criticism) I feel emboldened to offer another essay.

Your servant,
Ed

Picking on the professionals

I've been reading a young adult book, **Wildwood**, by Colin Meloy with fine illustrations by his spouse, Carson Ellis. Meloy is the lead performer of the Portland, Oregon, band called **The Decemberists** and **Wildwood,** his first novel, published in 2011, is **Book 1** *of the* **Wildwood Chronicles.** The publisher is Balzer + Bray, an imprint of big-house publisher HarperCollins.

I almost quit this book.

Two times so far I have talked myself out of just throwing the book against the wall in hopes of breaking its spine, and I am only just beginning Part Three, the final third of the book.

I do not fault the writer. We writers have bad habits, holes in our understanding of the fine points of language, and other concerns than doing typo patrol. That leaves the editors. They should have done a better job, and their job is typo patrol, word editing, and picky-sniffy stuff in general.

The latest thing to send me up the wall was an ugly use of apostrophe in a fanciful place name -- the **ANCIENTS' GROVE**. To begin, let us simply agree that the apostrophe here is technically correct but that usage allows for the dropping of the apostrophe in cases such as this, where the idea of possession is not the point of the phrase in question. Besides, as the creator and **bull-bitch tom-wallager** of his own alternative universe, Meloy can do whatever he wants with language. Anyone who complains can be simply thrown in the cells and allowed to rot while musing on the cabbage-headed king.

I blame the copy editor here. He was not doing her job.

The first thing to send me up the wall while reading **Wildwood** was not the mixed metaphor of bike tires carving through wet pavement. No, it was that 12-year-old Prue, who is important to the narrative, "found herself whiling time outside the coffee shop". I can tolerate the writer either leaving out or not knowing that the word **whiling** (is half-naked if not followed by the word **away**. Meloy's use of **whiling** is either a half-naked idiom or a half-naked cliché. In any case, all this exposed word flesh embarrasses me for the copy editor, who did not fix the problem. You could argue that **whiling time** is fresh and creative, but since you didn't say that it also makes sense and conveys something that readers will be able to follow, don't go there.

It was a mistake that no one caught.

I hate to pay for a hardcover novel with even one typo, particularly a book from a big house with lots of editors, but since I have grown fond of Prue, I continued to read through my irritation, past the occasional word or phrase that did not make any sense and that no editor chased, caught, or fixed.

■ ■ ■

Why do I care about poorly edited or poorly written copy to the point of throwing the offending book against the wall?

It gets me that I paid a big-damn publisher for a book that was released to the public while still in serious need of an editor's attention. That's half.

The other half is my visceral reaction to sloppy copy, or even slightly sloppy copy.

Well, you could reply, **as a copy editor, writer, and blogger yourself, to say nothing of your occasional lectures that you deliver off the cuff from an outline on an old envelope, you have done worse. God knows you have done worse.**

That is true.

Maybe that is what keeps me going with this otherwise fine book. I myself have done worse.

Amazing Grace. Roll the tape.

Amen.

■ ■ ■

What remains is a question with two horns --

■ How important is clean copy?

■ How can we as writers, self-editors, and bloggers produce clean copy?

And another stray thought. Perhaps it takes an entire village to produce clean copy. When you see an error or typo, you can send a friendly email to the author or publisher.

Ebooks, at least, can be fixed – even one error at a time -- without forcing the need for a new ISBN or edition change.

That helps, and the rest is a choice that a writer makes concerning how much crud he will tolerate in his own copy, and how she will edit the copy that will be born, she hopes, without blemish.

OhJim continues --

Luke and Jim were gloating when we returned, which I thought was the height of something, since we had an actual lead, again.

"Royce's parents," Luke said, "told us that their son, who was always in trouble, had fallen in with a man their son called **Petey**. This Petey, they said, was a big, violent man who was a lot older than their son. It was this man who led their son to the dark side, the way they see it, and it was at this time that they told their son to stay away."

"How," I said, "did they put such self-satisfied smirks on your ugly faces."

"They had a phone machine message from Royce, from just before the trip to Buffalonya. It was so weird that they saved it. This is the gist, "Luke said, reading from his regulation cop notebook.

"Mom, Daddy, it's Eric. I know that you won't see me and I guess it's Ok, but I want to give you something for all the bad stuff, you know? Let me visit when I get back from this business trip. It's on the level, and all. No more Peter and all that. Please. I'll call. If you don't hear from me, call this number."

"Did you?" I said.

"Sure," Jim said.

"And," Luke said, "we have an appointment with a woman named Janey Grimes. She lives in Shadyside."

≈ ≈ ≈

"I called Tommy with the news," Luke said, "and all he said was **ask her if her name is** Grimes **or** Grim. **Should be the sixty-four thousand dollar question**, Tommy said."

"Suffice it to say," Jim said, "we are curious."

"And on our way to see this mysterious woman," Luke said. "When I called Tommy back to follow up on his comment, I couldn't raise him, so we're going in blind but confident."

Jim nodded.

While the lucky pair were gone, Mister Ed and I called out for pizza and watched some playoff hockey.

"Grimes or Grim," I said. "Could Tommy be any more vague? **Bingo** would have been better."

"Tommy does," Mister Ed said, "as Tommy will. This we know about him and this is just about all that we know about him. The rest is not **need-to-know**. Goose has been very clear about this."

"My brother," I said, "is a liar and a damned liar, with a liar's leer."

"Tell me something I do not know," Mister Ed said. "Amuse me, my bald friend from over the hill and through the dell."

"OK," I said. "Do you know who ended up with Pop's watch?"

"I assume," Mister Ed said, "that you are referring to the gold-plated railroad-style fob watch that Mr. Pop got when he retired from the shadows."

"The very same," I said, "though it is not really a railroad watch. Just a gold pocket watch that keeps a version of Time."

I held the watch out, and Mister Ed took it in his enormous hand.

"My guess?" Mister Ed said. "You got the watch, and I have the time."

"Bingo," I said. "By the way, what time is it?"

"Time to go," Luke said, striding into the room. "We're heading back to Buffalonya, tonight."

Part One

This news story ran above the fold on Page 1A of this morning's **Daily Afterblatt, Lake Effect edition**.

Security lapse
Surviving bookshop attacker killed in his hospital bed

By Jane Carlotto
Senior Crime Reporter

A man authorities were protecting, to bring him to trial, has been murdered in his hospital bed, according to the Buffalonya Police Commissioner.

Peter Principe, 57, a Pittsburgh man who led a three-man attack on a used bookstore's owners and associates in mid-March, had been in an induced coma at an undisclosed hospital in the region, according to Police Commissioner Meme Shiva.

Night shift nurses alerted the police last night that Principe's life support system had been unplugged, Shiva said. She did not say whether there had been an audible alarm when this occurred.

"A man who lived by violence has died by stealth," Shiva said. "All good people deplore this sort of conclusion to what should be weighed in the court system."

Principe's two associates died in the attack on Caspar's Books and That, notorious as the meeting place and place of employment of a group of reputed former and retired espionage operatives who congregate at the bookshop.

The Eerie County District Attorney's Office has ruled that the two deaths in the attack were in self-defense, which will not be the case in the death of Principe, who was clinging to life after the abortive bookshop attack. Shiva refused to disclose the hospital where Principe was murdered.

When asked if the cause of death might have been negligence, error, or some other accidental cause, Shiva said that "we are quite certain that the coroner will agree that the man died because of the premeditated actions of a person or persons whom we are seeking."

Flanking the commissioner at her hastily called press conference this morning were Dets. Joe Blucote and William "Joe Bob" Schmidt, who had nothing to say. Their flanking of the diminutive commissioner, like bookends, was a stark contrast, at least for Blucote, who once ruled the roost, under the regime of Commissioner Tom Tonolody, who was murdered earlier this year, reportedly while under a witness protection program, according to certain sources.

Blucote's partner, Schmidt, was as usual taciturn to a fault.

In answer to questions, Shiva said that Principe died sometime overnight, between the hours of midnight and 4 a.m.

"He was okay and stable, according to chart entries at the change of shifts, but the routine mid-shift check revealed that Principe's ventilator and monitor had been turned off, effectively cutting off his oxygen supply and early warning system," Shiva said.

The detectives on the case are checking the hospital's security cameras to see if there are any leads from that quarter, Shiva said.

When contacted after the press conference, Dr. Bruce Backstaff, the county coroner, said that he would be doing an autopsy later in the day.

Shiva said that friends of Principe have been in contact with authorities concerning when and how Principe's body is to be returned to Pittsburgh.

Returned, sources say, to the city where he was born and lived a life of violence and extortion.

An Eerie County Grand Jury had handed down an indictment against Principe on charges of attempted murder and criminal conspiracy in the bookshop attack.

Editor's note: Tomorrow in the **Daily Afterblatt, Lake Effect edition**, Senior Crime Reporter Jane Carlotto will give an overview of two years of murder, official mendacity, and covert intrigue, with three articles to follow.

≈ ≈ ≈

Email from: Mister Ed
To Goose Grim

Subject: House of Verbs. Open again.

I rise, yet again, Mister Chair Sir, to offer another occasional essay on my favorite subject, which I am happy to report has garnered a second Fifth Column supporter, Jane Carlotto.

Hugs and a virtual rose from me to Jane, and this that follows for all.

Your servant,
Ed

A three-way mirror doesn't catch all my faces

In my life in play as an editor, I have noticed many trends, none more interesting that the trend that goes by the name of Print on Demand, or POD.

I am in awe of those who do their own publishing, for they do wear many hats. I made a list of the hats that I have seen on a single head, one after another, as a self-written and –published book goes from the writing to the printing, with many hats between –

    ... author ...
    ... editor ...
    ... publisher ...
    ... proofreader ...
    ... copy editor ...
    ... company blogger ...
    ... webmaster ...
    ... hardware guy ...
    ... software guy ...
    ... graphic designer ...
    ... cartoonist ...

... chief photographer ...

... print-on-demand (POD) expert ...

... legal eagle ...

... PR department ...

and something else I cannot recall.

Oh, yeah ... guerrilla marketer.

These folks even do **Windows**. And **Word**.

It is partly to honor these many-hatted persons that I choose to write about grammar and usage.

Why?

Because of this: --

Bad writing makes good readers angry.

If you don't know what an air horn sounds like, you may not know that you are about to stop a truck.

The hard way.

If your writing sucks, and you don't even suspect that there might be a few small problems, you will not suffer much, especially when compared to your readers, who may want to throw you under the nearest bus or truck.

Bad writing does make good readers angry.

This is a caution for the rest of us, who know just how typo-littered, usage-poor, and grammar-thin our writing can be.

So what must you do?

■ ■ ■

Well, those of you in my orbit can simply call on me. Others, who do not know me except as a virtual tool on the Internet, for their use at a fee, certainly do.

And if I can glean extra cash from my cover, using the excellent cover of the Internet, so can you, who write, augment your income using POD.

If you can afford to pay my mid-range rate -- current freelance editing rates range from twenty-five dollars to seventy-five dollars per hour -- I will fix what can be fixed and will tell you something about how to fix the rest. Your vocation will become a hole the size of a scream where all your money goes. Your significant other will cry ***STOP***!!! Even a light edit of your manuscript is going to cost you several hundred dollars.

[Note: I offer, as of now, a special discount for associates who can read these private tribal posts.]

Well, a few of you might say, ***who cares about a few typos? What's the huge deal, then? Sure, it is regrettable and***

avoidable, but my story is the thing, not my spell-checking! Don't be so anal!! I'm trying as hard as I can to drive the bus and here you want to stop in a bad neighborhood and talk about mechanics. Get off and get a life!!!

And I say, **Fair enough**.

I acknowledge my own fears of offering readers work that still needs a lot of work. Even if I had a book advance the size of an adjoining Zip Code, I still would want to deliver writing worthy of readers to the publishing machine waiting to print and publish my book.

That means fixing typos, which is harder than it should be.

That means slowing down my rush to be in print if I can see that yet another reading and editing of my manuscript is not only necessary, but also obviously necessary, and would be obvious to anyone who can scan **See Spot Run** and know that the topic is **jogging.**

That means finding someone who is willing to help either for free, or for **atta-boys** and **-girls** and a hearty handshake, or some mix of cash and barter of goods and services, plus making use of some tricks that I have learned along the way.

No matter what path I choose, I must admit that I am in recovery when it comes to clean copy and that I will never be free of this affliction. I err with every stroke I make. I err when I edit, making wrong choices and introducing typos.

I am my own worst enemy. I bear constant watching.

A writer can have skill as a storyteller but lack the gift of expression. If I cannot use words as the words, and people, expect, no one will understand me. So it is that I choose, among all the weeds in the publishing patch, to go after the weeds that cannot be avoided but that can be spotted and pulled if they sprout under my nose.

Problems with grammar and usage are weeds of this sort.

The good news?

By reading and thinking about usage and grammar you can learn almost all there is to know about grammar and usage. The rest of writing is mysterious and elusive. I cannot make you a writer, but I can teach you the parts that are teachable.

If you choose to be teachable, too.

Black/white and read all over

This news story ran across the bottom of Page 1A in this morning's **Daily Afterblatt, Lake Effect edition**.

Mystery Man, Daily Double etc.
Notorious bookshop stays at center of violence, intrigue

Editor's note: In the next four days, our senior crime reporter will recap and cast into the future observations concerning certain high-profile murders that seem to be linked in some way to a quirky, notorious Buffalonya used bookshop called Caspar's Books and That.

By Jane Carlotto
Senior Crime Reporter

Go back two years, to the string of three still-unsolved murders that became known as the "Mystery Man Murders."

Go back one year to the series of faux murders, two by two, that became known as the "Double Daily Double Murders."

Go back to mid-March, to what has become known as the "Big Bloody Battle of the Books."

Go back two days to the murder of Peter Principe, a man in a coma and under indictment for attempted murder and criminal conspiracy for his pivotal involvement in the Big Bloody Battle.

What common elements do you see?

Murder, certainly.

And in our own streets, homes, and businesses.

Many observers also see a thread in the involvement, in most of these cases, twisted around the various persons who form a community of former espionage operatives at Caspar's Books and That, a used bookshop in north Buffalonya, on Delaware at Junker.

"With the possible, probable, or actual (take your pick) exception of the 'Mystery Man' business, which no one understands, Jane, the bookshop has been at the center of most of the high-profile violence in our city," said one source, who demanded anonymity, citing national security as the reason.

Natch. Everyone does that.

Other sources, though less shy, are as vocal in linking the bookshop, its owner Eve Green, her common-law husband, Goose Grim, and a collection of aging and fading but still colorful characters who, according to a three-part series by this reporter written last year concerning the bookshop, are in some or many cases retired from service in our nation's covert agencies, of which there are more "than you can ask for or imagine," according to one source.

The immediate trigger for this series of articles is the murder of a man who was being kept in an induced coma in order to bring him back to health, to face an indictment listing charges of attempted murder and criminal conspiracy.

The dead man, Peter Principe, 57, of Pittsburgh, according to police reports, was the leader of a three-man death squad that broke into Caspar's Books and That, guns drawn. Two of the attackers died from close-quarters self-defense measures taken by persons in the bookshop. Principe had been in critical condition since the fatal day and in an induced coma.

Someone, police say, turned off the machine that was keeping Principe alive.

In the three articles to come, we will examine the "Mystery Man Murders," the "Double Daily Double Murders" hoax, and the matter of the "Big Bloody Battle of the Books."

We will chat with the authorities and listen to our unnamed but authoritative sources, to see what conclusions can be drawn.

Tomorrow, "The Mystery Man Murders, still a mystery."

Black/white and read all over
| 12May10 |

This news story ran across the bottom of page 1A of this morning's **Daily Afterblatt, Lake Effect edition**.

The 'Mystery Man Murders'

The question marks refuse to go away in three deaths

Editor's note: This is the second of four articles concerning certain high-profile murders that seem to be linked in some way to a quirky, notorious Buffalonya used bookshop called Caspar's Books and That.

By Jane Carlotto
Senior Crime Reporter

Wait a minute, you might be saying. Why link the "Mystery Man Murders" to that quirky used bookshop that keeps popping up in the most violent of places?

An excellent question, since no one has any clarity on the case despite countless hours of work by a pair of Buffalonya detectives, closely supervised by the police commissioner herself.

"Follow the book dust, Jane," one anonymous source said, "and you just might lead your readers into the light."

Cryptic, right?

This reporter thought so, so she went to Commissioner Meme Shiva for comment.

"The 'Mystery Man' mystery is like a pin cushion," Shiva said. "Anyone can pin any thing or any one to it and no one can prove them right or wrong or even say 'ouch'."

Eve Green, owner of the bookshop in question, refused to comment on the source's cryptic advice about the light.

However, sources agree that the case was a watershed, with cases prior and cases after being as different as night and day.

"There is a certain something about the progression from the 'Mystery Man' to the 'Double Daily Double' and on to the attack on the bookshop," Shiva said, "but it would be irresponsible, and actionable, to speculate in print or in private. So I will not, and I suggest the same course for others."

Shiva did have one thing to point out.

The body of the third person killed in the "Mystery Man Murders" and the body of former Police Commissioner Tom Tonolody were dumped in a dumpster behind a hole-in-the-wall bar in the downtown district going by the whimsical name of the Roll In & Crawl Out.

Tonolody's body was discovered, in mid-February, by the bartender on duty that night at the Roll In.

"I notice the overlap," Shiva said, "but my investigators have not been able to find any convincing evidence that would point in the direction of one perp."

The "Mystery Man Murders" case has three bodies, two John Does and one victim whose identity is known:

-- **First victim (i.d. unknown)**: On the evening of April 1, 2008, police were called to the scene of a bus vs. pedestrian accident in the dark, on a rainy night, near President's Park. The coroner later asked for and received, from a Coroner's Jury, a finding that the death was by misadventure, by a person or persons unknown. In other words, a homicide. The coroner was seeking to keep the investigation open, insiders have said. The coroner also pointed to the fact that the victim seemed to be frozen in the path of the bus, arms outstretched. This suggested some sort of impairment or coercion, the coroner had said. The name of the victim has not been discovered.

-- **Second victim (i.d. known)**: In early summer 2008, the body of Bill Zeohn, a freelance photographer known to government insiders downtown, was found in the middle of a street on Buffalonya's East Side. Cause of death was ruled to be blunt-force trauma to the head. Zeohn was probably killed at another location and dumped in the street, sources say.

-- **Third victim (i.d. not known)**: In late August 2008, a man's body was found in a dumpster in an alley downtown. This third body was linked to the other two by the discovery of a symbol drawn on the side of the dumpster with indelible ink pen.

Sources agree that the dumpster's appearing in two separate murder cases is an arresting fact.

"The odds that it was a random thing make the lottery look even worse than it is in terms of chances per gazillion," one law enforcement source said.

Thus, we began our three-part examination of the recent record with this baffling case.

Some insiders, when talking off the record, are willing to say that public officials act as if they don't care whether the truth ever comes out concerning the three Mystery Men, murdered in Buffalonya in the silly season also known as 2008.

Tomorrow: The hoax known as the "Double Daily Double Murders."

Black/white and read all over
| 13May10 |

This news story ran across the bottom of Page 1A of this morning's **Daily Afterblatt, Lake Effect edition**.

The 'Double Daily' hoax
Official lies, media outrage mark bogus murder case

Editor's note: This is the third of four articles concerning certain high-profile murders that seem to be linked in some way to a quirky, notorious Buffalonya used bookshop called Caspar's Books and That.

By Jane Carlotto
Senior Crime Reporter

The chill that descended upon the relationship between Buffalonya's media and Buffalonya's public officials this winter has not abated.

Although the cold tone cannot be seen as vast enough to contribute to so-called "global warming," those who feel the local chill say that it is a wonder that the exchange of information and inquiry, for the public good, has been able to continue.

Insiders say we should blame a murder investigation widely known as the "Double Daily Double Murders."

Why?

Because no one died, no one broke the law, and everyone who was mourned returned among the living, in time, with a story of a hoax that a variety of officials said was perpetrated to protect "national security."

Beginning in 2009 and continuing into 2010, various public officials reported, and the local media released, numerous stories concerning four citizens that officials said had been slain -- Nancy Chino, a 37-year-old actor; Chino's tenant Natasha Riga; and a couple who were once, sources say, spies – Goose Grim and Eve Green, of the used bookshop Caspar's Books and That, in the north section of the city.

These are the facts, or "faux" facts, fed to the media about the four "victims:"

-- The body of Chino, a well-loved local actress, was "found" in mid-April 2009 in the Aspen – Quarters Museum on the campus of Buffalonya State University.

-- The body of Natasha Riga, the elderly woman who was Chino's tenet, was "found" at the museum in May 2009. Both bodies had been "dumped" in the so-called "Cricket Room" inside the museum.

-- The bodies of Goose Grim and Eve Green were "found" in July 2009 in a dumpster behind the museum.

Police Commissioner Meme Shiva called a press conference, on Jan. 25, to "explain" why the police department and the coroner's office, at a minimum and at the highest levels, had colluded in the "Double Daily Double Murders" hoax that was explained to gathered and furious local media as a "pressing matter of national security."

In a move reminiscent of the little man pulling strings behind the scenes in the "Wizard of Oz" movie, as revealed by the clever little dog Toto, a shadowy figure at the press conference, shielded from the media by a screen, told the story of why the hoax was cooked up and "served" to a news-hungry public.

First, however, Shiva had to deal with the "servers."

After lodging a public disclaimer, the media decided to stay and listen.

The public's right to know trumped media outrage at being duped into "serving up" lies.

The Person Behind the Screen identified himself as working for an unnamed domestic security agency of the sort generally called a "Three Letter Agency," or TLA.

This is a summary of the story told by the Person Behind the Screen:

There has been, for a long time, in our city, a focused and covert effort to subvert public officials and departments and to influence their work in ways that were actionable if it were not for the volatile and sensitive nature of the sub-story that cannot be told.

Certain unnamed local officials were forced to tailor their departments' work to suit these forces from outside, the Person said, refusing to give any additional details except that the situation is now under control and that the staged deaths of the four persons had to do with the "Double Daily Double Murders" counter-effort that would remain largely secret in reference to details.

The Person added that Buffalonya's proximity to the border with Canada may be seen as a factor in the thinking of the persons who sought to corrupt certain city officials.

The Person refused to say whether the "Double Daily" counter-effort could be best-described as counter-espionage, counter-terrorism, or something else.

When asked for more information concerning the tie-in with national security, the Person refused to comment, citing the need for secrecy in such matters, in order that currently covert operatives are not only effective in the future but safe as well.

When asked if the sudden resignation and departure of the former commissioner of police, Tom Tonolody, was related to this covert operation, the Person refused to comment.

In January 2009, just months before the first of the four faux murders hit the headlines, Tonolody left town in great haste a day after making Shiva his deputy, then resigning without warning.

Unnamed sources say that Tonolody entered a witness protection program.

The so-called "Mystery Man Murders" were, in the minds of some observers, tied with the events surrounding Tonolody. This has never been confirmed or denied by public officials.

Tonolody's active part in the story ended this February when his body was found in a dumpster in an alley downtown, the same alley and dumpster where the third victim in the "Mystery Man Murders" had been found the year before.

Various media challenges to the handling of the "Double Daily Double" hoax are going forward, but none of them has yielded any results, according to senior media representatives.

Tomorrow: Book battle, blog blowup.

Black/white and read all over
|14May10|

This news story ran across the bottom of Page 1A of this morning's **Daily Afterblatt, Lake Effect edition**.

Book battle, blog blowup
Random acts of violence mirror virtual blog jousting
Editor's note: This is the last of four articles concerning certain high-profile murders that seem to be linked in some way to a quirky, notorious Buffalonya used bookshop called Caspar's Books and That.

By Jane Carlotto
Senior Crime Reporter

After back-to-back multiple-murder cases, Buffalonya in past months has settled down to hacks and the odd attack.

Who has not heard of the "Fried Buffalonya" blog site and *bologistan*, its owner, who "outed" the former spooks and their associates who own, work at, or just hang out at Caspar's Books and That?

And, more recently, who hasn't heard about what is being referred to as the "Big Bloody Battle Among the Books?"

Two of the three men who attacked the persons inside Caspar's in broad daylight, in late March, died in the attempt, with the third, their purported leader, ending up in an induced coma before being murdered in his hospital bed sometime Sunday night or early Monday morning.

Police say someone turned off his life-support machine.

The death of Peter Principe, 57, of Pittsburgh, in an undisclosed hospital in the region, brings our examination of the local tide of violence full circle.

Readers might wonder what connection that the blog site Fried Buffalonya has to the rash of murders in question.

First, the blog brought out into the open the quirky bookshop and its equally quirky crew, who were the subject of a an earlier three-part series by this reporter.

Second, the Fried Buffalonya blog site, taken over by a more seasoned hacker who co-opted both the blog site and the handle *bologistan*, was the scene of a hacker dust-up, pitting *bologistan* against a hacker calling himself *manram*.

On Feb. 15, *bologistan* posted a promise to tell the real story about former Police Commissioner Tom Tonolody.

"Stay tuned," *bologistan* said. "... we will tell you the real story about how and why Tom Tonolody is no longer the police commissioner and just where he disappeared to."

A day later, a hacker calling himself *The Man from Mars* hacked the blog site and took control. This hacker subsequently identified himself as *YentlBengie*.

A day later, the body of Tonolody was found in a dumpster behind a little bar in the downtown district called the Roll In & Crawl Out.

Sources close to the investigations say that all of these factors, by definition, form a constellation of a size and story that has not yet been charted.

One thing is certain, these observers say -- Caspar's Books and That touches every part of the untold narrative, either directly, as in the Big Bloody Battle, and in the murder hoax, where two of the four faux victims, Eve and Goose Grim, came from the bookshop, or indirectly, in ways no one can or will define.

Neither Eve or Goose Grim would agree to be interviewed for this article.

"Keep the faith, Jane," one anonymous source said. "The truth is a cur and will be whipped out of hiding, sooner or later."

Another source suggested that the virtual world of the hackers involved in the Fried Buffalonya dust-ups might offer clues and facts to further the unfolding of the story.

When asked to comment on this, Commissioner Shiva said that "police usually have trouble understanding, let alone penetrating, virtual hacker communities."

Last-known email addresses of *bologistan* and *manram* yielded no communications.

And no one knows how to contact *The Man from Mars* AKA *YentlBengie*.

Emails to *bologistan* and *manram* "bounced" back to this reporter's email inbox. Address unknown.

≈ ≈ ≈

Email from: Mister Ed
To Goose Grim

Subject: House of Verbs. Open again.

I simply cannot, Mister Chair Sir, resist bracketing the excellent work of our sister Jane with another of my offerings from the Planet of Grammar and Usage.

Your servant,
Ed

Time and chance - a witness for the words

I bear witness to many things that have changed in some of our largest institutions -- newspapers, the Church, book publishing -- and not just in the lives of persons but also in the sense of rules, permissions, and latitudes concerning language.

Others have responded to such Bay of Fundy tides of change with anger or anguish at the smacking around that our language (and institutions) must endure. Let us stipulate that persons are more important than words but that words, like pets, still need an advocate, for words cannot tell their own story.

Without persons who speak and write, and observe, words -- our words -- would be dead and gone. I care more about self and other persons, but I also prize words in themselves, like I love my cat -- less than my friends, certainly, but more than many other strangers or things.

Without words, how could I say, *I love you*?

▪ ▪ ▪

On balance, when I think of changes that I have seen, I feel happy, hopeful, and curious about what is coming next, more than I feel sad or angry or scared about what might come or has come already.

The words we speak and that many of us cherish as beautiful things in themselves are not **the real thing** nor do words come in for blame or praise. Words stand in for the realities that we wish to speak of in order to be more fully human, and especially in regard to community.

Words witness to human emotion as well as sometimes causing strong human emotion.

She walks in beauty like the night ... .

April is the cruelest month ... .

In the beginning God created heaven and earth ... .

Words can make us tall and handsome. Words can dress up our thoughts and feelings so that, no longer naked, we can go out of the house and meet other persons on the way to anywhere we are going. Words, as a vehicle for who we are, deserve to be valued, celebrated, respected, and played with, like children.

Like children of God.

And just like cats are people too, so too are words.

Just like people.

Like.

Words form the perfect metaphor. Words get us as close to shared meaning as we can get. And that is huge, that alone.

Godlike.

Godlike?

Some say that God is most powerful instead of all powerful, that God is, like a person such as you or me, moving closer and closer to who God wants God to be. This theological construct is meant to get at an answer to questions of why there is evil in the Creation that God made good.

What can be said of God can also be said of persons. Words get us ever closer to the meaning of who we are, together. And words, which form us, also inform us, when we tell our stories to one another, out loud or in print for all to see. Words thus can seem godlike in their power and utility.

The only thing missing is love. We supply that.

To words, and through words.

■ ■ ■

I have been reading at **Eats, Shoots and Leaves**, that bestselling usage book by Lynn Truss. How did we get from the thin but bracing air of titanic E..B. White's **The Elements of**

Style to an endless rant about the abuses of punctuation in public places? I am not going to rant about those who rant about language and its *bling* of commas, periods, apostrophes, and the rest. I recoil from the pick-sniffy air of Truss's book, and I have no desire to be known as a *stickler*. I am so much more than a rant-prone sticker, and I believe that you are, too. And Lynn Truss.

The challenge that sticklers take up is both personal and political. And important. Dangerous.

And just what, you ask, is the challenge?

My answer is this.

The challenge for those who love words the way that that little boy loved the **Velveteen Rabbit** is to learn how to hold our words lightly but well, like my father held the steering wheel of his logging truck with a firmness that he could sustain for the long haul -- with love, too, and civility.

Lightly and well, which came naturally to my father, who could lead what was attached to his cab while following the road. One who wields tons of logs in motion must be civil. As they say, somewhere in Africa, **When the elephants fight the grass suffers.**

Words, like children, demand and deserve special treatment. We want to hold words, and let go of words, in good time, to good effect. If words had no meaning or use, any cry or grunt would do, but you know what would happen. We would sort and discuss with sign language and file away the cries and grunts that we and others would utter. First an archive, then a dictionary.

If we had no language, we would build a sound one.

My reading tells me that there are four ways to vocalize words in Mandarin Chinese and that each way delivers its own category of meaning. Not only the words but also their delivery become precious and necessary to those who speak and to those who hear.

It is not that we do not do this in English but that hearing how others communicate helps us understand them, and us, better. We can see how others, in different ways, hold words lightly and well.

■ ■ ■

I love this image of holding words, like babies and steering wheels, lightly and well. Others, however, might say that I am a foolish old man of empty words about words – all words and no action. Our times, in the opinion of sticklers, strike a loutish blow against language that must be countered with blows of our own.

How quickly words can lead us to violence.

Those who use words the way male chauvinist pigs use women will laugh at my description of my gentle truck-driving father holding his steering wheel lightly and well. Does that erase my words, or empty my words of their power? No. Does that make me sad or mad, that my poetic and precise evocation of my father's memory could attract scornful snickering? Yes.

Do I therefore take up arms and counterattack?

Oh woe is me, so full of the woe of words.

■ ■ ■

Who, then, am I speaking to?

The choir, of course. The ones who sing from the same page as I do, making sweet sounds, at least in our own ears.

The challenge lies in being true to myself while encountering others as we swing like pendulums prone to collision.

The challenge is to give writers tools to live with in community, so they might sing for others songs of deep meaning and joy, as the occasion deserves and demands.

That you might be heard and understood.

I will write about the container, and the things contained, by us and in us. **Lightly**, I hope, **and well**.

Black/white and read all over
| 15May10 |

This piece ran in a three-column, 1-point box squared off with the lead story on Page 1A of this morning's **Daily Afterblatt, Lake Effect edition**.

Letter to readers
Hacker agrees to string for us re: blog wars

Dear readers,

It is one thing, and a bad thing, to buy news.

It is another thing, and a good thing, to pay freelance writers who can offer a unique perspective on the news.

We take this unusual but not unheard of position on Page 1A of our newspaper to share with you some special news.

As our Senior Crime Writer, Jane Carlotto, said in concluding her three-part series on our favorite bookshop and booksellers -- Caspar's Books and That, and Eve Green and Goose Grim -- the ins and outs of reporting on virtual things such as blogs, and even more, blog wars, are beyond most of us, Jane included (by her own candid and honest admission).

Jane also reported that she got no response to emails to the hackers who squared off over control of the shock blog web site "Fried Buffalonya."

This was true, at press time yesterday, but the hacker who calls himself *YentlBengie* initiated contact was one of the members of the Editorial Board, offering his services and suggesting a story explaining just what happened in the blog battle that he won over hacker *manram*, who lost control over the blog site when *YentlBengie* hacked the site and boxed him out.

(We call the two bloggers "him," but we acknowledge that on the Internet no one knows whether you are a person or a dog (to quote the famous New Yorker cartoon ... which reminds us of the other New Yorker cartoon that we like, where one dog sez to another, sitting at a keyboard in front of a computer monitor -- "Try *www dot someonefeedus dot com.*")

Our man in Blogistan, *YentlBengie*, though he promises a quick turnaround, does not promise to meet any particular deadline.

The piece will run on the Op-Ed Page.

We will alert you.

-- the editors

Meanwhile, back in the backroom
| 16May10 |

"While you were gone," I said, "a few things happened, my brothers."

While I am talking, Jeanne is busy licking the lobes (lurid red) and kissing the noses (a shocking shade of pink) of my two brothers Jim.

"And we have news, too," Jim said.

"Yeah," OhJim said, "and a straight-eight Olds that has a slight knock but a lot of miles left, like Mae West."

"Question is," Eve said, "who goes first, news or olds?"

"I don't know the answer to that," I said, "but I will say this. Brother Tommy has gone missing, which is why you were told to come back from Pittsburgh in such a rush."

A mere four hours have passed since my brothers jumped into the Crown Vic for a speedy trip home from Pittsburgh.

Jeanne walks over to David and wiggles into his lap, crossing her legs to dangle a brand-new black pump from her toes. My brothers, already pink down to their toes from Jeanne's greeting, take on that junkyard dog stare that prolonged exposure to Jeanne puts on your typical American male's face.

"I said," I said, "that Tommy has gone missing. Hello?"

"Gotcha," Jim said.

"Yeah," OhJim said, "and our news trumps your news, no question, Ace. Old news."

This, I though to myself, **should be interesting**.

Eve just smiles her Buddha Girl smile, to one side, and Jeanne smiles, bitter and sweet, to the other side.

Stasis.

Gotta love it.

There it goes.

Oh, well. I was getting bored.

I should have had faith in the way of life that we have chosen.

If you don't like the weather, we say in Buffalonya, **wait five minutes**.

At **Caspar's Books and That**, we say, **If you don't like what's going on, blink your eyes and duck**.

Marking the only time that a Goose is a duck.

≈ ≈ ≈

Email from: Mister Ed
To Goose Grim

Subject: House of Verbs. Open again.

I realize that these essays, Mister Chair Sir, have a strong personal element. I would be curious to see if any of my readers know which details are cover and which are what some might call real. Such as references to my "father". Clearly, the man was part of a legend. My legend.

Drop me an email. There is a prize.

Your servant,
Ed

When I'm in my write mind

I do not need to go back in my mind to the Reading-Record newsroom, silent witness to my days as a cub reporter. The rooms of the newsroom, the two of them, often are with me without bidding when I sit down and set out to write.

The mind, it seems, **anchors** memories with images. I learned from my reading that the discipline called **Neuro-Linguistic Programming** (NLP) speaks of this phenomenon in terms of its therapeutic applications. If you do not like the feel of a memory anchor, you can swap anchors in a simple mind process.

Basically, you close your eyes and pick a new anchor image. And it works.

I have noticed, for a long time now, that the mind anchor that accompanies many of my efforts at writing is that old Reading-Record newsroom.

A few details might help.

My hometown newspaper was, and is, the Reading-Record AKA the **Reading-Wreck** to certain of its critics, detractors, and employees, at least in my tenure at that newspaper. As a boy of 10, I begin delivering the R-R and kept my paper route until I was 17. Within a year, I was working the phones on weekend nights during football and basketball season. I talked with a lot of high school coaches and passed my notes and stats on to the sports editor and his sidekick.

In the lesser of the two rooms of the newsroom.

Sports and Society.

During the following summer, I graduated to the bigger room, and obits, and features, and press release rewrites. Plus an occasional school board meeting and anything else I was told to do by persons older and wiser than myself.

After securing a Bachelor of Arts degree in English Literature, I returned as a full-time editorial employee, first as a copy boy and quickly on to the copy desk. Four years later, I moved to Oregon and stayed there ten years on the copy desk of the capital's daily newspaper, going from the rim to the slot with time as night news editor on Sundays.

By going on to other work, I followed the advice of Ernest Hemingway -- that newspapers are good for a young person who knows when to get out and do something else.

The Reading-Record building anchored a short block on the edge of downtown at the edge of the steep slope that marks the lateral edge of the floodplain of the river than runs past the town. The building was made of concrete blocks. The newsroom's two rooms held a couple of sports reporters, the society editor, and the Green Sheet editor on one side and about six reporters and a couple of city and copy editors on the other side. The Editor/Publisher had an office off the main room. He was a patrician old man with a round face and red cheeks like hard drinkers develop in age. Those of us in the know knew that he was not really **Reader Rick**, who would write wry and amusing blurbs on local topics for the Saturday editorial page.

We all wrote **Reader Ricks** at one time or another.

The images that I anchor with when I write come from a visit that I made, on a hellishly hot afternoon, to the newsroom with a friend who let me in, to see the new computers that sat on the desks. The walls were a clean white and no posters or other untidy things adorned the walls. In my mind the place is deserted -- clean and white, with a hum in the background and dust mites in the diffuse light of the weekend-empty room.

I do wonder why these particular images and not some other images pop up when I sit down to write. After all, I also have anchoring images when I read novels, and they are different each time, and it is a surprise and a pleasure to notice the images that link up with my reading time. A set of images will persist until I finish reading the novel of the moment, returning if I put down the book for a while.

But why the newsroom? I was not particularly happy during that time. I was a piggy little SOB, frankly, who had a long way to go. However, none of that clings to the newsroom images. Decades later, the images give me peace and draw me into the mystery of creation.

■ ■ ■

When I asked my shrink, an older and wiser man who has forgotten more about NLP than I ever knew, he refused to engage with me on the subject.

"I don't know how people create," he said. "What is important is how you create. See you next time."

Me? I pick up my pen, or I sit down at the computer, and I write an essay or snatch of novel that I have been day-dreaming about. I anchor my mind with images that seem to be meant to occupy the parts of me that fret and prattle. I move along quickly without worrying much about my word choices. There is time for word-fishing when I revise, and I revise in rounds of polishing that have a charm of their own.

[**Note from Ed**: This is an exciting addition to my slight efforts to instruct and delight. When I shared my essay above with Goose, he put on his robes and gave me some words from the Rev. Mr. White on the topic in hand.]

As a person of faith and as a Minister of the Word and Sacrament, at least for the purposes of cover, and for those purposes, I studied as hard or harder than an other man of the cloth. I would say this about that, and I want to make myself perfectly clear. I find myself in awe of the flow from outside me, through me, and out onto the page, to you. My writing is a gift, I believe, to you via me with the Spirit in a consulting sort of role that some wise persons call **co-creation**. I write out of gifts that God gave me, I believe, and I cannot write or speak of this without tearing up, just a bit, which is probably tiresome for others but not for me.

I cry as I write, when I know that the writing is good.

This is what writing is like for me. I do not suffer from writer's block. My faith grounds me in solid skills of expression and the exponential perfecting of my work. I am a heavy reader, as well, and this paired with study, I believe, makes for an effective method of writing. I want to say it is like playing in the fields of the Lord, and it is, but the words of E.B. White come back to me, too.

About writing, White said something like ... **All of it was hard and some of it was fun**.

That is my memory, anyway.

■ ■ ■

My preaching has its moments, too, from a creative standpoint. In the many years when I was preaching, under the cover of the Cloth, the lion's share (what is the lion's share? ...

anything the lion wants!) was from an outline rather than a manuscript. I drew upon my writing, my reading, my day-dreaming, and my real-time grasp of language. I got up and started talking. I introduced an image or an idiom, or both. I told stories from my life, and I listened to the Spirit, for the Spirit's leading.

At first, preaching this way felt like tightrope walking without a net, but quickly it became a joy. My mentors taught me to monitor the flow of everything I hear or say, for sense and for adherence to certain core principles of language. As with my writing, my preaching came to me as gift and went through me, and did not stop.

When I preached, I was not usually aware of any anchoring images, but I frequently was aware of being in a light hypnotic trance (another piece of learning from mentors). From what little I know of hypnotism, I know that if I have achieved a light trance state, my listeners will be in a light trance state, too, if they enter into the experience and accept my leading.

This may sound hard, or odd, or whatever, but what I was aware of when preaching was the joy of creating stories and of speaking from my heart and mind, in the presence of the One who called me and gave me gifts.

■ ■ ■

[Note: Returning to Ed.]

I have been blessed in my working life. I have done creative work of many kinds, as a cub reporter, headline writing copy editor, book reviewer, and essay writer. I have grown from a piggy little SOB whom you do not need to know anything further about to be a person who can follow his inclination when speaking or writing. There is no finer thing that one can do with both feet on the floor.

I fell so grateful.

Anchored and free.

Time to catch up with the news
|17May10|

Like the huddled disciples that we are, we sit in the backroom at **Caspar's Books and That**, reading the newspaper and drinking coffee while waiting for the Spirit to light a fire under us.

"Looks like someone hurt Peter Principe," Jim said.

"They didn't hurt him," OhJim said, "they killed him."

The boys had been back but a day, and now this.

In fact, several surprises were vying for our attention.

- Tommy gone missing.
- Peter Principe whacked.
- Some story, yet to be told, that the boys brought back from Pittsburgh about the difference between **Grimes** and **Grim**.

Question was, should we start with the new news (Principe) or the new-to-you news (Tommy gone missing ... Grimes vs. Grim)?

Ma settles the issue as only Ma can.

"My Diamond and Ruby Jim boys, be gathering by me," Ma said. "I am of your telling about this Principe, in the newspaper this of the a.m. Is bad business and hoping I am that all of you are having the alibi."

Ma smiles her toothless rogue's smile to one and all.

"My view?" Mister Ed said. "No one here would have pulled the plug on Principe. It would not be sporting, or wise."

"The view from the heights," Jim said.

"Yeah," OhJim said, "our Great White Crane in the clouds."

"We're covered, Dear," Eve said. "Part of our quasi-criminal enterprise is the spin-off **Alibis 'R' Us**."

Eve gives Ma her best Buddha Girl smile.

"Besides, Ma," I said, "I am of the opinion that we were all in bed and sawing logs by midnight last night."

From David's lap, giggles.

"David and I have an iron-clad alibi," Jeanne said, smiling sideways.

"I wish I could say the same for my brother," Jim said.

"Yeah," OhJim said, "and how long have **you** been a poofter? You can go there if you want, but don't drag me along."

Tommy gets some slack from slackers
| 18May10 |

"You know Tommy," Luke said.

The agent shrugs his substantial shoulders.

"Bingo," I said. "We know Tommy, to the point where he disappeared."

"I'm missing something," Jim said.

"Yeah," OhJim said. "You have a point there ... ."

OhJim raises both eyebrows in the universal **help-me-out-here** signal.

"And," David said, "if you wear a hat it won't show."

"Yeah!" OhJim said. "Badda bing!"

David and OhJim meet at mid-room in a flying tummy-bump.

"I can see that we are all broken up about Tommy," Eve said. "I know that I am."

"Not," Jeanne said, smiling to the side.

"I'm still missing something," Jim said. "What is the story behind the headline, which as I take it would go something like, **Agent Bingo takes a powder**."

"Yeah," OhJim said. "Walk this way and you won't need to use powder."

OhJim stomped around. Eve and Jeanne gave him the finger.

"Let us come to orders," I said. "F-Troop meeting, eighteen May twenty-ten."

"Amen," Jim said.

"Yeah," OhJim said. "A women, too. Gotta be inclusive, Jim-bro. Women can take orders as well as or better than a men can."

"If I might, Mister Chair Sir," Mister Ed said, "then I will."

I nod to our other big guy in the shoulders department.

"It goes like this," Mister Ed said. "We were sitting in our places, with bright, shiny faces, just two days ago in Pittsburgh, at a certain safe house, when Agent Luke here walked in and shared the news that Agent Tommy, friend to one and all, was nowhere to be found. Luke said that he checked with this one and that one and a bunch of others whom we do not need to know the identity of. Nothing."

Luke shrugs his Mister Ed-size shoulders.

"The question is, Dear," Eve said, "-- has Tommy done this in the past or is this a first time for everything, in his case?"

"It is too soon to tell," Luke said, "but I can say that the players I talked with were guarded in their answers. The subtext was heavy and broody like the sky before a thunderstorm."

"It was enough for Luke to whisk us back to the motherhouse from Pittsburgh," Jim said.

"Yeah," OhJim said, "and we were hot on the trail of a big story."

"Yes," Jim said, "a big story that we haven't told you yet."

"Well," I said, "what are you doing in the next few minutes?"

≈ ≈ ≈

Email from: Mister Ed
To Goose Grim

Subject: House of Verbs. Open again.

The prize goes to David, who guessed, correctly, that there is no difference between what is real and what is cover. Good eye, young man. Your prize is a double discount for any of my editing services that you or anyone you choose may request.

And may I say, sir, that my emails say that your musing about the muse of the minister was a close second to my own humble efforts for the words.

Your servant,
Ed

Books in Review: *Words on Words*

John Bremner was a man of many faces and places -- priest, husband, professor, writer, friend. His usage book **Words on Words**, though not as popular or notorious as other titles, will be a sure map to the territory and with one exception, quickly fixed, will not let you down, lead you astray, or swipe your precious baggage.

That one exception was a misspelling that Bremner made in his manuscript for **Words on Words**. He misspelled the word **millennium**. When a copy editor called, he rejected the idea that he could have misspelled a word, a Latinate word no less. Bremner said the copy editor said something like, **Look it up, hotshot**, and hung up.

I wonder if she introduced herself as **Miss Spelling**.

Bremner was **1)** mortified and **2)** contrite.

This anecdote I heard in a roomful of copy editors. We were gathered to hear Bremner give a seminar on grammar and usage matters for journalists and their minders.

Copy editors seldom get any respect and usually get reviled for the mistakes that others make and that the copy editors do not catch. Being at this seminar was one of the few **atta-boys** I got in all my years of such work. I want to say that Bremner's throwing us that story was like feeding raw meat to sharks, but it was not like that. The response was the dull rage of the back-stopper.

Silence, and an occasional nod.

When Bremner had asked us if anyone knew what was wrong with the word he had written on the board -- a misspelled version of **millennium** -- a carefully dressed woman of a certain age, from the one metro in attendance, moved to the front of the class, placed her bling-bright reading glasses on her nose, and squinted at the word.

It should be m-i-l-l-e-n-n-i-u-m, she said.

Bremner bear-hugged her.

We back-stoppers smiled (though many of us also were grinding our teeth at not knowing the right answer; copy editors **are** competitive).

It is a memorable day.

Notice that I did not say that it **was** a memorable day. No. For me, it is memorable, like my last roller coaster ride, which also was my first. It is a memorable day in line with one of the many memorable things Bremner said on that day. Bremner explained the **sequence of verb tenses**, a principle of writing that one follows with or without using, knowing, or understanding the phrase **sequence of verb tenses**. For example, in reported speech I might write that "the mayor said that he was tired because he had been up all night with a sick aide."

The simple past tense of **said** is rightly followed by the more complex past perfect tense form **had been up**. In speaking and in writing, we do this automatically, but Bremner wanted the back-stoppers to know how to fix the thing if it got broken.

After filing a story on what the mayor said, later on I might be having a beverage with colleagues and say that "the mayor was in full bloom tonight. He really is a pompous twit."

Here the sequence of past tense verb forms yields to a universal truth on the order of "the moon is round" or "mean people suck".

Universal truths, even when part of the sequence of tenses usually used in reported speech, take a present tense verb.

"He said the sun is bright, and we said in reply that he was stating the obvious."

Other treasures that Bremner gave us that day included --

- using vivid quotes in news stories.
- placement of attribution for greatest effect.
- a term for meaningless headlines (**crinoline headlines**, which cover everything and touch nothing).
- and the roots of the word **ukulele**.

The day lives on for me like a beautiful rose that blooms in its season with a pleasing regularity.

■ ■ ■

John Bremner began as a priest and ended as a professor, at the University of Kansas. Bremner's students loved him, to judge from their public statements and their private stories. I worked with many of his students during my time in Oregon.

Bremner focused anger on lapses and blank spots in the use of words. I would say, after being in **The Presence** on two occasions that Bremner by his attitude said, **Join me in this anger ... focus your anger on fixing broken words and phrases in a broken world.**

Okay, that is a lot of me and a scoch of Bremner, but that is what I heard under all the zeal and showmanship. and all the stories of his students sitting beside me on the copy desk rim.

Bremner was large, expressive, and demanding. He had a vigorous salt-and-pepper beard that put out as much effort under his chin as above it. He taught his students through vivid stories and startling, thunderous pronouncements such as **Shit! said the Pope** or **Balls had I but two I would be King, cried the Queen.**

The papal pronouncement was meant to illustrate the choosing of quotes with punch. The queen's lament was meant to illustrate the importance of placing attribution for best effect -- **Balls, cried the Queen, had I but two I would be King.**

Bremner urged us to fix all copy that said anything other than some form of **said** in reported speech in news stories. He urged us to avoid the sports department's use of **would**, such as **In time on that day, Bremner would go on to say to us in closing, Meanwhile comma peace period.**

■ ■ ■

Words on Words, at just over 400 pages, covers most of the words that can make you look silly if you or someone else does not catch the error. The book rewards close reading. The book rewards those who use it like a dictionary. Sampling, even briefly, from this book will give you something of value. After all, who in their right mind would sit down to read a dictionary cover to cover.

Don't answer that.

Reading all of even the **Shorter Oxford English Dictionary**, weighing in at 20 pounds, give or take an adverb or two, would give you bragging rights to place beside your reading of **War and Peace** but also would give you an acute need for reading glasses. Your writing probably would be no better than it had been before you started with the A's.

Reading or reading at **Words on Words** will improve your writing.

Here is an example of the style that Bremner uses --

> **UKULELE**
> Note the spelling. Most of the time *ukulele* appears as *ukelele*. The word is Hawaiian for *flea*, from *uku*, insect, and *lele*, to jump, a reference to the fingers flitting across the strings. See also **ACCORDION.**

■ ■ ■

I choose to begin with Bremner rather than one of his many competitors because of my strong memory of him and the obscurity that his book **Words on Words** has in comparison to word masters such as Fowler or Bernstein, neither of whom will lead you astray. I choose Bremner in hopes that those of you who know the first tier will appreciate my gift of a new source of truth, trust, and joy.

Black/white and read all over
|19May10|

From this morning's edition of the **Daily Afterblatt, Lake Effect edition.**

Peter Principe

Funeral arrangements are pending for Peter Principe, 57, of Pittsburgh, PA, at Ikon-Saurin Funeral Home in Buffalonya.

Principe died as a result of foul play in an undisclosed hospital, according to Buffalonya Police reports.

A funeral service will be held at a time to be announced, in Pittsburgh, where Mr. Principe was a life-long resident.

He leaves a sister, Jeena, of Tampa, FL; a brother, Jim, of Pittsburgh; a daughter, Willa, of Pittsburgh; and numerous nieces and nephews.

The cause of death was linked to criminal activity in the turning off of Principe's life support system, without permission, by a person or persons unknown, according to the Eerie County coroner, Dr. William Backstaff.

A story worth waiting for
|20May10|

"I don't know what to make of it, but I do have a story to tell," Jim said.

"Yeah," OhJim said, "and it has a link to Principe, too."

"To say nothing of a link to us Grim types," Jim said.

"Well," I said, "take it from the top, then."

Jim looks at OhJim.

"Yeah," OhJim said, "I guess you're the storyteller here."

OhJim shrugs.

"Just before we were yanked back here to Buffalonya," Jim said, "Luke and I took a ride over to the Shadyside section of Pittsburgh to interview a woman with an interesting living situation. She went by the name Janey Grimes, but most people just call her the Rich Bitch, at least in the small circles we were moving in."

"OK," I said, "and the living situation?"

"Peter Principe's house," Jim said.

So many eyebrows shoot up that it looks like an entire herd of deer caught in the headlights.

"Well," Eve said, "and how did you come by that bit of info, Jim?"

"Well," Jim said, "We did it the old fashioned way."

"And?" I said.

"We asked," Jim said.

"Tommy's hint was a big help, too," Luke said.

"You shoulda seen," Jim said, "her face. Priceless."

Ma is of the remembering
|21May10|

"I am knowing of this Rich Bitch woman of the Grimes," Ma said, "but the knowing is not crisp like the toast, but still, knowing, like the bacon."

Ma grins her toothless rogue's smile.

"Do you remember when or where?" Jim said.

"This," Ma said, "is probably less of the helpful than silence, my Jim Ruby."

"Is it the nickname or the family name that you are getting a glimmer about, Dear?" Eve said.

"Both of these, Sweetness," Ma said, "and none of these at all the same of the timely. Someday this will be coming upon me, but not this days, here and the now."

"Well, Ma," Jim said, "I'll continue the story and maybe you will get some clarity as we go along."

"That's my clever boy Jim the Ruby," Ma said. "Continuing with the briefness of yourself."

"Well," Jim said. "Luke and I drove in the Crown Vic over the hill to Shadyside from the safe house in Highland Park, which meant driving across a corner of East Liberty and its extensive project housing blocks nicely paired with the needle spire of East Liberty Presbyterian Church, built by the Mellon family's millions."

Ma nods at this travelogue from her Jim Ruby.

"We drove up Murray," Jim said, "until we got to the address in question -- Peter Principe's house. The woman who answered the door put me in mind of no one more than our own Jeanne, but not in a good way, if you know what I mean."

"Yeah," OhJim said. " We read your nasty little mind all the time, Jim-bro."

Oh-Jim raises both eyebrows in the universal signal.

Help me out here.

Jeanne model-walks her way over to Jim.

Our Punk princess in strut mode is usually not a sign of good things to come for the man in her sights, though it makes for damn fine theater.

Jim, who knew what the model-walk meant for Tommy, in particular, quivers with half-expressed emotions.

At the last instant, OhJim throws himself in front of his brother, eyebrows still raised.

Stuck in SOS mode but ready to rescue.

≈ ≈ ≈

Email from: Mister Ed
To Goose Grim

Subject: House of Verbs. Open again.

Friends, I find myself in the odd or ironic position of introducing our own Goose Grim to the words that he has seen fit to share with me in kind reference to my own efforts of late to instruct and delight you all on grammar and usage, the two moons over my hammy, as it were.

Be sure to leave Goose comments and encouragement. Perhaps he will follow with more of the same, that is to follow. Right here, right now. Look down and enjoy.

Your servant,
Ed

Rambling about writers - content and process

Some writers make me larger, and some writers just make me feel small and inadequate. The best writers, however, take me higher and farther than I can go on my own. Being small, at least in comparison to a hill, dale, or mountain, I am easy to lift.

I'm thinking of Shakespeare, of Mark Twain, of Karen Russell, and of Orhan Pamuk. I can tell by the quality of my own writing when I've been reading one of my favorites.

The same goes for my preaching.

When I hear a dynamic speaker, I sound more dynamic in my own ears for a time. After hearing President Obama on television the other day, giving a eulogy at a memorial service for victims of a shooting spree in Tucson, I heard his rhythms in my own phrasing. Same thing happened after I heard a tape recording of William Sloane Coffin preaching. My delivery improved immediately.

. . .

You see, there is **content** and there is **process**.

Cargo and carrier.

There are ideas of power, and there are powerful ways of communicating those ideas. Sometimes, the words alone, in startling new order, have a power that exceeds content **and** process.

When you listen to Jesus, who knew how to stir up a crowd, you can see him provoking them with the whippy stick of the content of his presentation in order to make a sharper point about a process that he really wants them to understand. The tipoff is that after a catalog of outrageous sayings, such as **you must hate your mother and your father and your sisters and your brothers**, Jesus will use a summary sentence, such as *I came not to bring peace but a sword*.

The lucky ones among us get the point.

The rest of us wander in a guilt-ridden confusion.

If you get hung up on the provocative content that Jesus puts out there, you miss the process, which is the heart of the matter, and you wander down paths of pointless agitation.

Think of Jesus' saying that if your eye offends you, you must pluck it out. Sheer desperation can drive you to understand that a biblical metaphor is not a way of acting but a process of thought leading to a decision that guides actions in general.

I learned a lot about content and process from talking to Eve about her study and practice of psychotherapy. If the person across from Eve was telling a crazy and frightening story, she listened with divided attention for the themes. Otherwise, there would be two scared and confused kids in the room instead of one. Rather than solving problems, which is impossible anyway, Eve could help persons with their processes. If you decide something at process level, a lot of different and wonderful contents, or terrible contents, can flow from that one decision about the process, Eve told me.

The **presenting problem** is never the problem.

. . .

How can one writer both lift me up and run me down the way that Karen Russell does in her first novel, **Swamplandia!**? Russell has a wonderful feel for the words themselves. Watching her at play is a pleasure almost separate from the sense of her story, though her images are apt and do further the plot.

For example, in the book's afterword Russell thanks this person and that person and this person over here. And, oh yeah, the friendly family that put her up on their couch on many occasions --

... if this were interactive, I would give each of you an ovation and a Cadillac.

Reading **Swamplandia!** makes me happy and sad.

Content and process. The levels of the game.

Elation and envy.

■ ■ ■

I understand Shakespeare.

After all, I was an English Lit major.

Shakespeare cannot leave words alone but will worry at them like a cat with a hat or a dog with a scarf. Shakespeare wants to show the possibilities of words at play, the way meaning comes like a servant anticipating the master's summons.

Always the first to claim some pun-mined patch for Queen and Country, Shakespeare's footprints cover the map, even at the margins where it is written, **Here there be monsters.**

Twain reminds me that few things in God's green earth lack some pinch of humor. When Twain toured with friends (as told in **The Innocents Abroad**), he and his buddies got tired of local guides with names no one could say or remember. The three merry pranksters decided, by fiat, that all guides would answer to one name, **Ferguson**.

Ferguson was not amused and in some cases was rageful.

Thus does Twain mix mirth and rue to improve our humors.

Twain tells of getting a rubdown after a Turkish bath --

Please inform my family of my death, he said, **for I can tell from the stench arising from my body that this is so.**

Words to that effect, anyway.

And who has not heard some version of Twain's reaction to a false rumor concerning his health? I remember it as --

The news of my demise has been greatly exaggerated.

Twain describes how a sleepy river town comes alive for a while on a hot day when a steamboat puts in for water and wood to make more steam. Everyone, Twain said, was grateful for the **noise and confusion**.

■ ■ ■

Content and process. Jack and Jill.

I'm not absolutely certain of how this ramble of mine has any bearing on the subject at hand, which is grammar and usage, unless I offer it to you, at a discount, as a nod to matters of **style**.

Style in its many meanings --

- style as in typography.
- style as in tone, as in writer's voice.
- style as in the particularities of language ... such as style sheets.
- style as in Strunk and White's **The Elements of Style**.

■ ■ ■

The Turkish writer Orhan Pamuk, writing of and from Istanbul, amazes me. I am so much more glad that God is whispering fireworks of phrasing and cartwheels of ideas into Pamuk's ear than I am sad that my own God-given strings of firecrackers only hug the ground of their being and go **pop-pop-pop**.

Noise and confusion, silence and smoke.

Pamuk rewards the reader with work worthy of the name **literature**. His novels connect and cover the spaces among the dots, all the dots, no two alike. His essays do not merely assay or intend but come solid as gold and stay like diamonds set in the mind. We are made rich by Pamuk's either/ore, and we stand in awe of his Grammar of Gold.

Colors, patterns, intelligence, feeling, and cunning -- Pamuk's work in the service of the creator of us all. Only God can create, and only those with the ears to hear can try to tell us, in silence borne of letters, dumb until we bestir them for news from above, of the glories out there and down to here.

Content and process.

Pamuk, in his autobiographical book **Istanbul**, describes growing up in a wealthy family of privilege and of how the money ran down and the family prospered in its way though the mid-20th century decades of our life. Pamuk began as a fine artist but quickly switched from paintbrush to the press, of the pencil, on the page. His work earned him the Nobel Prize in Literature in 2006. His latest book to be translated into English, a slim volume titled **The Naive and the Sentimental Novelist**, gathers lectures that he gave in 2009 at Cambridge, Mass -- the Charles Eliot Norton Lectures. Privilege meets privilege, and we benefit from the riches and wealth.

Two things impress me about Pamuk.

First, that Pamuk's Istanbul has no western-style street signs, according to a map of the territory that I bought at the bookstore. One must hire a Ferguson to help one get around.

Second, that Pamuk writes at a location separate from his home and family, like a father going to his job, which is the profession of speech.

Orhan Pamuk's father was a writer of the hobby horse variety, and he wrote best in French, in Paris, far away from his wife, two sons, and legion of relations and circle of friends.

Pamuk wrote with deep compassion of his father in an essay printed in The New Yorker after Pamuk won the Nobel.

■ ■ ■

[Note from Goose: We return to Ed.]

When I was 10, my mother found a loose thread. When she pulled on it and pulled on it, our life began to unravel as she did. She found herself in the car, down by the river, trying to decide once and for all whether to jump in or go home and cook supper for six.

One morning during this time of unraveling, I was sitting on the porch in the cool of a perfect day in June. The last day of school, a half-day, was over, and I was waiting for my father to drive up in his logging truck, shattering the quiet of the street, and take me with him for the rest of his work day.

We thundered through the streets of our town and headed for the woods and a log landing two hours away, in the drainage of the Trinity River in northern California, way over by the tiny lumber mill town of Hayfork, which sat on the west fork of the south fork of the Trinity, or some such epi-geographical designation.

Remember Gertrude Stein's swipe at Oakland, California?

There was no **there** there.

Somewhere along the long way, thundering down a river road, we stopped at the spot where a 2-inch pipe stuck out toward the road at its clean end, delivering water from a spring in the gravel of a roadcut. A rusty tin can sat in the wet rocks below the dripping pipe. My father drank, and I did, too, realizing that a rusty can would not be something I should tell the others of when I described my day with dad.

Across the river road, past the pitch-perfect trailer load of Douglas fir lengths, limbed and bucked at about 20 feet -- tons of heavy chaos in a triangle stack of potential -- was an abandoned placer mining dredge platform. I guess you could call it a boat. Given water enough, it might float and it might stay upright. The placer miners who worked the riffles and panned the slurry for gold flakes, had shut down the machine and walked away, a long, long time before. They left behind berms of worked-over gravel that you never forget.

The water was sweet and cold.

Refreshing like a cool morning in June.

I was free until the fall, but not after.

Happy and uneasy.

That tin can, though clean, was rusty to a fault.

As my mother showed her iron will, my father showed me that can. And so many others.

■ ■ ■

My Editor in Chief in Oregon agreed to edit my book reviews before I gave them to the Sunday Editor. That was huge, all on its own. Editor OtherEd was dean, friend and colleague of John Bremner's for a time at Kansas. When the group from our newspaper had gathered with others to hear Bremner at a hotel in suburban Portland, Bremner came over and asked us in a resonant whisper, "Where is **The Dean**?"

OtherEd taught me three things --

● Book review must be the best writing in the newspaper.

● Do not use pronouns if you can avoid doing so.

● If you want to improve your writing, read good writers.

OtherEd gave me a year's subscription to The New Yorker. He insisted that I write no more than twelve column inches per book review. After a season, OtherEd passed me on to a staffer whom he admired, who ran the newspaper's morgue, where press clippings go to die. By then, I was writing tight, and I had a new confidence. My writing voice sounded right to me.

Jeanne's power-walk
|22May10|

Jeanne, in woven-leather pumps, is the same height as my brothers. Equal in stature but outshining them like the sun does the moon. She put one hand on Jim and her other hand on OhJim.

"Group-hug," Jeanne said, smiling bitter and sweet.

I guess that we can get habituated to drama and the crisis of the week, or maybe it is a matter of operant conditioning.

The Jeanne model-walk signals danger. Or did.

My brothers display a particularly lurid shade of pink after Jeanne releases them, in silence, and walks that walk, back to her chair next to David.

"Right," Jim said.

"Yeah," OhJim said.

Jeanne pops her right heel and bounces it on her red-toned big toe. Her arched eyebrows send the universal signal.

Help me out here.

Jeanne's power-talk
|23May10|

"Like I said," Jim said, "the woman who answered the door at Principe's house was sometime like Jeanne, but older, by at least ten years. But that isn't what I'm getting at. This woman was frightening. Yeah, beautiful, like a gypsy, with dense, curly-wavy black hair to her shoulders and just a bit more. Goth-like, too, in her stark contrasts of black and red. But she looked like she had been rode hard and put away wet. I dunno ... something like beauty but frightening rather than exciting."

Jeanne smiles to the side, and said, "Once you dig that hole, Jim-bro, go ahead and jump in. David will cover you over."

David smiles, all bug eyes and good will.

"Yeah," OhJim said. "I can dig it. Or David can. Makes me no never-mind."

"This isn't going well," Jim said. "What I am trying to say is this. Take it, Luke."

"I don't wanna," Luke said.

"Right," Jim said. "To continue, then. This woman was unsettling. That's it. Jeanne (he bobbled in her direction) is a contrast of the stark, the beautiful, and the good. This woman was the fulfillment of the outward trappings of stark beauty, but beauty like an orchard past its prime of scent. More Baudelaire than George Gordon, Lord Byron, more **Fleurs du Mal** than **she walks in beauty, like the night**."

Eve gave Jim her you-amaze-me smile, and Jeanne gave him her lemony sideways smile.

"I walked your way, Jim-bro," Jeanne said, "not to scare you but to empower you."

≈ ≈ ≈

Email from: Mister Ed
To Goose Grim

Subject: House of Verbs. Open again.

Good job, friends, in giving timely encouragement to our Chair, Mr. Goose Grim Sir. Goose has shared with me his thoughts on the creative process about the Grimoire series in particular, the books that appear out in the world under an assumed name of a hyphenated cast.

To wit, one Jon Rieley-Goddard.

Heaven knows where Goose got that name from.

This is the first of those efforts from the Chair. Note that I made an editor's decision to have Goose the writer talk about Goose the author as though he were another person who happened to also be named Goose. Good luck, and as always – enjoy.

Your servant,
Ed

The truth about stories that could be true

I came to see things differently while writing my first novel, like I had gone to the **Seeing I Store** and walked away with a stylish new pair of peepers.

The Mystery Man Murders, the first book in a series titled **Grimoire - the Bros Grim Breakfast Serial - a story in pieces**, started as daily serial posts to a blog I called **The Bros Grim Breakfast Serial ... have some crime with your morning coffee**.

The Mystery Man Murders is available on Amazon as a trade paperback or as an eNovel. The second novel in the series is in manuscript, and the third novel in the series is in your hands.

In the **Grimoire** series, I tell the story of the Bros Grim, three brothers of a certain age who grow up in a backward way, their three mothers long gone and their father on the job but seldom at home. Their Pop gives over the raising of his boys to a short, wide young housekeeper from the Old Country whom the boys call **Ma**, shortened from **Missus Mac**, itself a corruption of her married name, **Mrs. McFeather**.

This is from the **Grimoire** manuscript –

There is an ancient tradition concerning the **Grimoire** that says books are dangerous and that books set traps for the unwary. The only antidote, it was said, was to read the offending book backward, to free oneself of the spell.

The book in your hands is a Grimoire, too, because it is written by one who has the name of Grim, and because this Grim has wiles that may trap you, and because my narrative will require some unraveling before you understand it, and because it sounds like good, clean fun to tell my story backward as well as forward. ... I will proceed in a fairly straight-forward fashion. I promise (trust me?) that I won't jump around too much (whatever that means).

This friendly warning comes from Goose Grim, a fairly unreliable narrator fresh from the covert world of espionage. Goose, like his Pop, is a spook (forcibly retired). He is posting this or some version of his actual narrative to a blog over a Virtual Private Network (VPN) for his spook friends' amusement. Goose talks about the **so-called life** of the spook, where the backstory is a script and the spook is an actor. Early on, self yields to script and spook floats, for good, just slightly above his life as it was and now is and as it ever shall be. He becomes a story written by his handlers for reasons, not his, that are never specified.

A spook is an **Onion Man** with nothing at the core.

When Goose is thrown from the train after he embraces his cover story (he was cast as a minister named the **Rev. Mr. White** in an op called **Operation Beloved**), Goose has a shattering and re-forming conversion experience, which his handlers cannot accept since they did not write it. This puts Goose outside their control, they fear, so they cast him from the covert realm.

Spookistan.

Goose comes to himself face down in a muddy ditch of the mind. He is in exile from self, vocation, and his chosen covert community. A woman named Eve, herself an ex-spook, and a quirky used bookshop named **Caspar's Books and That** are what save him.

Adventures ensue.

Spooks have ghosts in their past like you would not believe.

■ ■ ■

In writing Goose's story, I came to see that our reality at some level participates in this self-denying, soul-squelching experience of the spook. After all, each one of us reveals and conceals, as each one of us decides what is fitting, politic, and wise to share, and others rarely get any clues when this work of redaction is going on. Each of us creates a safe self to meet other safe selves.

I have a hard enough time understanding who I have been, and I am as clueless as the next person is concerning who I am becoming. The public-self phenomenon comes naturally to anyone who has been abused as a child or who merely has been mistreated for being who she is and letting that show. Such persons create an **executive personality** and the true self goes into hiding – into exile. I believe that each one of us re-defines self for public consumption based on a secret list of omissions and commissions. All are exiles.

It has been said that extroverts are like generals who come out of their tent to meet and greet anyone who rides up looking to parley. Introverts are like generals who stay inside the tent and send out an aide to deal with the people outside. Perhaps your run-of-the-mill extrovert has put everything out there, but I doubt it. Being an introvert, I know that I certainly do not. And no person in public life, such as a politician or pastor, will or should share everything about herself in occupying roles that usually become fused with the sense of self, in parallel processes of **projection** and **introjection** -- people project an image on us, and we accept, or introject, their projections right back at them.

Bottom line?

Goose Grim is a lot more like me than I assumed, going in.

■ ■ ■

As I wrote Goose's story and began to see the links back to life as I know it, I did not feel uneasy. I realized that I was speaking the truth about living when I described Goose's habits concerning truth, certainly, and trust, too.

Question is, what bearing does this have on Ed's theme of grammar and usage? For the beginning of an answer, we can go way, way back, to that dreamer Pontius Pilate.

Pilate, a cog in the Roman Empire Machine, gets a bum rap in the gospel accounts of the trial of Jesus. There is a heavy but subtle judgment on him for dismissing the whole thing with a throw-away line. Actually, it is a really great line that Pilate gets to say -- **and what is truth?**

Pilate seems like a hip-flask swigging, cigarette smoking drunk in comparison to Jesus, who is regal and measured and who refuses to defend himself in the face of certain death if he does not. And Jesus only drinks wine.

As a minister in play, I was able to say with conviction **Jesus Christ, the same yesterday, today, and tomorrow** with the stentorian assurance of a train conductor shouting **All aboard!** I also could say, in all seriousness, **What is truth?** It is not that Pilate misspoke. His question stands as a test for all time, for all persons seeking beliefs that they can hold so dearly that they would take up arms and kill others for those beliefs. Who lives who does not yearn for meaning and purpose and understanding?

The truth, I believe, is that Truth has little to do with our values, our beliefs. We arrive at a set of values by other paths, such as early conditioning, deepest yearning, and sometimes direct revelation. I passionately hold and share my values, though I cannot prove their truth. Rather, I trust the mysterious paths by which I came to believe what I do believe and would fight for.

■ ■ ■

Perhaps the next questions, for writers, are these: Whether you agree with me, do you trust me as a writer? Do you feel that I have good intentions toward you as a reader? Even though my narrator Goose Grim is unreliable in terms of the version of his story that he is telling you at any given time, do you think that you could trust him? Based on my description of him, is Goose likely to speak truth into your soul, or would you see him as trying to blow smoke up your patoot?

You could say that this is all a bit dramatic and overdrawn, that you are only reading in order to fall asleep at the close of the day. I say that one can be vulnerable in the wardrobe that separates the waking reality from the sleeping reality. I am careful of who I allow access to my soul at such times. I believe that a writer has a sacred duty to respect his readers and to do them no harm.

This means that I choose words, ideas and images with care.

This means that I understand my intentions toward you.

■ ■ ■

No one but you knows whether you have good intentions toward your reader. However, the reader will sense many things about you, and she will read you, put you down for a time and pick you up again, or throw you against the wall without being able to say or even caring to know why she did that. This does not alter your charge as a writer or your value. You remain under the demand that you bear stories that could be true to a hurting and vulnerable world of persons who deserve your finest efforts to instruct and to delight.

Calvinist that I am (Calvin's notorious phrase is that humanity is marked by **total depravity**, but that is another essay), I leave a generous margin around the Fields of the Lord in which we writers plant our seeds and watch them sprout and grow. You will, I will falter and sometimes fail in our efforts to communicate words of essential blessing, but we will learn from our faltering and we will get help with our broken places, be they problems with grammar or usage, spelling errors and typos, or lack or lapses of respect for the other. We will treat ourselves with the same compassion that we will give our readers.

The contract that writer and reader sign has a section that concerns the little things such as typos, and a section that concerns the meta-questions of Truth, Trust, Intentions, Respect, and Compassion. At its most simple level, I as writer pledge to tell you stories that could be true, and you pledge to read my stories as you see fit.

We are not strangers, one to the other.

Blessings and peace to you, friend.

Jim starts with the outer trappings
|24May10|

Jim bobbles his bald head, warily, and said, "I'll just press on. It can't get any worse, can it?"

"Yeah," OhJim said, "can it."

"It was weird," Jim said, "knocking on the door of the man who tried to kill us all. And it was even more weird when we saw the woman who answered the door."

Luke nods.

"Way good looking," Luke said, "which did not surprise me. Principe would have had the best that his money could buy."

"The woman introduced herself as **Janey Grimes** and invited us in without asking to see any badge or identification."

"Describe her," David said.

"Janey Grimes," Jim said, "is Jeanne's height -- 5-foot-7 plus a few inches in her heels, call it an even six feet. She seemed to be somewhere in her 40s, which I would not sell at full price without getting a better look at her skin, hands, and feet."

"Horn dog," Jeanne said, smiling to the side like she does.

"Yeah," OhJim said, "you gave notice there."

"What I'm saying," Jim said, "is that she could be as old as I am. What I do know is that she was perilously good looking in a very well-defined way. And like Jeanne does, she was in black with red accents and had definite Goth leanings, which would seem to place her in the lower part of the probable age range."

"Yeah," OhJim said, "and what about her seams?"

"Another horn dog," Jeanne said, smiling like that.

"I'm noticing, Jim Dear," Eve said, "that you seem content to tell us about this beautiful woman's exterior, which is good as far as it goes, but I am also curious about the **Grimes versus Grim** question that the absent Tommy suggested that you ask."

Jim beams like well-aged bourbon.

"Well," he said, "you won't believe this but here goes."

What he said she did
|25May10|

When Janey X. Grimes answered the door, I did a double-take followed by one of the quickest recoveries in history. To her it probably looked like two eye blinks, but to me it felt like a simultaneous enema and lobotomy. I know that is easy to visualize and hard to follow, but there it is. Luke, on the other side, didn't react. I've had plenty of time to think about it, but in that moment of void and blankness I assumed that I was seeing Jeanne's evil older sister.

First thing that I noticed, in particular, after the general impression, was her smile. Well, I did take a peek at her heels, which were high, black, with cutouts on the side and perfect toe cleavage.

The next thing that I noticed was her smile.

Her smile started with her eye brows in the **help-me-out-here** position and ended with her lips sucked into her mouth, with a coda of a straight-forward moo of pursed lips. There was a touch of the clown, the child, and the vamp, in a TA mini-script enactment (Google it, Dude) that would stop Eve, even, in her transactional-analytic tracks.

I actually felt sorry for her, by the end of her smile sequence, and I guess that I also realized that someone with that tight and sad of a smile was redeemable. After all, I found out that I was, somewhere along the way. Who knows, we might be siblings, but I will let Pop's watch set the pace, once again.

"Miss Grimes?" Luke said. "I am Agent Luke Parmgartner and this is my partner, Agent James Baker."

Janey Grimes shook Luke's hand, with an up-from-under look that I'm sure that Luke gets all the time, being a hunk of a man and all. However, I swear on Jeanne's peep-toe pumps that Janey winked at me when she shook my hand.

"Thank you for agreeing to see us on short notice," Luke said.

Janey was a picture of stark elegance in a black silk dress. As I told the others, there was something evil or just scary about her, or perhaps, attendant upon her. Fact is, if my heart were not already Jeanne's ... but my heart is Jeanne's.

We walked in to a foyer that reached for the sky, falling short by just a few feet. Like all the other houses up and down this section of Murray, Janey's was old, well-maintained, simple, and expensive. The house towered above the street, forcing visitors to climb twenty steps to gain the door-knocker, faces upturned.

What he said she said
| 26May10 |

After a few preliminaries, we got to the point.

"Miss Grimes," I said, "an associate of ours said that we should ask you if your last name is Grimes or Grim."

"Yes, Agent," Janey said, "that might be a wise thing to ask."

She went straight to the moo.

"Well, then," Luke said, "which is it, Grimes or Grim?"

Janey's lips disappeared into her mouth and refused to come back out. She turned a lighter shade of pale. Her eyes were pursuing a phantom that only she could see, on the ceiling far above her head.

"**Grim**," she said, in a whisper through clenched teeth. "**Grim**."

"Spelling?" Luke said.

"**G-R-I-M**," Janey said.

For the second time in the space of a few minutes, I had that enema/lobotomy feeling. I wished that I had asked Tommy to tell me the next question in the event that she said what she just said.

Grim.

"My father's name was Grim," Janey said, "but my father was a bad and evil man whom I loathed. After he died, I petitioned to change my name to Grimes. I figured that I would be gritty but not grim. I was satisfied. Question is, how did your associate know to ask?"

I bobbled my head and shrugged my shoulders.

"I am in the dark here, feeling my way," I said, which I realize, at this remove, was not very professional.

Luke came to my rescue, as a good partner would.

"We make it our goal to have accurate data on the persons we interview," Luke said, smiling like a movie star. "And may I say, Miss, that we are sorry for your friend's condition."

Janey made her moo, which altered her deep red lipstick to a patchwork of glossy red and pastel pink.

"Thank you, Agent Parmgartner," she said, "but my **friend** and I have been estranged, though living in the same house, for several months. Still, he is my man, in some sense, and once upon a time I was certain that we were going to live happily ever after, but that was before I found out that he was **doing** my mother and a couple of her friends, before, during, and for a while, after, we fell in what passed for love and started keeping house here."

"Like they say on Facebook," I said, "it's complicated. Clearly."

Once again, Janey winked at me, or was it just a tic? Or both?

What he wrote she said
| 27May10 |

Between the wink from the beautiful woman and the nod to the name Grim, I went into a private place where I nodded and listened but did not attend. However, Luke, the perfect partner, was taking notes, which later he shared with me –

-- **subject wearing silk dress, Italian shoes, and expensive perfume.**

My comment -- check, double-check, check please ... .

-- **subject appeared calm but at a high price.**

My comment -- murder? lose? grief? terror? After all, two agents were asking her questions that she was not able to ignore, about her man, who was in a coma. She was keeping things together, but there were clear signs of strain around her eyes and mouth, and in the creases in her forehead (the kind that Eve calls **try-hard wrinkles**).

-- **subject family name Grim?!?**

My comment: I see your **?!?** and raise you three **!!!**s. In other words and symbols, it was a gold mine question and a solid-ingot answer. How many Grims are there? It is a common enough name, but careful follow-up is definitely indicated.

-- **subject evasive on questions about her father.**

My comment -- she refused to talk about him and we did not press her. Later for that, for sure, but this was a fishing trip. Next time, we just might bring out the elephant gun.

-- subject re: Eric X. Royce -- big, dumb, violent, amoral. Subject met him and the other muscle on a few occasions at the house and called the pest spray people after each of their visits, which were to see Principe.

My comment -- Janey follows the crowd here.

-- subject re: Gary Clyde Grant -- big, dumb, violent, malleable (sp?). See above.

My comment -- **m-a-l-l-e-a-b-l-e** is cq. See my comment above.

-- subject sometimes referred to Peter Principe as P.P., a nickname, by the sound of it.

My comment -- I love cop-speak. Luke is only pretending that he does not know for sure what P.P. is. I wonder what note Luke would make about the famous James Joyce pun .. **U.P. up** ... .

-- subject had obvious strong effect on my partner.

My comment -- Luke was not affected at all. Does that make him a poofter? R/O.

-- subject said she was not planning to see Principe any time soon ... said didn't care to and didn't know his 10-20.

My comment -- Luke better watch his 6.

-- subject wasn't smoking but butts in ashtrays and smell in the air.

My comment -- her skin is too fine for a smoker. Her face would look like sandpaper if she smoked. So who is the smoker and was that subject in the home while we were?

-- subject bristled at question concerning nickname Rich Bitch ... "no comment, move on" - quote.

My comment -- the shoe fit a finely turned foot. She was gracious to us, however, in the main.

-- subject had the black hair and general look of what many would call the gypsy.

My comment -- 10-4 ... but proper term is **Roma**.
... **B**oy **I**da **T**om **E**dward - **M**ary **E**dward ... .

≈ ≈ ≈

Email from: Mister Ed
To Goose Grim

Subject: House of Verbs. Open again.

My friends, I thought that when I began these interludes and asked friend and Chair Goose to post them along with the rest of the things that appear on the VPN blog, I did not anticipate that he and I would collaborate on my subject, that of grammar and usage.

It seems that more than one of us lives at the edge of the known universe on that Planet of Grammar and Usage.

I have taken emails from Goose and woven them with my own emails to him on the subject to come, down here and right about now.

Your servant,
Ed

P.S. A hint: Try to track the shifting ... *I* **... . See you.**

The truth about fact-checking

There are so very many reasons why I do not expect to be published in The New Yorker. As the demons said to Jesus, when he asked them for a nose count, **We are legion**.

I'll give you one bulky, big reason that stands in the way. The fact-checkers.

I write fiction and essays, and I hew to the line of storytelling in all the story-building that I do. A storyteller knows that he has a wide road to walk down with his listeners. **Stretchers**, as Mark Twain calls them, are allowed. Lies are allowed, too, but not Twain's category of **damned lies** (as in **there are lies and there are damned lies**).

As with my Grimoire novel series narrator, Goose Grim, I reside in one township and the facts reside in a nearby township. I visit but I do not stay.

That is one reason.

Another big and not so pretty reason for my probable silence in The New Yorker is this.

I simply do not remember all the facts about myself. In fact, sometimes I have to harmonize a story of my own, about me, based on my general sense of myself, being the one who knows me better than most do. When I began this **House of Verbs** project, I wondered (briefly, all too briefly) about the names of the persons who are central to the stories that I planned to tell. There also were questions about privacy and libel. By the time I had written a few pieces of this project, I could see that no one was in danger of mistreatment or libel.

I am using first names only because in a noticeable minority of cases, I cannot remember the last name of persons I'm pulling in. In one case, I cannot remember a first or last name, and she is someone whom I respect deeply and admire greatly to this day. The passage of 30 years has erased her name, but not her roguish smile and lovely red hair nor a chapter's worth of remembrances, to say nothing of her editing abilities.

For at least these two reasons, I am not likely to make the short list of persons published in The New Yorker.

Pity, that. I'm a huge fan.

■ ■ ■

My whimsy obscures some relevant points --

1. **Facts** do **matter.** I do not make up things that make me look better, and I do not do any violence to the spirit of

stories from my life. I silently pass over any conflicts that I might have had with the persons I describe, since libel does lurk in such corners. The last time I checked, you do not need to identify a person by name to fall into libel concerning that person. If the person's community recognizes the person from details that you give about them, libel can be proved even in the absence of naming.

The other standard for libel is malice, of which I intend none toward anyone I describe. Unlike stupidity, malice is not protection against a charge of libel.

A related principle concerning libel is that you cannot libel a dead person, though I would not test this in a book sold in the UK. Although you cannot libel a dead person, you surely can harm or piss off her surviving family. My decision is that life is too short to be taking cheap shots at old enemies, living or dead.

2. ***The mind does not respect the facts, ma'am.*** Experts say that the mind, like a harried bartender, tends to jam together in one blender aspects of similar experiences. That is only half of the problematic phenomenon. The mind also stores the blended, conflated version of things as a single memory and story, for retrieval. What works behind the bar on Saturday night does not work so well for writers who think that strict factual accuracy is possible and desirable.

The mind is a mindless blender of facts and fancies.

The mind is both more complex that computers and far less tied to **zeros** and **ones**. Instead of ***garbage in, garbage out*** (GIGO), it is ***garbage in, glitter out***. You may have walked down the alley to the corner store hundreds of times, but certain details stand out and are likely to have the look and feel of a single instance of walking down the alley to the corner store to get a Coke and a pie. To complicate matters, if your mind has stored a dream that includes walking down the alley to the corner store, that gets blended with the rest, as likely as not. The mind, rather than a database like a river of fact, is a deep, blue sea of fantasy.

What has a fact-checker to do with this?

The experts say this sort of thing about memory. I have validated the process myself, many times. My best friend has an excellent memory and fewer miles on her chassis. If she disagrees with my version of events, I listen to her, for I have learned that she is usually right in what she remembers. I am, by contrast, a storyteller for many reasons having to do with temperament and attitude toward the facts, including how I process and can them.

3. ***Truth and facts are friends, but truth has said privately that she would be just fine, thank you very much, if the facts decided to hang out with someone else.*** I had a parishioner in a church I served who was fond of saying that ***there are true stories and stories that are true, and the two are not always the same***.

I agree.

This distinction between truth and facts has long and strong legs for Christians, who can feel that they are being asked to give credence to some mysterious stuff. I side with those who see the truth in the gospel accounts, for example, as residing more in the metaphors than in a literal reading of the text. I think that it is wrong to argue from metaphors but helpful to live out the truths that metaphors bear. The gospels are stories that are true, as my old friend said, and the truth is in the interpretation of the story more than in the literal level of the language. Intent is more concrete than you might believe.

4. ***Life is precious and puzzling***. I love my life, and I love this world, and I often am puzzled by the things that I see, the things that others see that I do not see, and on and on. My eyes, as I have aged, play tricks on me. Like my mind does. I see a black garbage bag by the side of the road, hooked to a bush, and I assume, at first, that it is a small animal with sharp ears and teeth.

There is a saying among copy editors -- if your mother says she loves you, ***check it out!*** This was a Bremnerism, if memory serves. So often I assume that I know what someone else means without having listened well enough to ask a question or two. No one, I find, appreciates being told what they think or feel, probably because we guess at these things about others based partly on slim evidence and partly on a benign arrogance. Plus the usual projections back and forth.

5. ***Do not let the facts get your tongue***. Tell your story as you see fit. If it is a version of the truth, say so, if the form is not fiction. If it is fiction, say whatever comes into your mind. Write the story as you remember it, then write the story

as you wish it had unfolded, then write the most accurate account that you can.

That would be of interest to readers.

Who cares, really, about the fact-checkers?

Readers count.

■ ■ ■

The psychologist Carl Rogers (**On Becoming a Person**) had a saying about the course of psychotherapy.

Rogers said that **the facts are always friendly**.

If Rogers was concerned about a client who was acting out and where that was likely to lead, he would say so. If a client seemed to be heading for a psychotic break, he would say so.

The facts are always friendly, Rogers said. Being nice to your clients could be harmful to their health.

I would add that the facts tolerate our faulty memories. The blending that the mind does is a friendly process, at heart.

I would add that the writer and the reader can be friendly, too, and give one another a margin in which to tell and to react to stories in freedom on both sides.

The facts of our lives together are always friendly.

At heart, we wish one another well, almost always.

If I can be a friend to myself, I can befriend you, too, and we both can be glad for not just the noise and confusion of living but also of the facts as we see them, together.

Black/white and read all over
|28May10|

This piece ran in a one-column, 1-point box squared off with the lead story on page 1A of this morning's **Daily Afterblatt, Lake Effect edition**.

Letter to readers
Hacker's 'code of honor' on OpEd tomorrow

Dear readers,

Tomorrow we begin a new feature on our OpEd Page with a unique perspective and a distinctive byline.

The shadowy hacker *YentlBengie,* as reported at mid-month, will be helping us understand the virtual world of blogs and the blog wars that bloom like dandelions in May.

After reading a series of articles by our Senior Crime Reporter, Jane Carlotto, *YentlBengie* emailed to offer his writing services to help readers understand the new world of blogs and such, and the virtual reality of the Internet -- what some of us call history's biggest experiment in anarchy.

Jane's series was a three-part effort focusing on recent murder and violence in our city, linked to our favorite used bookstore and its spookish denizens (Caspar's Books and That and the owner Eve Green and her partner, Goose Grim).

Our Virtual Correspondent *YentlBengie* will consider the topic "The art of blog war" in tomorrow's editions of the Daily Afterblatt. Other pieces may follow, on an occasional basis.

-- the editors

Black/white and read all over
|29May10|

This piece ran at the top of the OpEd Page, in a three-column box squared off with an editorial cartoon, in this morning's **Daily Afterblatt, Lake Effect edition.**

Our Virtual Correspondent
Some thoughts on virtual time and why hackers hack

Editor's note: This is the first of a series of occasional pieces for this page that will address the Brave New World of Internet and subspecies such as blogs. The author asks to be known, only, as *YentlBengie*. Needless to say, the opinions that he offers are his own.

By YentlBengie
Our Virtual Correspondent

It's good to be back on the air, so thanks to the High Sheriffs here at the Daily Afterblatt for granting this forum to a virtual Bad Boy such as myself.

First off, and this is no slam on Senior Crime Reporter Jane Carlotto, but the record of local blog wars and principals is hopelessly scrambled.

The reporting on it looks like a dog's breakfast.

I will be unscrambling the offal and will give you a definitive list of the jousters who entered the lists and who fought over a small hilltop in Blogistan known as "Fried Buffalonya."

Some other time.

Maybe the problem that Ms. Carlotto tripped over has to do with people who see time as what a clock on the wall shows, so-called "real time."

"Virtual time" is nothing like that.

Virtual time is a matter of intentions, inventions, and disinformation.

And a few other things, too.

In its most simple and most accurate form, this is what happened in the local blog war in question.

A blogger calling himself *blogistan* started a blog that he called "Fried Buffalonya." In the course of pumping up his visitor stats (or "hits," as we call them), *blogistan* actually forced into the public eye a group of former spies who hang out at the used bookshop in north Buffalonya called Caspar's Books and That. A three-part series by Ms. Carlotto chronicled the dirty work that *blogistan* caused by his blogging.

In the end, *blogistan* was forced to flee by another hacker who went by a couple of names, including *manram* and *the destroyer*. This arguably stronger hacker took over Fried Buffalonya and issued a new promise of dirt to come concerning the absent, and now dead, former police commissioner, Tom Tonolody.

This writer, signing on initially as *The Man in the Moon*, hacked the blog site and brought things to a halt.

Why do such a thing as hack a blog site?

Why not?

Others would say that hackers are like the darwinian agents that make the natural selection of excellent hackers happen.

Others would point to one political stance or another.

Still others, including the hacker who revived Fried Buffalonya with the promise of dirt about Tonolody's quick departure and subsequent disappearance, do it for money.

I do it for the joy of the thing in itself -- hacking.

And, perhaps, because I am something like Robin Hood. It bothered me that an evil hacker was throwing mud on a much-decorated journalist and on a now-dead public servant whom no one has ever accused of anything more heinous than occasional bouts of indecision.

As far as the hack itself goes, I won't tell you any details, because you would not understand them in English, let alone binary, but the evil hacker would. It is not that he is not an able and dangerous hacker, because he is; however, I will not be the one to teach him how to thwart or beat me.

As for the illegal aspects of the Robin Hood work that I do, I am not concerned in that regard, because I sincerely believe that I am like the fog in that poem by Carl Sandburg that creeps in on silent feet and sits looking over harbor and city, and then moves on.

The authorities who could find me, or at least a version of me, have not tried to do so, because they have better things to do with their bandwidth, I am guessing.

After all, the only one who wanted Robin Hood stopped was the evil king.

Right?

That's it for now.

Watch your logs.

≈ ≈ ≈

Email from: Mister Ed
To Goose Grim

Subject: House of Verbs. Open again.

My friends, some of you have noticed, and commented, that Goose's emails that have been appearing lately seem to be a lot more polished than that.

Thank you for noticing.

You are detecting the fine editing hand of yours truly.

In this next piece, Goose discusses the admonition that writers should write about what they know.

Notice the delicious irony of Goose as the persona he publishes under talking about the life in the shadows from his viewpoint, that everyone knows about the shadows from what we read and see and hear in the media.

Goose, of course, knows the shadows from the inside. Those shadows are like the insides of his eyeballs.

Enjoy.

Your servant,
Ed

Writers should write what they know, right?

I posted daily to a serial novel blog that I called **Grimoire - the Bros Grim Breakfast Serial** for about three years. In serial posts and in my first-finished novel, **The Mystery Man Murders**, and in the **Grimoire** series that it introduces, I write about spies -- or **spooks**, as I prefer to call them -- and their far-foreign country, **Spookistan**.

I am not nor have I ever been a spook or a citizen of Spookistan. Still, I am writing about what I (and you?) know so deeply.

Espionage is woven into our lives by stories in print, on the radio, on television, and in the movies. We share a set of stories and expectations that are based a little on the news and a lot on the fictions we enjoy so much.

But there is more.

People, I believe, learn spycraft at a very early age.

We imagine worlds and populate them and interact in these worlds and make decisions concerning these worlds. Sometimes our outward reality enters into the floating world that we created and maintain.

It is one thing to imagine being interrogated by East German secret police. It is a faintly similar thing to be questioned by a pair of cops following up on a malicious neighbor's complaint. It is one thing to imagine the political maneuvering of the CIA and the politicos. It is a faintly similar thing to subvert the Suits in your own sphere of influence.

The impulse to hide and the impulse to avoid, and the mood one can feel when one enters a room are experiences that spies and children have in common.

There is nothing faint about this.

The wrong read results in more than a slap on the wrist.

. . .

Two poles emerge -- pleasure on one side and pain on the other side. The line stretched tightly between these two poles, like piano wire, can give a pleasing sound when plucked or can deal death or serious injury in the dark, in the park, with the sounds of pounding feet and labored breathing driving you to flee. The espionage stories that we read touch on these poles, and we remember the pain and the pleasure of our own stories. In espionage stories, we can find outcomes to suit our ever-changing psychological needs.

The reader brings a world of experiences and expectations, some real and some fanciful. The reader arrives eager to be delighted and willing to be instructed.

The writer makes and enters a world and populates that world with a range of believable characters.

When the pen pricks the page, all hell breaks loose.

And we are delighted.

. . .

Although I know little about actual espionage and have talked with few who have been spooks, I do understand the inner life of the spy. I have been a spy in the house of family and of profession, from the cradle.

My earliest memory is a violent one, and in a sense I have been running ever since. I have been living and surviving by my wits, and manipulating bigger and stronger persons, all my life. This is part of what I bring to **The Mystery Man Murders**, the story of my over-the-hill gang of cast-off spooks who run a dusty and wonderful used bookstore, **Caspar's Books and That**, partly as cover and partly as pleasure. I know the sensations of the spy and the tradecraft of those who survive, essentially alone, in hostile environments such as workplace and family of origin.

Public relationships. Love relationships.

■ ■ ■

Experience is the best teacher. The writer who engages readers uses **real life** as the starting point and as the way station along the race route, but the finish line will be a fanciful blending of fact and fiction. I write from the inner life of the cunning fugitive. I write as well from the top of the ever-growing mountain of my study of the relevant spook literature, print and film. This gives me a deep and wide ocean of common experience and expectations that I share with readers.

We know the territory.

We have a map.

We draw the map from memory.

Countless writers have told stories about spies, in as many contexts as you could list or imagine. The stories that endure have obeyed the rules and have stretched the rules in new ways, places, and directions.

Countless poets wrote of love, but only Ben Jonson wrote of the lover's fear of loss in terms of his **mountain-belly** and its fancied effect on his missing young lover.

Many writers have developed characters to fill the normal and usual slots in an espionage network, but only one writer could imagine George Smiley and give him such a fitting name and plausible backstory. Copycat writers would do well to understand the particular expectations that the English have about love and betrayal, and one's duty to respond with suffering rather than violence.

What is more sad and haunting than George Smiley, hiding in the shadows on a rainy night, watching his estranged wife, in the home he lately inhabited, touch the face of her lover while the mist outside makes a sodden mess of the little man whom many would kill for and even die for. We know George cannot react with rage and pull his house down. One does not do that. However, we also know that George is a lethal foe who takes his time. We know too that in America, the same scene would have an immediate and violent outcome. An American writer cannot produce George Smiley. Neither can John LeCarre produce Sam Spade.

Emma Peal, perhaps, but not Agent 99.

Or Maxwell Smart.

■ ■ ■

I do not know much about spying as it is done in the **real world**. However, I do know things that go on in other arenas, and I can bring to my stories an awareness of what it would be like to act as a minister as part of a cover story or to act the part of a journalist. I have been a journalist and copy editor and minister. I know the public self that the professional builds and acts from. The irony of building a role from commonly held expectations is an art that spies learned from whores (the first two types of professionals, according to many wags), a long, long time ago.

Or not.

The spy, the journalist, the minister, and the whore must understand the interplay of fact and fiction that their professions demand or they will be expelled by the people, and not for lying or manipulating or selling their bodies and souls but for refusing to honor the shared expectations that we live by. Social contract, call it.

As one who has been running all my life, I have no problem with this facade of reality. In fact, I embrace this reality, as a way of surviving and thriving in a cold and dark and dangerous world that started with consciousness springing like a scream from a series of unfortunate occurrences having to do with a 2-year-old, a bottle of black shoe polish, a brand-new hardwood floor, and a razor-sharp paint scraper in my mama's hand.

I bear a scared and scarred little boy inside me who knows how to survive and is not shy or retiring about what to do next. This is not all of who I am, but it is a part of my most fundamental and automatic functioning.

I have learned so much since coming to awareness at age 2. A two-inch zipper scar on my upper thigh commemorates the occasion. I have paid close attention at all points since and have learned how to survive by manipulations and later how to thrive by honest, compassionate interaction. I have fought the battles of office politics, and I have been cast aside by colleagues with agendas that reeked of evil darkness.

I have smelled the foul, sickening breath of mindless evil.

I survived, and I continue to thrive.

I write from a base as concrete as a bunker.

I can imagine the rest.

I find that writing about spooks is like writing about what I know best.

■ ■ ■

A person's first task is to survive.

The writer's task is to survive while noticing the details and noting the stories and obeying the drive to share stories.

The task of the minister, the used car salesman, the politician, and the whore is the same task. The best use smoke and mirrors more for the benefit of others than for self, though making a living is part of the picture.

One cannot survive on the kindness of strangers.

As a survivor, a journalist, and a minister, I could easily write of prostitutes and pimps.

I choose to write about George Smiley's progeny.

The choices that we make, as we walk through life, will sustain us, if we act from values that we would die for.

If my aim is to mouth the prayers and liturgies of the Church, as a way of tricking others into thinking that I am pious and worthy, I will fail.

If I act from beliefs so deep that I cannot utter them, I will survive, the people in my care will endure, and together we can thrive.

Life is sweet when meaning and purpose join hands and sing.

F-Troop circles the flagons
| 30May10 |

"The F-Troop will be so ordered," I said.

"I can take your order, Mister Chair Sir." Jim said.

"Yeah," OhJim said, "but will you give it back?"

"The only order of business before us," I said, "is who to send back to Pittsburgh to go to Peter Principe's funeral and take down names and memorize faces."

"If it is before us, maybe it will let us play on through," Jim said.

"Yeah," OhJim said, "we will be thorough if we get through."

"Well, Dear," Eve said, "I like sending Jim and OhJim, with Mister Ed to mind them this time."

"You mean," Jim said, "the other way around."

"Yeah," OhJim said, "as in we mind him, though we don't really. We do mind him and we like his company."

"Company?" David said. "I thought he worked here."

Jeanne smiles sideways at her man, who is giving us his bug-eye smile through his round glasses.

My brothers smile at one another with up-side down smiles.

Like little boys, they never like to share.

Jeanne, who knows this well, smiles to her other side.

They beam.

I don't remember them being this simple, but I have forgotten far more than I ever knew. At least Eve thinks so.

"You could send Sluggo and me," Jeanne said. "We do need the practice."

"And who," Jim said, "would mind you?"

"Yeah," OhJim said, "I don't mind you, but I will do anything you ask of me. Plus youse guys practice a lot already."

"Mister Chair Sir," Mister Ed said, in his indoor voice, where **indoor** is like a biosphere. "If I might and may."

"Yes," I said, "and yes."

"Thank you, Mister Chair Sir," Mister Ed said. "I rise in hopes of selling one and all on an ancient process such as was used by the Jews since before the beginning of time, almost. I refer to the children's game and the adult's refuge -- drawing straws, where the short straw wins."

"That sounds," I said, "like the only game out there that does not favor height, but that is neither here nor there, so why not?"

The others nod.

"Make it so, my friend," I said. "May the last straw be the beginning of a new chapter in the life of the Tribe."

Mister Ed goes in search of a broom.

One taken, one left behind
|31May10|

It was like the Rapture -- one taken, one left behind.

"I can see, Mister Chair Sir," Jim said, "that size does indeed matter, and never before have I rued the day when I would have the longer one."

Jim thoughtfully picks at his teeth with his chosen straw.

"Yeah," OhJim said, "and I am, for just this once, happy to be the shorter."

Jeanne smiles to the side, bitter and sweet.

"That is that," I said. "Jeanne, OhJim (wipe that silly grin off your face!), and Mister Ed will represent the Tribe , but softly, softly, at the funeral of our friend, our enemy Peter Principe and to do more skulking around in general. Agreed?"

"Yes," Jim said, "and grieved, too."

Jeanne kisses the hapless, eclipsed Jim on the nose, which brightened him considerably.

"Mister Chair Sir," Mister Ed said, rising like a crane, "second verse, same as the first."

"Take your time and your turn, my friend," I said. "We do not stand on ceremony here nor on stolid ground."

"Thank you for the wordplay and permission, Mister Chair Sir," Mister Ed said. "I rise in reference to the dearly departed Tommy. What news, sir?"

"Luke?" I said.

"Not dead," Luke said, "but beyond that, not anything to report. I continue to feel uneasy but my ears are not buzzing one little bit. Friend Tommy is gone, and the ground is silent, which is different from the other times he has gone where he knows, alone, for reasons that he does not share."

"I thank you," Mister Ed said, with a crane-like bow to the Agent in place, concerning the Agent misplaced.

"That begs the question, Dear," Eve said, "of our need to run some scenarios. For example, does Tommy's absence demand that we take extra care in dividing our resources among the two cities? My view is that we are as secure as ever, in both places, since we have nothing concrete but only that vague sense of quicksand that Luke reports."

Eve gives Luke her Buddha Girl smile.

"I remain," Luke said, "and though I do not have Tommy's access to intel, I do have such treachery as my age confers."

"Old age and treachery will win out over youthful exuberance," Jeanne said, with a sideways smile, "every time."

"Time to roll," Mister Ed said.

Steeling away softly, softly v. 1.1
|01June10|

Who was it that said comparisons are odious? They must have known what they meant, but I sure don't. I'm comparing my first trip to Pittsburgh with my second trip, and the results are in.

Second wins first.

Dig it. Three in the front seat, which is as wide as a couch and twice as comfortable, with a view out the window to die for. Mister Ed at the wheel, Jeanne beside him, and I beside her.

The first trip was two guys in front and two guys in back.

End of story.

This trip, we are just going and not worrying about what it looks like to have a massive senior citizen driving, a tall punk/goth beauty beside him, and a middling bald bobblehead beside her.

That would be me.

We don't talk all that much, but I cannot remember being quit so happy, for a long time. If ever. I guess that I have a so-called life most of the time, and before I came home to an instant family inside a community of like-minded people, I had a half-life, which was less than a so-called life and more like a heavy weight with which I did a credible imitation of Sisyphus.

Is it more notable that I survived or that I barely made it back home? I don't give a flying bleep one way or the other, and I'm betting that you are even less interested in the question than I.

I am resourceful, it must be said, and I do know how to survive, and I do so without sentimentality or despair. I thrive, but not much. I spit in the face of death, by my hand or anyone else's. So how did I get here? Anger fed me, and irony was my tipple. My friends did not speak English but had wings, or fur, or an insatiable taste for bone.

I was a pet's pet, and I loved the life.

I may sound pitiful to you, and you may even think that I play the victim. If that is your view, you have already written my story to suit your own ears and eyes, and I would like you to drop me a copy, because short stories are to my mind the height of the fictive art. I eat stuff like that with a soup spoon.

And how pathetic is it, huh? that I sit beside a beautiful woman half my age and worship the plush and plastic fabric upon which she sits and hang on every word, every gesture, that she makes.

Well, as my dear mama would say, if she had ever bothered to find me and talk with me, **Bleep you if you can't take a joke**.

But since you have read this far into this quirky, qwerty post, you also know me to be a funny and fun-loving straight man.

Who, I wonder, do you think is the real OhJim -- the angry, victim-prone loser or the knight gazing at the lady he will never posses not that he wants such a paltry and foreshortened end to such a blissful connection.

Did you pick the red pill or the blue pill?

Punny guy or angry loser?

How about a harmonization?

I am the **Red/Cross Knight**, OK?

Fits for me.

Sucks to be you.

How would I know?

Just a guess.

Pax.

Steeling away softly, softly v. 1.2
|02June10|

The bitch is riding bitch, flanked by Mister Ed at the wheel and OhJim riding shotgun. I didn't have it in me to make OhJay sit next to Mister Ed. Guys go nuts under that kind of scenario. So bitch it is, which a lot of people would say fits me like a size 8 pump of any heel height.

I already miss my man, and I hope he is improving the time until we get back from this trip to Pgh.

My first.

I'm looking ahead to the undercover thing and will be changing my punkish gothness for a librarian's look. That will be a simple matter of ballet flats, semi-sexy glasses, and no pierces or tats, of which I have none visible anyway.

My smile naturally inclines in OhJim's direction, which seems to please him. It is pleasant to be thigh to thigh with one of my biggest, or at least most fanatical, fans. I never have loved someone more whom I knew less about, but I did not survive what I have survived without being able to make an accurate, instant read based on things other than words.

OhJim feels safe, and I would take that to the bank.

As far as where OhJim has been over the decades, all I know, based on the eulogy that he gave for the third **Mystery Man** victim, the homeless one dumped in Buffalonya's busiest dumpster, behind Buffalonya's seediest bar, is that Oh was once homeless himself. Where, I do not know, and why, the same. He has a waif's way that brings out a maternal, sisterly streak that I did not know that I had. Like Sluggo, who brings out the woman in me in a way that I never thought would be possible.

Yeah, we're sleeping together, but neither of us will ever disclose how long my patient man had to wait before actually getting lucky. Some things don't belong out there in the open for anyone to play around with. The same goes for me. I'm done with being a plaything for anyone. Sluggo is the first man I've ever known who sees this as a good and healthy decision.

It does not suck to be Sluggo, I will say that.

Mister Ed, though he is not a fan, is a colleague. He feels safe, too, and deeply kind. Riding bitch certainly has its rewards. I feel wonderful sitting between these two.

One day I will also feel that I deserve such feelings.

Do you?

Steeling away softly, softly v. 1.3
|03June10|

Operation Next-of-Kin, part two.
Challenge pair –

> **Person No. One -- The grave's a fine and private place.**
> **Person No. Two -- That is something I can embrace.**

Talk about old age and treachery.

Me at the wheel of this Crown Vic.

Not the Punk Princess next to me or her man-pet beside her, but me.

Best available, I guess.

We drive in a comfortable silence, each of us turned inward.

Actually pleasant.

Jeanne, at roughly a third of my age, is unlike any woman I have ever known. I suppose that many women meet or exceed her charms and abilities, but, again, not in my experience, except for Eve, of course.

Eve. The beauty at the edge of night.

Jeanne. The beauty of darkness, darkness, draw me closer.

I knew a little girl once named Dawn, but she really was not much of a morning person. She was, however, a morning paper person, which meant she did her best work in the dark.

Musing, musing.

I wonder what will be the best approach re: Peter Principe's funeral. Maybe Jeanne and OhJim in their Sunday best. Question is, who are they to be? Friends of friends?

And me, in my shabby best clothes. A friend of the family.

Our goal?

Impressions.

Round-robin debriefing after, in some bar in the Strip.

-30-

Reference? Librarian
|04June10|

Jeanne turns heads as Punk Princess with Goth leanings. Consider --

• Her thick, black, wavy hair that makes frame-like comments on her picture-pretty face (actually, her hot, sexy, come-here-my-friend face, but that would have mixed my metaphor).

• Her figure, a near-perfect 3.3 + 3,3 + 3,3 = 9.9.

• Her wardrobe that goes heavy on basic black in lace, satin, jersey, and dotted swiss (black on black). A geography of the gothic inner landscape.

• Her shoes that come like Henry Ford's Model Ts in any color you want as long as it is black. Pumps, peep-toe pumps, kitten heels, spike heels, and slides, with toe cleavage sprinkled over all like capsicum powder.

• A related issue -- nylons, in any shade of black and in a number of textures. The heterosexual's favorite **swish**. NPC, I know. Sue me.

• Her fingernails and toenails painted deep red.

• Bling, usually pearls but sometimes necklaces that look like a magpie's collection of stolen objects saved on a length of leather lacing.

• Her signature smile.

The transition to Jane "Doodles" Doohey, recent grad (M.A. in library science) from SUNY at Buffalonya, necessitated the following alterations --

• No change in hair color but a slight change with the addition of a small Hello Kitty clip pulling her hair toward her right ear.

- No change in her 9.9 figure, the hide that cannot be hidden.
- Wardrobe -- Black yields to dark blue, with emphasis on soft cottons rather than satin and lace. Wool blends suitable for the summer season. Shirt-waist dresses with all buttons engaged (I know ...).
- Shoes uniformly dark blue and introducing "cute shoes" options such as ballet and other flats that go light on toe cleavage.
- Nylons go from black to blue.
- No change at fingers or toes.
- Minimal bling.
- Add eyeglasses in cute colors and shapes. Not optional to skip this step.

Tells for Jeanne to watch when she is channeling Doodles --

- Her signature smile.
- Any dipping or dangling.
- Any licking of anything except lips and that only sparingly.
- Any model-walking.

My change to becoming Brad "Doody" Doohey, the dad, a retired school teacher, was as easy as putting on a cheap suit and worn-in but shiny dress shoes.

My tells?

No puns, the word "yeah", aggressive stances reinforced by words used as a sharp weapon.

We tried our new personae on at the safe house, which seemed like a safe place to practice. Mister Ed allowed as he didn't need any practice to be a retired newsman from all over. With a slight drinking problem.

We will introduce ourselves, at the funeral and wake, or not, depending on the needs of the situation. And if anyone asks.

≈ ≈ ≈

Email from: Mister Ed
To Goose Grim

Subject: House of Verbs. Open again,

I received a favorable response to my book review and remembrance of John Bremner and his fine usage book *Words on Words*.

So I will hazard a second book review, this one comparing a later usage book with an earlier.

I hope you like it. In any case, there won't be any more reviews for now. I do have a few more emails from Goose that I will share when they are honed and shining.

Your servant,
Ed

Books in review: White +/- Fish = ?

Into each life, a little bit of E.B. White should fall. Chances are, a little will grow to be much more, as your growing interest pays dividends. White wrote the book (**Elements of Style**) on the craft of writing, for the 20th century, his fans say, and it is also true that White had a knack for children's stories for kids of all ages (**Charlotte's Web** and **Stuart Little**).

The Elements of Style, though thin and pinched when compared to the rest of White's work, is the tip of the spear that White chucks at us, in all high seriousness and glee. Oddly enough, when we get his point, more often than not we are grateful for the prick, so to speak. In the many years since White released **Elements**, at mid-century, a multitude of us have used that spear to make a point with writers in need of help with the mechanics of writing. It can be no surprise that many readers do not appreciate **Elements**, perhaps because of small scars in the midsection and across the back at shoulder height.

I stand with those who love the **little book**. I have read and re-read the book, and I have multiple copies including a Dover edition of the original William Strunk version (1918) that White edited and added to many years later. Strunk taught White at Cornell, and White teaches us -- all over, all the time, any place.

However, I am getting ahead of myself, for there is a third group that is larger than the fans and detractors combined, the group known as **Other**. Most people in need of White's attentions have not heard of him, I'm guessing.

So.

The Elements of Style, published in 1957, revised a booklet on style for students at Cornell University in the wilds of upstate

New York that Prof. William Strunk wrote early in the century. White fondly recalled Strunk when a friend sent him a copy of that little old booklet, decades later. White undertook the job of adding to and taking away from Strunk's little book.

If reading about grammar and usage is your passion and joy, **The Elements of Style** will be among the ten books you would not be without should you ever find yourself on a desert island in need of some editing (note the **squinting modifier**).

White shows writers how to be clear and concise and shows editors how to bring fuzzy writing into focus. If you have not read **The Elements of Style**, you will benefit from reading it. No doubt about it, and I do not even need to see your stuff to say this.

■ ■ ■

If you do not appreciate the tone or approach of **Elements**, or if you simply enjoy reading from the category that White all but created, for our time, a smallish work of recent birthing that you might enjoy is **How to Write a Sentence and How to Read One**, by Stanley Fish.

Many of you will know of Fish from his appearances in The New York Times.

I know of Fish from the angle of being an English major at UC Berkeley. Fish, who had just published a book of literary criticism titled **Surprised by Sin: The Reader in Paradise Lost**, visited my senior seminar class on John Milton. It was a stimulating and challenging hour that we spent with this man of many letters, who went on from lit crit to become a professor of law. His little book on sentences is a response to problems that his law students have with their writing.

Fish's book offers a quote from The New Yorker on the back flap of the dust jacket -- "... whether people like Stanley Fish or not, they tend to find him fascinating."

I would agree.

I never have forgotten the point on that one occasion that I was in his presence when Fish told a guy across the table from me, who had been doing a lot of talking with his hands, "You have a very sloppy mind."

■ ■ ■

In the push to publicize his book, Fish appeared on National Public Radio's Talk of the Nation program. He said that White's **Elements** does not attack the question of writing from an assumption of innocence. You must be on your way already to benefit from White's book, he said.

Well, that is true.

However, Fish's little book does not do so, either. Fish has written a strong book, but the level of engagement demanded is far beyond what one would want to bring to a first reading of **Elements.** Truth is, if you can read and write, you can benefit from either of these books.

The question of their relative merits has no charms for me.

I have read both books and am glad that I did.

Fish's command and recall of literature is awful.

That alone recommends his little book to your attention.

A hint: Words ending in *-ful* can be seen as saying "full of ..." or "... worthy of ...".

Awful, which is nothing like **terrible**.

On balance, I prefer White to Fish. White does what he sez he will do; Fish sez he will do one thing but does another. IMHO.

No sloppy, mind you.

Not sloppy at all.

The point is to read early and often from anyone you can find who writes well concerning grammar and usage.

Good mechanics are hard to find.

OhJim continues --

Lengthy debriefing to keep a wake
|05June10|

After attending the Mass of Christian Burial for Peter Principe, the three tribalists returned to the safe house on Hampton Street in the Highland Park section of Pittsburgh.

"What was that church?" OhJim said. "The Fourteen Hefty Helpings? Something like that."

"I believe, my funny friend," Mister Ed said, "that the church is called the **Church of the Fourteen Holy Helpers**."

"Are you sure, Ed?" Jeanne said, smiling to the side. "Wasn't it the **Powerhouse Church of the Blinding Light?**"

"Not in this life, Four Eyes," Mister Ed said with his big, horsey grin aimed right at Jeanne.

Jeanne was radiant in her librarian's togs and electric blue reading glasses, and the men were presentable.

If it were not odd to say so, one might say that a good time was had by all at the wake after the funeral.

At least our guys had a good time.

"Impressions?" Mister Ed said.

"First on the list has to be running into Tommy, in the flesh," Jeanne said. "Hands down."

Lengthy debriefing to keep a wake
|06June10|

"Go with that," Mister Ed said. "Since we were incognito, you were the only one who talked with him."

"Yeah," OhJim said, "I didn't talk to him but I did eavesdrop on him."

"Well, don't be stingy," Jeanne said. "Spill."

"Well," OhJim said, "I noticed that Tommy was talking with Janey Grimes, the grieving widow-equivalent, so I lurked behind a handy potted plant. Tommy called her **Sis**, and he asked her how **Mom** was. 'You know Lailah ... she will expect you to ask her yourself,' Janey told him. It was all rather confusing and left me with the impression that Tommy and Janey are siblings and their mother is someone named **Lailah**. If you think about it, this is the first personal information that we have about our Agent."

"Well," Mister Ed said, "did you get a look at this Lailah?"

"Yeah," OhJim said, "I sure did, and I'd like to see her again. And again. And a bit more. For an old broad, which she has to be -- do the math -- she look more like Janey's twin sister, the hot one."

"Which one?" Jeanne said.

"Take your pick," OhJim said. "The temperature is constant."

Jeanne slipped off her heels and put her feet up on the coffee table in the living room of the safe house, a brick-made Victorian dwarfed by twin Tudors, one on each side. Mister Ed and OhJim had loosened their ties and shed their shoes, though this was not the high-value production that Jeanne effortlessly made.

"Get Eve on your cell phone and tell her of our sighting," Mister Ed said, "if you will, my dear."

"On it, Dear," Jeanne said, as she punched at the cunning device in her lap. "I'll also tell her about Oh's eaves-droppings."

"Yeah, do," OhJim said, "or doodoo, as it were."

Jeanne just smiled over her reading glasses, bitter and sweet.

I could watch her all day long, I swear.
Checking out the librarian.
Long overdue.
Lost in the stacks.

Lengthy debriefing to keep a wake
|07June10|

"Ok ... gotcha ... right ... bye," Jeanne said.

She flipped her phone closed and stretched.

"We go home tonight," Jeanne said, "to give our report in person, especially about Tommy."

"What's the buzz?" OhJim said.

"Luke is scratching his head and muttering in some foreign language," Jeanne said, "and Ma is carrying on, too, in her personal idioms."

"That's my Ma," OhJim said. "She has made a separate peace with words and sentences."

"I wonder," Mr. Ed said, "if we have any other things to flag from the wake."

"Yeah," OhJim said, "I didn't tell you yet about getting up close and personal with this Lailah person."

OhJim was smiling, and he clearly was enjoying being the one with the information.

Fact is, he's a natural. It's the one who others don't remember who collects the best intel. And OhJim, for all his many fine points, is has a dial tone of a face and a meek manner when he turns off the charm.

Jeanne, in contrast, stands out like a beautiful woman who lives on in the memory for years after the fact. Her genius, though, is exercising the art of distraction that keeps the eyeballs in her direction, dulling the defenses, while OhJim sidles close to eavesdrop.

The two could not have worked better together if they had planned it. OhJim's oblique, sideways moves mirror Jeanne's captivating sideways smile.

Mister Ed, as an aged peak among hills and plains, stands out like a talking horse at a Toastmasters convention. Ed has to use his considerable wits and instincts to gain his ends. His genius is in directing his henchmen and -women to likely targets in a room. From his superior height, he does not miss much.

Miss Much?

I once knew this buxom little barmaid by that name ... .

Lengthy debriefing to keep a wake
|08June10|

"You know me and beautiful women," OhJim said.

"Yeah," Jeanne said, "I resemble that comment."

"According to me," OhJim said, "yeah."

You might be noticing that without the pairing of the two bobbleheads, Jim and OhJim, puns were in short supply, like a punless indulgence. You might also be noticing that others cannot plug that dike, lift that bale, or put their nose to the grindstone, their shoulder to the wheel, and their ear to the ground.

"My bobbling friend," Mister Ed said, "we are hanging on here -- the dangling man and the dandling woman. Tell us the story of one Lailah, last name, possibly, Grim."

"Sculpted jaw line," Jim said, "like a super-fine line in the sand, reminiscent of the sands of Northern Africa, and wild dark hair (but to call it black would erase a rainbow of highlights from silver to white to pale, pale transparency, with a body that knows the language of love and has been speaking it for decades beyond comprehension, and my weakness of kicking high heels in a tiny size."

Jeanne smiled to the side.

"So much, and more, for the surface, my pet," Jeanne said. "Now animate this pretty stick figure with some dialogue."

"Yeah," OhJim said. "I guess I got carried away. What happened was I noticed Tommy Agent talking with this Lailah maybe Grim, so I sidled over and hid behind a clutch of people. Although I could not hear what they were saying, I could interpret a lot from their faces and where their bodies were, in reference to one another. If I didn't know better, and it strikes me that I don't, it looked like a conversation between a mother and her child."

"Clearly," Mister Ed said, "we have a lot to learn about not only Lailah but our associate Tommy maybe Grim, too."

Lengthy debriefing to keep a wake
|09June10|

"You might want to put your seatbelt on, OhJim my friend," Mister Ed said.

"Yeah," OhJim said, "and maybe it might help to actually be in like the car."

Mister Ed raised one eyebrow.

"I don't know all the details," Mister Ed said, "and mind you, your Ma knows the whole story, though she may have forgotten it, but there was always a rumor that your Pop didn't bother to refute that he had a family and wife, or common law wife, in another city."

"Maybe Grim," Jeanne said.

OhJim bobbles for a moment.

"Nothing that I have heard or seen or felt or imagined about my Pop has ever made much sense. To tell the truth, when I found out that he was dead, when Goose found Jim and me over the Internet a few years ago, I was glad, because I knew that the target had stopped moving."

Jeanne gave OhJim her very best lemony smile, bitter and sweet, which perfectly matched the climate in the room.

"I guess," Jeanne said, "this goes toward explaining why you seemed uninterested in some provocative information that has suddenly appeared."

"Yeah," OhJim said, bobbling all the while, "as Tommy would say --."

"Bingo," Mister Ed said.

"**B13**," OhJim said. "That's **B13**."

≈ ≈ ≈

Email from: Mister Ed
To Goose Grim

Subject: House of Verbs. Open again,

Thank you, my friends, for your kind comments on the book review of White and/or Fish. I realize that the Bremner piece had more power, but I encourage you to glean the goodness from the White/Fish piece, too.

What follows in a few lines from now is the first of the two emails from Goose that I mentioned a while back. The text includes my additions and subtractions.

As always, watch for the ever-shifting "I". Three of us use the same "I" in the piece that follows.

See if you see them.

As ever, and always, enjoy.

Your servant,
Ed

Some editing needs to be second-rate

It is challenging to edit my own writing. I must do battle with a tendency to fall in with the cadence of my prose like a good toy soldier on parade, counting out **one, two, three, four … one, two … three, four!** I look up from editing to realize that I have been more intent on admiring and far less intent on improving the text. This familiarity never breeds anything approaching contempt.

And come to think of it, a copy editor should never have contempt for the writing that is at hand. An attitude of alert and even hyper-alert attention paired with lodged suspicion will get you where you want to end up when you sit down to edit. Contempt will poison your spirit and drive off your business.

The late Prof. John Bremner said it this way: ***If your mother says she loves you,* check it out**.

Now that is suspicion.

Another piece of aggressive good advice from Bremner was this: Imagine, he said, that you are tossing a child into the air, and catching her, and tossing her into the air and catching her, and tossing her into the air and catching her, and … well, you get the idea. When you stop, and you put the child on her own two feet, what does she say?

Do it again!

This, Bremner said, is ***The Thrill of Monotony.***

In your editing, practice The Thrill of Monotony.

And, I would add, suspicion.

■ ■ ■

I am not exactly certain of my main fictional character Goose Grim's attitude toward my hyper-alert and suspicious way with his precious daily blog posts in the novel series ***Grimoire: The Bros Grim Breakfast Serial - a Story in Pieces***, but I do know this. As the author persona Jon Rieley=Goddard, I am the better writer and (need it be said?)the better editor. I take steps at all turns in the plot to make sure that this is true. Goose is good, and I am better.

Goose is my creation. In his genesis, I decided that I would let myself go when I wrote in Goose's voice and that I would allow Goose all the puns, purple prose patches, and semi-retired clichés that he wished to use. Goose writes like I do, since Goose I am, but Goose does not get the final edit where puns, purple prose patches, and semi-retired clichés would come under fire from my relentless and suspicious scrutiny.

For Goose, I suspend The Thrill of Monotony.

If Goose misses the mark, that is fine. After all, that is the way my man Goose writes. He is a bit uneven. Just like me.

■ ■ ■

When I edit my own work, I too have the same goals that I have toward any other editing job where someone is paying me to edit their work. I hope to do no harm to this other writer's voice. I make changes that will seem subtle to this other writer, by learning to hear her voice, to celebrate her voice, and to make her voice as perfect in pitch as I am able to. This is much more than catching typos, and it is **not** making her prose conform to my self-satisfied and rigorous standards of usage and grammar and style and form, to say nothing of function.

If the work that I am editing is a dissertation, I will apply all the academic standards for formal writing, including conformance to the style guide of her discipline. If her writing that I am editing is personal in tone, I will hunt for her voice and that will be the standard. The same goes for her fiction. The rules will conform to her voice.

■ ■ ■

There is a lovely freedom in editing Goose's fiction. It is amusing and refreshing to stay my hand and allow all the little and picky things to slide on by. If Goose uses a parallel construction, I will allow him to leave out the crucial word or words **that** give the reader a clear signal **that** two trains are running on parallel tracks and **that** the sense of the sentence revolves around those words.

Goose is uneven at the best of times, usually in subtle ways. Sometimes he puts the signal words in and sometimes he goes with the first instance and leaves out the second. A lot of writers do not understand or value such signal words. Associated Press copy is often edited in a way that ignores signal words in parallel constructions, and I am convinced that this approach is so familiar to us that we will use that approach ourselves and will assume that we are doing the best we can, in imitation of the ubiquitous AP tone. It may be all that you know.

AP copy, however, often ignores AP style. As does Goose.

■ ■ ■

In my essay writing, I include the signal words in my sentences. Otherwise, the reader will look up in the middle of things and realize that she has no idea where she is or how she got there, like a driver who leaves his GPS at home. My writer's voice tends to produce complex sentences that do not always intend to create either straight or forward progression. I want you to have an experience along the way and a clear sense in the end of what I am saying and where I have been taking you. I want you to wander but not wonder.

Goose probably understands these things, at some level, but he has not been trained to do this or to fix his stuff when it strays from a clear standard of guiding the reader.

Some of you do not like fictional Goose. You think Goose is pompous and controlling, though I doubt that he would say that about me. I could fix that problem that you has with Goose, effortlessly, but both of us would mourn Goose's passing and I would have Goose's inky blood on my hands. I do not want that and neither do you. Nor does Goose, even if he has never come out and said so in print. And Goose would miss fictional Goose, too, obviously.

■ ■ ■

How does one find another writer's voice? This is the first and most important question to answer. If you can detect that other voice, your editing choices will flow from what you have decided you are hearing. It's not preaching, or surgery, or rocket science, but your ability to hear, respect, and assist another writer -- including those whom you create in your fiction -- will be of ultimate concern for that writer. You are not like a surgeon holding her beating heart in your hands, but you are a kind of midwife who can assist or get in the way and do terrible harm, depending on your gifts, training, and intentions.

I cannot teach you what you need to know, but I can show you what I do, and if you are willing to give yourself up to this process, long on example and short on rules, your own editing will improve. I guarantee it.

■ ■ ■

One of the most helpful things that an editor can do is to mangle another writer's prose. The teaching moment comes when you stand before a pissed-off colleague or friend who has your editing changes from yesterday's newspaper, let's say, in her rage-shaking hand. What will you say, how will you listen, and what will you learn?

When you let yourself down, you know it, too. When your book is in print and you read it, you will see countless places where you have faltered in ways that no one else will ever know or detect.

But you will know.

What to do?

As Goose would say, **Get over it.**

Do better next time.

Laugh.

Laugh particularly if you messed up. Laugh to keep from crying, and learn from your mistakes, too.

There is no other way.

The darkness surrounds us
|10June10|

"Four hours max," OhJim said, "from safe house to home. It's good to be back."

OhJim bobbles in agreement with himself.

I can see that our trio are tired, but it cannot be helped.

Let us be," I said, "in short-order."

"Ham and wry," Jim said. "If it please you, Mister Chair Sir."

"Yeah," OhJim said, "but please not a Panini, for Pittsburgh is still too much with me."

"The darkness approaches," I said, "Let us improve the time."

Eve smiles her Buddha Girl smile.

"It may even be," Eve said, "that the darkness surrounds us."

Jeanne gives Eve her sideways smile full-on for a 10-count.

"We bring stories to push back the night," Jeanne said, from David's lap. "We also come in search of other stories to help us see what is dark to us."

"I am of the opinions," Ma said, "that you will be asking for me of the stories that I cannot be of the remembering. This was of the truth thing before, but be of asking."

Ma's smile is a rueful version of her usual rogue's impishness.

"I know, Darling," Jeanne said, "but at least we can tell our story and see what responses arise."

Luke frowns a spook's frown, which to a blind horse may be as good as a wink or a nod. but to the rest of us signals something a bit more somber.

"Tommy giveth and Tommy taketh away," Luke said, "and no one is the wiser about where he is or what he is about."

As I said to my friend ...
| 11June10 |

"By your leave, Mister Chair Sir," Mister Ed said, "I will begin."

I nod.

"Thank you," Ed said, "and greetings from our sister city to the south. We had a short but powerful visit. The wake for Peter Principe was of particular note for us all, and the news has reached you before we did. We went armed with the knowledge that Janey Grimes had changed her name from Grim to Grimes, after her father's death, because she felt soiled by the association. Perhaps, in itself, this was provocative."

OhJim bobbles.

"Yeah," OhJim said, "I for one was provoked by the mention of the family name and its linking with someone called **father**, but frankly I do not think of such things and men willingly."

Ma, sitting between her Ruby Jim and her Diamond Jim, put s her hand on OhJim's shoulder.

"My besty boy," Ma said, "you are the one of whom is being said that the Pops was not in the graces of goodness for you. I am being right here?"

"Yeah," OhJim said, "and I cringe in this company to say so, but the news of Pop's death, in my absence, was something that I hoped very deeply had not been exaggerated. I feel ambivalent toward him, at best, and this is something that I have not said out loud in this place."

Eve gives OhJim her Buddha Girl smile of healing.

"Pops," Eve said, "was a hard man, Dear. I am reminded of that story about the scorpion, where the point is that **it is in the scorpion's nature to sting**."

OhJim bobbles.

It dawns on me that you might not know the story. It goes like this. A monk crossing a river grabs at a soggy log to float himself to the other side. But there is a scorpion on the log that strikes at the monk every time he tries to hold on to the log. When the thoroughly wet and tired monk reaches his friend on the other side, the friend mentions the scorpion's aggressiveness. *Why didn't you brush it into the water? I would have!* the friend says.

Ah, my friend, the monk says, **I bore it no ill will, for it is in the scorpion's nature to sting.**

... because I am always talking ...
| 12June10 |

"So, Oh," I said, "it would be a challenge but perhaps not a surprise if we were to discover that our Pop had yet another family in another city, complete with wife and children whom one presumes he loved more than he did the three of us."

"Yeah," OhJim said, "something like that."

"Mister Chair Sir," Mister Ed said, "to continue my sharing of the story that the three of us have pieced together, I turn to the wake and several startling things we saw and heard and (in the case of OhJim) overheard. To wit, that Tommy in conversation with Janey seemed to be referring to her as **Sis** and to someone in the room as **Mother** and as **Lailah**. Further, we saw Tommy in conversation with a woman whom we three all assumed fit that description. I believe that Jeanne sent an email ahead sharing these facts, so what we have here is a need to communicate."

When Mister Ed says **Lailah**, Ma's head jerks up.

"Wodka," Ma said, "I am feeling the needing of this."

David runs to fetch the bottle from its hiding place up front, near the always-absent-from-our-proceedings Mr. Red.

Shouts and murmurs from the front attest to the success and the difficulty of David's errand.

"Is better," Ma said, taking a sip. "Is best, as of the well. This name Lailah is ringing the bells up in my belfry and the bats are making the contact with my temple. **Lailah** is speaking of the desert, this I am knowing of it, and is of something more than."

Ma shakes her head in rue.

"But," Ma said, "I am not the retriever after this name. Still, **Lailah** is in there, among the grey cells of the head. I am getting only from the letters **L-A-I-L-A-H**."

... Jim, I said, the darkness surrounds us ...
| 13 June 10 |

Ma's willingness and Ma's inability to recall were of a piece. I am not surprised by the attempt or the failure.

"The story," I said, "divides along the fault line of the earth-shaking news that Tommy surfaced at the wake for Principe and the earth-shaking news that he calls someone (one Lailah) **Mother** and someone else (one Janey, known to us), **Sis**. Further, there are conclusions to rule out or embrace, such as the possibility that we are related to these persons, including Tommy, in ways that we never knew."

It costs me nothing to say this at this point.

"Yes, Dear," Eve said, "and that is the personal dimension. The larger dimensions divide from the merely personal, on paper, but in reality the two are intertwined and cannot be separated."

"Yes," I said, "our investigation into strangers has branched into a search for our roots as well, it seems."

I half-expect Tommy to appear in the doorway and say, **Bingo**, but he does not.

"I'm getting the same sort of chatter from up and down the line as before," Luke said. "No one knows what to make of the Tommy sighting, and I was careful not to share the personal stuff about his apparent family connections. Such things are largely out of bounds and would have nothing to do with his case names or legends."

"Right," Mister Ed said, "and like our wives and girlfriends, may the two never meet. But Mister Chair Sir, I ask the obvious question. Where are we with **Operation Next-of-Kin**?"

Outside, in the dark, the dogs of irony raise their voices to mock the moon.

... why don't we, and why not ...
| 14 June 10 |

When next I look at the doorway, after hearing but faintly the little bells at the front door, and a murmur and a meow, who appears but Mr. Black and Nancy Chino.

Late but never not welcome.

"Friends," Mr. Black said.

He gives us his highway-in-the-desert smile.

"Hey," Nancy said, smiling her smile of secret sorrow, "good to see you."

David moves two chairs up into our circle.

"Hello, Dears," Eve said. "How goes the Beer Bore Wars?"

"Any victories in such wars are the sort that we cannot afford to win," Mr. Black said.

"So here we are," Nancy said, "fresh from Bee's being on the phone with Tommy."

That grabs our attention.

"He wishes," Mr. Black said, "to commend us on our efforts to learn of him by stealth and he bids me remind you that not all that glitters is gold nor are all those who wander lost."

"Weird, huh?" Nancy said. "It makes no sense to me either."

Jeanne begins to pace around the circle behind our backs.

"It would seem," Jeanne said, "that Tommy is advancing the idea that what OhJim heard is what Tommy wanted him to hear, which begs the question of where the truth lies."

Jeanne smiles sideways and sits.

"The truth is a liar," Jim said.

"Yeah," OhJim said. "You said it, Jeanne -- the truth lies."

... get a bleeping big car ...
| 15June10 |

Mr. Black as usual betrays his usual private amusement at the machinations of others. Nancy, as usual, is pretty and perky, and sweet, like a child when compared to Mr. Black's darker purposes.

"What else," Jeanne said, "did that Tommy tell you?"

"Nothing I needed to know," Mr. Black said. "He spoke, he hung up."

"Again," Nancy said. "I agree. Weird."

"And what," Jeanne said, ignoring Nancy, "do you make of it?"

"Nothing," Mr. Black said, "beyond what I have said. But if you are asking me my thoughts, I would say that the big questions are the ones that we need to pursue -- who is trying to kill some or all of us, and why are they doing that, and when will they try again, and how and where?"

Mr. Black looks at each of us in turn.

"Focus on the donut," Mr. Black said, "not the black hole of questions about murky personal stuff like Pop's libido and the likely or unlikely outcomes of it. if you have kin, they will become known to you, as a side effect of maintaining your focus on the big things."

"And if we detour to chase after the smaller concerns," I said, "we will lose sight of everything and probably find out nothing."

"Bingo," Nancy said. "I agree. Weird, huh?"

... drive, he said, look out where you're going
|16June10|

"To that end, Dear," Eve said, "I proposed that our best course is to send another team back to the safe house with the aim of picking up the threads that have appeared, including interviews with this Lailah and Janey."

"Yes," I said, "whom shall we send, and who will go for us?"

"Here I am," David said, "send me."

"The Lord loves a volunteer," Jim said.

"Yeah," OhJim said, sing-song, "and Jeanne loves David."

Jeanne smiles, bitter and sweet, to the side.

"Davey is a good choice," Mr. Black said, "because he is not a known associate of anyone. I suggest that myself and Goose can round out the crew, with the brothers Jim moving to the **Roll In**. Nancy will be in and out. She has a gig with the Bard."

"Done," I said. "And just beginning."

≈ ≈ ≈

Email from: Mister Ed
To Goose Grim

Subject: House of Verbs. Open again.

I am gratified that friend and Chair Goose is getting as good or better than I am from our audience.

What follows in a few lines from now is the second of the two emails from Goose that I mentioned a while back. I

blended my thoughts on editing with Goose's on writing and shared one "I" between us. You know what I mean.

As ever, and always, enjoy.

Your servant,
Ed

Cookie-cutter advice for that dial-tone voice

Many writing how-to writers -- including one or two who have something worth reading -- stand ready to help you pick a cookie-cutter approach to writing. You will receive guidance, for the type of writing (usually non-fiction), the subject (something you understand at depth), the goal (making a profit), and the method (everything from beta testers to web sites and blogs, to having (can you believe it?) a My Space page.

But.

I am here to tell you that you must find and respect your own writer's voice. Without a sense of your writer's voice, any advice about how or what to write will mean little, if anything. If you do not know your own voice, you can write anything (to no real purpose). If you copy some other voice, you will sound flat.

Who wants a writer's voice that sounds like a dial tone?

None of us does.

So what can you do to find your voice?

- Read good writing of the sort you want to produce.
- Write on a schedule of your own choosing.
- Seek feedback on your own terms.
- Learn from your mistakes.
- Forget everything and just write.

Read good writers

I read a lot of fiction roughly divided among mystery novels, spy novels, and novels of any stripe, especially first novels. Plus books on social media and self-publishing. I read a lot of books.

Writers write, and writers also read.

My first reason for reading is pleasure. Good writing delights me. My second reason for reading is instruction. My preaching, as well as my writing, suffered when I ignored my needs and allowed myself to squander my focus.

I read at least two hours a day, on most days.

I also read bad writing.

It is easy to improve when you can spot bad writing and know something about what you would do to fix it. I will not suggest that you do this as an exercise (unless that is how you learn). Simply become aware of these things while you read. The explosion of eBooks at prices as low as 99 cents ensures you a steaming heap of bad writing. Listen and learn. Stop when you can't stand to read another sentence. You are only out a buck, and you got a penny back for your piggy bank.

Write on a schedule, any schedule

The books that tell you how to write books are likely to tell you that you must write every day, at the same time, and hit the same word-count goal each time. If you hang out at churches you will find many people who will tell you that you must read the Bible every day, at the same time and for the same length of time. They will say the same about prayer.

I have never found it possible or rewarding to read or write or pray according to someone else's aggressive good advice. I notice, however, that I tend to write seriously about once a week. That is my rhythm. Notice that I am not talking about editing or revising. I do that constantly.

The point is to know yourself.

You do need to write, on some kind of schedule, if you wish to go beyond telling friends and strangers that you are, or want to be, a writer.

Writers write.

Although I tend to write at a weekly interval, I did post daily to a blog for almost three years -- an online serial novel. I wrote two-and-a-half book-length (300 printed pages or more) manuscripts for my Grimoire series. I found the discipline to be much more than tolerable. I got results from an hour or less per day of effort. In fact, the first book manuscript, **The Mystery Man Murders**, after a year of daily posting, totaled 700 typed pages. The final edit produced a book of half that size.

I learned what one day at a time could do for my writing.

A blog allows you to put **something** out there every day or every week or on some other schedule. Or at random. It is your blog and your choice. The blog potential for exposure is worth a lot to you as a writer. Not so long ago, a writer would write in silence for months on end and at some point begin looking for agents and publishers while continuing to write into the void. This is the most lonely of places for writers.

Even if you restrict your blog to a few readers who participate by invitation or password, or if you have only a few readers that find you, you still will be amazed and gratified by your results, and you will not be alone, at any point in your process.

Seek feedback on your own terms

All those who would tell you how to write a book will usually agree that you must submit your precious stuff to others who are solemnly charged with giving you honest feedback.

No one who is healthy enjoys this, on either side.

Still, outside opinions are crucial if you want to grow in your ability to instruct and delight your readers. I was blessed by many years of newspaper work, from two years I spent part time as a cub reporter to 14 years of full-time work as a copy editor on two daily newspapers.

Somehow you need to find readers who love your stuff. There will be and must be also readers who scorn your stuff and seem to extend their scorn to you yourself. These two categories of readers are not only helpful; they also are inevitable. If you write for your own pleasure you have everything you need, right now. The rest of us need readers, including pissed-off readers who gleefully say they are **former** readers. We also need editors and mentors and copy editors, and someone to compare the page proofs to the ms.

How you do this is your business. Your call. Your cash.

Learn from your mistakes

Mistakes that concern writing come in at least two flavors -- making mistakes in your own writing, and mess up the writing of others. Both flavors are tart and unpleasant but avoidable.

You will learn from the inner work of noticing yourself as a writer. You also will learn when you get feedback from others.

Hate your mistakes and see them as sin, even, if that will be helpful for you. Resolve to do better by having a sense of what you did wrong the last time.

I have benefitted from therapy in my adult life, and I have learned as much about interpersonal dynamics as I have about personal dynamics. I have had many mentors and some detractors, and often in the same person, in my newspaper work.

Seek friends and foes, and as the singer says –

No one can harm you; feel your own pain.

Just forget everything and write

Any time you wish, you can just sit down and write. Listen for the still, small voice inside you that knows what it wants to say. Listen for the voices outside of you that want a hearing. Tune yourself to the Spirit and write what you receive as gift.

It is not so important what you write.

It is important that you write.

You can always clean up later.

Part Two

Goose muses on Pop's other watch
| 17June10 |

My **Bro-Oh** may well have **Pop's watch**, because he took it and claimed it, since no one else wanted it, and I believe him when he says that he keeps the watch under his pillow while he sleeps, **but** I am the son Pop set as a watch over his **Ticking Time Bomb** that usually goes by another name, like an operative on a covert mission who carries a selection of passports.

The Vault.

And **scrub your *but***.

Goose muses on Pop's other watch
| 18June10 |

This last advice -- **scrub your *but*** -- comes to us live and direct from Eve in her therapist persona.

Pop would have understood but would not have appreciated the humor or the pun. Pop, you see, did not laugh at anyone's jokes but his own. And that is another thing about Pop -- his successful effort to continue laughing at his own jokes from the **Other Side**.

I can hear him as we speak, like the scream of the butterfly or the sound of one hand chapping.

And just because Pop would not laugh at your jokes, for fear of giving away even a gram of his power, that does not mean that Pop shunned puns or scoffed at wordplay.

Am I not my father's son?

Case in point.

Pop created a pipeline to connect him to **This World** and called it **the Vault**. The pun is dormant without its referent, which is a quote from Pop. He would say to me, again and again, that **they will jump when they see you coming, and when you say jump they will say *how high*?** Pop also would say that **a Vault is useless without a Pole but you are more like an Englishman who came over by way of the Baltic**.

But that just confuses the issue, so let it pass.

Goose muses on Pop's other watch
|19June10|

Since comparisons are odious (and remember that line and its source, Dogberry in **Much Ado About Nothing** by the Bard himself. Nancy will have need of it soon.) ... I say, since comparisons are odious, I will not compare my watch made of dawn and the middle ground of the dark of night with OhJim's watch made of gold knit by the central metaphor of human existence.

Why?

Partly because this is not about me or OhJim but about Pop.

Partly because we both have a relic of **the one truly cross man**.

Jesus was Cross by Choice, but Pop was Cross by Nature.

I was but a mannish boy of some 20 years when Pop found me in some seedy bar and dragged me off for what these days goes by the charming name of **detox**. And yes I know right well that there is a pun there, but I will leave it up to you to detach it from its source and parade it through the streets.

You disappoint me, Pop said. **I expect much more dissipation from a son of mine than you seem capable of, Goose.**

Oh retched, retching man that I was. Who would deliver me from my body of sin? Who? Pop, that's who. Pop, who was more sinning than sinned against, by his own report.

Wipe your snotty face, Pop said. **I have a job for you.**

"I already have a stinking job, Little Man," I said, sticking my index finger in Pop's chest with some force when he made to strike me. "And I am my own boss, not you. Do that again and you will be breathing through a scab, A-hole."

Pop and I did not mince words or stand on ceremony or share with one another the Cup of Salvation or of Forgiveness.

I hated the Son of a Bitch.

Ah youth!

Ah wilderness!

Goose muses on Pop's other watch
|20June10|

Pop, being older, manifestly, and wiser, as would become clear to me in time, ignored my verbal and physical provocations and like a matador moved in to place the banderillas right in the midst of my bull.

This job of which I speak has excellent benefits, longevity, and a pension to die for, Pop said. **There is only one catch.**

"I grow, I grow," I said, "interested. Continue, please."

You will follow in my footsteps, Pop said, **for although I do not like you, I do love you, as I am able, and I see that you have certain skills at least in potential.**

Now you might think that I would ask Pop what it was that he saw, but remember I was young, dumb, and full of alcohol at a level that demanded that I let the dog drive or call a cab.

So I just nodded my head, and Pop took that as a green light.

You and your brothers, Pop said, **and certain others whom you do not need to know, or know of, yet, will depend upon you as a steward of a sort. As a keeper of the cave where all the secrets that others had hoped were dead will be, rather, just hiding and lying in wait.**

"I do not intend to be a semi-connected, proto-human traveling salesman, Little Man," I said.

So you really do not know what my line is, Pop said. **Natasha said none of you boys did. I didn't believe her. I guess that the middle finger really does describe your collective I.Q.**

I raised up to smite him, but it was just too much trouble.

Or I took a swing at him and he ducked.

I don't remember.

Goose muses on Pop's other watch
| 21June10 |

Are you always this touchy when someone tries to give you a blessing? Pop said. **Listen. I have a story to tell you and an offer on the table. Will you listen, or will you walk?**

With effort, I nodded.

As you will you be, Pop said, **if you say yes, I am what is known as a spook. Others hearing my story would insist that I am a spy, but to me it has always been about the shadows and the ghosts and the wishes and dreams that I detect, and distort, and redirect.**

In the course of a lifetime of such work, I have gathered to myself a growing, healthy, and potentially noisy flock of geese. These little birds of scandal and shame would fly away if I did not clip their wings and keep them in check. And

those from whom I have taken these bits and pieces of guilty information know that I have husbanded their secrets in a place that I know and they do not.

The Vault, I call it, and it is more like the gates and the lower levels of hell for those who would wish that I and their secrets were burning in the hottest place in that place where one must abandon all hope but enter nonetheless. And you, my sodden young thing of darkness, my drunken Caliban, I choose as the keeper of the secrets and the keeper of the knowledge of the location of those secrets. In exchange, I will see that you are trained in the dark arts of the spook, given a lifetime of work to do in the shadows, and the number of a Swiss bank account with resources beyond your imagination.

What say you?

I nodded, once again, and that has made all the difference.

Goose muses on Pop's other watch
|22June10|

Pop kept his word and all that he promised was mine -- the job, the secrets, and the resources (though it was not until he died that I gained access to that Swiss bank account).

From that day in 1980 until the day Pop died, in the first decade of the 21st century, he mentored me and sheltered me.

It was not a coincidence that I was cast from Spookistan not long after Pop died.

He favored my alliance with Eve and he knew her as a fellow traveler in the shadows and protégé of his old and dear friend Caspar. He initiated Eve into the secrets of the Vault, as a hedge against the volatile nature of human dreams and wishes and the usual life expectancy of your average spook, and he was very fond of insisting that I was a very, very average spook.

OhJim was embarrassed to say that he had hoped that the news of Pop's death had not been, in the words of Mark Twain, greatly exaggerated. I liked Pop even less that Oh did, or anyone else, but I also knew him better than they did and I did respect his tradecraft and I was, in the fullness of time, a big fan of the Vault.

It was simple, elegant, and dangerous, and volatile like a cache of bomb-making supplies or a neighborhood meth lab.

Everyone who needed to always remember and never forget about the Vault and their orphaned secrets understood the dangers that the Vault that Pop built posed for them and their children, even to the seventh generation.

It was all-but-biblical in its power and intention, which were demonic.

And Pop was like some long-bearded prophet without remorse, grace, or pity.

And I was his heir.

The Watchman standing in the gap.

I did not even know everyone that I was shielding, but I was going to find out, as would all the others as well, but that is getting way, way ahead of ourselves, isn't it? Like Pop's watch?

Yes, it is.

So, watch me, now. And, as ever, trust me.

Honestly.

Goose muses on Pop's other watch
| 23 June 10 |

Pop taught me, and Eve, too, that the Vault is strong if certain conditions are met and maintained --

- If it is not used (think **atomic bomb**) except as a deterrent.
- If it remains secret as to its location(s).
- If it receives regular infusions of new secrets with proofs.
- If those threatened understand that erasing the keepers, and even their dwelling place, would not erase the secrets, since the secrets, even if palpable and actual, such as pieces of paper or computer disks, are likely to be hidden in multiple locations that would be disclosed to the new keepers by actions set up in advance, like trip wires connected to shotguns aimed at your head.

Pop lived long enough to understand the gift that virtual information meant to the Vault. Virtual storage of proofs could be endlessly cloned. There could be no defense against this viral spread of guilty information.

Pop taught Eve and me that the most fundamental threat to the Vault itself was indifference and its evil twin, distraction. People who no longer care about exposure or who have been frightened by other stimuli will no longer be in the Vault's orbit.

Finally, Pop taught us that one did not collect or store the secrets of one's friends or family. For a man who had almost no empathy or ability to distinguish love from lust or utility, Pop did value his friends and associates.

Pop would understand, and approve, of the Tribe.

Pop would understand, and approve, of its self-identity as a quasi-criminal enterprise.

Pop would oppose, with lethal force and the cunning that age confers, any idea that a Tribe would use any remedy except murder for those who broke faith with their friends or family.

Pop was wired that way.

I used to be.

Eve, too.

Goose muses on Pop's other watch
|24June10|

Pop appreciated that the data aspect, the proofs, if you will, of the Vault were all but invincible.

Only fire can erase the threat of digital information burned onto the silicon surface of a hard drive. A heavy hammer could re-distribute the information stored this way but he knew that special machines in the hands of special people can retrieve information from silicon in any form short of smoke.

You can break a hard drive into pieces but you cannot predict what blocks of information will be retrieved in the lab, nor can you begin to guess how many clones of the information are out there, somewhere, and intact.

Pop was much more concerned about the safety and the viability of the keepers of the secrets.

The Watchmen.

Pop's strategies for the safety and survival of the Watchmen revolved around the ideas of protection, regular and rigorous training of the next generation of Watchmen, and clever use of disinformation.

This last idea may need some assistance here.

The disinformation that could protect the Watchmen would be to appear to favor and protect one Watchman over another. For example, Eve and I are the only ones who know who is more important to protect when push comes to shove. No one else knows the answer to that question, and the VPN blog that we post to and read each day, in certain scrubbed versions, is always available for the needs of disinformation.

You know that.
This tempers the edge of your trust in my honesty.
Pax.

≈ ≈ ≈

Email from: Mister Ed
To Goose Grim

Subject: House of Verbs. Open again.

For those of you who have been asking me, privately, whether I will ever take back the narrative baton from friend and Chair Goose, I say that you must be patient. For Goose, my friends, is on a roll.

I realize that Jim and OhJim would pun on role vs. rolls by farting in a bag of Parkerhouse rolls. I will take the high road and not do that.

Enjoy my brother, and his persona, Jon R=G, as I do.

Your servant,
Ed

Approaches to writing the novel - *clever and dense*

Markets are conversations.
-- Doc Searls, writing in Linux Journal

If you think about it, puns cause laughter or groaning without inflicting much injury or insult. This cannot be said for the other forms of humor, where the cleverness pivots upon disaster in some form, like a ragdoll-dressed ballerina losing her focus in mid-twirl and falling quick and hard to the floor like a crumpled rough draft flung from a frustrated writer's hand, missing the wastebasket.

If there is not a banana peel to slip upon, no one laughs.

Don't like puns? How about wordplay? You do like Shakespeare, don't you? If there is no wordplay, there is no Shakespeare.

I'm thinking about that line from **The Taming of the Shrew** that goes, **The oats have eaten the horses**.

If that ain't word-playful, I'll eat that horse and chase its rider.

One of my favorite Bible verses says, **My people no more will be put to shame**. Although I am as amused by shame-based humor as the next person, I do think that self-deprecation has the edge over scatter-shot shaming, even if it is sham-shaming. It is the difference between the pratfalls of frequently falling comic actors and shock-troop stand-up comics who see audiences as target-rich environments.

That brings up another aspect of humor, the need for distance. When the water from the upstairs neighbor's overflowing shower drain is filling my ceiling light fixture's covering dish, it is hard to find any humor in the situation. When yours is the foot that leads the body into disaster atop a banana peel, it is hard to laugh on your way down.

One person's floor is another person's ceiling.

* * *

So much for cleverness. And density? That would be the part of writing that mixes the fun of wordplay with the satisfaction of things such as genre-bending, unreliable narrators, and simple love of words at play.

You might wonder where the title, **Clever and Dense**, comes from. It is a phrase that the marketer in me made up while talking to a friend about my first novel, **The Mystery Man Murders**, which she had just finished reading.

She quickly pointed out and I as quickly agreed that the novel is as concerned with language itself as it is with furthering the plot.

Dense, I suggested.

But in a pleasing way, mind you, she indicated.

I know what, I said. **We could say that the book is clever and dense**.

Her reply was the short, barking laugh of amused agreement.

Another friend told me that she was starting over with the book and had reached page 60 without incident. She suggested that my writing style was something like that of Thomas Pynchon. I replied that I had started many Pynchon books and while I had enjoyed them very much had yet to finish one. She said that her son loves Pynchon. **Maybe,** she said, **I should give him your book.**

Another friend, whom I usually talk to about DIY projects around the house, told me that my novel reminds him of film director Woody Allen's way of introducing and describing characters. I was nonplussed, since I have been told that my sermon delivery is reminiscent of the pacing of the actor James Stewart. This friend also noticed and appreciated the tone of hard-bitten noir detective in some of the narrator's speech.

Others have noticed that there is a juxtaposition of a tight mystery genre story and the simple love of watching words at play. Same goes for the spy thriller genre, which undergoes even greater violence from my love of language-as-language.

Dense.

Since I am ten times a writer as I am a marketer, I have no firm ideas about how one would market such a book, except to warn readers in a friendly way that the book is more of a novel than a mystery or thriller while still being both mysterious in turns and thrilling at whiles.

One friend found that after studying painting to the level of a master's degree that her vision of what a tree looks like was generally not pleasing to the people who came to art-for-sale shows in her backwater community in the wilds of northern California. I am happy to report that she did not change her way of painting trees, or faces, or anything else.

She was more interested in her vision than in making sales.

***

When I talked with my wife about how to market my novel, she encouraged me to point out to prospective readers that there are a number of large themes in general and most particularly the theme of redemption. Yeah, I said, and added my sense of the importance of using a framework of blog posts that allowed me to play with time, narration, and point of view. Yeah, she said, there is a lot of good stuff going on that people would be glad to know about.

I wanted to write a book about a guy who had been a spy and who had been thrown from the train and under the bus by those whom he had allowed to create who he was in decades of covert work. I wanted to show his anguish and rage and impotence in the face of hands far stronger than his own. I wanted him to win.

I wanted to let him speak, at length, and to repeat himself and contradict himself, and expose the dirty deeds he had done.

I wanted him to find peace and healing, and not a sword.

Redemption.

***

I remember reading a column by Doc Searls, circa 2000, in Linux Journal. **Markets**, Searls said, **are conversations**.

Wow.

I quickly preached a sermon about how churches, like markets, are conversations. It suddenly made so much sense.

At the time, Searls was senior editor at Linux Journal and had just co-written the book **The Cluetrain Manifesto**.

Searls, as I recall, cited those whom he said gave him the seminal idea about markets as conversations. It's like the laying on of hands, what we in the church call **apostolic succession** and what others call **each one teach one**.

Humans can't not communicate is the way one of my mentors in the practice of pastoral care and counseling put it. One of my professors, David Steere, wrote a book titled **Bodily Expressions in Psychotherapy**.

We talk, and our bodies talk, both verbally and nonverbally. No one can stop this, no one can avoid this.

Like God, we even communicate through our silences.

***

Writing is even more of a conversation than painting is, and I am struggling with just what it is that I am seeking to find in writing and sharing my work in print, blog, and POD. As resident theologian in two churches that I serve as pastor and as co-pastor, I know that some modern theologians say that God would be God with or without us. By extension, I ponder the alternatives of having or not having readers with whom to share my writing. I cannot imagine myself writing without the sense of at least one person **out there** who is reading my stuff with interest and occasional satisfaction or irritation. And in biblical terms, where two or three are gathered, there is a conversation going on, with a spirited fourth person in the midst.

That is my goal in sharing my stuff, I guess. A conversation.

That conversation has been a large part of the joy of releasing my novel to the **out there**. It is fascinating to hear what people make of my golden and precious prose. This conversation is ego-stroking, certainly, and also stimulating, but it is not the entirety of the matter. The conversation I am imagining is also a **marriage of true minds** sort of thing -- a mysterious joining of energies in the void of consciousness as well as a face-to-face meeting of writer and reader in the quotidian.

My writing, after all, begins in my mind and is partly a transcript of my internal conversations with God. In a real sense, I am passing on to you what I hear in my heart and attribute to God with whom I am pleased to claim in these magical moments as my partner in co-creation.

I say this without ego because it is simply the way writing can be for me, when I am flowing and recording and creating in a place that must be a lot like what people mean when they talk about heaven.

I could no sooner write without sharing my writing than my friend could paint a sinuous tree on the wall in her closet and shut the door when she was done and walk away empty-handed.

***

I figure that my way of writing down my conversations with the Spirit of God may sound **woo-woo** or weird, but the conversations that I have with most of my readers are stranger still, because most of my readers are strangers to me **out there** and our communication, though a conversation, is one-sided on each side.

I know what I want to say. I have no idea what the other wants to say. This channel is not open for me in the way the woo-woo channel is.

Writing is both mutual enjoyment and solitary vice.

This is not likely to change.

Thank God for the voices in my head.

The check is in the mail
|25June10|

Since I expect to be busier than a rabbit pulling fur, I will post in one piece when we return, or I will ask a friend to do the honors.

Yours,

Goose.

P.S. Happy Midsummer's Eve! We'll be up all night. You, too?

≈≈

Hudson does a friendly takeover

|13August10|

Someone please post ...
It's **Friday the 13ᵗʰ**, and I'm taking over.
It's the only way.
Summer is almost gone and still we are not saved.
You have been like ice.
I'm your summer, glorious summer.
Your sun of York.
Good luck.

-- **Hudson**

Hudson breaks the ice

|14August10|

This will take some explaining, and a bit of negotiation, but
Hudson is right.
I've been frozen. Stuck. Speechless.
Hudson will explain.
Hudson?
Ah, yes, Hudson.
Hudson goes by the nickname that Jane gave him. The rest of
his name is **Carl X. Otto**, and Jane calls him **Hudson** because he
is as big and comfortable, and overstuffed, an ottoman and **otto**
as a '41 Hudson settee and sedan.
Pun alert ... too late.
You might recall Hudson as the owner of the **Bookplate Cafe**
and Jane's particular friend and invention. Hudson and Jane, in
a word, are as close as one brain cell is to another.
To call him her boyfriend would only hint at their connection. It
would be like saying **Jack and Jill went up the hill, end of
story** -- leaving out the water that they went to fetch and the pail
that they packed there. To say nothing of the fall, the head injury,
and the **tumbling-after** Jane, coming in second but safe. For
Hudson and Jane have is a fairytale romance if ever there were
one, and a classic case of opposites attracting, beginning with the
obvious disparity between **the Hudson**, fat as Falstaff and as
wide as a tugboat or a '41 Hudson motorcar, and **the Carlotto**, a
low, sleek, and nasty Italian-made chassis in which you gamble
every time you get behind the wheel.

Here be irony
| 15August10 |

Here be irony.
Yes, Class, and what is irony?
OhJim? Yes?

Irony, Mister Chair Sir, is the felicitous disparity between what the writer knows, what the reader knows, and what the story (as in the characters thereof) knows. Irony, Mister Chair Sir, is like a three-way contract that gets broken with alarming frequency. Should I continue?

No, Oh. You have spoken well. Stop before you fall in and cannot get out.

Thank you, Mister Chair Sir, and may I say, Sir, it's grand to see your words once more.

Here be what the irony be
| 16August10 |

Irony.
Iron.
I.

The irony (as in, **Who knew?**) is that Hudson's crossing my bow with a writerly warning shot has put led in my pencil and has unloosed my tongue, like the swan that dying unlocks its throat.

Relax, I'm not dying. Just blabbering.

Glorying in the sound of my voice.

Here's the deal
| 17August10 |

This is the deal that I made with friend Hudson, who does drive a hard bargain.

Hudson will pick up the threads of the narrative where I put them down when I left for Pittsburgh.

I reserve the option of picking up or putting down whatever strikes my fancy, and I absolutely will tell Pop's part of the story in my own voice, and my own words. And I will add comments, provide details, and I will make endless digressions -- as needed or tolerated.

Hudson will be Hudson, and part of my task as I see it and as I negotiated it will be to clue you in on what **that** means.

So fasten your seatbelts and we'll take the Hudson for a spin.

But first, a few more of the details that Hudson and I decided. Digressions, like.

Or as the pitcher said to the catcher, **If I don't throw it, they cain't hit it.**

Which reminds me of the similarities and differences of the **writer's digression** and the **pitcher's change-up**.

I'll bracket that.

Fact is, I already used that one.

Agreed on method?

Here we go.

It takes two to digress
|18August10|

Hudson demands that he be the one who explains why it was that the cat got my tongue and I stopped posting.

Fine.

My demand back is as I have already said -- I'll post as I wish and when, and about whatever.

You, Friend and Stranger, stand to gain.

You have not lost a storyteller.

No, you have gained a fairly reliable narrator.

Good luck.

With me back in the mix, you will need it.

Hudson backs into his story
|19August10|

Right now, before the story I am about to tell unfolds, I make the following promises to you the Reader:

• First, I will not lie to you or withhold information from you. I will inform you if my words are altered or edited after I send them on to the VPN blog maintainers. I will not mislead you, and I will not misuse your trust.

• Second, I will assume that you come to my words in trust and that you will continue to trust me until I earn your suspicion or I should say until I lose your trust because it is going to happen at some point. I will tell you right now that I cannot keep you from becoming suspicious of me. However, I can "act" out of my "superior" or simply different knowledge.

• Third, I will not overuse commas. I will not knowingly engage in what others call "wordplay." I will not use boldface type to indicate emphasis. I *will* use italics. I will not structure my sentences to avoid the use of "he" or "his," etc., to indicate men and/or women in third person collective noun situations. For example, I will not say that "every *person* is the author of *their* own destiny." As you can see, I will not place punctuation outside single words or partial sentences in "quotes."

Come on back, Hudson ...
| 20August10 |

Walt Whitman, the 19th century American poet, wrote that *this is no book/ Who touches this touches a man.* I say that the one who writes a book holds the Reader in his trust like a lover holds his beloved. I will be telling you a story (a piece of "*faction,*" if you will) that Goose would treat as fiction and that I will treat as truth. Once I begin, "I" will step back and you will simply hear the story. If "I" feel the need to interpose comments, I will use footnotes or will break the narrative to muse on whatever in a separate post.

Straighten up your wheels, Hudson ...
| 21August10 |

Who am I? Who is it that you hold as you hold this book? *

---

* Carl X. Otto is the owner of the Bookplate Cafe, a used bookstore in North Buffalonya on Hertic Avenue, the best cross-town ride in the city. Otto is the author of a popular series of mystery novels featuring the feisty amateur sleuth Hannah Anna Gaeleag. Otto's friends call him "Hudson," in apparent reference to the automobile sedan by the same name.

That's fine, Hudson! *sound of glass breaking*
| 22August10 re: 25June10 |

Goose Grim, former spy and current bookshop hanger-on with enduring ties to certain "Three Letter Agencies," sat in the front seat of the early-model Crown Victoria sedan being driven by his long-time friend and covert associate Mr. Black. In the back seat was a young man in the employ of his common-law wife, Eve Green, owner of the notorious used bookshop Caspar's Books and That. This young man's name is David. No one knows his last name, which strikes one as strange. David is speaking.

"What's the plan, my Elders, when we get to Pittsburgh?"

"Why, the same as it was when we left the others behind in the backroom at Caspar's," Mr. Black said, glancing with a frown into the rear-view mirror.

"What do you think has changed since then, Grasshopper?" Grim asked, turning around to fix the younger man with a stern look. Then Grim chuckled, stroking his white chin whiskers and looking fondly at David.

"I don't know," David said. "Maybe you have some stuff that you held back from the Tribe. Stuff they didn't strictly need to know?"

David's voice went up at the end of his sentence in that pseudo-question tone that is the affectation of youth. David added this overworked inflection to a unique array of smiles, bug eyes, and general though slightly tiresome good will toward his fellow man.

"Confine yourself, Davey Jones, to patrolling that expanse of fabric known as the 'back seat'," Mr. Black said through straight and pinched lips. He stared ahead as the capacious sedan passed the exit for Slippery Rock University.

The three men had been on the road for just under three hours. David's questions had marked the end of a hundred miles of solitude. The taciturn look of Mr. Black and his rigid head, facing relentlessly forward, were clear signals that he was returning to silence -- the silence of rock and tree, of fields of corn and stretches of hardwood forest as lush as rainforest on this midsummer's eve. Impish Grim, however, remained in profile to David, while he had his old and dear friend in profile as he drove.

"Here," Grim said to his young friend, "are things *you* need now to know."

Grim sings a gladsome Pop song
| 23August10 re: 25June10 |

With his invisible grin, Grim continued in this wise: "My papa was a rolling stone, young David, and wherever he laid his head and his hat was his home. Some said that he lived out his days in Pittsburgh, that he had a second family there that no one knew about but the sprites of the air and certain nosey spooks who didn't get it that family is always off-limits and private. I for one and more than that for all of that ... I, I say, never believed that story. Hell, I don't *believe* anything. I do *believe in* things -- or people, I should say. That's it. I *believe in* people. But not Pop. He was a person, and a person I never did trust. Now where was I?"

Goose had stopped talking and was looking intently past Mr. Black's nose, at the passing pastoral scenes of northwestern Pennsylvania. The man looked like he had fallen into the muddy roadside ditch.

"You were 'dissing' your Pop or were about to do so some more," David said.

Grim gave his protégé a teacher's frown. "More the teller of tales about Pop, young David, than simply one who would dump on his memory while pissing on his grave. There *is* a difference and I would have you know it."

Goose's stern tone was in voice only.

His eyes twinkled like Peter Pan's.

Who is this Goose Grim guy *et al*?
| 24August10 re: 25June10 |

Who is this man? To tell you would take too long at this point in the story, so you must settle for a description of the man whom others know as 'Goose Grim.' Grim is fond of saying that only he and God know the name God knows him by though Grim has forgotten.

Goose stands, loosely, at just under six feet in height in his boots. He slouches when he stands, so one must guess at his size. In his 50s, Grim looks older than he is, with his monkish bald head and white facial hair of the sort commonly referred to as a 'goatee.' A half-smile or a stern frown are the lines that his face takes in repose. This day he wears casual clothing of tweed sports coat and blue jeans, with hard shoes of the 'crossover' variety. In his chosen uniform, he is angular of face, but those who have seen him in the locker room say that he runs nimbly toward chubbiness.

And what of Grim's old friend Mr. Black? He *is* angular, and fit, and not just seeming so. This day he wears the same uniform as Grim but with much, much more attention to detail such as cleaning and pressing. Although he is much nearer 60 than 50, Mr. Black looks much younger than his friend Grim.

And what of young David? He is twenty-some and of a deceptively slight build, according to his friends and employers. His sandy hair has a mind of its own, going where it will and when it will. His eyes bug out at one through round wire-rimmed glasses. Men would say that David is "handsome." Women say he is "cute."

Goose offers his own profile for consideration
|25August10 re: 25June10|

Goose looked sidelong at David, presenting his face in profile to both of his road companions. "I know that OhJim, brother supreme, returned from his trip to Pittsburgh with tales of gypsy women and Tommy, but that is what I make of that -- tales about some tail of the twitching female sort that caught Oh's fancy, which frankly is not hard to do if you can but pass the physical. I am keeping an open mind on what we will find when we start interviewing these folk who might, just might, be kin."

Goose's half-smile did not match his rigid accommodation to the stories that his "Brothers Jim" had brought back from Pittsburgh. The rest of the Tribe had been in a "dither'" of speculation.

"I will believe it if and when I see it. Until then, I will wait in peace and hold it, too," Grim said.

David's eyes grew bigger and even more bug-like.

"Are you playing with yourself *again!*"

Mr. Black glanced in the mirror in a frowning manner.

"Don't be pert, Puck."

Two paths diverged into a wood ...
|26August10|

Right.

Hudson takes a different route to get to the same destination. He likes the fast roads; I the surface roads, stop lights and all.

That semicolon is for you, HudBud.

And that is just about all the metaphorical dalliance that I can manage now.

Right.

I once knew a writer who had a block so strong that she could not produce a laundry list. As for crafting a single sentence, she simply said **I can't**.

Can't or *won't?* her shrink said.

Bleep you, she said. **Leave the wordplay to the experts**.

Of semicolons and other orifices
|27August10|

Our flighty friend still is dealing with his clipped wings, which leaves you to me, who does not trust flight but sticks to the ground of things.

This is my gift. I offer for your appreciation a set of webbed feet that will lead you through the swamp of as-yet unexpressed details and anecdotes and unvarnished truths that have piled up in the way of our bird-like colleague -- son of the Mother (Goose, that is).

Please note, Dear Reader, that I would never write such florid things except in ironic, splenetic excess borne of irritation at my intended target.

"Semicolon," indeed. He would not know one if it punctuated his speech balloon and smoothed the edges of his cartoonish life. As for "HudBud"...no comment. I will not be mocked, sir, nor will I stand by while you butt in and beg off just shy of doing any of the heavy lifting.

Are we clear? I can't hear you!

Two preachers got up to preach
|28August10|

The story is told of two ministers who traveled together to an event where both of them would be preaching in the course of a daylong gathering around the topic of "The Preacher's Path: Ways to Go."

Tyro preachers still in seminary sat in rows of folding chairs, awaiting the first interlude of actual proclamation.

The designers of the event had set a rhythm of lecture, proclamation, lecture, proclamation, lecture.

The first of our two preachers strode to the pulpit that sat in alien splendor amid the metal chairs and harsh tube lighting of the cold white room. Let us call him the Rev. Mr. Black. In the interest of time, we will not dwell on his words of proclamation but rather on his method. Black had no notes, no manuscript. Anyone standing next to him might notice a sticky note that he had slapped down on his text from Scripture. That was all in the way of notes for Black. His Bible was open to the proper place and his reading glasses were standing by. He made eye contact with his listeners in a random-seeming way and started talking about the text. When he was done, he stopped, closing the Bible on the sticky note in a punctuating move.

A few hours later, when the chairs confronting the pulpit in the cold white room were once more filled with the faithful, one of the event spokesmen stood up and walked to the pulpit.

"The Rev. Mr. White, whom we were to hear now, has sent word that he is unable to be with us around the Word. He is still at the airport and is still trying to locate his baggage and, thereby, his manuscript for this occasion as well. He begged me to say that he so very much wanted to preach to you today but that he cannot make the attempt without his manuscript. He assures us that he will be with us if and when he finds what he is looking for. The Rev. Mr. Black has graciously agreed to preach for us once again, and those of us who preach from a manuscript, in awe, fear, and a bit of trembling thank him for this heroic standing-in for his colleague and friend the Rev. Mr. White."

When a honker cannot blow his horn
|29August10|

The Hudson has developed a nasty hiss that seems to be coming from the tail pipe. What we need is either a good mechanic or a dedicated proctologist.

Right.

The irony of it all. Goose, the honker who always has a thing to say, unable to tell the greatest story that he has ever seen or been part of.

Mr. Black, dour and precise, deliberate and possessed of a faint smile that telegraphs dark amusement at the things going on around him -- Mr. Black as hero, Mr. Black as **goel**, Mr. Black redeeming his pale friend's broken promise.

I brood over the uselessness of letters.

And I hear you, Hudson, and since I am hearing mostly rhetorical questions, I have no response. As for your anecdote, message received loud and clear, and just let me say, Friend, that you are a real bitch for telling that story. I bring you into the light and give you voice and vote, and this is how you say thanks?

Bitch.

I'm done now.

I'm Ok. Hudson is OK.

No more semicolons.

Just checking in on the new ride and driver
| 30August10 |

Just one more thing, my friends.

I trust that Hudson is giving satisfaction.

Right? Good. Glad to hear it.

Sit back, and enjoy the ride.

Hudson will be your driver for a time yet.

I know there are loose ends that I had meant to pick up, but later, much later, for that.

I'll do what I can as I am able. I am still stuck at the airport, in the mud beside the runway, or upside down in a roadside ditch. All my baggage, which I cannot yet discuss or describe, continues to elude me. Until then, I cannot speak of the contents but only seek to find the container.

I ape the art of the storyteller, but my words lack that certain something that would take us deeper, much, much deeper, into the darkness that surrounds us. I cannot yet make friendly that which now causes me to quail.

Drive, he said.

And I immediately pulled over and could not stop shaking.

I'm a passenger for now, and my eyes are open to nothing.

My mind is a blank. White-line fever.

The blue-lined page is monochrome.

Would that I could say to that macho Macbeth of thought --

I have no words.
My tongue is in my sword.

And cut his bleeping head off.

I have no words.

My tongue lies like a butcher's trim ends.

My sword is silent.

I skate on the surface.

The depths rise up to trip me.
My pen skips and skates away from the story that I would tell.
If I could.
But **cant**.

Upon arriving at the Safe House well after dusk
|31August10 re: 25June10|

The Safe House on Hampton Street seemed to the three friends to be frowning in the darkness leavened by the odd street lamp on a standard at regular intervals down the hill. Perhaps it was the permanent experience of being slightly hunched in appearance in contrast to the two hearty Tudors, one to each side of our diminutive Victorian, up the hill and down the hill.

"She looks just a little bit pissed, doesn't she?" said young David as he walked behind his elders up the walk to the front door that lurked at the far end of the dim and deep front porch like a burglar in a cute cat suit. Such, anyway, was Grim's thought on that head. Never one simile when two will do.

"Why 'she'?" asked Grim of his protégé, grinning.

"Because it seems so to me," David said. "And because I miss a certain Miss who looks stunning in basic black and heels."

"Did someone say my name?" Mr. Black asked, stepping into the house. "Not my name, perhaps, but certainly my hue was the cry that I spied."

"By his tone will you know him," Grim said, motioning his young friend to enter before him. David glanced back as if in fear of a trap or trick, or guy-to-guy practical joke. One expected Grim to goose the youngster and say "... a quart low by this gauge" while holding his finger aloft, or some such, but Grim simply kept his hands and thoughts to himself.

The house, which was doomed to be free of constant occupation when certain governmental persons picked up its title and deed, gave up an aroma of dust, stealth, and broken promises laced with regret, but its stories it kept to itself. Or so said Grim to himself as he entered. By arrangement, the three weary men went to the rooms that they had assigned themselves in their reveries of the long ride there. The day was done and the morrow was at a distance. Now, they were tired, like their silent hostess, who was stunning in her Victorian garb. She was a woman of a certain age (Grim again, musing), who knew only too well how to give hospitality and a taste of something else that only great age in its infancy can confer.

And so goodnight, sweet dreams, if you are able, but rest, for tomorrow comes of a pace either fast or slow, but with a grinding of glacial intention not to be stopped but always to be awaited.

Or so Grim said to himself as he stumbled up the stairs.

His last thought before oblivion was "ice wine."

The street takes on its night-time life in secret
|01September10 re: 25June10|

Outside, the street's lamps played the one tune that they knew and the light air was the accompaniment to the mighty dance of the good, the bad, and the ugly who sleep not but plot without ceasing in the dark under trees. In another part of the city that knows no flatness, two women slept, one by herself and one with her memories, dashed hopes, and dark dreams that inclined to violence and revenge and hopeless warding of threats only imagined but strongly so nevertheless.

A threat is as good as a fact when it comes to lying awake, she said to herself, lying alone about the past and getting ready for any number of futures. Such was her way, and beauty sleep was her constant need and occasional lack. Still, the pillows would have smiled, if such were the way of them, to hold her pretty head with its once-black and still lush curls. Whether she stayed or strayed, her scent remained on their slack-jawed faces.

Tomorrow, when it came, would be a collision of like and unlike, of the sort that mothers and children, or children and other children, would endure when fate drew them together, only to watch them recoil in fear and trembling, or was it rage and loathing?

One day becomes another like stars and suns
|02September10 re: 26June10|

"Morning," David said, "becomes electric."

He stretched in a way that would cause Grim, in particular to have hot pains in the back and the bursa.

The ever-fit Mr. Black, like young David, would have noticed nothing.

"I think you," Grim said, "mean that 'mourning becomes Electra'."

Grim put dismissive air-quotes around the correction, which the youngster dismissed with a "whatever" of a shrug and a sweet and bug-eyed smile through his wire-rimmed glasses.

"Where to?" David asked.

"First," said Grim, "we stop for coffee and a bagel. Later, after we conclude our first interview, we will have a Coke and a pie."

"What my loquacious brother in Christ is saying," Mr. Black said, with a frown as faint as his smile, "is that you don't need to know anything until we have chased away the cobwebs, with hot coffee sans adulterants, and thrown wide our arms to embrace this rosy day, as in *I took a shower and felt Rosy all over*, if you know what I mean. And so I, for one, can already say that *this is the day that the Lore has made*, etc., etc."

"And so, my young friend," Grim said with an ironical smirk that mocked itself sick, "let us rejoice and be glad in our ignorance."

Grim slammed shut the door and led the way down the steps to the elderly Crown Vic, which was at the curb, waiting for its morning stroll.

The Safe House looked on in frozen tableau, empty once again like a lover left behind, already listening for the sound of his key in her lock.

TLA all the way
|03September10 re: 26June10|

All the way to their interview with Lailah X. Batavia, whom the three friends had at the top of a list that drifted into the laps of the Tribe in a process that was *TLA all the way*, in Grim's mind, they talked of this and of that.

"Who is this 'Lailah Batavia'?" David asked with one eyebrow akimbo *(like a hairy sumo wrestler*, Grim said to himself).

"Don't know, really," Mr. Black said. "Luke was our final source on this, but the genesis of it was no more than just a beginning."

"And in the beginning, Grasshopper," Grim said with his sly smile, "the earth was a formless void of undifferentiated solids and liquids. Don't be sense, Boy."

"That's the spirit," David said, "but the movement is of another sort."

"More thunder mug than thunder, more straining than brooding?" Mr. Black asked rhetorically with his straight-lipped glower of a smile.

"Watch," David said, "that your blast be not also blasphemy."

This said as usual with eyes bugging out like a child in desperate need of potty training, Grim said to himself.

I dish up this drivel, Dear Reader, in a spirit of full disclosure. Certain others might add, in a spirit of "malice." Whatever. Anyway, why should you get to avoid what I cannot escape?

With the sturdy and still-dangerous, steady hands of Mr. Black at the wheel, the three headed for an address familiar to others.

The horses under the hood know the way
|04September10 re: 26June10|

Well might one ask, "Why did not anyone warn them that they would find the woman Lailah X. Batavia in the company of one already known to the Reader -- Janey Grimes? Indeed, the home of Peter Principe, as was.

As our three fellows trod the steep treads made of quarried stone up to the front door, they were in two cases "oblivious" and in one case "circumspect." The "why" of this will take some effort to explain, but that chore can be discharged later.

Although I give but a sample of the conversation, such as it was, the ride from the Safe House to the house of Janey Grimes and of Peter Principe, until his untimely (?) death, was short. It was the equivalent, in Buffalonya terms, of the daily trip that Grim took in getting from his home on the west side of town to the bookshop, in the north part of town. About ten minutes, all told.

The route from Highland Park to Squirrel Hill goes from stately old houses down hill and up again, to the flats and project blocks of East Liberty. One does not quite recover from that contrast, since the home and hills of Squirrel Hill shading into Shadyside and Oakland, are more steep in both price and geography. Or so Grim mused as they rode. Little did he know, but the interview to come would be a contrast of a personal sort that he would barely survive with his already-dodgy sanity intact.

The lady drops *rich* in favor of *bitch*
|05September10 re: 26June10|

The woman who answered the door was young-seeming and beautiful. She led the three visitors in silence to a large room with many windows, toward the rear of the massive house, which in the irony unique to architectural types, is known as a "Craftsman Bungalow."

"Greetings ... -- Gentlemen," said another and even more beautiful woman of an age and ambiguity only to be observed in surprised wonder by those who are meeting her for the first time.

"My daughter, I believe, is known to certain of your associates as, I understand, the 'Rich Bitch.' I have no doubt, if you run along the lines of most people who see us together, that you will divide her fanciful appellation in halves, like Solomon, and leave the 'rich' with her and attach the 'bitch' to me."

This was said with a self-satisfied smirk that sat surprisingly well on her lovely old face, or so Grim said to himself and, one assumes, would have you believe.

The lady drops *rich* in favor of *bitch*
| 06September10 re: 26June10 |

David, shorn of speech like some ironic "Samson," looked as though he had met his "Delilah." Mr. Black had no visible response. Grim laughed in tones that suggested a startled sort of delight.

"Ah," Lailah said, -- that girlish name being what she insisted that they call her -- "my 'Sonny Grim.' Your report, which has gone long before you, does you justice already, at least in this regard. Your father would have frowned, it's true, but he would have owned you, at least, as his 'thing of darkness.' But he was a difficult little man, no? A mother would never say such a darksome thing. Ask Sister. She will agree."

Lailah gave Grim the same smile as the spider would to the fly.

Grim nodded in a bewildered way. His mouth had opened like the sally port of a car ferry but no words or cars came forth. A veil fell over his eyes as Janey silently and with a gentleness palpable to see guided Grim into a chair conveniently situated behind his knees. It was as if, Grim would say (much later), the two "Black Widow Beauties" had scripted and choreographed Lailah's salvo and Grim's fall.

"And the redoubtable Mr. Black. As handsome and dangerous as ever," Lailah said with eyebrows arching like two synchronized swimmers whose gaze is locked on the middle distance just before they dive and their butts appear, in lockstep. Mr. Black took Lailah's hand and bowed slightly as he kissed her left temple, next to her evident, perfectly incised crows feet.

"You are a magnificent bitch, Lailah, as ever, but I did not expect you to sell the farm. Try to behave yourself, Darling. Be a 'Barbie' to your 'kin'," Mr. Black hissed in her ear.

If the magnificent (as so she was) Lailah heard or attended to Mr. Black's provocative hiss, one was not aware that she had any response. Mr. Black, one suspected, had met his match. Grim certainly could not ignore the proof of a prior relationship of some strength, intensity, and duration. After all, Mr. Black did hiss loudly enough in Lailah's ear for the others to get the gist.

The Black Widow Beauty turned to young David.

"And last, least, and most handsome David," Lailah said, with an eye-flutter that hit him in his manly package (as David would say later). "The report of you that reached our ears was accurate as far as it went but deficient in those details that a girl so likes to hear, but we can see, can't we, Sister Dear, that the young man represents himself as well as one could wish and certainly better than those who do not sit in his skin."

"Yes, Mother," Janey said, "and perhaps you might allow your guests to insert the occasional question or comment into the conversation."

This the younger woman said sans smile.

"Thus my dear daughter, Gentlemen, "Lailah said with pretty shrug that would have sat well on a mall-crawling little home-wrecker in cute shoes and a string-strap top vying with boldly displayed bra straps for the right to claim the greater provocation.

"Janey pretends to forget why I asked for this meeting."

With each word that Lailah said, Grim registered the impact like a dead horse fallen on a domestic battlefield but still catching the bullets aimed at those hiding behind the carcass.

"Get my erstwhile 'Son of York' a beverage, my Dear," Lailah said. "He is uncharacteristically silent, *n'est*-ce pas?"

Janey said a curt phrase in a dialect one seldom hears in polite society, but she also complied by pouring Grim some brandy from a drinks cart at hand.

"And you, friend Black," Lailah said, "what is your pleasure?" Lailah winked at Mr. Black in the lascivious way of the courtesan. "Still the same, I'm guessing."

Mr. Black, in his stoic non-responsiveness, smiled his usual frown that others have described as resembling the broken but arrow-true white line of a highway in the desert.

"And our 'young Lochinvar'?" Lailah asked, pursing her lips out in a burgundy flirtation that you have to see to believe.

David, bald as a baby in terms of his ability to speak, shook his head in a fashion suggesting not so much pesky house flies as unbidden thoughts.

"This is going well, Mother," Janey said "sotto voce" with a daughter's ironical smirk.

"Of course," Lailah said, "it *is* going well. As I assured you that it would."

Turning to the others, Lailah said, "You will have to excuse my daughter. She is in a sort of mourning that has to do with Grimlins and such. It sits on her prettily like the hen on the egg that she has produced and currently both conceals and traps under her skirts."

Lailah pushed forth her perfectly formed and painted lips. The effect was much as the old girl had intended, for she was very like Peter Pan in her still-potent refusal to grow, either "up" or "older."

Dear Sister Janey looked on with a face too frozen to allow any rolling of the eyes.

The look of the two widows
|07September10 re: 26June10|

The two women who set the tone of the interview shared many things. Both were black-haired widows, and both were cheating Time of the revenge that Time visits upon all whose bones play host to flesh that not only is vulnerable but also responsive to the tick-tock march of Time. So would friend Grim have said if he could but think or speak.

Janey looked like a trophy wife of some years standing, so did her mother. Janey seemed to be a woman of thirty or forty, though she was more like fifty, and her mother in the diffused light of morning, looked like Janey's twin or as one a few, and a few years only, older but not wiser. For the younger woman was clearly the mother of the older woman, just as the son is said to be the father of the man. (Quoth Grim again, as if you could not tell.) But I digress, and in tone and phrases almost alien to my wonted cadences. It seems that Lailah had caught me in her web, too.

Yes, the two widows shared so many things. One did notice that the mother's moo of pursed lips was answered in the negative by her daughter's smile, which began in earnest with the same pressing forth but ended with her very pretty lips sucked in and suddenly tucked out of sight.

Janey had black hair of a ropish quality in regular ringlets and of a length and lushness that strongly suggested the gypsy, to quote from memory one of the other brothers Grim. Lailah's hair, of a black modified by Time in still-pleasing highlights of silver and white, was severe in cut and bangs, without curl, like a high-born Egyptian woman in ancient artwork. "Look at what Time hath wrought," one said to oneself, and one marveled at the beauty of it, even after one had heard this beauty speak, for it was not the pleasing tone of her voice but the biting and satiric words she chose that were the issue here. One almost felt sorry for friend Grim. Almost.

Janey wore a simple dress of black silk and expensive heels of black in a woven leather as only the Italians seem to understand. Lailah, resplendent in a snug frock of virgin wool in a muted tweed of royal blue with hints of the sun and stars, wore heels of Cuban influence in a height all but fetishistic, bringing her ram-rod straight torso to nearly six feet in height, if she would but stand. In repose, Lailah was as God made her -- a woman of medium height, sitting very straight, in very, very high heels. The few persons who had ever seen her in her bare feet reported a girlish effect suggestive of vulnerability.

Time had touched, with Love and Forgiveness, this perilously beautiful and thoroughly terrifying Mother, or so Grim would say, much later when he ended the long journey back to the land of the living where friends and family did not hold secrets but told stories that could be true, one after another, to erase the shock of discovery and in the interest of a renewed policy of candor.

What passes for a benediction
|08September10 re: 26June10|

With a gesture of dismissal, Lailah said to her guests, "My daughter returns with you, she tells me, to do those things that seem to her to be of importance. I leave to her, as the older and wiser in attitude if not years, the content and the intent of her mission among you. I remain here, in my exile, with my dreams and memories."

Janey's mouth thrust out, then back, and after briefly hiding her lips, or so it seemed, said to her mother, "Yes, Darling, and you shall wait for your other 'Son of York', who lives for your ease and works to your weal and not your woe, or so say you when you tell the truth with little or no varnish."

Grim looked in bewildered silence from sister to mother. It would be some time before he could put into words the horror of the moments that he endured in their presence on that day. In this space of time, one did feel a certain something for him -- who refused for a time to feel for himself.

It takes an entire village to tell this story
|09September10 re: 26June10|

Jane tells me that my work is done here, because others stand ready to take up the baton of narration. It is just as well, for you and for me. I have little patience for friend Grim, as you have no doubt noticed, and I have, as you may not know, the highest regard for Jane's pronouncements, particularly when they impact directly on our relations together. Jane may not be high but she is mighty, and I am not a fool, my friends.

Pax.
Hudson.

Part Three

Goose muses on death and dreaming
| ... any date will do ... |

I seem to recall that once I had a life, and once I loved that life, more than life itself. Then I remember seeing a sight that I could not credit with my eyes, or anything else at my disposal. After that, I wandered in desert places where there was no way, let alone a straight way.

All was lost.

Me, too.

And then, as once before, I heard a voice, and for me it is a voice that I would die for, except for the determination of the voice that I **stop being a wanker and start living again**.

Eve.

My New Day.

One more time.

How much time has gone by, I cannot say, so let us simply agree to continue the story from this point and dispense with the cutesy dates and headings.

Chime in if you have something to say.

I know that David wants to say a few things.

There may be others.

Here is the deal. Just interrupt the previous speaker by typing three hash characters like this -- # # # -- and starting talking. It is going to take the entire tribe to finish this story. Oh, yeah, and identify yourself. It would help if you remind yourself that you are up to no good, but your mileage may vary on things like the fundamental nature of persons.

Me, I'm a Calvinist.

Total depravity and so on.

Just saying.

I would like to thank Hudson for taking my mind for a spin and not denting or scratching what cannot be fixed. I would like to, sure, but I also would like to kick his fat ass into his forehead and see if Athena jumps out.

Hudson has said all that his has to say.

By my definition.

Eve tells me that I have a mother and a sister that I knew nothing about.

I hasten to remind her that I brought that bit of data home in my kit bag. Never mind that I was in no state to know anything beyond shapes and muffled sounds. Lailah got in under all my defenses, and played around as she would. That woman is evil, my friends. Evil. And the rest of us are little if any better, too, I am sure.

And Pop?

Weasel. A dangerous little animal, the weasel.

Eve tells me that my brother in Christ Tommy is still absent or missing. I do not know why, yet, but I figure that he probably should stay away for a while, until I sort out just who is family and who is not. And decide what I will do with these sheep and goats after I have sorted them out in my own mind.

# # #

David.

I mean, this is he.

David. Me.

I can't get her voice out of my head, and I can't shut off the sight of Goose going down, and out.

"Can't hold his own, I see," Lailah said, nudging the fallen Goose with an expensive, lethal looking high heel bearing up a shoe of woven leather that left little circles for her black hose to peep through.

I don't know how she does it, at her age, but Lailah is a thoroughly dangerous woman.

And Goose's own dear mother.

We all heard what she said, and we all read between the lines, though it was hardly necessary, and we all gasped, though Goose also bonked.

I do not blame him.

If I ever find out who my parents, my real parents, are, I probably will bonk, too. If I ever, that is. I'm in no hurry.

"Well," Laiilah said, "yet have I one son who knows what is due his mama."

"Yes, Darling," Janey said, "yet have you two sons, and a daughter. Why you do is a mystery to me, but indeed you do."

Lailah once more poked Goose. He got the point this time right in his wallet.

As one who knows only too well what damage a high heel can do, I bend down and put myself between the kick and the pants, so to speak. I checked for pulse, I looked at Goose's eyes.

"Alive, I trust," Lailah said.

I nodded.

Mr. Black grabbed Goose by one arm and I grabbed the other arm, and we lifted Goose to a couch.

"Magnificent," Mr. Black said. "No one can cut a rug or pull it out from under an unsuspecting volunteer from the audience, Lailah, the way you can. When are you going to pick on some other family?"

"Are you volunteering?" Lailah said, "because I am tiring of these Grim sorts. Look at him. Not a smile for his mother, or a bunch of flowers. I could be a picture on the wall or a face in a mirror, for all he shows me."

"Leave the mirror out of it," Mr. Black said. "No one sees you in a mirror. Most of us see you in a coffin with a wooden stake through your heart, when we consult our own wishes."

Lailah smirked. She stepped lightly back to her chair and sat, crossing her legs. Once again, let me say, let me just say, that Lailah has far too much style and flair for her many years. I for one find the comparison to be permanently unsettling, like a husband who finally admits that his mother-in-law makes his wife look like a cleaning lady. Or a mother who looks more like a sister to her daughter.

"I think we should be going," I said, to the room, since I did not have anyone's attention. Goose was in a self-induced coma or some nearby Zip code, Mr. Black was locked on to Lailah's eyes in a motionless, silent standoff, and Janey was looking from one to the other with a go-to-hell look on her stark, beautiful face.

"Sit down, Junior," Janey said out of the corner of her mouth. "It ain't over until the skinny broad sez so."

I sat.

"That's right, Boy," Mr. Black said. "Lailah rules the roost, Lailah hatches all the eggs, and Lailah decides when the cock crows."

I looked at my mentor in some not inconsiderable wonder. Mr. Black does not back down, from anyone. At least the Mr. Black that I hold in my mind does not. I would have to observe this version of the man to see if any modifications were in order.

"Pop was a dear man in his own little way," Lailah said, to no one in particular, though unlike me she had everyone's attention, save Goose. "He would have wanted his son to go to his grave in ignorance of who he really was. Pop really did not have many thoughts that others would applaud, but he did have a delicious sense of irony, perhaps in spite of himself."

Mr. Black, released from the basilisk stare of the dangerous old sister, sat across from Lailah.

"No," Mr. Black said, "Pop was not politically correct, or normal, or blessed with any sweetness. He was, however, just in his dealings. Just look at you, Lailah. We all know what you deserved at Pop's hand, and he stayed the sentence we had agreed upon, and took you to bed."

"Better he than thee," Lailah said, with a snarl.

"Believe me," Mr. Black said, "though I was not much older than the boy here, I certainly never was smitten by your dark charms, Lailah."

Lailah smiled like a demon.

"You were not," Lailah said, "and I often wondered why."

"I do my thinking with my brain," Mr. Black said, "and not my crotch, unlike the dear and departed Pop. He had no brains cells that were not soaked in semen and testosterone. It does things to you that you cannot outwit or outlive, though Pop did his best."

Janey sat down on the couch, at Goose's head. I could see that she put some thought into placing herself between her mother and her brother. Why she did, I do not know.

"Getting close to the one who killed your man?" Lailah said.

"Stuff it, Darling," Janey said. "My man was yours and every other person in a skirt. This is me mourning his timely passing."

Janey spoke soften and without anger or any other emotion that I could detect. The effect was as unsettling as her mother's crafty speech and demonically winsome ways.

"You seem to have gone to a great deal of bother," Mr. Black said, "to try and kill your son. Why didn't you just catch a bus north and do it yourself, two years ago?"

"I believe in hiring the handicapped," Lailah said. "Dear Peter was so out of sorts. He needed cheering up."

"Most women would offer oral, Darling," Janey said, "but you had to take it to the extreme."

Lailah looked at Janey with thoughtful attention. Apparently they were walking together over dirt that had long since been plowed and replanted. I had nothing to compare this to. Nothing that had happened since I walked through the door had made any sense to me.

"Motive, opportunity, means," Mr. Black said. "And what is the motive?"

"You," Lailah said, getting up, "can guess."

Lailah walked in a demonic exaggeration of Jeanne's model-walk, right out of the room.

"Yes," Mr. Black said to her back, "but that will not close the case."

Janey stood.

"Let's get this over with," Janey said.

"You get our hats," Mr. Black said, "and we will get the Goose."

# # #

You could say that I have been largely absent, and you would be largely right, and if size matters to you, I am guessing that you will see this as a good thing of sizeable proportions.

Me?

I am just trying to get by, frankly, and I am only slowly putting together one and one and getting a quotient of two.

This woman who seems to be my mother, or my birth mother, has shaken me in ways that I did not know I could shake. She has exposed to me painful places in places that I did not know that I had, and I have to simply get on with my life and try to make some sense of this, and not only for myself.

The Tribe's life, too, hangs in the balance.

As you can see, I have decided to throw words at the problem.

An to repeat as necessary.

Oh, you might ask me what is the large deal, and I would struggle to tell you the truth.

This, by the way, is me struggling.

What do you do when your mama sends people to kill you?

Do you retaliate?

Huh? Pop?

If Pop could talk, what would Pop say?

And what would I say back, and more important, as Eve assures me, with a pressing gentleness, what would I **feel**?

I know this, that it would be somehow more comforting to have a big zipper scar on my ass than to try to make sense of the heard but not seen message that I get from the one who, I believe now, gave me life though grudgingly while muttering curses my way.

Am I supposed to feel grateful to her, for making me in order to have her dogs hunt me down and tear me limb from limb?

Do I sometimes play the victim?

It is clear that my precious feelings are part of the picture. However, the clear and present danger that has been in place for a long (long) long time deserves my immediate attention, in view of the new information (and how sterile that sounds) that I am in possession of.

I find that I can speak again, and write after a fashion, but I still feel like I am recovering from an interview with Satan.

Pop was in on this, certainly. In like flint, in the biblical sense, and then in a pattern of disinformation and lying that stretches back fifty years and more and forward for the foreseeable future.

This is my mother we are talking about.

My brothers, though they are deeply interested in the matter, have a layer of distance, since they don't have a mama to fear and loathe in the flesh.

I guess it really does right now suck to be me.

Or so it seems.

Yes, Pop was in on the whole thing, and I find that I cannot find it in me to be angry with him.

I already knew that he was the spawn of the devil,.

(What do I really know about his parents, my grands. Nothing.)

So why do I quibble over his consort, and why is it a matter of concern that you know that I see her, who made me, as evil and beyond redemption?

OK, that was harsh.

So excuse me.

Yeah, I lure you in by playing to victim, then I kick your shins.

Eve keeps telling me to claim my feelings and to seek my healing, and I hear her, clearly, and do not act. Indeed, for a long time I could barely speak, to her or the others, and as I slowly come back to a sense of myself in the present moment, I realize the size of the debt that I owe to Eve and to the Tribe. There have been no meetings of the F-Troop, no strategy sessions, no puns from the bobbleheads named Jim. I seem to recall a good deal of satisfaction from these simple things, and I have wandered in places that I thought I only could find in a godless wasteland like Spookistan.

I keep thinking back to the many conversations that Pop and I had when he was breaking me, and breaking me in, to work in those shadows. Mostly I remember how much I hated him, and how indifferent he was to how I felt about him or anyone or anything else. Pop and Lailah do share that glacial indifference.

***Don't* waste my time, Boy, just do not do that. I am sending you to places where my attitude toward your juvenile self-absorption wills seem like a dotting father's love to you. So just don't do it.**

And so I remember, and in remembering I find that my sense of numbness is worse, not better, as long as I am casting about in my memories for a sense of who this **little bastard** really was. Just as the son is the father of the man, I realize somewhere along that road that I can look to myself to have some sort of understanding about who Pop was and what drove him.

I know why I began in the life of the spook, and I know what it was that sustained me after my initial naïve attitude ended up in a muddy ditch, tits up and floating like a man who had fallen among thieves, banged with terror.

The usual wisdom is that a person can be recruited into the shadow ranks either from ideological motives or monetary motives or motives of revenge, or an addiction to adrenaline. This much we all know, from a steady diet of spy stuff in print and on the big screen and on the television. What is harder to pin down is what keeps one such as myself in the business after all these years, and so long after the death of all my hopes and dreams. The old ones,.

The short answer is survival.

Once you start, you continue, and if you want to get off the merry-go-round you will find yourself trampled by rearing horses with dead eyes. You could not stop being a spook, and live, anymore than Larry Welk could turn off-a the bubble machine.

I notice that I did not answer my own question. I did not tell you why I started in the work – politics, finances, revenge, or addiction to the racing heart and panting lungs.

I will have to think about that, for I never have done so before. When you hang out with spooks, no one thinks to question your simple but effective wardrobe choice. No one says, **I don't get the** eye holes and the mouth hole. That just doesn't seem to be *you*.

So, Uncle Goosey, tell us why you became a spook.

Backstory (-ies)

There is a suggestion on the table, that I tell you why I became a spook. I have a better idea, and it will take us to the same places as the question on the table would take us by its own merits.

Simply put, I need to figure out what the bleep is going on, and whom I can trust and whom I cannot trust. I have spent many dark hours revolving the facts and fictions that pitched me into the abyss. The next step is to systematically examine all the principals to see what we can see.

If this were a novel, I would be throwing plot out the window and under the bus and over the moon. Let us simply call these backstories, and let us simply get going.

I suspect everyone and no one, including especially myself.

In the end, we will find a new beginning.

A note on method: I have made a list, and I fancy that the list is intuitive for my loosely stated goals and true to my dark inner voyaging of late. I will not deviate from this list. Ready for it?

David
Jeanne
Jim
OhJim
Mr. Black
Nancy Chino
Joe Bob
Jane Carlotto
Mr. Ed
Mr. Red
Eve
Goose
Pop
Ma
Tommy

David

The first thing to settle about David is the matter of his last name.

That is a fair question with a foul answer, since the question seems to be out of bounds You can hit that ball but it will not stay in play.

So David came to us in a way that seems, now, to me, to be suggestive. Of what, I am not certain.

The old guys of the Tribe, aware of a certain faltering in the physical arena, began to talk about ways in which we could continue to provide safety for Eve. We wanted a way to give ourselves and our Lady the peace of mind that comes with youth and vigor.

We looked around for a young and vigorous young man. Friends and friends of friends became aware that the bookshop crew was looking for an intelligent protégé who could also provide some on-site security. After waiting to see what shaking this tree would do, we finally decided to go into the forest and pick another tree..

Eve, though she thought that we were being silly, did us the favor of putting a sign in the front window of the bookshop --

Help wanted – bookshop clerk – must be intelligent and a quick learner – inquire within – ask for Goose

"This," Eve said, "will get you in touch with the right population. That is, the people who come here for the books."

It goes without saying that Eve was right.

I remember the day that David showed up, asking for **Goose**. I took a look at him and wondered what sort of security he would be capable of providing. After all, David though tall is slight of build and eager to please, at least on first acquaintance. We chatted, and I finally realized that I recognized him from his previous visits to the shop. It turned out that he was a college graduate of some months' standing. Even better, he was an English major. That was half the battle right there, so I called Eve in.

Eve and David hit it off from the moment they met, and that has always been my fundamental touchstone when it comes to David. Eve likes him, and that is golden (just as sometimes I will give a customer an extra 10 percent off because I have noticed that Wild Billy likes her). It may seem arbitrary to you, to base my decisions on such vague indicators, but I have to rely on something. I am under no fantasy that I can pick and chose accurately. Only time will tell that tale. So liking, cat or human, is usually a big plus in these matters.

We hired David with the understanding that he would sit at the front and take people's money and that he would be our first line of defense in the event of any trouble.

"What sort of trouble did you have in mind?" David said.

"Oh," I said, "that is a very good question and shows a lot of initiative. I wish I could tell you an answer that would make any sense, but the reality is, if someone comes into the bookshop and you decide that they are up to no good, you are to call for backup."

"Yes, Dear," Eve said, "and since this is a smallish shop, simply clearing your throat and calling out a name should get you all the backup you need."

I explained to David that we were especially concerned that he take Eve's safety as his first and last task. David, with a warm and toothy smile, all bug eyes and good will, said he would take his job seriously indeed.

"That is good," Eve said, "and since I write the checks, being the owner and all, I will need you to show me your driver's license and fill out a W2 form."

David was quick to comply, and in the first blush of getting to know the new guy, no one thought to ask for any name but David. After all, we all have a number of names and the passports and other documents to support them, so in the back of our mind we assumed that David indeed had a last name and we indeed did not really give a rip what it was, since he was as capable of making up names and providing bogus papers as the next person.

And you might think that we would be suspicious of a young man who makes up names, and you would be very, very wrong. Such behavior would have been reassuring for us and would have made the process of getting to know how much and how far we could trust David that much easier. As it turned out, we had to accelerate the process of vetting David when the **Mystery Man** murders started piling up and Jeanne showed up at our door.

The need to evaluate Jeanne on the spot put David on the same fast track as Jeanne rode in on, and both of them assumed the same level of liability.

Things would go hard for them if we regretted our trust.

Two years later, we have no regrets and we have had no regrets. The youngsters have been everything we hoped for and more.

So why do I still not know what David's last name is?

The short answer is that Eve said she promised David to keep his last name to herself and that for the rest of the Tribe it would be **need-to-know**.

"And trust me," Eve said, "Goose, you do not need to know such a paltry fact about the boy. He has a thing about the name, and that is all that I can say, at this time. Trust me, Dear."

So I do, and so I shall.

My Buddha Girl has never let me down yet.

What I know about David is what I have seen and what I will see, combined with what I ask of him. However, what I ask is a weighty thing not to be squandered, and the goals of my current inquiry into the facts about my associates does not at this point demand that I sit the boy down and say **David what**?

≈ ≈ ≈

So, to be brief, this is what I have observed about David.

David gets along. That is his gift and his charm. And that will be the ground and being of his tradecraft, always. And make no mistake, he is a spook in his soul.

Come on.

We don't even know his last name and we trust him.

That is pleasingly tricky.

David's smile is a bug-eyed magnificence. You are put to rest and have nothing but good will toward David after you see him smile. At first we had little else to go on. For many months, David was the smile that greeted customers and took their money. And that was enough. We were uneasy at a pre-cognitive level about the boy's physical ability, so it was only a mater of time before one of us made up an excuse to see how much game David had.

Mr. Red was the one who gave us that bit of intelligence, though it was not a thinking thing that motivated Red but an emotional thing. Face it, no one can please Red, and he is not shy about his disappointments. One fine day, David made a mistake. Not a big mistake, but a mistake nonetheless. A customer had a pile of books that David was checking out, and David picked up a copy of some math whiz's autobiography and put it in with the books that the customer had purchased, thinking it had been part of the pile.

Well, Red was furious.

"How are you doing in the brains department?" Red said, in a voice meant to shake the timbers in the walls and put the boy in a state of panic. "I am thinking you are of the stupid variety."

David just looked at Red with an air of self-possession.

Red turned purple, but before he could say anything from his higher state of color-coded rage, David put up his right hand.

"I have already," David said, "apologized for my error, and I am on my way out the door to meet up with the customer and get your book back. You can stick your sputtering rage over this where the sun don't shine, sir. I am doing what I need to do to make amends."

It is probably a good thing that the only other person in the room at the time was Eve, who has a special relationship with Red. His **Eveie** can do no wrong.

"Put a sock in it, my friend," Eve said, "for David is standing on the higher ground. If you leave your personal books laying around in a bookshop, someone sooner or later is going to sell one of them or give one of them away."

Eve, I am sure, at this point gave Red her Buddha girl smile.

"Goose," Eve said later, "it was a wonderful thing to see such a young man have so much quiet confidence in the face of such loud rudeness as only Red can generate. I declare that you have chosen well in this young man, and you can spread the word to that effect. I am sure the rest are wondering, Dear."

The first thing about David, then, is his quiet strength nicely balanced with his evident good will toward all.

The category, ladies and gents, is David, and more to the point, what I know about David based on observing him and working with him for two years and more.

Jeanne is the next thing that I know about David.

Theirs is a storybook romance, and we all have been glad to see them become lovers and all. It makes it that much easier all around when we get our needs met without going outside the Tribe, or outside at all for that matter. If either of them had to go out to get intimacy, then both of them would have to, and that is two big security holes, holes which are not there because of the romance between the two.

Jeanne is a handful and more, in any sense you choose to pursue. She is smart, desirable, and fearless. She is a natural-born leader. She is not shy or quiet, and she does not hang out in the shadows, though she is perfect for the work that only goes on in the shadows. It would be interesting to speculate on just what kind of man Jeanne would look for, and knowing what we know about her, we might assume that she was not looking for any man at all. More on that in a while.

Suffice it to say that David is the other tone. If Jeanne is black, David is white, and together they made a negative that produces fine prints. Jeanne would not be able to share the Alpha Dog position with any man or woman, when it came to her deepest intimacy. She would need a man who knew how to be strong and assertive in ways not immediately apparent while at the same time accepting her leadership day to day.

Jeanne needs a man who is strong enough to follow her lead while being himself. Jeanne has other needs that, as I said, we will turn to soon.

David can, and must, watch while Jeanne dominates a roomful of men by dangling her shoe from her pretty big toe. David can, and must, remember that he is the one who enjoys all of Jeanne all the time.

The second thing that I know about David is that he has the stuff that an amazing and wonderful woman is looking for, and that what he has is a quiet strength that does not insist on its own way.

In a world of punning old men of a certain cunning, David was slow to unbend and join in, but once he did, we all appreciated his wit and charm. He only had to flag his jokes a time or two before we began to anticipate what his contributions might be. Paired with this ability to get along, however, is a stern quality that emerges when the Tribe is involved in unraveling a mystery. David asks hard questions and does not tolerate a lot of slop in the mechanism, a trait he shares with Jeanne.

Along these lines, David works well with Mr. Black and has take his turn on the barstools of the **Roll In & Crawl Out**, Mr. Black's self-selected forward position and home away from home. And although David does work well with Mr. Black, I cannot say that he works well with Tommy.

Another Alpha Dog.

Tommy's lack of cute shoes is a big negative for David, I guess.

Tommy does not work well with men compared with how he works with women. He has a string of women in his network but few men,, really. David tends to be stern with Tommy, in group processes, as does Jeanne. Tommy could not care less, to look at him, but I happen to know that he is privately pleased that they have taken none of his bleep. And make no mistake, Tommy is full of it and he is going to let it go, frequently. Tradecraft, again.

So the third thing about David is his general ability to get along and the wrinkles in that fabric.

The next big thing that I know about David has to do with what went down right here in the bookshop not so many months ago, when Peter Principe and his two thugs attacked us from both the front and the rear. We all had to step up to answer the attackers, who were screaming Ma's old case name **Natasha Riga** and moving to find her, to her detriment, one assumes, though we still do not know why Ma would be their target. So put that on the list of things to ponder.

List of things to ponder

■ **Why was Ma the one the thugs were looking for?**

After all, ladies and gents, the subject is what I know about David.

And after that bloody big damn day, I know a lot more about everyone who was there, including David. He was a step behind Jeanne, who was armed with one of her spike heels and hobbling ahead of him to meet the threat. Jeanne did not pause to talk or hesitate. She put that spike in Royce's eye and David followed up with a deadly blow with a length of pipe he had stashed where he could get his hands on it when he had to. Very good job all around.

So, yeah, I know that David, like the rest of us, is a resourceful killer at need. However, the killing is not the heart of the matter. David did not set out to kill. He set out to defend. And it is the aftermath, now, that is more important, and the question is whether and how David will deal with what he did and saw. Eve and I had a sit-down session with David, and David continues one on one with Eve on a schedule that seems random. Neither of them tells any of us what they talk about, so I only have what I see and hear to go on. What I see is a young man with a solemn but steady gaze, in his private moments, when no one is watching, or so he assumes. I watch him, at these times, and I see things that reassure me. Or I should say, rather, that I am pleased by what I do not see. I do not see David trembling, or depressed, or anxious, or rageful. I see the same youngster but now a man.

None of us will soon, or ever, forget that day, and most of us add it to the memories of similar times of violence and survival. As far as I know, David does not wake up screaming.

I wish that I could say the same about myself.

So the fourth thing that I know about David is that he has seen the devil and lived to tell the story, in a firm voice with no stuttering.

David, and Jeanne, are the franchise players. They are the future and will replace us in the fullness of time. That was always the plan, even when we had more hopes than facts or understanding about our new young friends of such ability and potential. This is the time-honored way in which we spooks procreate. We shun marriage and we shun close relationships, especially when we are still in play, as Tommy for example is. We make sons and daughters from the material at hand, though ours is no godlike begetting or making. We simply pick and choose, and hope that we choose well, for the traditional remedy of poor choices is to blame the one chosen not well, to blame with extreme prejudice. Eve and I have decided to walk away from tradition, and to enforce sanctions that allow others to live, and to outlive, our poor choices.

Gentle Ben Wick is an example here. He quickly showed himself to be unsuited for our work, so we found him a home with our friends Baldi and Luce, who were in need of a nerd just like Ben. And Ben, removed from day-to-day interaction with the Tribe. has shown himself to be ruthless and apt as a hacker in our corner.

The new ways have been good to us.

In summary, then, David is a mystery to me as far as his last name is concerned, which means that I know nothing about his parents or upbringing, but on the other side of the ledger, I have watched his feet, and I like how he moves and what he has done and not done. I am proud to be his **papa in the shadows**. If it becomes necessary to know, I will know all that Eve knows, so for now this assessment about David of mine is enough. So add that to that list.

List of things to ponder

- Why was Ma the one the thugs were looking for?
- What bearing, if any does David's last name have here?

Jeanne

We know Jeanne's last name. It is Wheenin. And when we know that, what do we know that we didn't know before?

Not much.

Jeanne, however, is a bit more than much. She is more like a double helping of feminine goodness. And that is just the horn dog talking. Jeanne is so much more than her outward promises.

We were in a fine mess when Jeanne walked into the bookshop and demanded to be made a part of us. Although that sort of thing does not happen every day, we deliberated only for a while before accepting Jeanne on Jeanne's terms. We are glad that we did.

Jeanne adds spice to the mix, and she melds well with our reigning Lady, Eve. Some of the Tribe would die for Eve, and the rest would not count the cost. Jeanne has earned the same intention.

It is hard, after two years of getting along swimmingly, to recall the details of our first encounter. We had just come back to the backroom at the bookshop from an undercover operation downtown, where Jeanne had been covering a coroner's inquest for the **Daily Afterblatt, Lake Effect edition**. Mr. Black had gone missing, and we wanted to figure out if he was the unidentified victim of a bus vs. person collision with homicidal overtones.

It could be said, and defended successfully, that journalism was not exciting or (more to the point) demanding for Jeanne, who has a fine mind. Rumors about the shadow side of the bookshop and its colorful hangers-on attracted her. When she saw Mr. Red sitting outside the courtroom, ion a cheap wig, she followed him back to the bookshop and crashed our party. Since we were thoroughly spooked by the sudden disappearance of Mr. Black, we realized that our unwillingness to exposure ourselves to our usual sources made Jeanne's offer of coming aboard attractive to us. She had contacts that we could use.

The high heels were a bonus. Still are, and will be.

Jeanne, although she is not a small or thin woman, is blessed with what some might call hotness. And wonderful legs. She quickly became a favorite among us, including Eve, who simply refuses to notice the junkyard dog effect that Jeanne has on us.

My brothers in particular were smitten like Snow Whites dwarves.

Jeanne in time made us understand the depth of her experience with men, beginning at too early an age, and we grew in a new appreciation of her ways. Jeanne had decided to use the hotness that God gave her to level a playing field build and maintained by men who were bent on using her but not ever knowing her. The fact of her early abuse and subsequent adaptation is known to all of us, but Jeanne has yet to tell us the particulars. However, as Eve says, **abuse is abuse is abuse**, and the particulars are of no concern to us and are Jeanne's to share or withhold as she sees fit.

Jeanne's sharing will meet a need for Jeanne, not us.

Jeanne did tell us that she was not going to share anything about the length of time that David had to wait before becoming a very lucky man indeed.

Now we still appreciate Jeanne's model-walking, her shoe-dangling, and her ear lobe licking, to say nothing of her general hot appearance and manner. We celebrate these things because men celebrate such things about women, and at the same time we admire how she has turned the tables and gotten the upper hand rather than suppressing or distorting her story.

The implications for her tradecraft should be obvious, and if they are not, shoot me an email to **goose at bite me dot com**, and I will ignore it.

Although we know Jeanne's last name, we know few of her particulars beyond the fact of her graduating locally with a B.A. in journalism and a lifelong residency in Buffalonya. We know nothing of her family. She never talks about parents or sibs, and she says that the Tribe is her family, and the only one she has ever had.

Judging from the total lack of any contact with strangers that might be family, I am guessing that Jeanne is a orphan.

That, as I have said, is not a problem for us, since we evaluate one another on the basis of **trust**, renewed every day. Or not. We do not put much value in **truth**, since no one of us is capable of spending much time even alone without spinning a lie or two just to pass the time. Life in the shadows teaches one the value of cover stories, and we still write them and live into them, to keep our hand in.

We may lie endlessly, but you could trust us if we wanted you to.

Another tribal quirk is our vast tolerance for sitting around in the backroom, drinking coffee and reading the newspaper and listening to my brothers swap puns like survivalists at a gun show swap guns.

Their humor is that deadly.

Jeanne, and David, fit right in. Not everyone likes inactivity as much as we do, and few others get the chance to indulge enough to actually see if such a life would suit them. It is a pleasant fantasy for the usual work-a-day sort of person, to imagine the backroom sort of life, but I know that most of such ones would be homicidal in just a little while of our constant chorus of **do-*Be*-do-*Be*-do**.

When we must, however, we do work, and the work we have been doing for the past two years has involved us in the higher circles of corruption of the public-sector sort. We have not engaged in nation-building, certainly, but we have done some king- and queen-making. Jeanne has been invaluable in these efforts. She has worked well with David in leading our group processes and debriefing us with a critical eye and demanding demeanor. The one who said that a child will lead them might have had these two in mind, for the youngest among us are frequently the sharpest, loudest voices of adult skepticism. And once they get their teeth into something they do not let go. This has been a big help in dealing with Tommy, who can be a little on the controlling side and who sometimes does keep us in the dark and feed us manure. The up side of our relationships with Tommy, however, has made this more than tolerable. He often seems like a magician, or a woodland sprite, appearing at the moment that we most need him to be with us. If he ever demands his freedom, we will be lost. Or so we believe. However, Jeanne, though she appreciates Tommy's access to persons and intel, also does not tolerate his crap.

It was Tommy who first elicited that now-familiar model-walk that Jeanne does to vamp things up and also to signal that someone is just about to get sandbagged. Tommy falters when Jeanne begins to walk his way. The effect is amusing, and also subtle and wonderful. Keep in mind that Jeanne is no more than half-way through her twenties. Genius dawns early out here in the shadows.

Jeanne's genius was apparent in her journalistic work as well. If it were not for the fact that she chose all on her own to throw over her budding career for work as a clerk in a used bookshop, which is what the world sees, if would be easy to feel guilty for enjoying her presence as we do. Jeanne could do so much better in the world's eyes, if she wanted to and if she had any need for the world's good opinion. She does not.

That attitude of hers is a key to understanding why she has embraced a world of shadows and tradecraft, with continual need to provide and maintain safety against threats no one can locate with any accuracy. I firmly believe that Jeanne is a spook among spooks because she feels, finally, that someone understands her and values her for all of who she is. All of who she is, both on the lovely surface and the wounded interior. We share that with her. The outside is whatever we need to make it, and the inside is always in need of attention that we barely know how to provide for ourselves. Jeanne finds in the Tribe a safe place in which to feel unsafe while working toward a day when safety is not her constant concern.

Do you understand what I am saying?

Jeanne, by her own report, was a distraction to the men around her from the time that she became aware of herself and others, almost. Certainly by the age of 10. She said that the calls from friends' fathers started about then. It is easy to watch a beautiful woman, or a girl for that matter, and lull yourself into thinking that she is in control of herself because she certainly is in control of you. When it is woman who pulls out this kind of response, it is normal and usual, only a bit more so. When it is a 10-year-old who is exciting this kind of thought process, it is tragic. Make no mistake. Such abilities at an early age are won at a cost that would terrify you if you got a window into what had gone on.

Jeanne is a survivor, a cancer survivor, if you will. She told us that she decided to always remember and to never forget what had been done to her, when and by whom. She knew the dangers in suppression, and someone loved her enough for her to never have to descend into that blind and terrifying place of orphaned feelings.

I realize as we speak of Jeanne that I do not know who that redeeming person was for her. Perhaps it was Jeanne herself. Knowing who that person was, who loved Jeanne in such a way that she never quite lost sight of her value as a person, could be a helpful thing to know as we sort out what has been going on and who has been trying to destroy us. Don't ask me why, because I could not tell you. It is just a sixth sense sort of thing. Any loose detail or hidden motivation in the Tribe has a potential for understanding.

Anything.

However, this too is need-to-know, so I will simply at this point add it to the list.

List of things to ponder

- **Why was Ma the one the thugs were looking for?**
- **What bearing, if any does David's last name have here?**
- **Who was it who loved Jeanne enough for her to survive and thrive?**

This thing about Jeanne is more important than ever, in light of the events that day when the bookshop became a killing field. I and others, especially Eve, who has extensive training in counseling, continue to watch and wait, to see what effects from that experience will endure and what forms they will take, in Jeanne and in David.

Of the five of us who visited violence upon the three thugs who invaded our sacred space, the two youngsters are the ones worthy of concern. Mr. Ed, Mr. Red, and Goose Grim know the cost, the demands, and the eternal damage that violence visits upon those who endure it and who dish it, whether offensively or defensively.

That makes no difference.

For abuse is abuse is abuse.

.

We old guys have gone down this road before, and we have the quirks and ticks to prove it, the bravado that the meek have no need of, and the recurring nightmares to seal the deal. There is little you can do for me, and there is little that you can do to me that has not already been done. I am strong in the broken places, and my broken places make every breath that I take a tortured thing of desperate intention.

I would not wish this on anyone. Anyone.

And I led my little ones into this very danger that I would not wish on Satan.

So I watch and Eve watches, and we pray and wait. No one can predict the outcome, and no one more than we can could bring any healing to these youngsters with blood on their hands.

It is, as they say, complicated.

And it is not like I can draw upon anything from my own Pop to deal with the waiting and to be ready to assist in the healing. It is a torture to wait for the sores to appear, and to wonder what they will look like and where they will reside and to what extent they will scar. About the time that we forget that we are waiting , the damage will manifest itself. That much I do know.

Only those who have lived through the giving and receiving of murderous violence can make a difference for ones such as Jeanne and David. Wounded healers who watched with interest as their own wounds were bound and healed, so they can do the same for others down the road, are the ones who can heal them.

This is what I mean by someone who loves you enough to save you, for that someone must sit in your presence and break the bones that are broken in you, in order to learn what you need for your healing.

Are you willing to do this?

The one who was willing to break herself to heal me was Eve, and the depth of my love for her is packed in a zeal that easily can become violent toward anyone who threatens her safety. The zeal of the mother for her pups is nothing compared to the gratitude of one who has been made whole again, or at least has been restored to one piece of humanity instead of a reeking pile of crap fit for the thunder mug.

You might be wondering what it was that led Eve to this place, to do this for me. After all, I am bald and can grow hair only in the unmentionable places, and I am over the hill and under with weather and beside the point much more often than not.

No, it was not something that I earned or deserved or got because I was sexy or good-looking.

Eve healed me because someone had healed her.

It is that simple.

Would you be able to do this and see the value in this?

I think that you can, stranger though you are.

It is possible to go through life without any real understanding of what love is. What a tragedy that is, but if you do not embrace the truth, that you will need to learn how to love, because loving is foreign to the rest of what it takes to survive, you will not ever really love anyone, even yourself. Yourself in particular.

What an irony it is, that those who can love are so damaged that they often cannot survive. Jeanne and David will survive, by healing one another, out of a love that they brought with them from the shadows that visit even the young and that have no regard or respect for anyone of any age. Eve and I, and my brothers, will do what we can, when we can, but the lovers will learn at the hand of the other, how to love.

This, too, is the secret light that shines in the punk/goth trappings that Jeanne has embraced. Short of tattoos or pierces. Light does shine in darkness, and those who are driven into dark corners by the coldness of broken people who should know better, find more than just a mutual taste for mutilation. They find community, and their outward trappings betray nothing about what goes on inside. It takes a scope that has not been invented to chart the ways of the inner person, so we hang hints from ourselves, like lip bling or prison-rough tattoos.

Jeanne is like a beautiful statue with no arms because some vandal has broken them off and probably left them when they fell. It is not what is missing but what remains that we see and know to be beautiful, and more than enough. If you look at the eyes, and keep your focus there, you will see a universe of such beauty that your heart will skip a beat.

And so I muse on my muse's young friend.

Pop would hate this kind of talk, and he would rightly feel that he had failed in his efforts to bend me into a pretzel that could be of some use for the ends of the body politic.

So be it.

Pop isn't here.

I am.

It is a fruitful question to wonder how much of this Jeanne understands. My conviction is that Jeanne understands the whole picture.

Why? Because she is alive and is learning how to thrive, better each day.

The quick and the dead.

Simply put.

Jeanne may not be able to articulate all that I have said, here, but she will see the truth of it and anything that she could not have said is simply not yet risen to her consciousness but still pooling in her depths and sending the occasional dream and such-like message to the surface. For we do not need to understand everything to be judged to have a place among the wise.

Jeanne has an honored place among the wise.

But does David?

In so far as he has chosen very well, David shows wisdom, and in his reticence to share his story, even with his Tribe, I sense a wisdom that is probably his own. Certainly the love of one such as Jeanne, just as I have been loved by one such as Eve, will bring David to healing, be he wise now or only seeming so.

It makes no difference, at least to the wise.

Love is like mercury.

Love is quick and can be deadly.

Explosive in ways that either heal or kill.

Love is no respecter of roles.

Love can make loving parents of any human stock.

Love grants family privileges without respect to DNA or bloom.

Love never dies, but those who have loved always do die.

Either before or after that instant we call death.

Some of us know what love is, and the rest of us long for something we cannot quite define.

That is love.

That longing.

I may be getting at the heart of things, even if I have strayed some from the subject at hand, ladies and gents.

And that subject is Jeanne.

I am convinced that Jeanne knows, in her depths, what is going on and who the threat is, and what needs to be done.

Why?

Because Jeanne has been present for the whole thing. The same could be said for the others in the Tribe, but with one exception, David, we are old and jaded, wise in the ways that lead quickly to death. It is no idle dream that it is said that a child shall lead them. And who knew that an abused child will be the only sort who can lead us out of a buried and potential wisdom that is already born but still hiding.

The goodness of old age is that treachery is like the air we breath, and we thus are capable of much more than we understand. That is our genius, waiting to be born in us, like Abraham and Sarah, in time, creating new life out of old bones. Our genius is in the nurturing of those children who will lead us out of our old bones.

And thus it is that I look with both longing and love, with great confidence and expectation, to Jeanne and to David, and in that order.

Watch these two, for they are our future, and they will need our love and healing, so we too will be loved and healed.

No wonder I value trust over truth.

I sound like a New Age snake oil salesman.

No sound and fury but lots of bromides and bull.

The truth, however, is in there, somewhere.

Trust me.

Honestly.

Jeanne and David do.

Jim

You probably think that I finally am talking about someone I know.

You would be wrong.

I do know a version of my brother Jim. A young one. I can tell you story after story of Jim as a boy, but as a man Jim is a mystery to me.

I am noticing a trend here.

Jim, as you know, is the toe that kicks the ball. OhJim, my other brother Jim, is the paddle that smacks the ball back at Jim.

Jim likes to make light of anything and everything, for if he is not laughing he is likely to start trembling with a fear that never really goes away.

It is a Grim business being Jim.

Or OhJim.

Or Goose.

Poor we.

Three motherless boys who grew up together and scattered to three points of the compass. I was right there with them, right up to the scattering. After, I was by myself, in the shadows that Pop introduced me to. My brothers found their own shadows, and OhJim told us a bit of his history when we had a memorial service for the **Mystery Men**, but Jim has kept himself to himself.

Sometimes I realize that Jim is irritatingly shallow, and that he bats away any and all feelings. He meets any attempt at intimacy with a pun or a raspberry.

However, he is my brother and as such he can do no wrong.

If he has intimacy issues, and who of us three does not, then he must have a good reason for being a shoal sort of guy. OhJim seems to have a rapport with Jim, anyway. They have this twin thing going on, though they had different mothers. Or so we believe.

I have a largely public relationship with Jim, and that is as it is, I guess. I cannot say that I would like anything else.

Simply being able to hear Jim's voice, after a lapse of more than 30 years, is a simple and surpassing joy for me. My brother who was lost is found, safe and sound, more or less. I am happy about that, and I will be happy about that for a long time. I never thought that I would see my brothers again, because I did not expect to survive the shadows myself.

I have Eve and the Internet to thank for finding my brothers. Eve did some searching, on the sly, and presented current contact information to me about both of my brothers. Email addresses.

Email addresses tell no tales.

I emailed them, and I invited them to visit. They came, with battered old suitcases. One apiece. That tells me a lot right there. Free to come and go, and free of attachments and stuff. But was that by choice?

I cannot bring myself to ask.

For all I know, and in my most paranoid moments I do wonder, just what kind of moles these brothers are. Of course, I will take them as they are, and be glad, and who but a spook who has been thrown under the bus would ever doubt his own brothers.

A son of Pop, that's who.

The trend that I am seeing can be stated in the negative or as a positive thing. I can say that I do not know where Jim came from, or I can say that I have watched him, from the moment he walked into the bookshop and sneered at me and shot off a one-liner, and bestowed his best leer on Eve.

Long time no spree, Big Spender. Who's the Frail?

That is Jim, a wise-ass turned inside-out, farting from his mouth and jumping out at you like a talking fartbag.

And I love him more than anyone, save OhJim, Eve, and Ma, plus the other members of the Tribe, of course.

Because I love Jim, he is safe and warm in my mind for ever. Because I am a paranoid git with a bad case of the shakes, I watch him like a hawk. Not because he deserves my suspicion but because my suspicion keeps its own counsel and its own hours, and has its own credit cards, passports, and values. And its own last names.

Simply put, I watch everything and everyone like a hawk.

Since Jim has not escaped my obsessive attention, I have noticed a lot about him, and I know him in ways that cannot be easily uttered, but I can try.

I notice that Jim bats away anything even remotely resembling intimacy. He is happy in his space, and he is well-protected. For a shortish, slight man, Jim is fearless. If you piss him off, he kicks your metaphorical shins and will not back down.

Jim has no wife and no kids, as least that he talks about. From the time I invited him to visit until he arrived, three days passed. The fact that he came to visit and never intended to leave tells me the same thing. No one other than the Tribe would care if he lived or died.

No one.

That has to hurt, and that has to be a big part of the laughing at everything and making jokes and puns without end like a snake eating itself from the tail backward.

The Grim's family crest, the **Grimoire**.

There is one thing about Jim that I would not want him to change, and that is his love for Eve. Jim may have called Eve a

frail when he met her, but he was smiling when he said that, and he kissed her hand and looked at her with that steady bobblehead focus that he shares with his twin-set OhJim.

Eve, for her part, treasures my brothers and would be furious with them if they had ever done anything but come to visit and never go away.

Even more than Jim's respect and regard for Eve is his love for Jeanne.

When Jeanne came into our midst, Jim went into a tailspin that lasted for days. He would just stare at her and mutter sounds that did not rise to the level of words. He became a bobblehead.

Jim is a male chauvinist pig if there ever was one. And the phrase **politically incorrect** was coined to describe Jim's essential nature. He likes Jeanne's look, and he has never made a secret of that. He simply digs the woman's ways, and when it comes to Jeanne's shoe thing, well, Jim is a lost soul with no thought of looking for the way back. Shoe bop, shoe bop, shoe bop.

That is half the story. The other half of the story is that Jim loves Jeanne for who Jeanne is, and he is devoted to her as a person and not a plaything. And Jeanne, who knows exactly what she can and will do Jeanne finds that the brothers Jim are safe.

That is something for them to be proud of.

Jeanne has explained her sense of this, and she probably trusts Jim and OhJim more than anyone else except David. She liked to be liked, and she likes to be liked for being hot and beautiful. She likes being liked for her gifts of intellect and insight. The Jims, like David, can do this, all the time.

Jim fits the form perfectly, and not because he tries but because of who he is. How many men do you know who could do this? How do you imagine you yourself would be in Jeanne's orbit day in, day out? I assume that Jim, who is a person that you could have left out in the rain, came quickly to an understand of self and other and situation when he first saw Jeanne. He had nothing and he had nothing to lose. Now he has a lot and he has a lot to lose, and Jeanne fits that form effortlessly.

It is a daily source of quiet joy to see the man, slightly shorter than the woman in the striking heels, nonverbally communing in a space they share with one other, OhJim.

Snow White and her two dwarfs.

I have noticed that Jim has significant tradecraft. He has an aptitude for the work. He adapts quickly to situations and has an amoral sense of the possibilities of situations. He can lie like a rug and you would swear that he was the most sincere and wonderful guy you had ever met, if he wanted you to feel that way toward him.

It has been a joy for me to see my brother's gifts fit for the work.

Sometimes I wonder just how he came by these abilities. He is Pop's son, however, and that is enough to account for the gifts. Pop didn't make junk. He was junk, mind you, but he didn't make junk. I and my brothers, regardless of how you feel about us, are far from junk. We may be a little pack of horse thieves, but we ain't junk.

I think it was Jim who said that he was glad when he heard that Pop was dead. Pop could no longer hurt him or use him or ignore him. That was his feeling, and OhJim and I knew exactly what he meant by that.

I notice, too, that Jim is the Alpha Dog of puns, and OhJim follows his lead, but in terms of social skills and general likeability and even in terms of cleverness, OhJim has a definite edge, which is another story soon to be told. But for now I notice that the Alpha Dog grabs the prime spot but misses the brass ring. And that he is content with his gains and losses. Why? Because he makes no bones about who he is and what he expects, and he has never shown any remorse or any resolutions to change and be a better person.

That means that Jim is rock-bottom solid and trustworthy. I know who Jim is and I am certain that I can depend upon him to be as he was in the future, if you know what I am saying. Jim will not drop everything and go searching for enlightenment. If he ever encounters a guru, he will kick his metaphorical shins the same way he kicks every other puffed up person he encounters.

In a Tribe with no followers, only leaders, this is an important fact.

I notice something else about Jim, and that is his love for Ma. Jim does not talk to Ma a lot, and he does not expect anything from Ma, but I know what Jim would do if you menaced Ma. The last thing I saw as I ran out of the backroom and right into Peter Principle was Jim and OhJim back to back, right in front of Ma. These guys had no weapons, but the look on their faces would have turned you into stone. To hurt Ma, you would have to get past these two bobbleheads who have this amazing ability to turn themselves into snarling junkyard dogs. If I did not know them, and wanted to get past them, I would pause in wonder and unease, and I would wonder what they could do to me.

Which brings us to a subject that is near and dear to me.

Me.

Jim although he is an Alpha Dog about puns and such, accepts my leadership. He always has, and this has always been very important to me, for a leader without followers is a nothing more than a delusional loner. I was the leader of the F-Troop and my brothers Jim would follow my lead. They always did, and they never complained. That is huge in itself, and it speaks of a certain deference, certainly, but also a certain solidity. They did not feel diminished by following another whom they knew and trusted. That takes a set of values and beliefs about self that many persons do not understand or possess. When leaders become followers, there is a power in that. A great power.

I remember Jim as a child. He was quiet, most of the time, and he tried to avoid Pop whenever he could. Pop did not pick on Jim any more than he did OhJim or me. You can see what is coming, though Pop picked on each of us, and the three of us together, whenever he was in town and home with his boys. We for our part were much more happy when the thing that we saw was his back getting smaller, and we were not happy to see his face getting bigger. Nothing good ever came of our interactions with Pop, and Pop never gave us anything other than crap. That is my memory.

What parent would give his child a stone if he asked for bread?

Pop would.

That simple, evil reality reminds me of another thing that I notice about my brother Jim. He is normal, or close enough, and he is capable of attachments, at least a few, and those few attachments are strong, genuine, and enduring. Jim is someone you are glad loves you, if you are among the few who can claim Jim's love. Pop's evil ways and sneering nastiness toward his boys did not break Jim or distort him. though there was some deflection.

The amazing thing is that Jim not only survived but thrived, after a fashion anyway. That outcome was never sure or certain, but someone loved Jim enough, and that someone was Ma. And now Eve and Jeanne, and the adult version of his two little brothers.

One could do worse that Jim has, and one has done worse.

Hell, Jim has, too.

The point is, Jim lives and we are glad.

A number of us, and as many as Jim wants or needs.

List of things to ponder

- **Why was Ma the one the thugs were looking for?**
- **What bearing, if any does David's last name have here?**
- **Who was it who loved Jeanne enough for her to survive and thrive?**
- **What secrets does Jim have that cold bite me and mine on the butt?**

OhJim

What is it about this man? He is a lot like his brother Jim, but OhJim gets more than half of the warm, fuzzy stuff.

When we were growing up, it was the same way. OhJim got the **love**, and Jim got the **like**. And I got the hind tit.

Not really. I probably got both.

The one person who treats my brothers Jim equally is Jeanne. She loves both of them in a special and powerful way, and they respond with a middle-aged fever that you have to see to believe.

As with his brother Jim, OhJim came to us in a hurry, and has been in no hurry to leave. Not that he should, mind you. The days of being estranged by ennui are over and done with. We are the F-Troop once again and will ride that horse to the end, together. Like three amigos or three tenors or three junkyard dogs.

OhJim gets a thimbleful more of love than Jim or I, but it makes no discernible difference to OhJim. He is the same yesterday as he will be tomorrow, and today he is being himself.

How many people can say that?

OhJim is who he is and he cannot be another, nor does he want to be. His may seem like a small life to you, but he beams contentment when he is with you, and especially when he is with Jeanne. She pulls from OhJim, and Jim, a gentle sort of humor in stark contrast to what the rest of us get, day to day, from the punishing duo.

Ma makes much of OhJim, as she does of me and Jim, for that matter. Her **Diamond Jim** and her **Ruby Jim** and her **Goosey**. We would have been bleeped without Ma, no question about it. Ma saved us, and she was the one who loved us enough.

OhJim, when he spoke at our small memorial service for the **Mystery Men**, told us about being homeless, about beating a man for spilling the last swallow of Tokay, for setting abandoned buildings on fire to stay warm and alive on frigid nights. OhJim said he knew what it was like to have no one who cared whether you lived or died.

As shocking as his story was, the more shocking reality is the fact of it. How did my brother fall away from all love and family? Who and what brought him back from that brink?

Another thing that we know is that **Pop's watch** is in OhJim's care, and made it intact through those dark days, and we also know that OhJim sleeps with that watch under his pillow the way Pop would be more likely to sleep with a gun under his pillow. That of course is speculation, but we do know exactly what our fecund father put on top of his pillow.

OhJim is the underdog, and underdog always wins. That is what Eve tells us.

When Pop gave out names and nicknames, OhJim did not get the **Jim** name as Jim did. He got the variant of **OtherJim**, when Pop tipped his hat to the mystery/thriller writer Ross Thomas and his manipulative character **Otherguy Overby**. Pop was also thinking **This is my brother Darrell and my other brother Darrell.** What was no more than a chuckle for Pop was a life sentence for us. Three sons of a sociopath. What do you realistically expect from the sons of a sociopath? That seems to be OhJim's life stance, and I say that in love and without rancor toward my brother.

I save my rancor for my father.

And mother, but I am seriously far from ready to discuss that.

OhJim does not know his mama, though as I say again and again he does know his Ma, bless her.

I have had both of my brothers Jim take a turn at posting to the VPN blog that the Tribe shares over a secure connection, and I have to say that I have enjoyed OhJim's voice more than Jim's. Just as I think that OhJim's follow-up puns are as good or better than Jim's initial efforts. And which is harder, to dream up a pun or to react to someone else's pun with a good or better one of your own on the fly. OhJim, I am saying, is quick, and to look at him you would not expect him to be quick. Like Jim, OhJim is bland and aging, and bold as his brother, come to that.

Tradecraft, that. OhJim has you wrong-footed from the moment that he comes into your awareness, and it goes south from there endlessly. This is a valuable trait, and OhJim uses it to listen in on conversations, particularly, since no one really sees him when he is in a roomful of strangers. For although he is interesting and vital, he certainly does not look that way.

Eve loves both of my brothers Jim, but she also admires OhJim's occasional revelation of poetic and scholarly depths. He is the one of the two Jims who gets my Buddha Girl's **You amaze me** smile.

I try to imagine my brothers as men with wives and children, at least in their background, since they certainly do not have either of those at present. Never mind that I do not have nor have I ever had a wife or children.

I do however have a life partner, and that makes a huge difference.

None of us three boys had much social life, and no one ever came around to chat and laugh in the way that teen-agers used to did. We were nerds without portfolio, and the other nerds gave us a miss in school and at home. No one ever came over for a sleepover. With the three of us, every night was a sleepover,, though, and Ma was tolerant to a fault, which makes it something like being raised by wolves. We were the only humans that we had to obey.

Everybody needs somebody to love, somebody to kiss, just like this, as the song says, and I take it on faith that my brother is not a 50-year-old virgin, although I am largely figuring back from the fact of his high heel pump fetish.

Let us face it. People are like icebergs that pass in the night, and we all have depths and secrets galore down where the water gets dark and embarrassing and dangerous.

When you do not love and do not lose at love, you seem drab and semi–transparent to others. It is easy to feel superior to those people.

Tradecraft.

It strikes me that I would not be surprised if OhJim and Jim had worked for Tommy, as so many others in the Tribe and nearby have done. Of course this is paranoid, and of course it is possible. Delusion is the near miss. It only works as such if the facts can bend its way. Facts, in my life, have been like spaghetti.

No way, you might say, Jose. The Jims could not keep that secret from you.

Tommy-made spooks certainly could.

Once you notice and bracket my paranoia, you have to come to agreement on this at least. Someone taught them something, and if so, taught them very well indeed.

One could do worse than to be an agent under Tommy.

To what ends would such duplicity serve?

And how could I be so blind?

Stop laughing, all of youse.

Look at it this way. Mr. Black clearly has agents in place and clearly is himself an associate at some level of Tommy's. We know or sense that, but no one is getting up on hind legs to protest that as an obvious breech of trust.

I'm just saying.

And also, a further word about Pop's watch.

I keep Pop's watch in a way that no one else can or does. I walk out the portfolio that Pop stuck where the sun don't shine, and I feel that to this day. This accounts for my awkward gait.

OhJim keeps Pop's watch, literally. He keeps that watch safe and he makes sure that watch is ticking by grasping it by its little topknot and twisting until he can twist no more without breaking the mechanism. If he cannot stop his hand, from anger or rage or fear, or whatever, the watch will stop ticking and its message will stop. Time will not stop but Pop's message will stop. And what is Pop's message – *I'm still here, in your heads, you little bastards*.

OhJim, the test of Time shows, was the right person to end up with Pop's watch, because that watch continues to keep its watch, and continues to tick tock out Pop's Time-bound influence. I would have driven a rusty spike through the face of

Pop's watch and followed that up with a blow from a sledge hammer. And perhaps a trip to a blast furnace for the remains.

So yeah, OhJim was the better choice. And what are the implications? First for me, is this. The gift, call it that, bestows a mantle of poor-me on the one who receives and more to the point, accepts, the gift. The gift weakens the receiver, so the giver would want to bestow the gift on one who has the bend profile of one who would not fight back.

OhJim has that streak of compliance in him, and that streak is not present in Jim, nor in me, though I will have to do some explaining, for I carry Pop's suppository like Papillon and his special *plen* where he kept his valuables while in prison.

I am, simply, Pop's ass.

That sounds like the streak that OhJim has and a further indignity as well. Never mind that I am the one who chose the image. Ok, I will try on the idea. I have that streak of compliance and that faint air of poor-me just like OhJim does.

Eve would call this a breakthrough.

Pop was our father who molded us, and molded us to his purposes. I cannot bring myself to express that in any other way. So what was Pop's goal for Jim? I think that Jim's role is to ridicule OhJim and me when we show the family flaw.

The taunts make us cling to the flaw.

Another question tumbles on the heels of the one just past. What is Pop's own profile? Did Pop have the flaw? The quick answer is absolutely not, but upon reflection I say that perhaps he did have that poor-me thing going and that all his evil schemes were meant to mask it and make it go away. I certain would like to deny the gene. You saw me do it. And OhJim? I simply do not know that man, though I do know the father of the man, and not Pop. The child, remember, is the father of the man.

OhJim can feel a connection with Pop and can tell himself that he is special in being the one who has gotten the gift. I can see that my initial scorn for Oh in thinking about the gift has swerved into a growing feeling of compassion for my brother. I am not a compassionate person by nature, but I can be compassionate by choice. I must overcome the Pop influence to do so, but Eve taught me how to choose, a long time ago. And what does it matter, really, whether one is or chooses to be good as long as the outcome of one's thoughts and feelings lead to good?

I do not have an answer for that question, though my shoes seem to have a resolute sense of what they intend me to walk out. The tongue in the shoe never lies. I have used that chestnut many times in my preaching, when that was the role that I was living out. Perhaps I am still in play, as OhJim certainly is, and Pop as ever is our handler, and we hate him with a purple passion because spooks can do nothing else but hate what they do and hate who points them and pulls the trigger.

OhJim either accepts the gift of Pop's watch or cannot say no, or some combination of the two. From the reports that I have from Jim, I would say that OhJim feels a secret sense of difference and specialness in keeping the gift, and I also believe that the motion of placing the watch under his pillow is indicative of a needy gratefulness that something tangible ticks and tocks in his ear like love. The watch, though it is not a person, like a loving mother or a loving father, or both, if you can imagine such a thing, is proof of something good and saving, and in its motion and its voice the watch reminds OhJim that he is not alone and that he is if not loved at least tolerated and allowed to live.

I am reminded of the advice to pet owners, to put a loud-ticking clock in the basket with a whining pet, to give the pet the comforts that sound and repetition can bring.

This may be the sound of darkness and the sound of silence for you, and you may go away, muttering about how dark and dreary all this is. I cannot stop you and cannot care that much, because right now I am talking to myself and I are behind a curtain, listening and growing uneasy. If I wanted all this to be common knowledge, I would post it to the VPN blog so everyone could laugh at it and wonder what version of the truth I was bending and breaking this time.

That Goose!

OhJim keeps the watch going, by assent and by necessity, for when the watch stops, he dies inside and the strain of love in him drifts like smoke on the wind.

This is no small thing.

My tradecraft demands that I explore all the implications.

The implications for the rest of us include the admission on my part, at least, that Pop's influence can reach beyond the grave and grab us by the neck just like he did when he was mean and we were small and malleable. I and the Tribe will ignore this at our peril. I would be silly to say that Pop is gone and that Pop's malignant influence for me and others, particularly my brothers., is gone.

Eve has assured me that avoiding one theme in a family by substituting other behaviors will ensure, ironically, that the hated and original family theme will be transmitted to the next generation. For example, if a father is passive and the sons of that father hate his passivity and swear that they will be different, they will find that when the chips are down, they will replicate what they saw and learned from their father, who himself may have been trying and trying to deny what his father had taught him. The saddest part of this is the subterranean way in which these things perpetuate themselves. Eve would also say that we have choices, and I have to believe that she is to be trusted.

Otherwise, the love in me would be like smoke on the wind.

So it is true that OhJim's fault is in me, too, and that Jim's standing apart from us to jeer at our weakness is all of the same piece. I want to say, as I have said over and over that this is proof and presence of Pop's evil seed sprouting and growing in us, his three sons whom he never had a good word for but always had an agenda about. I can continue to allow this rage-born conviction to circle the drain of my personal sewer, or I can decide to make other associations and decisions.

First, I decide to work for the good, whether I myself am good or only playing a good person. It strikes me that my goodness is in my intentions toward others, and that I can be good if I work with others for a common good. In a group such as the Tribe, a lot of good can flow from the spaces between each one and the others.

Second, I will take back my projection on OhJim and reclaim his poor-me stance as my own, that I have in common with him. I will look to his strength and goodness and trust in that. I will stop sneering at him in secret, assuming that my scorn does not leak like battery acid.

It is, after all, in the nature of dry-cell batteries to leak acid.

Third, I will think differently about Jim, for his sneering is not of his making, though he may have accepted that projection. Jim is simply my brother, and I need to cling to that, and that alone.

Finally, I will look at Pop in a new way. I will not deny his evil influence, but I will focus on its outcomes rather than my rage that Pop was evil. He simply was, or he was enough that I cannot change that nor would want to try. I will focus on my values and the outcomes that I and my Tribe desire.

As Jim would say, as a sort of benediction, **Good ruck with that.**

List of things to ponder

- **Why was Ma the one the thugs were looking for?**
- **What bearing, if any does David's last name have here?**
- **Who was it who loved Jeanne enough for her to survive and thrive?**
- **What secrets does Jim have that cold bite me and mine on the butt?**
- **What are the depths of OhJim's connection with Pop?**

Mr. Black

To talk about Mr. Black is to talk about his network of irregulars.

For starters, anyway. For to talk about Mr. Black, once I start, will take a very, very long time unless I assert some sort of filter.

Let us see how I do.

Mr. Black is a man with a plastic face. He has no name that I know, and I know him better than I know anyone except myself and Eve.

Mr. Black and myself, as Mr. White, did a not of damage as minister colleagues going back a long way in **Operation Beloved Community**. It was only our actual and life-shattering conversion experience, unique to each but occurring in tandem, almost, that brought our collaboration to a halt when we hit the brick wall of our handlers' aims and needs. Our handlers needed us to obey them, and we needed as of a sudden to obey **Someone Else** whom they had absolutely no control over. And since they realized that their control over us was suddenly and fundamentally in question, they threw us under the bus on its way out of the shadows, and as far as we know they have never looked back.

We, however, have, and it was a long time before Mr. Black and I had anything approaching the trust that we had shared for so very, very long. I with Eve's assistance and Mr. Black all by himself, one assumes, survived the cessation of who we thought that we were.

Puppets in the hands of The Man.

Well, spooks in the employ of the State who were reasonably in sync with the aims of the agents of the State.

Our handlers.

One stark difference between Mr. Black and I is that he always had his network of irregulars, and I always was a Lone Ranger by comparison. I chalk this up to the one, Pop, who trained me in tradecraft, though Pop also was the one, come to that, who trained Mr. Black in tradecraft. Perhaps, then, it was, and is, more a matter of personality, style, and modes aimed toward specific goals.

Mr. Black is magnetic interpersonally, though inside he is a void in certain essential senses, and I am more prone to lead that to cultivate others, though inside me at those times there was a void in those same essentials.

One cannot be a spook and expect to have organs and blood and all the other things that make people vulnerable to Time and to one another. Pop, as all other handlers before and after him, was a demonic refining fire that burned from his charges all of their humanity, at least as far as they were able to sense. If you cannot live in the void, you cannot do the work. If your attention is divided, your worth is halved or worse.

First, Pop said, **I will break you. Then I will remake you in my own image, and you will think that you have been reborn.**

It may seem odd that one would tell another person what he was going to do, but the telling made the reworking that much more difficult to alter, later, and that much more enduring when the object of all this refining had enough understanding to assent to the process.

You have to want the void for someone else to put you there.

Any other way of getting to the void makes you useless to yourself or the State and its representatives who will be handling you. If your brain is washed without your complicity, you become a zombie instead of a spook, and there is a universe of difference between the two.

Your nieces and nephews understand this. Ask them for details.

The Rev. Mr. Black and the Rev. Mr. White were agents of subversion at the level of the local congregation, with influence extending to the higher bodies of the church. We generally in all that we did thwarted the Christian impulse of our sheep and our colleagues.

We were very good at what we did, and we never talked to one another about the details, only the need-to-know stuff of living out someone else's values. We did not know what those values were and we did not care what those values were, and we had no sense of our own aims or values.

These things became submerged, and merged, with the aims of our handlers, with whom, I cannot say often enough, we had a conflicted relationship.

Like mules kicking in our stalls, we simply resented that another mule was kicking in our stalls as often as he wanted to. It was like a testosterone thing, and hormones probably do go a long way toward keeping spooks in the grooves set out for them.

How else can you account for the spookish impulse? The impulse may have its genesis in greed, or zeal, or love, but how can you explain the way in which the spookish impulse endures and thrives in a climate that is hostile to life of any sort for any reason? As one who has lived in these shadows and who has survived the experience of being blinded, at long last, by the light of what others call reality, I can say nothing helpful about the process beyond the awareness that I assented to becoming a spook at deep levels that I cannot touch.

It was the experience of being blinded by my sudden sense of God, like Saul on the road to Damascus, that stopped the madness and started the searing pain of healing, such as it has been and will continue to be.

Who more than a spook can understand the idea of forgiveness? Who else really can understand the Christian idea that anyone including Hitler, or any other monster you can imagine, can find the way to God's loving forgiveness?

And since I do not understand my own darkness and cannot speak to it, so too I cannot explain the perilous light of God's love. God has forgiven me for all that I have done and all that I have left undone. That work is done. My work of living into that healing Light is hardly started, for I am a willful subject at the best of times, and my assent to this Light and the refining of me by this just and beautiful fire is fundamentally restricted by my sense of my sin. I must need the notoriety, but for whatever reason, I resist the One Who loves me more than I can love myself, in any fashion.

Does this sound familiar to you?

Mr. Black did as was done to him, much like Tommy is still doing and has been doing. This is no testament to their difference, but really is rather a testament to how similar all spooks are. We wear the sheet and we see through the round holes, and we all are a void inside. Spooks on the outside and zombies on the inside?

Do you remember the song that has the little girl saying that *there's a hole in daddy's arm where all the money goes/ Jesus died for nothing, I suppose*.

I know the feeling, from both sides now.

The irregulars of Mr. Black were the way in which he did the work, and my way, though solitary, was every bit as effective, for we were meant to be, each of us, only half of the loaf that together resembled bread, though living bread we were not, though we also were not dead inside, only missing in the line of duty and not likely to return alive, though we did return alive against all odds.

Thank you, Jesus is only the beginning of an exploration of that.

When I was reborn as Eve's consort and became in some sense a redeemed version of the sun of the morning star, I kept my stripes, for a tiger cannot change his stripes or would he want to. And Mr. Black on his own became a redeemed version of that same dark star, and he too retained his stripes.

His network.

In the absence of need, and simply because it was what he did and what he understood how if not why to do, Mr. Black came to a sense of himself as he walked out of that dark wood, and he looked around himself and began to pull together a new network, like a leader who cannot imagine following but must always lead.

I found the love of one person, and Mr. Black found many who might not love but always would follow him. For you can fancy that you have a deep regard for Mr. Black, and Mr. Black will encourage you in this feeling, but you will find to your chagrin, that you were deluding yourself. Such of course is the course of human love, and decidedly so when you deal with a person whose charisma is little more than the human depth as defined and confined by the human skin.

When I realized that Eve's love for me had sharp limits, I was able to go deeper because of the Light that shined over me and in me. I speak of Mr. Black in a contrasting way, but I would not trust him if I did not sense that the same Light had penetrated his iron heart.

We really are talking about personality, and tradecraft, for one hath need of these things in this vale of tears, this plane of existence, where we may long for the Light but usually only remember its strength and warmth and healing essence. To be loved and forgiven does not take us off the Wheel of Fortune or make the revolutions any less sickening. The roller coaster cannot be anything but a roller coaster and still go by that title.

And so I tend to work alone, and Mr. Black tends to run agents of his own choosing.

My leadership of the Tribe is a stark contrast to this dichotomy, and I only started, or retuned, to this childish practice when I was reborn as a person and no longer a spook, though I continue in the work, certainly, by choice and for good now, in a way that I am aware of and have a measure of control over. I am, simply put, my own handler now, in consultation with Eve.

Jesus is my copilot is how others might say this, but the phrase seems sickly sweet to me. I have been too long and too far from sweetness to use such a phrase in such a positive way.

Pax.

Before talking any further about Mr. Black's irregulars, it is time to also talk about the man himself.

Mr. Black exiled himself for a year, a years or so back, in order to protect the bookshop and those in it, who are precious to him, for whatever reasons. And we cannot know those reasons except by noticing Mr. Black's behaviors because Mr. Black refuses to talk about his feelings and he will not willingly share his deeper thoughts. I infer from what he did, to protect the Tribe, by disappearing, that he had and has, for that matter, regard in good measure, and more, for the Tribe. Mr. Black used the wounded- mother-bird move to led his attackers away from us, and by doing so he was alone except for his network, which I guess is a powerful argument for having a network -- or friends if that is how you think and speak.

We are still working out the implications of who was attacking him and us and what we must do to stay safe, sane, and alive, together. But in terms of motivation, it was Mr. Blacks choices under great strain that set this trajectory for us all. If he had simply taken care for himself and no one else, we would be mourning the loss of not just Mr. Black but also many if not all of us.

Mr. Black is strong in body despite the down-drag of his years and has a youthful quality that is in contrast to the mature and fixed sadness and wisdom that sit in his eyes and in the straight and thin equivalent of a smile that Mr. Black usually betrays. It is his stern reminders that we are at war with an unknown enemy that have saved us more than once in the months that have marked our floundering around in a sea of unknowing. It is for this reason that Mr. Black occupies a barstool at the **Roll In & Crawl Out**, which he calls the Tribe's forward position, and which we all have taken a turn in manning with him, all of us, woman and man.

I know that many of the Tribe do not understand this image of the **forward position**, for nothing much seems to go on there (which is an understandable distortion). The **Roll In** is our forward position because Mr. Black occupies that position, whether he is sitting and drinking there or living and moving and having his being somewhere else.

Mr. Black is a magnet for the iron hatred of our enemies.

They seek to hurt us where we are most strong.

He like iron will draw them to himself, and no one knows this better that Mr. Black does. This awareness is what drives him to maintain a network. For if you are going to attract the tip of the spear, you will need help in withstanding the force coming at you. Indeed, you will need knowledge to avoid what is otherwise as inevitable as the attraction of iron and magnet. You need help in repelling that iron. Those are the poles that define you, and you never forget what others always stray from, and that is the constant threat to who you are.

That is the attraction of Mr. Black.

List of things to ponder

- **Why was Ma the one the thugs were looking for?**

- **What bearing, if any does David's last name have here?**
- **Who was it who loved Jeanne enough for her to survive and thrive?**
- **What secrets does Jim have that cold bite me and mine on the butt?**
- **What are the depths of OhJim's connection with Pop?**
- **What will Mr. Black's network do for us, and to us, in the time to come?**

Nancy Chino

NancyPants. Nancy Chino. The way Ma's mind works.

We first met Nancy in the **Double Daily Double Murders** of fanciful generation. I still do not know what to make of the mess that we inflicted on the public, and I only was glad that no one actually died, though public trust in the media was sorely stretched.

Talk about tradecraft. Nancy has an actor's ability to be anyone she needs to be. Nancy is a master of disguise, using words and gestures, and a few items of clothing, from an old closet, to sell a character. Who could be a better half for Mr. Black, who can change his identity by changing his tie. The two make a charming couple, perched on their adjoining stools at the **Roll In**. Nancy hangs there with her **Mr. Bee** as often as she can, and it is always a treat to see her at meetings of the F-Troop, for she is chatty and fun and full of crazy talk, for the real Nancy, if you will allow me to use that fiction, is funny and vulnerable and pretty and wise. Her smile – **her smile** – is weary and wise in a way that breaks your heart and reforms it for her.

Nancy as Nancy has a **can-you-bleeping-believe-it** sort of charm that also draws you to her. She is candid and blunt and funny. She has indicated to us that she and Bee go back a long, long way, to an age all but shocking in its low number. This connection, we understand, is how she came to be the landlord of Ma when Mr. Black and Tommy brought Ma to us in a hurry, never really explained, from Pittsburgh in the time of their skulking around there last year to try and figure out who was trying to erase the Tribe. As a logical extension of that long connection between Mr. Black and Nancy, she went the extra step and called in dead, along with Ma, Eve, and me for the **Double Daily Double Murders**.

The subterfuge made a lot of sense at the time, but we are not that far along in understanding the threat to the Tribe, though I sense that the threat to my personal stability may very well prove to be the same threat. Which is why I am slowly and systematically (you didn't get that, did you) looking at my family and associates to see what I can see, and to find what I can tolerate finding. So far, I have had constant reminders that when one embraces trust over truth and the need to know, one puts oneself in a singular bind. I find that making a list of the many things that I do not know about my friends and family is becoming a sore subject for me, and I have had to insist with myself that I will maintain the decision of not knowing what I do not yet feel certain that I indeed do need to know, right now, or yesterday, whichever comes first.

I feel like two persons, who do not agree on truth and trust.

So back to the drain.

Nancy was mourned by her colleagues and the arts community in general, and they were overjoyed to get her back in one piece. Nancy has told us that she has done work for Mr. Black from that early age when he recruited her, and this makes her the one member of his network that we will name and spend time with. The others you have met, in their roles in the two murder rounds that have marked the past two years. Just think gypsies, tramps, and thieves, and that bald bartender at the **Roll In** and you will just about have it.

Nancy like so many others in the mix is a life-long resident of Buffalonya, though she seems to have moved in other circles than, say, Jeanne. The two did not know one another before last year. The same goes for Eve and I, and Red and Ed. But Mr. Black knew her then and knows her now. Theirs is a traditional relationship of strong, silent male and twittery, compliant female, though one wonders what the real Nancy thinks about this. I suspect, from the independent way in which Nancy discusses sensitive things among us, that the compliance is partly cover, and I notice that I am comfortable with the idea that Nancy would have a cover story concerning her interactions with us, for I trust

Mr. Black with my life, as I always have, and I will gave him all the rope he wants, and I will not complain if he uses my rope to tie my hands in certain unexplained directions.

If I wanted to know all, I would run away and join the circus and seek out the swami.

Ok, that did sound a bit shrill.

Nancy also has indicated an early connection with our brother Tommy, which brings up the question of the largely covert but also very clear connection around being in play that Mr. Black and Tommy share. I am not ready to examine Tommy closely, so I will simply note that and try to forget it for now.

Nancy and Ma took to one another quickly, and Nancy seems to have a genuine regard for Ma, and Ma for her. This will go a long way with me and my brothers, and my brothers like Nancy a lot, being that she is a woman and more than just a little bit pretty. My brothers can be incredibly shallow, but that is part of their charm, and -- who knows? -- may just be part of their cover. Which is another line of inquiry that I am seriously far from ready to follow out. Noted and moving on.

List of things to ponder

- **Why was Ma the one the thugs were looking for?**
- **What bearing, if any does David's last name have here?**
- **Who was it who loved Jeanne enough for her to survive and thrive?**
- **What secrets does Jim have that cold bite me and mine on the butt?**
- **What are the depths of OhJim's connection with Pop?**
- **What will Mr. Black's network do for us, and to us, in the time to come?**
- **Why is Nancy under a cover story to cover her time with the Tribe?**

Joe Bob Schmidt

Det. William "Joe Bob" Schmidt is as we know the largely silent

partner of the blustering Det. Joe Blucote. That was in the beginning, anyway, but last year we found out a truckload of additional information about Joe Bob. He told us that he has been an agent of Tommy's as well as having the public job of being the first Native American detective on the Buffalonya force.

In the time it took to hear just the first mention of that covert connection, we went from scorn to affection in a hurry. And with the advent of this new information, we saw a side to Joe Bob that surprised and pleased us.

Joe Bob was at pains to make sure that we understood that Blucote did not and could not know his covert role in our brother Tommy's work. That was fine with us, since Blucote is a windbag of gigantic proportions.

Joe Bob's role seems to be mainly that of being Tommy's man on the inside for anything Tommy might require, and I am betting that there are a lot of Joe Bobs out there making Tommy look like he has second sight. Tommy's info has no equal, and we have come to rely on his producing the pregnant fact at the timely hour, again and again.

Tommy BTW continues to be among the missing. No comment.

Jane Carlotto

Another associate of our brother Tommy is Jane Carlotto, senior crime writer for the **Daily Afterblatt Lake Effect Edition.**

This is another case of Tommy putting in place the ability to collect, and to affect, the flow of information.

Jane has the ear of the community, and when she agreed to help manufacture the **Double Daily Double Murders**, she already had been working closely with the Tribe through Tommy for more than a year.

Jane, as we found out, has a portly boyfriend, Hudson, who writes when I cannot and who runs a little bookshop called **The Bookplate Café**, which is not at all like **Caspar's**.

I would like to be grateful to Hudson for taking over the posting duties for a season after my disastrous trip to Pittsburgh, but he was worse than a loose cannon.

No more of that.

Jane, by contrast, delivers at all points with no noticeable downside.

She has squared her covert aims with her overt ones, I presume.

This cannot be easy, and I wonder what it is that drives her.

Is it just the magnetism of our brother Tommy?

Somehow that does not seem to be enough.

Something idealistic must be in play as well, though Jane and I have never had a private conversation.

However, I can say, once again, that personal magnetism is not enough, and the idea that women as agents would be any more inclined in that direction is a distortion worthy of scorn.

That would be a piggy way to think.

Meme Shiva

Meme Shiva, a longtime associate of Tommy's, rose through the ranks of the Buffalonya Police Department with a speed that can only be described as supersonic.

Early on, when Shiva was a walk-the-beat cop, she was the subject of a profile that Jeanne wrote for the **Daily Afterblatt, Lake Effect Edition.** This piece served two purposes, establishing both women as persons to watch -- Jeanne for her skill in writing and reporting, and Shiva for her skill in grabbing public attention.

Shiva continues to grab headlines, and Jeanne no longer is a player in that public game, though as a full member of the Tribe, Jeanne continues the work of making Shiva look good.

To begin with the outer trappings, I have to say that Shiva is a pleasant and attractive young woman. You should have seen her in her clubbing clothes when she used to have the time, inclination, and public indifference that allowed her to have a life in public that included tight and short dresses, sky-high heels, and that lurid red dot on her forehead.

All of these things have done the way of the snail darter.

Today Shiva runs the Buffalonya Police Department, and she rides herd on the once-prominent duo of Dets. Blucote and Schmidt. Blucote in particular shows the strain of losing the public exposure, but he knows what is what, since he and Joe Bob were there when we made Shiva the new commissioner and sent Tom Tonolody into exile AKA witness protection via the work and zeal of Tommy and certain of his associates and superiors.

Shiva was able to garner the support of the rank and file, as well as the mayor and his minions, because of the singular ineptness of Tonolody, a truly wretched human being who only saw the insides of his eyelids, most of the time, and saw only himself emblazed on the negative impression of his selective orbs.

We still do not know who killed Tonolody and dumped his body behind the **Roll In**. And we do not give a bleep, either, except as it impinges upon the question who has been trying to kill off the Tribe.

By **we** I mean the Tribe.

The local authorities have even less information, and zeal, than we do about the unsolved question of Tonolody's murder.

Same goes for Peter Principe's murder.

Someone is out there, doing terrible and dangerous things, but that is the nature of things, isn't it? No change there, so we adhere to the usual protocol. The zen of survival. Being ready and not ready at the same time, and trusting one another until we get evidence to the contrary.

I guess that we are behind on that, but there will be time for such things when my mind is right again. All the way, I mean.

I will let you know when that happens, or you might notice on your own.

List of things to ponder

- **Why was Ma the one the thugs were looking for?**
- **What bearing, if any does David's last name have here?**
- **Who was it who loved Jeanne enough for her to survive and thrive?**
- **What secrets does Jim have that cold bite me and mine on the butt?**

- What are the depths of OhJim's connection with Pop?
- What will Mr. Black's network do for us, and to us, in the time to come?
- Why is Nancy be under a cover story to cover her time with the Tribe?
- Where and why did Tommy recruit Shiva?

Gentle Ben Whick

It is hard to talk about Gentle Ben Whick without talking about the OhTribe that he is part of.

That is, The Other Tribe, composed to Baldi and Luce Cleanue and their girl with the Glock, Jo-Joe. Ben hangs with these three and provides computer security and actual security in coordination with Jo-Joe, who provides the muscle. The two work very closely, if you know what I mean.

We do not hear from the OhTribe often, but Ben is always with us in a virtual sense, and he stays in touch on all fronts and universes with Jeanne and David.

Ben keeps the virtual **Roll In**, just like Mr. Black keeps the actual one. Both occupy forward positions for the Tribe and probably give the lion's share of our safety their attention.

Pop quiz: Just what is the lion's share?

Triple points if you said, ***Anything the lion wants***.

Ben in his various on-line guises put Manram in mothballs and took over the notorious blog titled ***Fried Buffalonya***.

It is very good that Ben was able to make the transition from the Tribe to the OhTribe without paying a premium that he could not afford, like a driver who gets into trouble and has to be switched to a more expensive and less helpful insurer until he is deemed to be back in good graces by paying higher premiums.

Insurers hate paying out a penny.

We hate having to terminate persons who do not work out with the Tribe, and Ben was our first survivor, so to speak. Eve and I had decided that we would go against the grain of the shadows and find a new way to be safe and not sorry about recruits.

Ben is happy, and we are happy, and all of us are very happy.

That is Ben as Ben.

His associates bear scrutiny, too.

Baldi and Luce are friends who go back to the beginning of the Revs. Mr. White and Black.

Baldi was a minister before becoming a millionaire, and Luce worked in non-profits. After they hit it big and then some in the Lottery, they took up a hobby.

Spook work and detection in general.

No one save us knows much about the work that Baldi and Luce do, for the same TLAs that we sleep with, and it has been, now that I think about it, a long time since I checked in with them.

Baldi has the worst comb-over that you can imagine. Which is to say that his hair is as silly as that of anyone who decides that no one will notice if he pastes three or four hairs over his bald spot and calls it good. You gotta love a guy who presumes on thee kindness of strangers to that degree.

Luce is big in every way that you can imagine. She is a delight to the senses and a gladness to the heart. She is like a version of Jeanne, but Luce does not have the darkness that Jeanne does, and that makes her difference and wonderful in her own way.

List of things to ponder

- **Why was Ma the one the thugs were looking for?**
- **What bearing, if any does David's last name have here?**
- **Who was it who loved Jeanne enough for her to survive and thrive?**
- **What secrets does Jim have that cold bite me and mine on the butt?**
- **What are the depths of OhJim's connection with Pop?**
- **What will Mr. Black's network do for us, and to us, in the time to come?**

- **Why is Nancy be under a cover story to cover her time with the Tribe?**
- **Where and why did Tommy recruit Shiva?**
- **If we open a new front with Ben's virtual gifts, can we win?**
- **Who can expect to rely on the loyalties of Baldi and Luce?**

Agent Luke

Luke Parmgartner works with us, and sometimes for us, in the shadows as we know them in Buffalonya.

Luke, like Tommy and Mr. Black, is one of the few who is currently in play.

Luke like so many men of reasonably good taste and inflated self-concept, which would seem like a prerequisite for spook work, fancies Eve and fancies that he has a chance with her, if I would only dry up and fly away like the leaves that turn and flee in the fall.

It is a running joke between us, and is as funny as a runny nose or dripping faucet.

I would like to call the plumbers to put a wrench in his pipes, from the end to the beginning.

Joke.

Luke has good looks and large size, as large as Mr. Ed and a lot younger, though he is not young per se. We call on Luke for his brawn in the hope that his brains have not slid into the sea. So far, so good.

And Eve does like Luke, by the way, just not in the way he wants.

Isn't that the way of all flesh?

In the growing absence of Tommy, we have come to rely on Luke for the pregnant fact at the climactic moment but generally have been disappointed and frustrated by his inferior package of gifts in that regard.

There is not substitute for Tommy.

And as to where he is, and was, and shall be, you will have to wait for the return of my full recover. I know. I'm praying, too.

Mister Ed

If you were named for a talking horse, would you keep your name or go to the trouble of changing it?

Our Mister Ed has never neighed a peep about his having the same name as the horse who owned Wilber and who appeared in the golden age of television in the usual shades of black and white.

Mister Ed has a long history of working as an editor in ops in the shadows, first in Spookistan and last in Buffalonya.

Ed has a voice as large as all outdoors, and his indoor voice, frankly, is no softer. You can ask Ed to use his indoor voice, and he will not take any offense, but if you do you will still need to cover your ears.

Ed's voice in all places, inside and out, is pitched for the top of the main mast on a dark and stormy night. I would like to say that I am used to this, but that would be a lie.

No one is.

Despite this considerable challenge, Ed is a favorite, for his slightly courtly if not portly demeanor and his gentle and thundering ways. No one knows Ed's real name, but I suspect that it might have been Zeus.

Out of his bounty and goodness, Ed plays the parliamentarian when the Tribe gathers to the gavel of Mr. Chair Sir, yours truly. Ed accepts my leadership in this and in the other areas of the life of the Tribe. He has no problem that Eve chose me, and he works for the common good, always.

Among Ed's special relationships are his ancient connection with Ma, and with Mr. Red, from the post-war days. **Operation Poison Ivan**, they called it, and we still do not know the details beyond Ms's case name of **Natasha Riga** and their common goal of subverting refugees from the communist counties who can\me across in droves.

Ed and Red fancy themselves to be the parents of Wild Billy. Their antics on the bookshop cat's behalf make the Odd Couple seem somehow boring and small. You have to hear it to believe it.

List of things to ponder

- Why was Ma the one the thugs were looking for?
- What bearing, if any does David's last name have here?
- Who was it who loved Jeanne enough for her to survive and thrive?
- What secrets does Jim have that cold bite me and mine on the butt?
- What are the depths of OhJim's connection with Pop?
- What will Mr. Black's network do for us, and to us, in the time to come?
- Why is Nancy be under a cover story to cover her time with the Tribe?
- Where and why did Tommy recruit Shiva?
- If we open a new front with Ben's virtual gifts, can we win?
- Who can expect to rely on the loyalties of Baldi and Luce?
- What do our close associates such as Ed and Red keep to themselves?

Mr. Red

The first thing to say about Mr. Red is that the veins that throbs over his temples tell a frightening story of one who is no stranger to violence. Just look at him. He is about to blow.

Always.

Red is the most violent and murderous of us all, and that includes the considerable skills of men such as Mr. Black.

What is Red's edge?

Rage.

We call him Red for two reasons, for his beginnings behind the Red Curtain, and for his face, which goes from its bedrock red to its purple extreme with the ease of a slingshot in the hands of a boy like David.

Not our David. That David.

Red is always one for contrasts. Take the reactions of Red and Ed to the sudden appearance of Ma among us. Ed was contrite. Red could not be bothered.

He simply continues as he is, in all situations.

You always know where you stand with Red. He hates you with a passion that can go purple at any moment. And you had better remember that small packages can kill you. One of the three thugs who attacked the bookshop hade that mistake. He is no longer with us. Red is to blame, with a little help from his friend Ed. As the song sez, **Don't let the glasses fool ya; stand beside me when you measure my size.**

Two things modify Red's rage. Three if you count Jeanne.

And you should. Count Jeanne.

Red, as I said, has a parent's dotting love for Wild Billy. His other love is Eve, whom Red calls his **Eveie**.

When I say **Red** in a warning tone, he says **bleep you** back.

When Eve says **Red** in a warning tone, Red stops and listens.

No one else can do that.

No one.

When David returned with Red's book that he had given to a customer by mistake, Red glared at David but accepted the book like a peace offering. David got no other notice, though I have noticed that Red in his treatment of Jeanne, which is marked by a strange but wonderful degree of respect, extends that good will, or whatever it is, to David, too.

David, for his part, has taken to asking Red for lessons in higher math.

I suspect that Red is secretly pleased to continue his special brand of tutoring in the language of love that is numbers, for him and his countless ilk.

David doodles, and Red rages. They may even be happy. Go figure..

Eve Green

In dealing with Eve, there are two things to avoid.

Jokes about Adam and Eve.

Mother Green jokes, as in –

Question*: **Is that Mother Green?***

Answer*: **No, it's just the way the light hits it.***

There are at least two things about Eve (references to **all about Eve** do not bother her, by the way) that we should talk about.

Her Buddha Girl smile.

The Vault.

Eve pairs a predilection for calling everyone **Dear** with a smile of such sweetness that it reminds you of the Buddha's smile upon holding up that flower.

The smile, since it is a matter of the lips, speaks for itself.

The Vault, however, cannot.

This is a fortunate thing for Eve and I, who are the keepers of The Vault, a little thing of great potential that Pop created and made Eve and I the keepers of.

One of us is the primary keeper and the other is the secondary keeper. If you want to crack The Vault, you had better know which of us is which. And a bunch of other stuff as well. You really didn't think that I would tell you how to crack The Vault, did you?

You did?

Pity.

The Tribe is the Tribe and the bookshop is the fort and we are who we are, in all our arrogant glory and tiny stature, The Vault is what makes us big and dangerous far beyond our many years and considerable abilities. Many have rued the day that they ever saw Pop, and ever lost control of little bits of information. Pop stuffed the Vault with lots and lots of embarrassing little documents and photographs and dossiers. After a life in the shadows, Pop had trunks full of the stuff, and he hid them in many places and made us the sole keepers of the details about location.

That is our story anyway, but if you think that killing Eve and I would neutralize the Vault, you are even more naïve than you were a moment ago when you were waiting for me to sell the farm. Suffice it to say that bits of information have become bytes of information, cloned at will and hidden in plain sight, all over the world and the digital abyss also known as **the Cloud**.

Bleep it, let's hop on a cloud is more than just a stoner's mantra.

It is our mantra, too, repeated endlessly.

Others still have speculated on what is in the Vault, and they divide into two schools, those who think that I should give examples and those who give me tips on just what a good and tricky Vault would contain.

Again, you really should do something about that juvenile strain.

As much as I would like to tell you about the last time we used the Vault, I won't be doing so, but you can depend on it that the Vault is the black hole down which many a bad person has tumbled.

Now that I am a day closer to being able to talk about my Mommy Dearest (there, I said it), I realize that I wonder what she knows about the Vault and whether she is included in its files. Since Pop isn't and I am not, nor is Eve, or anyone in the Tribe, it is not likely.

Or is it?

Pop was not perfect, in morals or in tradecraft.

In fact, he was arrogant and slipshod, and if he could get you to do his work, well that was a good thing.

As I have cast around for reasons why my own mother would be out to kill me, I have made a tentative list, of sorts. The Vault is actually at the head of that list, and that is because the Vault is amoral. It will bleep anyone and bleep with anyone, and talk about it in all cases, into the mike and from there into the Vault.

The next questions becomes this. What could be so damaging to her and hers? Since I do not know her, despite participating in her DNA and passing through her portal , so to speak, I cannot find out the answer to my simple questions of motive, opportunity, and means.

As Pop's main squeeze, she certainly would know about the Vault, and to know about the Vault is to fear it. That much is true, but it is true for all persons and all cases. That does not narrow things down much.

The only one I left out is God.

I may not know Lailah (there I said it – her name), but I do know Pop. What would Pop do with any information that he had about Lailah or anyone else he cared about or loved (if such a word can be applied to the little bleep)? The answer seems obvious to me. After all, we have the example of what he did with bits of information about his enemies.

He hid them and used them.

When Pop hid and used those bits of information, they all had to have a physical form to be of any assistance to Pop or anyone he knighted, such as Eve and I. Bits of information that Pop was the steward of, such as embarrassing files, photos, and receipts. Pop had the option of destroying these things, but in many cases the damning information could have been a part of the files that damned his enemies. If his friends had made mistakes or had proven themselves to be evil or amoral or lawless, he could not have separated that information from the information that would serve the ends of the Vault. There could be Vaults out there that I do not know about. How is that for paranoia?

That leads me to the conclusion that the Vault is a two-edged sword that can cut friend as deep as foe. Further conclusion – I need to look at the files and see what I can see, with the new eyes of paranoid faith.

There still might be a trove of damning stuff that Pop could not bring himself to destroy, even though it was of danger to his friends and family. It make be counterintuitive to you, but I can see why Pop might do that and put it in a corner and forget it.

Who more than a spook would agree with the statement that there are, in this life, no permanent friends and no permanent enemies?

If you agree with this statement, then there need be no further reason for Pop's hoarding of any and all information, in one dump. The only challenges that Pop had were to choose his hidey holes well and his heirs better than well.

So, to continue in this high plane of reasonable musing, I would say that Pop's Vault has put all its subjects at odds with all others. In most cases, that is unknown to those persons, but in the case of Lailah and I, we are lined up like jousters on mail-clad mounts.

I suppose that whatever Lailah is afraid of, in reference to me and mine, does not necessarily have to be in the Vault. She may have some secret of her own that she wants to keep from us, and killing us may seem to her to be the better course of behavior.

It also is possible that she is plain crazy as well as sociopathic.

You might ask me, sage as you clearly are, why Lailah did not take out a gun and shoot me when I was in her presence. I have wondered the same thing myself, though the presence of several witnesses, half of whom would favor me over her, were also present.

Another thing that I assume about my darling mother is that she is or was a spook herself. Pop would have no access, or interest, in anyone else. You just would not be of any interest to him. After all, those who torture small animals mix the boring with the disturbing in a way that repels most of us, and you might be surprised to learn that I would assume that Pop would not have any interest in small, twisted minds. I am just saying.

Now if you have a large, twisted mind, Pop would have already been in touch. The Vault is like that.

To return to the question of Lailah, I repeat my assumption that she is, and was, of interest to persons like Pop. Her timeless, elemental appeal alone would snare Pop like a horny weasel, though persons who are damaged in the ways that Pop is damaged quickly lose interest in the merely physical. Your hotness, ma'am, is a door that Pop would walk through in order to see what you were like on the inside. Based on what I have seen of Lailah, I would say that Pop would be hopelessly snared by her exterior charms and interior darkness. After all, Pop was a friend of the Devil, and his mantra was ***a friend of the Devil is a friend of mine***.

Pop and Lailah were a match made not in Heaven but in Hell, I have no doubt, and like the friends of the Devil that we know so well from film and novel, those fiendish friends would persist well beyond the grave. That gives a present to their past, and not just because Lailah lives, and cheats time with her timeless sheen of beauty, like a bad orchid of evil, able to trick and enslave the children of light, let alone a dark horse like Pop.

I suppose I should have put a stake through Lailah's heart when I had the chance, and Pop's as well. My failing with Pop was that I often wanted to kill him, but I did not ever think that I would have had to so that in a particular and ritualistic way.

Clearly, I have gone somewhat beyond Eve, strictly speaking.

Goose Grim

You cannot talk about Eve without talking about Goose, sooner or later. Eve and I form a universe with two halves, of roughly equal size and abilities and concerns. If you want to know about Eve, you could start with me, as easily as any other. Choosing me is probably the best, if you keep in mind that people are not exactly geometric but that some metaphors about people do benefit from reference to lines and planes and triangles.

Especially triangles.

What form, when place on its side, has more strength that the triangle, and what form, when followed by three persons, has more enduring potential for rage and sorrow?

Think about it.

While you do that, I will pick up the thread of my narrative.

After roughly seven hundred pages of posts turned into two novels, you may fancy that you know a lot about me, and that is because you do, or there is the potential for that, anyway. But think about it. In all that material there is precious little about mama and mama.

There is, I will grant you, a lot about Ma and me, but not much, up until a moment ago, about me and mother.

Lailah.

This is fresh meat, new vistas, geometry gone wild.

Lailah and I have the most simple of connections, that of Points A and B. A straight line, because if you hitch two horses to one rope, the rope will quickly be stretched and often severed by the initial encounter of two forces in opposition. In this case, Point A wants to kill Point B, and has had this goal, I assume, as a thing of at least two years' standing. Otherwise she would have had ample opportunity and means to do so when Point B was just a little dot of a guy.

The original connection between Points A and B was a cord that gave me life, in the womb. Her womb. The next connection is the first of a series of metaphorical connections. I can see, from looking back on an empty stage, that Point A quickly lost interest in Point B and either forgot to maintain the connection or actively sought to sever it. Pop. I assume, was the agent of change here, and perhaps Lailah was the catalyst. Pop made the break for Lailah, based on her powerful chemistry with him, and Lailah was not changed by the reaction in the beaker, though Pop was.

Lailah did not care whether I lived or died. I was not a blip on her screen or anything more than an impurity in her test tube.

Pop did care, at some level, about whether I lived or died. I have no idea why he would care, but I just checked and I can attest to the beating of my heart and the bellows effect of my lungs.

I live.

Pop would have reason to hate me, since he might have actually had something like love for me, but Lailah will never see me as more than a problem, like a thorn in the side that one cannot pluck without assistance. And it would be amusing, if it were not so evil and dark, to wonder what Pop would have done if his connection to Lailah had come into conflict with his connection to me. Pop thus becomes Pont C, and we move back to the metaphor of the human triangle, commonly called the **love triangle** and not commonly seen as a way of charting the relationships among a mom, dad, and child.

In the common run of things, parents love their children and wish for them good things. As Jesus said, **Who among you if your child asks for a fish would give him a scorpion?**

I see that Lailah has raised her hand.

Thus does the web become tangled, when what is the curse of adults becomes the curse of parents and child, with all the misery, rage, and terror attendant on your typical love triangle.

Still, the equilateral triangle is the best image, the right image, for so many of our human connections, for the triangle sitting on its intended base has Point A at the top and Points B and C on the straight line at the bottom, both of whom are meant to focus on and hold up Point A. This focus is as irresistible and solid as a geometric truth, most of the time, but when Point A is one of the Parents and Point B is the child, we have problems, at the outset, all along the way, and in any configuration forever more. The other way to address this misshapen situation is to tip the triangle so that the Child, whatever its letter designation, moves to the top.

Other will applaud the restoration of the natural order of things, but the deposed Point A, now on the bottom, will secretly, and probably outside awareness, grind her teeth and desire revenge.

When parents compete for the child's position, the chemical reaction will normally be explosive. All it takes is a match, and I do not mean a match made in heaven.

Have I made you feel uneasy? Are you feeling like I am painting a dark picture with little detail discernible and no beauty at all?

Good.

Good?

Yes, good, because you are beginning to understand how twisted and dangerous, and painful, this position is, was, and ever more shall be for the three points of the love triangle.

Now to switch the metaphor somewhat, let us rename our triangle the **Drama Triangle**, and assign the three points these roles – Victim, Persecutor, and Rescuer.

Let me say, at the outset, that this is not my own concoction, like the pervious was. The Drama Triangle is a staple of the Transactional Analysis system of Eric Berne, of which Eve is a practicing adherent.

You could ask why she has to practice and can't just get it right, but I would have to hurt you, so just do not go there. Ok?

Here is how the Drama Triangle works, according to Eve. If you enter the Triangle as one of the three players, you can only exit if you take on the role of another of the players. For example, if you enter the Drama Triangle as the Victim, as I have, as the wronged child in my story, I have two choices for exit. I can switch to being the Persecutor or the Rescuer. This switch, by the way, is a basic part of Berne's social game theory.

Notice that there are no good options here. In Berne's game theory, Eve tells me, there are no good outcomes to the games, since the games are designed to help us avoid the pain of intimacy with others. That is bad because intimacy cannot be ignored in this way if health is the goal.

So I can **persecute** Lailah or I can **rescue** Lailah. I can switch between the two roles at my whim while staying on the drama triangle. I can call her evil and chase her down, and drive a stake through her heart. Or I can rescue her and make excuses for her behavior and ignore all her provocations and always seek to show that she was not really at fault but was the victim herself of her own inherited circumstances.

Or I can simply refuse to enter the Drama Triangle.

Which pill will I swallow?

That is the question, and an active question with vast and grand implications for myself and all others in my orbit.

Pop

I never knew his real name, not really. For how would I know it when I heard it, and what documents can I trust and what documents can I discount, when it comes to this man, my father? He did not want me to know him, and I did not want him to know me, at least in the early years. After he recruited me, I had to modify my stance, partly because he modified his toward me. It was a play, of course, but I pretty much had to go along with him on that.

Do like I teach you, son, and you just might make me proud. And if you don't, you little bleep, I can always have you whacked. Har, har har!

Who was this man? My anger sustained me through this time of forced closeness and false gaiety. The image of my hands closing off his windpipe as he jerked and flailed at me was oddly comforting, like a mother's kiss on my brow.

I was, you can be assured, young, dumb, and full of sperm, and that is no surprise, given my father's well-documented and -hung exploits in those categories. I have always had to put up with the raised eyebrow, or eyebrows when Pop comes up, depending on the coordination of the persons involved.

Don't let the bastards get you down. And don't forget that they will try to get you down, just to see what you are made of. And the poofters are the worst, son. Do not, I repeat, do not turn your back, ever, do you hear me? on a poofter.

Pop was amused to call his instruction in racism, sexism, and gender bias by the name of **tradecraft**. A lot of what he told me was offensive, even to this son of a monster. I guess I fell a little farther from the tree than he would have liked, but close enough to struggle at times with the ever-shifting thing most folk call **normal**.

No one in the shadows was, or is, or shall be, what you might call normal, or moral, or empathetic, or sensitive. Any of these traits if indulged in would get you killed.

It's Ok to be a poofter, just so long as you do not think, act, or smell like one. You can be any color you want as long as it is black. Henry Ford was right after all. Understand me, son, I do not give a flying or a rolling bleep on a stick about who you really are, or were. All I care about is how you identify, and kill, who you are in favor of who you will be asked to be and who you will have to become.

It was not the usual sort of father-to-son imparting of wisdom. After all, Pop was ten years and more late in sharing, and he was a lifetime away from anything that Dr. Spock ever wrote for his peers and pupils in the parenting line.

Pop had a lot of interest in the **simple act of bleeping**, but he had no interest in loving or raising the little bleeps who popped up from time to time.

Three times, to be exact. Well, as exact as I am able to be.

Pop seems to have a daughter, Janey Grimes, and Lailah seems to have a son, the man whom I have been pleased in a mindless way to call **brother** in the two years that I have known him.

I'll even say his name.

Tommy.

That didn't hurt a bit.

In fact, I cannot hardly feel anything at all.

I have become comfortably numb, I suppose.

Listen up, boy, and live. Watch out for your friends as much as your enemies, because where you will be going, you will not be able to tell the one from the other. And don't smirk at me, you little bleep. It's not like you really know what I am saying. This is a lot more than some exhortation to rotate your tires and clean the leaves from your gutters in the fall after the trees are bare.

Pop was not the only one who attended to my acquisition of tradecraft. He was, though, the only one who added a lot of aggressive and unwelcome good advice. The others were generally civil and professional. After all, they did not have to live in the shadows. Spookistan they knew only by report, from those who had been there and in most cases were going back. Your support staff do as they are told, and the genius involved comes from other quarters. Your typical handler, though, is a veteran of the shadows and has done his work so well that she can no longer go there because his cover is blown.

These, my friends, are particularly bitter people who are hideously demanding and unreasonable. And that is saying nothing of the legend writers, the backstory corps. They are truly unreasonable in the roles that they gave us and the amount of time we had to become someone we had never met or been or conceived of.

We did have a set of tools that made the transitions smooth. Things about where people are vigilant and where they are oblivious. We learned how to stay in that zone of oblivion as much as we were able. For example, most people will remember the face of the last pretty girl or handsome man they saw, but they will have no recollection of the drab guy who jostles them in the subway or the plain jane woman who cuts in front of them in the line at the coffee shop.

Get rid of your clothes, boy, because you chose them for the wrong reasons. To stand out. From now on, you will blend in, and you will wear what you are told to wear, and you will say what you are told to say, and you will improvise as necessary and along the lines of the legend you are living that day.

I can't say that I had a girlfriend, or friends as such at this time. I had **bed buddies** and **bottle friends**, and we met in bars and left alone. I was all of twenty-something and I never had had sex in the prone position, in a bed, sober. I guess you might say that I was perfect for my new career path, because I had been rutting in the bushes by the side of the road for most of my young adult-equivalent life. Pop could not have been more pleased.

You don't want no stinking girlfriends, boy. You want your basic one-night stand. Your local sex workers are your best friends, and your only friends. Well, sort of. Actually, you will have no friends that your handlers don't tell you that you have. Marriage and children are for the squareheads and their beach-ball wives and snot-slurping brats. They are the ones you will be protecting, son, so you had best avoid them like they were diseased. Which they are. There will be times when you want to be one of them, despite the obvious down side. Find a quiet place and lay down, make your mind blank, until those feelings go away. Everything you will touch will turn to crap, so do not touch. The only people who will be able to stand you are other people who come alive in the dark. That is just the way it is. What, no smirks?

I pointed out the Pop, with a great deal of heat and profanity, that he had fathered three sons and done a lot of stuff that he was telling me to avoid. If memory serves, this is where that persistent fantasy about squeezing my hands around his dirty little weasel neck started.

For many years, I followed Pop's advice, and my friends were sex workers and bar stool brokers, and I lived out my days in a dream being dreamed by people who were always behind me, watching me become the man they wanted me to be. I had no feelings, only appearances that included an array of feeling-like sounds and movements. My waking hours were like a never-ending soap opera, and my sleep was the sleep of the zombie, with no dreams and nothing remembered. I would scream myself awake almost every night, and go right back to sleep. They taught me so well to be someone else that I rarely had to deal with my own feelings. Sensations, though, were a constant and belittling irritation. I could have a sensation, but it could not come out. My only good days were those when my sensations and my script called for the same array of appearances and behaviors.

And now I have feelings, and I am getting to the point where I can feel my own feelings without pretending all the time. I only pretend some of the time, now, and it has been Eve's steady influence and guiding hand that have brought me to this better place. Just as some demonic guys including Pop had to teach me how to be a zombie without looking like one, others such as Eve have had to teach me simple things like love and fear and sadness, and gladness. I would like to say that I am healed, but I know that I will always struggle with the simple implications of just **what is normal** in any given situation.

And the screaming myself awake?

That will continue, though the frequency has changed.

And so my Pop, who taught me to be a walking vanilla pudding ready to take on any flavor and harmonize with it, somewhere along the way fell off that turnip truck and into the arms of a woman named, shall we say, **Lailah Batavia**. Clearly that is not her real name. It fairly screams **legend**. However, that does not need to be an impediment. I have seen her face, and it would be hard indeed for her to simulate that. She looks like someone named Lailah Batavia. I will give her that. She even looks like my mother, but then any woman could, since I have never seen that face for sure, for the lion's share of my days.

I am happy to report that I do not, yet, have any fantasies toward Lailah that include my hands and her neck. That I suppose might be of some comfort to you, but for me, I am used to surviving on my anger, and I can and will produce anger whenever I need it, even if I have to gut another feeling and stuff anger into the shell.

I feel angry toward her. I have the sensation of anger as well. Part of my anger, I know, is manufactured, since I cannot imagine felling anything positive toward her. And some of my anger is congruent, a word that Eve is fond of when she puts on her therapist's costume. When you think about it, though, the feelings and sensations are nothing compared to **my intentions**.

For example, do I intend to return evil for evil, and try to destroy the woman who has been trying to destroy me and my friends and family? Or do I intend to forgive her, to embrace her, and to try to get to know her after all these years? I do not like the look, or feel, or taste, or aroma of either of those alternatives. I may not need to decide, because it is a question that my Tribe could answer in a vote, where a simple majority will win the day and the rest will struggle until they are in concurrence. Except for Mr. Red and a few others, who don't really play nice ever.

It would help to have more information, but that is not available to me. I suspect that many of my Tribe have information about Pop and Lailah that they are not sharing with me, even though I really do need to know more than I do now. I and they are under no compulsion to share the truth, since no one of us really cares much about truth.

Trust, then. What about trust? And I still do, and always will, trust my Tribe. I have nothing else in this life. You could bring me up short with a timely and pointed question about Eve, but the answer is the same. I and Eve are two people. We share a feeling, a constellation of feelings, called love, but we do not share one body and we rarely are of the same mind on even the most trivial of things.

No, if I am to find out more about Pop and his woman, my mother, I will need to search on my own and ask for what I cannot imagine. Sounds like work cut out for a spook, doesn't it.

Ma

I was trying to think about the things that I have told you about Ma. Of course, I have not told you everything, since I have a store of memories that would make a book in their own right and length. No, I was wondering what you know that I know and have told you, versus what I know and have failed or avoided or forgotten, to tell you.

Let us make a list.

I told you about the early years, when Ma was housekeeper and our stand-in mother to an absent father who would have done better if he had been a stand-in parent like Ma.

I told you about when Ma came to Buffalonya last year, and the circumstances of the **Double Daily Double Murders** hoax.

I told you about the *Big Bloody Battle Among the Books*.

I have sprinkled my posts about Ma with hints.

I have given you samples of Ma's wonderful way with the English language and idioms.

What I have not told you is any sense of Ma's position in the story of **Kill Goose and All His Friends and Family**. I suspect that Ma's position is central, pivotal, startling, and hidden.

I have been thinking hard about Ma. She was present in the beginning of Pop's time in Spookistan, post-WWII, when she played Natasha in **Operation Poison Ivan**.

Ma was in play.

Ma had, and has, tradecraft. Ma, thus, has secrets.

To hear her speak, you might decide that the woman is an idiot, a lazy immigrant who refuses to learn the language of the host country that saved her and gave her new life. You would be in serious error, and you probably would want to check to see if your wallet is out behind where it should be or up in the darkness where you will not want to go looking for it.

Ma's considerable tradecraft moves on your assumption that she is an airhead.

When Ma was younger, and we knew Ma when she was close enough to that youth, she was rudely red and flushed in a healthy peasant glow. Ma was never pretty, but she was attractive in a big-boned and -breasted way that never fails to attract attention.

Ma and Jeanne share this, with certain allowances for different contents. The process is the same. Hot women confuse men, and other women, when they pretend to be less intelligent and more pliable than they are.

I can tell from the few things that Red and Ed have said that Ma was a double handful for them and a valuable ally in their efforts at subversion.

Ma has her secrets, and she had access to the secrets of Pop, Ed, and Red, at a minimum. And when Ma came to us as our housekeeper, scant years beyond **Operation Poison Ivan**, she could as easily have been in the employ of the state organs of secrecy as the apparent arrangement, a financial one between her and Pop. The first, and covert, option seems to go further in explaining Ma's ability to commit to the three little boys she enveloped in her embrace.

I do not and cannot question Ma's zeal in mothering the three of us, and I do not know how it would have changed things to discover that Ma was still in play and doing work with Pop and against Pop, at the same time.

This would put Ma in possession of secrets that Pop may not have know that she knew, even though Pop would not worry overmuch about such things, since he would have wanted to keep Ma close – keep your friends close and your enemies closer.

Still, Ma may be keeping secrets that are not in the Vault, concerning Pop at a minimum, and also Lailah, for all I know. After all, Ma and Lailah both lived for many decades in Pittsburgh, and if A knows C and B knows A, then B may also have known C. In other words, if Pop knew Lailah and Ma knew Pop, then it is possible and would be something to rule our or use in a provisional sense when running scenarios that Ma knew or knew of Lailah.

And if Ma knew Lailah, then Ma might have known that Lailah was my mother, and if that is the case then Ma decided, or was told, to withhold that information. Why? I do not know.

A related question is whether Ma is in possession of her memories, or not. Certainly, last year, Ma could not tolerate any question on any subject. And then, she was able to hear and answer questions. We never questioned at any length why or how that could be. We were just glad when that strange array of behaviors lifted. I could ask Ma, directly, for the truth of the matter, but if she is continuing to conceal information, or facts, about me and mine, then why would she stop doing that in the absence of any inducement? Clearly, she has squared her love for us with her zeal in keeping secrets. So the strongest inducement, that of love, is already part of the mix and already in place to conceal rather than reveal.

You might think that I am farting in a bag, here, and just grabbing goofy stuff out of the air, and I might have sympathy for that assumption, since I do like to play around, and I do reveal and conceal silently and you are none the wiser.

However, there is one fact that comes into play here. Think back to the **Big Bloody Battle Among the Books**. What were the three thugs shouting as they invaded our bookshop.

They were shouting **Natasha Riga**, over and over again, to find her, yes, and also to terrorize us. In other words, the thugs in the employ of the person or persons who want us all dead, were sent to kill, first, Ma. That puts Ma right in the center of things, and we have not been unaware of this. It is not like I an suddenly saying, **Oh yeah, whuddup wid dat!**

What is different is that I am being more accurate and less distracted about who this wonderful woman is and was, and shall be, too, and not just saying some version of, **Since Ma is precious, by rule, we must protect her at all costs**.

There may be more at stake than our love for Ma and the continuation of our decision to love Ma and enjoy her forever, or at least for a very, very long time. It may be that our precious Ma is a threat to our enemies and this makes her a threat, so to speak, to our happiness, to say nothing of our safety and our ability to be a quasi-criminal enterprise operating in plain sight at the behest and the sufferance of the TLA elephants with whom we lie down with.

I am identifying what is what, according to the information I have and the scenarios that I can see as flowing from that information and from any implications that seem either possible or probable. It would be fair to say that I know little if anything more than I did before, but I do feel more ready to react to situations as they unfold.

Not if they unfold, but when they do.

I have talked to Eve about the Vault, and she has agreed to check to see what if anything is in there that might apply to the questions that I am chewing on. I wish I could explain to you how she will do that, but it would put you in a bind, so I won't.

Ok?

One thing I can do, I realize, is to tell some stories about what it was like to grow up with Ma.

I remember the day when I figured out that Ma and Pop were not married or anything like that. I was 4 years old, and my brothers and I were playing in the yard with a girl from next door named Sally. We were sitting in the backyard, shouting and jostling one another like kids do when they play. It is all about aggression and being right.

Sally was saying that at least she knew who her mother was, and then she crossed her arms over her torso.

"What?" I said. "Ma is my mother, dummy."

"That," Sally said, "is not what my mother says, and my mother is always right. My dad says so, and he is a very smart man."

I looked at my brothers, and they looked at each other, and we all shrugged our shoulders and picked up dirt clods and started throwing them at Sally, who screamed and ran. We didn't hit her, of course, but it was not because we were not trying. I suppose I was mad at her.

I remember talking to Ma later that day.

"Sally says," I said, "you are not my mother, Ma."

Ma just looked at me with this kindness and shook her head.

"Your Pop will be of the talking for you three of the boys."

Pop did not waste any time with kindness.

"You three little bastards," Pop said, "Front and center."

I looked at my brothers and they looked at each other.

"It has come to my attention," Pop said, "that that brat Sally is telling you tales about your mama. As hard as it may be to hear it, Sally though a little bleep is right. Ma is your mother in the sense that she is raising you. The details will have to wait until you can understand what I am talking about. Now get out of my face and go play or something. Make yourselves useful. Find a cure for cancer or something."

That was enough for that day, and we went about our little guy business without seeming to notice. When Sally would come around, we would pick up some dirt clods and she would run, but when we were 7 instead of 4 that did not seem to work for us. So we went to Pop and he gave us the speech about our three moms and what bleeps they were, and that is when he gave us our nicknames of **Goose**, **Jim**, and **OtherJim**.

That is about the time, too, that we started having meetings of the F-Troop and dreamed up the special sign of two thumbs up, middle fingers touching.

Ma was home when Pop had that talk with us, because Ma was always home. She didn't drive and she didn't have any friends that we ever saw, so she was always around. We did not see how weird that was, because we went to school and we had each other and Ma loved us, so we assumed that our loving her back was enough for her and more. We figured that she had so much love that she could have sent some of the surplus to the Old Country or to those starving kids in India that Pop was always inserting sideways in our virtual patoots.

Kids know a lot, and a lot of what kids know is the covert stuff and the unspoken stuff, and the rules to live by that *just are*, but kids have blind spots, too, when it comes to things like empathy and altruism. I would assert that a child continues in self-centered confusion for as long as it takes to understand that there are big words such as **empathy** and **altruism** with at least a working definition of what those words mean. The really bright kids even may not know how to spell those words.

So when does a kid develop empathy? I guess I really don't give a rip about the answer to that question, but I do know when I had a sense of things like empathy. My brothers and I had a touch of that when we were 10 or 11, but it is probable that it was hormonal changes that put us over the top.

We always knew that we loved Ma, but it was only when our nether regions kicked in that we realized that's we loved Ma with a great deal of passion that kicked up a feeling that we learned to call gratitude.

When Pop was mean to Ma, when we were little, we told him not to be a meany. When we were 16, we told him that we would kick his narrow ass if he didn't stop, and when we were 18, we basically did just that and climbed over his tightly tucked body to leave home for good. In all that, Ma got lost in the hormonal stew, so we sorta, kinda forgot to say **thanks and see you later**. We just left, and in three directions.

A lost touch with B and C, and D and E, and each of the three of us was a more lonely lone letter than we knew.

I had meant to tell you three stories about Ma, but it just is too painful. So I stop.

Tommy

There were two people who laid me out on that day a while back when my buddies and I went to see Lailah and her daughter in their home in Pittsburgh.

Lailah certainly did me in, and I don't remember much after that for quite a while of wandering in the dark wood where the straight way is lost.

Tommy, though, runs a close second in this race. From what Lailah said about her other son and what we figured might be possible from the funeral wake for Peter Principe, I was also struggling with the fact that my mother who I had not known also had a son – and a daughter, come to that – and that this was a man who I had called **brother** with as much awareness as you would say **have a nice day**. That is to say, almost none.

I notice that I do not include Janey Grimes in this list, and it is owing to her not having lied to me or wishing me dead and actively working toward that outcome. I do not know Janey, so it would be hard to feel the sense of betrayal that I do toward Tommy. I guess it is true that I do not know my mother, but that in itself speaks of betrayal. She just did not care about me and that is obvious. Janey may not have known about me at all.

But the subject here is Tommy, and the goal of these profiles is to glean produce from the margins of the field that may be right under my nose and rotting away unharvested.

Tommy is younger than I am, and he has the same father and mother, it seems fair and fairly accurate to say. When I was 15 or so, he was born, making him thirty-something to my fifty-something. Pop got busy with Lailah and Tommy was the second issue of their efforts, a few years after producing a daughter, Janey. I was the first, and for whatever reason I was largely abandoned and Tommy and Janey at least knew who their mom and pop were.

Why me and why them? Such questions have no answers.

And I try and try and try to find answers.

Tommy was recruited into the same shadows that I was, though I never have heard any of the details. Perhaps he was recruited by Pop. It all raises the question of how it was that Pop was such a desirable asset that the powers that be and had been were willing to ignore Pop's fleshly faults. And not only that, but to pay Ma to keep his three sons on the straight and narrow.

Tommy seems devoted to Lailah in a Tommy sort of fashion, with that mixture **of hail, fellow, well-met** and **hey, mama, looking good**. Tommy from the reports that my brother and Jeanne gave, seems to have a close but also strained connection with his mother. Tommy is still among the missing, and I have not bothered to ask why.

That is the crop.

The implications are vast, and they will take a while to understand and to understand in terms of action. It is probably for the best that Tommy is not among us, for it would tip things in a quick and probably violent direction, as likely or not, if I am the one who would do the choosing. Others, it is true, would have clears heads and would seek to control me and my darkness.

The answers to the questions are these --

- **Kill Goose et al**. Tommy is either in line with his mother on this or is trying to modify or block that outcome. I would assume that if Tommy was convinced that I had to go, that he would have found a way to get that done without any trail back to him. Does that mean that I should kiss him and say thank you?

- **Lie to Goose et al**. Tommy is clearly taking the idea of need to know for a joyride. We have embraced him and brought him in to the fold and done good work together. Our stories are intertwined to the point that the punishment for one would be shared by all. Does this mean wee continue to work under the usual rules of engagement – trust over truth. The truth is, I could trust Tommy, if I can get over the other stuff.

- **The happy family option**. If Tolstoy is right, then unhappy families are each unhappy in their own special ways. If I decide to declare war on my mother and my brother, I know the implications of that. If I decide to forgive them, I do not know the implications of that. If I choose to forgive as well as forget, I will need chemical and surgical assistance, Thorazine and lobotomy.

I like the option of knowing everyone's story and thus having a basis for trust and forgiveness and the giving and getting of sanctions and reparations.

How do we get there?

Who will go first?

The Happy Family

A one-act play

Characters:

Goose Grim, a spook,
Eve Green, a spook and Goose's wife
Pop Grim, a ghost (or is he?)
Lailah Batavia, Pop's Puck
Ma AKA Natasha Riga, a Sibyl, or prophetess

Scene A bare stage save for a wooden table at the center.

Goose: (slamming a big, ugly handgun down on the table): You know what Chekhov said, right?
Eve: I have not been with you all this time and not heard this one, many times. So, yes, Dear, Chekhov said that if you introduce a gun in the first scene that someone had better fire that gun before the final curtain falls.
Goose: I see three choices here.
Eve: I will expect you to list them before the final curtain, Dear.
Goose: As I said, I see three choices.
Eve: I see a pissed-off partner, Dear, who does not usually play with guns.
Goose (putting the gun to his temple): This, I think, is Option Number One.
Eve: I can see that this is no play, but real in a disturbing way.
Goose (pointing the gun at Pop Grim, in academic robes, who

enters with his Puck, Lailah, dressed in a skimpy little tutu): And this is Option Number Two.

Eve: Thank the Dear, Dear, that you mentioned a third option.

Goose (gesturing to the stage and the audience): This is Option Number Three.

Eve: I see, Dear, and I hear you. So the play is the thing after all. I had my doubts for a few lines.

Pop Grim: Put the gun down, boy.

Goose: Silence, Shade. I will pull your cord when I want sound or sight from you.

Lailah (to Pop) : Always the little prince, ain't he.

Stage note: As the scene progresses, Lailah addresses herself only to Pop.

Goose (to Pop): You look a hell of a lot more like a spook than a ghost, old man.

Pop: Your mother and I, well, I, anyway, have been meaning to talk to you about that, but the time by my watch never seemed to be right.

Eve: It is time, Dear, to wind things up. Perhaps a bit of honest oil of a sweet nature might get things ticking and tocking once again.

Goose (to Lailah): What say you to that, Mommy Dearest?

Note that Goose still holds the gun in his right hand.

Lailah (to Pop): Must I deal with this irritating man-child?

Pop: For once, you lovely, evil bitch, yes.

Goose: I must say that I am of two minds here. I applaud your facility with language but I deplore your treatment of someone who seems, but perhaps only seems, to be dependent on you like Puck to Prospero. Even this mock of a mother of mine.

Ma (from a corner of the stage that had been in darkness): That is the being of my boy. My boy! Not the son of some tutu.

Lailah (to Pop): She always did talk too much. It still is not too late to stop her gob. Ask of your son his gun. Do it!

Pop: We are done with tricks, Lailah. We are one happy family here, and you are part of that happy family. Don't be introducing murder in this mix. No more. The Happy Family murders no more.

Enter Jim and OhJim. (OhJim wears Pop's Watch on a chain around his neck.)

Jim: Well, look at this. A gun, a ghost, and a girly-girl. Talk about your timing.

OhJim (grasping the watch like a weapon and taking a step forward)**:** Yeah, but not just yet, Jim-bro. Not until we figure out who is the Big Hand and who is the Little Hand.

Jim: Call me crazy, but Goose has the big gun.

OhJim: Yeah, and Pop was always the little one of a weasel cast. Still, though, it is time to settle this question.

Lailah (to Pop): They are still three little bastards with a collective I.Q. of one centrally raised finger.

[Enter Tommy, with Janey Grimes on his arm.]

Jim: Well, look what the cat dragged in.

OhJim: Yeah, one stepbrother and one stepsister. Or, a hairball and a puss.

Goose: My brother.

Tommy: And so you have said from the start.

Eve (to Goose): The time has come to make it official, Dear. Forget not, too, that you have one here that you can call **sister.**

Tommy (giving Pop a fist bump and putting his arm around Lailah): Always good to see you, Eve.

[Tommy, Pop, Lailah, and Janey form one group. Janey has nothing to say. Goose and Eve form another group, with Jim and OhJim standing, like comedians in a strip joint, between the two groups.]

Ma: I am of the thinking that you all of you are being of the impressing that you are having all the informing that you need, in ordering your bad selves around the idea of this being, this Happy Family. I am knowing better.

Goose: Ma, you are making perfect sense, but the time is out of joint for me still. I see much of my family arrayed against me or simply standing at a distance.

Ma: My boy, my darling boy, is of the suredness that I am telling you soon a story of amazement. This is not being just all about you. Is of everybody.

Lailah (to Pop): Finally the old bag is popping. You wanted to see everything out there. Look, it is spilling out and will be rolling from her like effluent. Kill her now. Do it!

Eve: I see that there is a ranking here, and you, Goose Dear., are as usual, and by our own efforts and report, in the lead. Rankest of all. Or, more like, the least of these in rank. Everyone, including me, I guess, knows more than you do about you, and yours.

[Eve gives Goose her very, very best Buddha Girl smile.]

Goose (slamming down the gun onto the table): Edify me.

[Enter Jeanne and David, hand in hand. Jeanne is doing her model-walk, and David as always is finding a way to stay up with her. They stand with Goose and Eve.]

Jim: And now is the winter of our discontent made glorious summer by this Daughter of the Sun.

OhJim: Yeah, if Jeanne is the heel that goes tick-tock down the street, then David is the sound of one heel tapping. Both welcome and well-met.

Jeanne: Part of the problem, Mr. Mother Goose Sir, is that you were sleeping with eyes open for a long time after you met your mama. Being awake, we all had a chance to hear the story. Now it is your turn. Be glad and attend. Give up the conspiracy theories and hurt feelings. Leaders do this every day.

[Jeanne gives Goose her bitter lemon smile to the side.]

David: You really do **need to know** all that you will hear.

[Enter Mister Ed and Mr. Red, who holds Wild Billy.]

Mister Ed: Mister Chair Sir.

[Ed bows from the waist like a crane in the air.]

Mr. Red: Bleep you, Consort Man.

[Wild Billy walk tail up over to Ma and jumps onto her shoulder like a familiar. Ed and Red stand behind Goose and Eve.]

[Enter Mr. Black and Nancy Chino, with Joe Bob Schmidt, Meme Shiva, and Jane Carlotto. They form a crescent behind the two groups, shading slightly in the direction of Goose.]

Jim: You are all probably wondering why I called this meeting.

OhJim: Yeah, I missed that. What did you call it? Mystery Meatheads? The Happy Family menu medley?

Mr. Black (striding forward and pushing the two Jims to the side, with some force): Maybe we should call this The Happy Family Murders.

Mister Ed: *Murders* noun or verb, Mister Black Sir?

Mr. Black: Both, and I will speak to that if I can get a second.

[The lights go down and there is a lot of noise and confusion. When the lights come up, the characters are in the backroom of the bookshop Caspar's Books and That, sitting in a circle. Goose, with Eve beside him, sits with the handgun in his lap.]

Mr. Black: This meeting of the F-Troop will be in my order.

Jim: Or in chaos, if the Chair be so easily overturned.

OhJim: Yeah, and in odor, since that stinks like a foot stool.

[OhJim, his usual lopsided grin in place, holds his hands slightly apart.]

Mister Ed: If I may, Mister Chair Sir, I will make like the second one who intends to take over your task, to wit, as that of one who acts like the father of us all and who calls us into being and who gives us work to do. You, in a phrase, Mister Chair Sir. But, as many are noticing, you are the subject of this gathering and as such cannot be expecting, nay, cannot be allowed, to rule the roost as is your right, by goose and by golly. For the nonce. I rise to suggest that **Robert's Rules of Order** makes provision for such a fix. You simply can turn over to another, of your choosing, the role of Chair (the **foot stool** reference, though related, was unfortunate) for this one occasion. And may I say, the one who has already come forward and in effect laid claim to that role may very well be the one who you choose. I would allow that, as parliamentarian. He can and could call on others as needed to tell the story that you now **need to know**.

Goose: So ordered are you by him that *so ordered* shall I be, too.

Mr. Black: It is to each to tell Goose what you know, and what you have held back. I will start.

[Mr. Black stands a comfortable distance from Goose.]

Goose: The time is here. Show me your hands. One and all.

Mr. Black: We have been like two shadows against a darkling background, you and I, for many years as the Revs. Mr. Black and White who dealt in lies that seemed like stark clarity to those who heard them. From the day I met you, I knew who you were and where you came from. It is for others to flesh out the story. I offer no apology, nor I think, should any others. You did not need to know, then, and you do, now. We need enough truth in the mix to restore trust.

Pop: You were right, Goose, to say that I look more like a spook than a ghost. You were more right than you knew. I live, and this Puckish beauty beside me has put up with me for a very long time. Many others, mostly in my loose grouping, have known this. What you need to know is that my death in your eyes was necessary for the aims of others who continue to pull the old and creaky strings that animate me. The withholding of critical information was operational. For you, it may be another thing entirely, judging from your long absence in plain sight.

Lailah: You meant as little to me as the pea meant to the princess. I am not wired for affection. Just ask your father. I convinced him, and your brother, or so I thought, that you needed to be kept in the dark, and I thought that I also had convinced them to neutralize that old windbag, too, but it was only a seeming sort of thing. They did things to give me the illusion of control, and for a few years I though that the outcome would be the silencing of the old woman who always and still threatens to play the prophetess. I was willing to murder her, and you if need be, but the others were not willing, only seeming. Did they bother to tell me of their caveats? Clearly, no. I could give you a mother's love, but look at the love, some might call it, that your brother and sister enjoy. Are they smiling? Do you want a helping of that?

Mr. Black: And Eve?

Eve: You probably are curious, to put it mildly, Dear, just when I came into possession of these so-called truths and facts that are unfolding before you.

[Goose, who looks like he has seen a ghost, can barely

move, but he finally nods. Once. Eve continues.]

You see me as your savior, Dear, and as a metaphor I am willing for that to stand, provided you, too, stand, on your own and by your own power, like a boy who becomes a man and claims his own spot in the sun. Like an author who writes his own story. In brief, I too learned the truth while you were present but beyond our reach, after you came back from that meeting out in the Cold with this chilly, chilling woman, your mother.

Mr. Black: To make this more simple, Goose, there are but two others who knew from the start. Tommy first, then Ma.

Tommy (who rises to stand at a comfortable distance from Goose): I was astonished, when we met over that body under the tarp outside President's Park, a few years ago, and as we got to know one another, that you seemed to trust me like a brother from before the beginning. It was like you had no tradecraft at all, and this did not square with the man, the brother under the spook's sheet, that I knew so well by report. I, yes, knew you as my brother, from the start and before. The reasons for my silence and my seeming to dupe you, are few. One, actually. I saw no other way to save you, from the designs of our mother, who has a unique ability to throw all humanity aside and make decisions based on her wants and desires alone. I am her son, and I give her my duty-bound love and support, but I could not allow her to follow through with her plan as she laid it out, and I subverted her and protected you, sacrificing Tom Tonolody and Peter Principe along the way, and if anyone needs to apologize, I am in the unique position of needing to ask both combatants – you and Lailah, that is -- to forgive me. You, I know, would do so. Mother, I know, would do so, and she would make me pay. That is as it is. I do call you, brother. My brother.

[Tommy turns to Jim and OhJim. He continues.]

And you, and you, with your wise-crocks and hidden watches. I call you, brothers. My brothers. And that is half of the story, for I know your papa but not your mamas. No one does, and lest you feel bad, just look at the love that this mama you can see has for all her children.

Mr. Black: And, at last, Ma.

Ma (who follows Mister Ed as he carries her chair to the center of the circle): My boys, my three little boys. I am being the mother of you, that you never are having. That is this which is never being over. I am coming to you many years ago, and I am staying as I always were, and being of your mother in the sense that I am having the love for you. Goosey, you must understand, that I am not telling you of the truth about your mama because I am not going to be the one who is telling you that she is being a monster. I also am of the avoiding from an ancient curse. Tell him and kill him, and live to always be the remembering of his agony. I am living and being of the stupid, and making such of you so you can be from the living and never knowing. This is loving you. Me. This is being my way of savings. Other secrets are for other times. Now is for the saying of sorry.

Mr. Black: And so, Goose, the choice is yours. That gun which you introduced in the opening had better go off before the final curtain.

> **[Goose nods, with a little more vigor than before. He takes the gun and removes the clip and tosses all the parts to the floor.]**

Goose: Go off, you. Someone say **kaboom!** and someone say **amen!** And someone make a motion that we are adjourned.

[Goose raises his hands, thumbs up and middle fingers touching in the *F-Troop salute*, which is taken up by all. The curtain falls with a loud noise off.]

This Is the End

The **Grimoire's** end is its beginning -- like the self-swallowing snake of dreams, the **Uroborus**, eating itself from the tail forward in an ever-tightening circle like a noose.

In this circle of life, all happy families are alike, noun and verb.

Email from: Mister Ed
To Goose Grim

Subject: House of Verbs. Closed for a while. Open again.

Friend Goose and friends all, I have enjoyed giving you a taste of my world, which I directly share with Goose and indirectly have shared with all of you, fellow tribalists.

I have been mining a vein of material (dare I call it gold or silver?) from the manuscript that I wrote a while back and that has been sitting on the back burner.

The material that I have shared so far goes under the name of *General.* **The second section of this manuscript, about 60 pages, and called the** *Specific* **section, appears at the final section of this book. I have opted, after discussion with Goose, to leave this section intact. That means the shifting ... I ... will continue to squint three ways, to me, to Goose, and to the writer of record, Jon R-G.**

I hope you like it. It was fun to write, in the spirit of the great man himself, E.B. White. I give specific guidance according to the principles that we have laid out for you in the occasional pieces that are sprinkled over the beginning and middle of this book like salt and pepper on a salad of greens and reds.

This side comes free if you order the Happy Family medley.

The manuscript, as presented, has that shifting ... I ... that I warned you about. See if you can separate me from Goose and Goose from the person he published under the name of in the world as they know it, the world that stands over against the shadows and like a flash photo has no shades of gray but only black and white.

[Extra credit for those who can say if my use of *gray* in the paragraph above is correct, of if I should have said *grey*. Look it up, Google it, or ask Goose.]

Need I say, once more, enjoy?

Your servant,
Ed

House of Verbs
Grammar, Style, and Usage for Writers

Part Two: Specific

Some thoughts about the current crisis

No matter your stance was toward William F. Buckley, he did not disappoint.

If you hated what he stood *for*, he still would deliver fresh material every time that you heard him speak.

The same was the case if you loved the guy.

Many of us loved his go-to-hell manner and mannerisms, and hated his politics.

And we loved his loving, extravagant way with language.

I could enjoy small doses of his **Firing Line** program on public television. Buckley would hold his head back and look down his nose at **everyone**. His was the best rendering of **snob** that you would ever see.

Somewhere along the way, I read that Buckley had one title for the speeches that he gave on the nationwide talk circuit --

Some Thoughts on the Current Crisis.

No matter how many months ahead of his appearance, that title would always hold up to the events of the moment.

Past, present, and future walk into a bar

> *Past, present, and future walk into a bar.*
> *It was tense.*
> *It was a sequence of tenses.*

I borrowed the first and second lines from someone somewhere on Facebook via my wife. The third line is all mine.

■ ■ ■

I'm a classically trained copy editor/reporter/writer. In other words, I studied other things in college and learned on the job, during and after school. I am still learning.

Part of my training was an understanding of the **sequence of verb tenses**. Due to the timing of this training and the age of the teachers, **sequence of tenses**, though it is as important today as it was then, goes by different names now or no name at all.

Verbs, however, have not changed or gone out of style.

As long as there are verbs, there also will be the ordered or disordered sequence of verbs in sentences.

Here is an example of a sequence of verb tenses --

Jon said that he was trained on the job.

The verb **said** (past tense) rules the next verb in sequence, **was trained**. The sequence is from simple past tense to **was trained**, a more complex past tense form. If you begin with the past tense you continue in the past, most of the time.

We are all deeply blessed by the fact that largely successful following the sequence of verb tenses in English has only one requirement -- a nodding, or better, acquaintance with English, either written or spoken or overheard.

Although sequencing verbs is as easy as drawing water from the tap in the kitchen, you can benefit from reflecting on what you are doing. Like thinking about the difference of drawing water from a well rather than a tap.

We will be defining terms and looking at how sequencing works in newspaper stories, general nonfiction, and fiction.

Defining terms

The phrase **sequence of tenses** harkens back to earlier times. The venerable and durable H.W. Fowler (**A Dictionary of Modern English Usage**, 1926) has an entry on the subject. I understand that when Ernest Hemingway worked as a young man at the **Kansas City Star**, a few years before Fowler published his usage book, the in-house style guide at the Star featured prominently the admonition to "follow the sequence of tenses." I got this information courtesy of the one who taught me about the sequence of tenses, the late John Bremner (v. his **Words on Words**). I also am drawing upon my memory of two day-long seminars of Bremner's that I attended while working as a newspaper copy editor in Oregon.

Since verb sequencing is intuitive, as well as rule-guided, you can be your own expert, if you wish.

Or you can let the rules rule you.

You get to decide which verb forms to use based on your intentions and your understand of the language from reading, speaking, and hearing it.

You can say --

He said that he was old.

He says that he is old.

He said that he would be considered old.

Each of these sentences is correct, and each sentence has its own intentions. Each sentence covers the territory in part but not in full, and each sentence says something true about the territory. But just as a map is not the territory, so too are these sentences narrow in their foci. And true, each one.

Here is another example --

He said that mean people suck.

In this sentence, we have an eternal truth about mean people. When you state an eternal truth, the second verb in the sequence will be in the present tense. Try out the alternative --

He said that mean people sucked.

Although the sentence is proper (it has a subject and at least one verb) it is not helpful. The implication is that mean people can stop being mean, but that seems like expecting a tiger to change its stripes. Rather than stating an obvious, eternal truth the sentence stops short of providing the additional facts that would make this lame thing dance and sing.

For example --

He said that mean people sucked eggs when they could get them, especially by theft or fraud.

Now we have a sentence that at least is trying to be helpful, but choosing the past tense will never get us to the place of truth and simplicity of --

He said that mean people suck.

Newspaper stories

Think of a typical newspaper story --

John Doe, 49, of Buffalonya is in jail today, charged with cruelty to animals.

The police officer investigating a complaint against Doe alleged that Doe "bit his dog on the ear in a fit of rage over some spilled kibble."

Anyone who has written a story of fact for publication can use intuition to sequence the verbs that appear --

The PTA Auxiliary will meet at 7 p.m. Monday at the Roll In and Crawl Out, in the downtown mall, to enjoy a spread of beer and peanuts.

"The bar will be open, and closed, if you follow my drift," said John Doe, the auxiliary's press officer. "In other words, bring some cash."

Anyone who has read a newspaper for any significant length of time could write a story as competent as that one. The verb choices border on the archetypal. In fact, it is my belief that must persons of my age learned how to write from reading daily newspapers.

Non-fiction

Verb choices in non-fiction do not stand out as much as verb choices in fiction. Perhaps it is the reader's comfort in knowing that what she is reading is **true and real**, so to speak, that makes most readers float along on the typical non-fiction writer's current with little awareness of undercurrents such as verb tenses. Fiction demands our attention lest we be led astray by some unreliable narrator or deviously playful author. We bring a different set of filters with us when we read what is **made up and fanciful**.

The sequence of verbs in general non-fiction such as personal essays is, as before, a matter of matching your verbs to your intentions.

For example, take a personal essay such as **A Native Hill** by Wendell Berry.

This is the beginning --

> The hill is not a hill in the usual sense. It has no "other side."

Berry chooses this construction to build tension and interest. The reader sees **The hill ...** and immediately is wondering **what hill?**

Hooked already, and wanting to hear more.

The alternative would have worked well enough --

> The hill was not a hill in the usual sense. It had no "other side."

There is nothing wrong with that construction, but there is no tension or interest for the reader compared to Berry's choice of the present tense. The alternative, if it gets some help, will probably have to go in another direction than the one that the author intended.

Fiction

In fiction the sequence of verb tenses is a more complex question, and other important questions such as dominant verb tense (will you tell the story as **unfolding now** or as a memory from the recent or not so near past?) and narration -- first, second, or third person -- will vie for the writer's attention.

Consider a current (fall 2011) bestselling novel, **The Night Circus** by Erin Morgenstern.

The first thing that I notice is that this writer like all others makes choices about the dominant verb tense. **The Night Circus** uses the present tense as the dominant form, instead of a past tense choice.

Occasional breakout pieces are in the second person.

Using the present tense as the dominant verb form gives the story a more immediate tone --

> They sit in the oak tree in the afternoon sun, the five of them.

As a reader, I'm already thinking, **Tell me more**.

We meet a controlling girl named Caroline, her three friends, and her little brother Bailey. Caroline forces upon Bailey a game of **Truth or Dare**, and Bailey -- who wants to fit in with the others -- chooses **Dare**. Caroline assigns Bailey the task of breaking into the circus compound, which the five can see from the tree in which they sit. Bailey is to bring back something tangible as proof that he did as he was dared.

The story that follows is forced by the writer's intentions to use past tense verb forms to give the back story, but when Bailey arrives at the compound just as we are getting the last of the details from the past, the writer switches immediately to the dominant present tense --

> It takes Bailey the better part of ten minutes to walk all the way across the field … . The gates are easily three times his height … .

When you write fiction, you must choose the dominant verb tense -- the tense that best-serves your purpose. You can ignore this, certainly, but your manuscript will be in the historical-past tense, probably. Most of us write in historical-past tense when we are in a hurry or when we are not thinking about the art of what we are doing. If you have moments of lucidity, you probably will switch to verb tenses that work better for both you and your reader, but if you slide back into auto-mode your story will demand a lot of work in the revision stage. Once the story is told, problems such as verb tenses will jump forth in bold relief, demanding attention.

· · ·

When I wrote the first draft of the first title in the **Grimoire** series, **The Mystery Man Murders**, I was in auto-mode. My verb tenses flowed from my non-fiction writing habits, and I was using the past historical tense to record a story that the narrator was telling in daily blog posts, an especially immediate and present form of expression. I-talk of the sort seen in most blog posts is always immediate, especially to the I doing the blogging.

When I began revising the manuscript, I could see that a story that I wanted to tell in an immediate way was sliding again and again into the past-historical tense whenever my writerly back was turned. This put much too much distance between the unfolding story (which is as fresh as a blog post from this morning) and the telling of the story. I was using past-historical tense, the verb tense that one uses when recalling at ease events from the dim past, where all or most of the feelings and principals are dead or lost or defined to the finest detail.

It took hours and hours of effort to edit the manuscript to reflect the immediate aspect of the story.

What person?

When you think about the verb tense that you choose as the dominant one for your story, you begin with your goals in telling the story, and you will quickly be looking at the narrator, too. What voice will you use? **The Night Circus** uses a standard third-person narrator, a faithful and reliable teller of the story of **he**, **she**, and **they**.

It may seem odd to say that the narrator of a work of magical realism is reliable, but it is so in the case of **The Night Circus**.

In **The Mystery Man Murders**, which purports to be the real-time chronicle of a quasi-criminal enterprise based in a used bookshop, I chose first-person narration. My generally unreliable narrator, Goose Grim, is a throwback to pulp fiction voices of the noir sort. You can tell a hard-bitten noir mystery or thriller using third-person narration, but all the noir touches will be confined to the dialog. That would be like putting a splint on one leg of a runner and expecting her to finish first.

In noir fiction told in the first person the fun stuff appears in both the dialogue and in snide side-comments from the narrator.

For example --

> I was lurking in the shadows, like a hungry shark that has forgotten what blood in the water tastes like, when she appeared before my starving eyes -- tall and blond, thin in the places where thin is best and substantial in the places that grab a hungry man's attention.
>
> "Got a match?" she said in a husky voice laced with perfume and guttural purpose.
>
> "Your face and my camera," I said, blinding her in a flash. Another cruising wife in the can.

I just made that up.

You get the idea.

. . .

The Night Circus does not suffer from its third-person narration, partly because the dominant, relentless return to the present tense keeps the reader in the now and maintains the jarring tone.

Occasional set pieces using second-person also keep **The Night Circus** firmly in the present --

> With your ticket in hand, you follow a continuous line of patrons into the circus ... .

In second-person narration the narrator tells you the story of **you**. This cannot be sustained without running the risk of seriously pissing off the reader.

No one appreciates being told what to think or do.

Summing up

It is natural to follow a sequence of verb tenses, because that is the way speakers of English speak and write. If you want to write in a buttoned-down, academic style, or must, you can closely consult the authorities such as Fowler and Bremner.

Know that you have a great deal of freedom in the verb tense sequences that you choose or simply use.

Let your well-tuned ear tell you when the sentences are good.

Sin boldly. If God does not like your choices, God can send your stuff to literary hell.

It is much more likely that God is indifferent to these matters.

None of this is essential for salvation.

However, you will not enjoy making a fool of yourself in print for all to see. It matters not whether you do this from inattention or ignorance.

That is not what a writer seeks.

That is what a writer seeks to avoid.

The dangling man

It's past time to talk about modifiers, those words and phrases that make simple things less simple and more rich. The flip side is important, too, since getting these things wrong makes what is simple also absurd or misleading.

In particular, we will be looking at **dangling modifiers** and **squinting modifiers**.

Along the way, we will discuss the nature of attribution in matters of grammar, style, and usage. Just who, in other words, is the expert here.

Dangling modifiers

When I was a young man, I wanted to be a poet. This is a sample of my efforts --

Walking down the hill,
the bright edge
of dark clouds behind me.

It was supposed to be a haiku, and I guess that it is. Fourteen syllables with a focus on nature, with a sudden turn.

It also is an example of a dangling modifier.

The idea is that if you begin with a phrase such as **walking down the hill (comma),** the word that follows the commas is supposed to be the subject of the sentence. In my poem, the subject is **me**, but my construction indicates that the subject is **edge**. No big deal, right? Well, it is a big deal, since edges, even edges of dark clouds, cannot walk.

To fix the grammar, and probably do violence to the poem, I could say something like **Walking down the hill, I sense the bright edge of dark clouds behind me.**

My example, though I did not know it at the time, is close to a popular way of explaining the absurdity that follows a dangling modifier --

Walking down the street,
the moon shines brightly in the sky.

Such a clever moon, to be in two places at once.

This error can be fix in a few ways. If the subject of the sentence is **I**, you can say, **While walking down the street, I saw the moon shining brightly in the sky.** Or if you want the focus to be on the moon and its brightness in the face of the darkness, you can say, **The moon shined brightly in the sky,** *making my steps sure and certain in the silvery world of a bright night.*

Why is this important?

Dangling your modifiers is high on **the list of the top ten things that make writers look dumb**. No one seeks an outcome like that.

Squinting modifiers

If you get this one wrong, it is both more apparent and less damning than dangling modifiers.

For example --

> **The moon in its glory, the sun cannot touch --
> these things are true and also will be so**.

A squinting modifier looks both ways, and this causes confusion for the reader. In my example the phrase **the sun cannot touch** operates in two ways. As you read the sentence, the phrase seems to set up a poetic contrast between the beauty of the moon and the sheer power of the sun, which for a nanosecond is a pleasing thing, but the rest of the sentence makes it clear that the writer was listing two things, largely unrelated, that he sees as true yesterday, today, and tomorrow.

The best way to fix a squinting modifier is to be clear with yourself on your goals and recast the sentence to remove the problem. For example --

> *The moon in its glory, the sun cannot touch,* I said to myself in awe of the silvery landscape of darkness before me. **Darkness, darkness**, I sang, **draw me closer.**

Another example --

> The day's theme, to be clear, said a lot about the weather and the speaker.

The phrase **to be clear** seems to operate as the idiom that it usually is, or does it? We also seem to be talking about a speaker's announced topic that may or may not be, **To Be Clear**.

Fixing such a sentence is a matter of erasing confusion and penciling in clarity --

> The speaker's theme, **To Be Clear**, said a lot about the speaker and the weather. It just happened to be a lovely day of the sort that makes sitting and listening a chore. It is a good thing that the speaker was compelling and passionate. And clear.

Although the fault in the original sentence may seem small, you only get so many chances to engage your reader and keep her interest. Even small goofs can send her on her way. Readers keep score, and their tolerance varies, so our job is to be clear. That means hunting down and altering our goofs.

I would put dangling modifiers in the top half of **the list of the top ten things that make writers look dumb**. I would put squinting modifiers in the bottom half of the list.

Truth is, anything on the list will make you look dumb, so the rank may mean little.

Just who is the expert here

I own a number of books about herbs. Something that I noticed after reading a number of such works is that the authors borrow and steal from one another and from other sources without any attempt to cite their sources in any fashion. It was amusing and also slightly irritating to see a myth such as **herbs should be grown in poor, rocky soil like they do in the wild** get copied and offered as gospel again and again until someone finally points out that his herbs grow like weeds because they get rich soil and lots of water.

Books about grammar and usage have similar challenges. I became competent as a copy editor by learning from other copy editors and from reading books about grammar and usage, and by looking up every word I did not know how to spell or define. When I sat down to write this book, I could see that I was going to need some help. I have tried to stick to the dictionary (Webster's II) and my favorite usage experts -- Fowler and Bremner -- and I have given simple credit where due if I have had to go further afield for answers, usually to Wikipedia.

It goes almost without saying that one must assess the truth of answers that one finds on the Internet, even Wikipedia. You must assess the experts' accuracy. What does that make you?

However, no one is really an expert on language. Language is free and easy. Language is either growing or dying, and everyone or no one is an expert when it comes to language. Still, there are agreed-upon norms that writers do well to understand.

If you are bent on breaking the rules, first you should know what the rules are, in fine detail, or you will be seen as a dumb writer rather than as a fresh or bond one.

No one wants that.

Besides, it is more fun to break the rules when you actually know what the rules are.

Subjects and Verbs – happy families are all alike

When **Subject** and **Verb** agree, everyone feels a gladness.

If any one or any thing can express gladness, it would be the **Parts of Speech**, inanimate though they be. Without these Parts, our speaking and writing would be far less than even partial in effectiveness. We would be dumb, in all the senses of that short, wide, blunt word.

When Subject and Verb disagree, no one is glad.

No one.

And sometimes, the disagreement sulks just under the placid surface of the pond of our prose like an ugly family secret hidden from all eyes.

Oddly enough, the Parts of Speech, so eloquent on other occasions, remain silent in the face of slightly submerged faults. This is when you step in and make things manifest and fix all errors. To do this, you will need tips and tricks.

Here are a few --

■ Notice that I said **Subject**, not **Noun**. The subject of a sentence can be any one of a number of things other than a simple noun referencing a person, place, or thing, or animal, vegetable, or mineral. Phrases in particular can act as nouns.

For example --

Of Mice and Men deserves a place on your bookshelf.

■ It is true right now and likely to continue as true in the future, as it was in the past, that the subject of a sentence will never be found in a prepositional phrase. This bear trap with bone-shattering jaws awaits your blundering step in its direction. For an example we need go no further than what I wrote a moment ago --

> Oddly enough, the Parts of Speech, so eloquent on other occasions, remain silent in the face of slightly submerged faults.

The actual subject of the sentence is **Parts**, and the functional subject of the sentence is **Parts of Speech** taken as a phrase acting as a noun.

The real subject of the sentence?

Flip a coin and take your pick.

The important thing here is that the noun **Speech**, falling within the prepositional phrase **of Speech**, cannot stand as the subject of the sentence. The subject is plural, not singular.

All verbs should make a note of this, and you can, too.

■ The subject of a sentence can be the presence of an absence. That is, the subject of a sentence can be assumed by the context. For example, I could say --

> Am I right?
> You know that I am right.

Or I could simply say --

> Right?
> Right.

... and you would know the meaning, and the subject, of the sentence by the kind of detective work that anyone who speaks or writes knows how to do without thinking about it.

■ Finally, in a few cases you must make a choice, if pressed, or if you are diagramming sentences. Is the subject of the sentence the noun **Parts**, which gets the nod by function, or the phrase **Parts of Speech**, which gets the nod by its function as a noun phrase?

Oddly enough, the Parts of Speech, so eloquent on other occasions, remain silent in the face of slightly submerged faults.

Usually, no one will give a rip.

. . .

The question of subject/verb agreement makes my list of **the top ten things that make writers look dumb**. There are two reasons for this.

The first reason is this. Many readers – the better ones -- will judge you by subtle things such as subject/verb agreement.

The second reason is this. When I was a young copy editor, our Editor one fine day called the news editor and copy editors into his office and gave us an ultimatum. The next person, the Editor said, who allowed an error in subject/verb agreement to appear in the lead paragraph of any story printed in the paper would be fired. The five of us took this threat seriously. The Editor was a vain and proud man whose social skills were eclipsed by his my-way-or-the-highway style of management. No one of us (and **that** chunk of speech -- no one of us -- is a good example of the problem we copy editors were dealing with) doubted that the Editor was deadly serious.

As much as I disliked his threat, I also felt embarrassed.

We copy editors did what we could to amend our faults of the past, We conducted side conversations and general conversations about troublesome lead sentences, especially for the first week of sudden-death copy editing that followed that visit to the Editor's woodshed.

Several things became apparent --

■ Lead sentences that included the word **one** were to be hunted down and recast. For example --

Nobody and no one -- none of us -- wanted to be fired.

The pitfall in this example is that the sense of a word like **nobody** was the equivalent of saying **no body** -- one could argue that this is a singular subject. The alternative phrase **none of us** is a tricky way of saying the equivalent of **no one of us.** Also, in effect, singular rather than plural. Remember, nouns inside prepositional phrases such as **of us** will never be the subject of the sentence.

The extreme example was not the kind of thing that any of us wanted to fight for, with the Editor, even if we were right.

We could be right but end up wrong, at the Editor's whim.

For example, consider these two alternatives --

None wants to be fired.

And --

None want to be fired.

The word **none** is a functional contraction of the phrase **no one** (a singular noun phrase). That was the correct version, not **None want to be fired** (which is the same as saying **No one want to be fired**, which puts subject and verb in disagreement. Each of us on our own decided to simply recast any such sentence rather than run the risk of debating points of grammar or usage with the Editor, who was of the school that said you win all arguments with those you have power over by escalating by any means necessary until the point is carried.

The take-away is this. If you look at a sentence and suspect that it is in error, rewrite the sentence in a way that you can prove is correct, at least to your own satisfaction.

As we went through that first week of post-threat fear and trembling, we copy editors noticed others words and phrases that deserved banishment or recasting. For example --

Two inches of snow is the forecast.

If confronted with this sort of lead sentence to a news story, we might have quit on the spot and switched our line of work. Two inches ... is it an **it** or an **are**? If you get it wrong in the eyes of the Editor, right or wrong you know the probable penalty. And notice, too, that the example has an inverted structure -- it can be argued that the subject is **the forecast** but the structure of the sentence has been turned inside out, making the copy editor's job difficult indeed. The best fix is to rewrite the sentence like this --

The forecast is for two inches of rain.

That makes for a clearly singular subject that demands a singular verb. Done.

Some of us argued that the order in which the words appear is the ruling factor, leading to the absurd but technically, they said, correct version being this ---

Two inches of snow are the forecast.

The rest of us had two things to say about that.

■ When you fix a sentence to be correct but also make the sentence sound absurd or look ugly, you need to recast the sentence rather than fix it by the book.

■ The phrase "two inches of snow" is a single idea and thus must be treated as a singular subject. Although we were on solid ground here, none of us wanted to debate the choice with the Editor. That snowball had a rock tucked inside it.

Thinking about this sort of thing led me to the **Jack and Jill Test**. If you can substitute **Jack and Jill**, a known plural subject that is the equivalent of **they**, you have a plural subject that demands a plural verb. For example --

None of us wants to be fired.

... becomes ...

Neither Jack nor Jill wants to be fired.

The following sentences by this test would also be correct --

Jack does not want to be fired.
Jill does not want to be fired.
Jack and Jill, as a team, do not want to be fired.
Neither Jack nor Jill, as individuals, wants to be fired.

■ ■ ■

In the end, no one of us copy editors was fired (or, **in the end, no one of us copy editors would lose his job**).

What happened was a gang of language outlaws learned how to work together despite in many cases loathing one another. We also had a lot of fun talking about Jack and Jill in some funny situations. And mean old Mr. Editor had to find other ways to be our Lord and Master Even Unto Death.

In short, a good time was had by all.

This is my final thought on the subject -- if you can, have fun with your editing efforts.

If you find that you cannot have fun in this fashion, build into your budget the cost ($25 to $75 per hour) of hiring someone who will both have fun fixing your writing and take your cash.

Or accept that the work of editing yourself, though the equivalent of eating dirt, is still less sickening than watching some stranger play with your writing and your gold.

No one really wants an outcome like that.

This just in: My copy now is clean

I started this book project about a year ago, with one goal from the start -- address the dirty copy issue that so many print-on-demand and electronic books suffer from. I wanted to make that problem my own and offer a solution for all. Sounds grandiose, but that was my goal. In setting such a goal, I set myself apart from the dirty masses and made them out to be the asses.

After all, I would be the one with then clean-copy solution.

I was angry. I bought an eBook that promised to teach me how to sell my books. All I remember, now, is all the typos and grammar/usage mistakes. My wife told me about a popular thriller writer's latest book, published by one of the big-name houses in New York City.

Same problem. Mechanics.

I got a copy of the thriller, hoping to put another poison arrow in my quiver. I decided that the thriller writer had demanded upon the strength of several best-selling books that the original back-story manuscript be published, presumably to do something for his ego.

It is common for writers who score big to make such demands about book manuscripts that got no respect in their early days.

The big house printed the thriller writer's manuscript, warts and all. Each page has its own little embarrassment. No editor was harmed, threatened, or even present for the making of this typo-ridden book.

As we say in the Church biz, be careful what you pray for.

Thriller writer got the gold mine; readers got the shaft.

I decided that I was going to give writers tools to build better worlds than the ones I was encountering. I was reviewing, editing, recasting, and proofing my own novel manuscript – **The Mystery Man Murders**. I was more determined than I ever have been to produce clean copy. When I finally published the novel in December 2011, after four years of solitary confinement with the manuscript, I was confident that I had a clean specimen. Instead of a mere workboat, I had crafted a museum piece out of hull cloth.

Then I began to get feedback of a different sort.

One early reader of my novel, a church friend whom I had given a complimentary copy, told me that he saw a number of typos but had not marked them. He remembered seeing about a dozen typos.

I considered paying him to re-read the book and flag the typos, but I was not willing to create a dual relationship. The only right relation with this person was person and pastor. My faltering resolve was made firm when my wife, also under the same ethical imperative concerning dual relationships (we are co-pastors of this congregation), spoke against the idea.

I began to repent of my high-horsey attitude toward the mistakes that others, who actually received cash advances, had rushed into print. I was, I told myself, with some heat and a good deal of scorn, no better. In fact, I was worse. Rather than seeing this as evidence of low self-esteem, I saw it as accurate. I resolved to re-read the manuscript myself until I found those typos. This time, I said sternly to self, no nodding off in the middle of sentences.

Me, myself, and I knew the probable outcome.

I love my own words with an extravagance that is only matched by my inability to stay awake after an hour or so of editing those words, golden though they be.

While this fond hope of staying awake and being ever watchful while self-editing fed my fantasy life, my brother-in-law, without my knowing, was making a list of my boo-boos – a spreadsheet, no less – and checking it twice. He emailed me a treasure map that told me just where to dig. He had found twelve typos, one of which was more than my usual fault of dropping the final letter in a word that still passed the spellchecker but did not make any sense. I had said **confident** when I meant to say **confidant**. I know better; my fingers, however, are mindless in their scurrying around the keyboard like a bored-silly squirrel in a cage.

Why do I single out this one mistake of twelve?

No one else would know that I knew the difference between **confident** and **confidant**. I was at some level mortified.

I also at some level tend toward the dramatic.

Beside the twelve typos and where they lay, my brother-in-law gave me some thoughtful editorial suggestions.

In sum, priceless.

That was the word that came to mind as I made the fixes and uploaded new files to the various virtual places that my novel is available for purchase.

Priceless.

When I did the math of comparing his finds with my church friend's impressions, I decided that my book was most probably, and at long last, clean.

What a relief.

Writers who go the traditional route cannot make changes as easily as print-on-demand writers can. The high-tech printing press that puts out our POD books does so in about a New York minute, and we can bespeak as few as one copy at a time.

From order to boxed and shipped – less than 24 hours.

Those of us who do our own publishing work can fix a problem in less than 24 hours, with most of the time being the lag between uploading a new file, and getting the all-clear that the new file will indeed fly, from production traffic controllers at places like Amazon and Smashwords. Although traditional writers cannot do this high-speed fixing, their minders usually produce clean copy the first time. Otherwise, the only chances to make fixes come with later printings. If there are no later printings, the errors stand for all to see, forever.

In the case of that thriller writer, it was a matter of *who knew? I forgot that gaffes are a petty crime against readers.*

No fixes on the fly there.

By printing a book with a dozen dumb errors in it, I felt like I had failed in a fundamental way, and I expected to feel that way after I finally received, passively, a way to fix the problem.

Not so. I feel grateful and humbled, and I have a renewed confidence in my novel. It now is the best book that I could write, when I wrote it. As I reviewed the formatting of the newly fixed and uploaded book file, in a desktop utility that emulates the turning of pages, a father's fond smile dawned on my face.

I am so grateful for my brother-in-law's support. All I did was give him a copy of the book, as a Christmas gift. He did the rest, quietly and completely. I emailed him as follows – *I love you in all caps, man!*

He doesn't always check email, but he will read this.

As one with an editor's eye, I sometimes will alert bloggers and writers to problems that I encounter in their work. The response varies. Some say *thanks, I needed that* and some say nothing at all. The hard thing for me is busting past my own self-talk. I easily convince myself that people will see me at best as a tight-ass and at worst as a mean, negative pick-sniffer. The argument that works for me, against me, is realizing that I would want to know if my blog post or novel or whatever had errors that I could fix if someone would simply show to me the kindness of the stranger.

I encourage you to alert others in a frank and friendly way about errors that you find, especially if you only find a few.

You can start with me.

I still don't know what to say to a writer whose copy has more wrong things in it than right.

I'm working on that, in recovery.

Jerks and quirks: Stuff I do cuz I can

Setting aside the examination of actual errors, let us take up the subject of apparent errors.

Such as *cuz*.

As in *Jerks and quirks: Stuff I do cuz I can*.

It just looks wrong, almost.

What I did in choosing *cuz* was to think of the word **because** and reject it, since it is a word that I overuse. I wanted to introduce an apparent error right away, and I think that *cuz* works well here. It is a bastard contraction of **because** and as such should rightly be rendered as **'cause**. This I rejected as being about as stirring as an all-white church choir singing operatic versions of negro spirituals. I moved on to **cuz** and dropped the apostrophe. After all, I was by now in the land of coined words and could do as I would.

The working title for this essay was ***It's My Bleeping Book/Blog/Website, or IMFW***. In earlier days of the Internet, you might have seen the acronym ***IMFW*** alongside such old favorites as ***IMHO***, ***YMMV***, and – my favorite – **RTFM**. Since I am bound (another example of stuff I do cuz I can) to avoid four-letter words of a frank nature, in view of my work in the Church, you might be better served to Google any of these acronyms that you don't know or cannot puzzle out. My use of the word **bleep** to mark such occasions does not move you any closer to understanding ***JFGI***.

Just Bleeping Google It does not honor the original.

One of the joys of walking on the waters of language is knowing where the barely submerged rocks reside. When you know the rules, the bending or breaking of the rules becomes second nature. And let us face it, you are free to do as you will. My one bit of advice is to count the cost of your choices when it comes to bending or breaking the rules and conventions of grammar and usage. Know what rules you are breaking.

Language itself, in its constant tumbling in the marketplace of writing and speaking, changes again and again without end. When a variation gains widespread use, the grammarians among us call the result an ***idiom***.

An idiom is a slang phrase that has moved uptown.

You are free, here too, to choose whether you will use idioms or not. In your doctoral dissertation, you probably will avoid most idioms and related forms such as slang and four-letter words of a frank and startling nature.

Once you can call yourself ***doctor***, you can cuss like a trucker if you choose to, particularly if you have tenure.

Dr. John Bremner was a master of the startling phrase.

When Bremner said, ***Balls*, cried the Queen, *had I but two I would be King!*** I paid attention. At the same time, I have yet to explore than amusing phrase in my preaching.

Not only do we make choices about rules and conventions concerning words and phrases, but we also make choices about typography and style.

For example, the book that these suggestions about grammar and usage will be part of will be printed in ***Bookman Old Style***.

Why? Well, it pleases me and so I chose it, when I was wearing the hat labeled POD publisher. My first novel is printed in a sans serif typeface called **Trebuchet MS**. Why? It pleased me to challenge the Old Saw that says serif typefaces, the ones with all the little index marks, are easier to read. I wanted to form my own opinion based on a book-length sample. I liked the choice of Trebuchet.

A good example of a serif type would be **Times New Roman**.

This sentence is rendered in **Times New Roman.**

This sentence is rendered in **Trebuchet MS.**

This sentence is rendered in **Bookman Old Style.**

Notice how the Bookman Old Style, though a serif type, is also lively and lyrical, especially when compared to the old and tired Times New Roman. The Trebuchet is lean and strong like a gymnast. The point, however, is that I get to choose the typeface that I use, and I get to challenge long-held conventions about typography. It helps that I have a nodding acquaintance with typefaces, since I am determined to do something bold.

While I break one rule, I do adhere to another rule of typography, that a book or newspaper or a slinger that you put under all the windshield wipers of all the cars on your street must be confined to one typeface for the body type and one typeface for the headlines and such. I generally confine myself to a total of two typefaces but form a variation by using the headline type as the type for the indented material. I could easily break this rule and use a different headline typeface on each page, but the result gives a book an air of freaky holiday, which is seldom in sync with content.

Another rule that I bend and/or break is to shun the use of italics in favor of bold plus italics.

For example –

This sentence is rendered in italics.

This sentence is rendered in bold plus italics.

There are two reasons for my choosing to use bold plus italics rather than the traditional italics alone –

■ I cannot pick up italics easily on a computer screen. By adding the bold, I can see the words treated this way and I still can understand at a glance that the bold plus italics means the same as italics does in traditional printed materials. I also think that italicized words on the computer screen look more pixilated and TSR 80-ish than the bold alternative.

■ The addition of boldness makes the page look more interesting and lively for the reader, who needs all the help he can get from the writer and typographer to maintain interest in a world that spins much more quickly than once it did. I am such a reader. I read fat, boring paragraphs only if the material will be covered in the next pop quiz.

I could add a third reason. I do these things cuz I can.

My use of journalistic paragraphing is a choice that I make that is related to this idea of helping the reader stay awake, alert, and engaged. It helps to know the rules and conventions. In general, formal writing will make use of paragraphs that start with a periodic sentence of subject followed by verb that states the assertion or aim of the paragraph to follow. Such paragraphs end with a sentence that sums up what has come before. A hint of whimsy is tolerated here, but only just.

Pity, that, but formal is in the end formal.

A journalistic paragraphing style will make use of single-sentence and even single-word paragraphs to highlight the important or amusing stuff.

Really.

Journalistic paragraphs usually won't rattle on for more than a few sentences before a new paragraph begins.

By contrast, my copy of the stylebook aimed at psychologists says that one will not use single-word or single-sentence paragraphs. One will not use single-word sentences. Ever.

Fine.

I have sought to mix the two paragraphing styles.

You will be the judge of the effectiveness or lack thereof.

Many so-called rules have long-since been retired, such as the rule that forbids one to end a sentence with a preposition. Sir Winston Churchill, who did as much to save the language as he did to save the free world, had this to say about that –

That is something up with which I shall not put.

Another venerable rule for writers and speakers says that one must keep the parts of a verb together.
For example –

To go hopefully forward ...

... becomes ...

To go forward hopefully ... .

Following the rule makes of a phrase that has poetic and metaphorical possibilities become a phrase of plodding banality.

My advice? If your copy editor is a slave to the rules, find another copy editor. Especially if you write fiction. Being right by the rules is wrong when the music of the sentence dies. Characters don't always speak the King's or the Queen's English. Narrators of fiction can and should vary in their training in grammar and usage.

There are a number of rules and conventions of typography that do not make sense to me. I put a space before and after ellipses ... and if the ellipses end a sentence, I add another space followed by a period ... . The traditional approach...is cramped in my view, and the use of four periods like birds on a wire to denote the end of a sentence seems nutty to me....

Traditional typography makes use of **em dashes** and **en dashes** and jams everything together—a practice that gives me claustrophobia. I use two hyphens -- and I put a space before and after. My software usually jams the two hyphens together and I just go with that.

I use typography to help the reader, not to punish her.

I use a dash instead of a colon, in most cases where I want to set off examples.

For example:

My eyes simply do not see colons in type.

Same goes for semicolons; I rarely use them for fear of losing them.

What I want you to take away is a sense of the freedom that can come from assuming the yoke of rule and convention for an initial period like an apprenticeship. Once you know as much as your elders know, you can play with that knowledge, and all will be pleased.

If you break rules like a mom who runs over the bike in the driveway because she is too tired to see it, your elders will be more likely to frown than to smile.

There is a joke about a priest, a rabbi, and a minister. The three holy men decide to go fishing. The priest and rabbi, as old hands in the community, want to get to know the young minister who has just recently come among them.

So they go fishin'.

After a few hours in the rabbi's boat, the priest announces that he feels the call of nature and must seek a bathroom. He calmly steps over the side of the boat and walks over the water to the shore.

The young minister is startled, to say the least.

After the priest returns, the rabbi makes the same trip, over the water to the shore, to answer the call of nature.

After the rabbi returns, the young minister decided that if his colleagues, who after all believe in the same God as he does, can walk on water, he should be able to do so as well, particularly if he makes of his faith a platform and steps out upon it.

Or so he tells himself.

However, when the young minister steps over the side, he finds no footing and sinks into the water, over his head. When the priest and rabbi fish him out of the water and place him back in the boat, the minister sputters a question.

Why couldn't I do what you did?

Ah, says the priest, **it helps to know where the rocks are**.

To which I would add, **Let those with ears, hear**.

Signpost words - marking the straight way

Some words, be they ever so small and shy, provide a big service – they serve as signposts for the reader. Many writers take away these little words when they should be adding them to mark the path to understanding in the dark forest where the reader can become lost. The writer's task is to provide good guidance. If a reader gets lost, it is the writer's fault. That is the unspoken rule, or covenant, or contract.

Even if you the writer won't see this and sign on --

- You are the guide.
- The reader is in your care and follows you in trust.

One of my mentors, a wise man who guided me during seminary, was fond of using the image of a massage, and the image of the proper petting of cats, when he talked about how to lead. In both cases, he said, you keep one hand on the person or cat at all times. This is for reassurance and for being grounded to avoid static electricity.

Think of what happens when you pet a cat on a dry, windy day in spring. Or when you reach out to touch your cat, with love, on its wet little nose.

Sparks fly.

It amazes me that my cats allow me to touch them after a few of these poorly grounded incidents.

Perhaps readers are like cats. You maybe can get away with startling them in unpleasant ways through inattention.

I doubt it.

Cats, as smart as they are, cannot form the thought-with-powerful-feelings-in-tow that goes like this --

How dare you!

Cats can't, but readers can.

If cats could read, our readers would adore us in exchange for treats. Our readers have less adoration and make more demands on us than our pets do.

The best practice for writers flies in the face of the rigid rules that writers have received, or embraced, or introjected from self-sealed, so-called experts of the dim past. To help readers stay on the path, you must be sure that certain words such as **that** are present in longer sentences.

For example --

He said that writers need to be kind to the little words and that those little words have a big job to do.

About now, many of you will become aware of a voice in your writerly head that says --

Write tight. Remove extra words. Search and destroy.

Like most inner voices, this voice batters you with stern advice that actually has some merit. The problem comes with the extra zap of static electricity. That jolt has the effect of forcing compliance at the cost of making your brain go flat. All you care about is being compliant lest you get held up to the class as a dunce. Maybe you experienced that fear often enough to make you a good little writer who always follows the rules and who never does dumb things that make you stand out from the rest of the class.

What writer wants to blend in and not be seen or heard?

Raise your hand. We will ignore you.

The drive to conform runs over the one who desires the benefits of conformity -- it's a form of auto-abuse. Some so-called expert made sure that you would continue to inflict upon yourself her harsh rules after she was long dead and gone.

Instead of watching out for the reader, in fear you watch out for yourself. This, my friend, is crazy, and this, my friend, is something that all writers do. The saving grace appears when you can see what you are doing and stop.

Here is the way to get out of this impasse over whether to leave in or take out the little words that create and maintain the rhetorical structure of your sentences. When you hear yourself spouting rules that others have forced upon you, stop like a mule. Sit in the crossroads. Refuse to move. Say **hee-haw** if you wish. Just do not continue down someone else's narrow-minded path. Do not move until you have made your own decision about the rules thundering in your head.

The story is told of the baseball pitcher who suddenly stops and simply stands on the mound. He looks at the two runners on base who are there through a combination of his poor pitching and some fielding errors. The catcher calls time out and runs out to the mound. He demands to know why the pitcher won't pitch.

If I don't pitch it, the pitcher says, **they cain't hit it.**

I will be the first to agree that becoming mulish is not the entire strategy here. Sitting down and refusing to act on someone else's rigid rule is a way of reminding yourself to think for yourself. The next step is to identify the rule in question.

Write tight. Remove extra words. Search and destroy.

You just know in your bones that this voice in your head hates words like *that.* Such words, being optional, must die.

The next step is to ask yourself, ***Have I ever at any level questioned this rule?*** If the answer is no, the next step is to question that rule, right now.

Why must I always remove words that aren't necessary?

When might I want to add words that seem unnecessary?

How can I restate the rigid rule in more helpful terms?

If you follow the steps, if you question authority to the end, you will arrive at the conclusion that there will be times to remove and times to include words that may seem to be unnecessary. Optional does not mean unnecessary.

Now. Here is my view on those words, which are usually small and unassuming in their size (but not in their intent), and which give the reader critical guidance at confusing points.

These are some categories of signpost words --

- Parallel constructions.
- Synonyms (or not).
- Redundant words that say things twice.

Parallel constructions

The world would be a simple place if writers would stick to sentences having a subject followed by a verb followed by a direct object --

```
See Jane Run.
Run, Jane, Run.
See Tom hit the ball.
See Spot run after the ball.
Run, Spot, run.
```

Most writers will vary the tone, length, and structure of their sentences, and this laudable goal will quickly find the place of impasse if the writer ignores the importance of signpost words. A long sentence with inadequate and partial attention to signpost words is like a guide who gives you a box of matches when you arrive at a branching of three paths in a cave. Good luck, he says, and runs out on you.

For example --

I want you to know when you are breaking a rigid rule, and I want you to know what your own and not someone else's opinion is in the matter. You, too, are an expert.

When you want to be very, very clear about something, the best approach is to repeat yourself to set up a cadence of authority for the one whom you seek to educate. Not only will you repeat words, but you also will repeat phrases.

Can you stand it?

If you take out some or all of the repeated words -- the signpost words -- sense will fly out the window like a bird on the wing.

For example, to edit the example above, which has signposts --

I want you to know when you are breaking a rigid rule and what your own opinion is.

This is the sort of sentence that one writes when one allows someone else to rule their writing. **Do not repeat the same word in a sentence**, the voice in your head thunders. **Do not use unnecessary words. When in doubt, take it out!**

When in doubt, take it out is a poor way to write sentences that readers can follow to the end. As the mighty poet Dante says, **In the journey of the middle of our life I came to myself in a dark wood where the straight way was lost.**

And what does Dante do? He takes on a guide.

Look at the sentences in question. The first sentence is sturdy in a subtle way, like a stool with four legs. The second sentence with signposts removed is vague, though on the surface it is a sentence and not a fragment. The words that were removed were optional by rule (but crucial to sense). The fault is that I have removed one of the four legs of the stool without rearranging the remaining three legs in a three-point stance for stability. If your reader sits on this three-legged stool, she will end up on the floor.

I have weakened the structure of my sentence, which in turn has muddied the tone of the sentence. By weakening the formal structure of parallel elements, or clauses, (**I want you to know**), I have discounted the expert tone that I wanted to use. The alternative sentence is shorter, yes, and vague. And absolutely banal and irritating, like a warm spit bath on a hot, dry day.

If I go with the shorter version of the sentence, I will give away the power of my convictions so I can please some rhetorical jerk who moved on a long time ago.

The reader seeks a feast but gets a snack.

Synonyms (or not)

It may sound like heresy to you, but repeating words rather than taking out words is usually the better choice. One famous example comes from the book *The Careful Writer* by Theodore M. Bernstein. He cautions us to avoid **synonymomania**.

For example --

> *I went to the garden shed to grab a* **shovel,** *but my son had taken my* **spade** *with him to use at his house, so I went next door and borrowed Bill's* **earth-turning implement.**

One must not ever repeat the same word in a sentence. Right?

This is an extreme example, I grant you. For everyday errors of this sort, listen to the news on the radio or television.

For example --

> Europeans are worried today about the Euro. It seems, the experts tell us, that the common currency is facing some new problems. And these experts add that the beleaguered coin of the realms may never be the same after all is said and done.

Your mileage may vary, but I would much rather hear the same word -- Euro -- twice in that sentence, or even three times. Circumlocutions take us to the edge of the circle and away from the point. Being specific, by repeating the key words, keeps the reader's feet dry. Circumlocutions put the reader's feet right in the mud at the side of the path.

A final example --

> Word surfaced today that the President has made an unannounced trip to Afghanistan.

> The leader of the free world arrived in the war-torn nation just after midnight, sources say.

I have seen benighted editors and reporters help one another think up these crazy circumlocutions.

Talk about your air of freaky holiday.

Redundant words that say things twice

This is where you can take away words and leave a sentence in better shape than when it started out. And if you occasionally fall into the error of repeating yourself unnecessarily, it is not a large deal. Your reader will either not see the small fault or will readily forgive you.

However, if you say things like the **circular ball**, the flat **pancake**, the **thin veneer**, or the **tiny blip**, one after another, the reader may decide to quit you and move on to someone who knows how to write tight in the best meaning of that phrase.

You are being redundant when you add detail that is already included in a word's definition.

For example --

Haven *vs.* safe haven.

A haven, by its dictionary definition, is a safe place. If you say **safe haven**, and you will do so if you think it is the right choice because everyone says it that way, you have fallen into not one but two errors. You have 1) been redundant and 2) jumped out the window after all your loser friends.

And that is not all. You have implied that there is such a thing as an **unsafe haven**. Why would you specify that some havens are not, er, safe but unsafe?

If you suspect a redundancy, turn the phrase around and see if the opposite makes sense. If it doesn't, fix it.

If your word choices and your excising of helpful words make your readers sit down in the crossroads like mules and **hee-haw** about what you might have meant, and about where the path continues, be certain that that is the response that you want. Maybe you think that your readers will thank you for their long, floppy ears and braying voices.

Your reader is right behind you.

Lead or get out of the way.

Inclusive language – BOMFOG under attack!

I love the acronym **BOMFOG**, which stands for **Brotherhood of Man, Fatherhood of God**. If ever there was a bombastic acronym, BOMFOG has to be at the top of the short list.

Long-standing and now-leaning rules of grammar say that when referring to persons, one must use the male pronoun forms to indicate mixed-gender groups.

The debate over this in the Church goes by the label **inclusive language**. The wider debate gets folded into the overworked phrase **culture wars**.

No one fights more fiercely than Christians among themselves, in my view, so I pick up the narrative there.

In the Church, matters of the male-as-genderless pronoun have importance on two levels. The first question is how to treat biblical references to persons. The second question is how to treat biblical references to God.

If church talk of any sort gives you the fantods, you may go now. But I do hope that you will stay. I'm not your mama's churchman (don't even know her). Plus this is good stuff.

I know one minister who would argue with anyone who thought that inclusive language is a load of crap or a serious challenge to traditional authority. She was fired from her first church over this very subject. Church people, it seems, feel strongly about their male pronouns.

To use another trite phrase, this was a hill like Calvary that she was willing, and did, die on.

In the wider culture, inclusive language takes on other labels. We talk about the fitness of using the male pronoun for all uses that refer to both men and women – words such as **mankind**, which can yield to **humanity** with little fuss. Or to give a specific example, in sentences like this –

Every person should be free to worship at the church of his choice.

When this sort of restrictive sentence surfaces during worship when my wife and I are sitting together (which happens seldom, since we serve different congregations at the 11 o'clock hour on

Sundays) I lean over and whisper, **Sorry, Honey, just the guys, I guess. Better luck next time**.

Which brings us to the crux of the debate, whether in the pews or on the streets -- the feminist critique.

Feminists, male and female, have fueled the fires of creativity concerning alternatives to using the masculine forms as also the inclusive forms.

Let it be stipulated between us that there is no grammatical alternative to pressing the masculine forms into this double duty. What we have are several ways of breaking the rules, a few workarounds, and at least one coined word.

Breaking the rules

Many of us, particularly in informal writing and speaking, will say something like, **Every person should worship at the church of their choice**. It is a flouting of the rule in question – the double duty of the male forms – but we really don't worry overmuch about that.

The challenge comes when we write for others or when we write formal things such as dissertations. Flouting the rules of grammar just isn't wise when a supercilious committee or a pompous boss or client is involved. The alternatives are to use constructions such as, **Every person should be free to worship at the church of his or her own choice**.

That alternative is grammar-legal, and banal.

Another alternative is to say, **Everyone should be free to worship at the church of their choice**.

Sticklers will insist that the apparently plural **everyone** is another way of saying **every one**, which is singular.

Soon we are beyond the banal and into the heart of the absurd.

his will happen when we apply rules to words, which like birds can be hard to keep in cages with rigid bars.

A few workarounds

Probably the best solution for one who is opposed to the use of the male pronoun to denote both men and women is to rewrite the sentence.

For example –

Where I go to church is my choice, and the same goes for you.

That is fine but has a different aim than a sentence concerning the church of one's choice. What started out as a philosophical utterance that is delivered over cigars and brandy has become loud words from atop a soapbox.

Another example of rewriting the sentence –

Every person should be free to worship at the church of one's choice.

This may work for some of us, but the tone has become snooty. Substituting **one's** for **his** distances the reader from the sentence, which had been emphatic in its rule-bound form using the male pronoun **his**.

Coined word – a penny for your thoughts

The one coined word that has been struck in this debate over word genders is **s/he** (or **(s)he**), which some of us advance as a better way of saying **he/she**, or **he or she** and related forms of that kind.

I suppose one would pronounce it **she-he** (with a never-ending wrangle over which gender gets the emphasis).

That sucks.

And that is a shame, because the faults s/he is trying to fix do need fixing.

■ ■ ■

Language as a changing art can and should be allowed to solve such questions through the way we talk to one another. We have not allowed the language to police itself in the way that all languages do, in the marketplace, at the dinner table, and upon the marriage pillow. Language drives mindlessly toward resolution of rule-bound concerns by finding compromises from among the things that real persons say to one another. This process can become political, and when it does some subset of the population, in this case, women, will suffer and continue to suffer consequences.

It is not acceptable to refer to half of the world's population using conceptual male forms when the persons in question are actual female forms. Just because it is **only words** does not make the debate any less sharp or important. I believe that language is a window into the soul, and if I am happy to call women men for some rigid rule that is man's and not God's, I am also going to be ashamed of myself and of my culture and of my church. To insist that we must follow the rules puts rigidity above equality and justice, and perpetuates social forms that continue to put women in the one-down position.

This is real, this is ugly, this is wrong.

That said, I tend to use the male pronoun when referring to God, even though I am fully aware of the many good arguments against this practice. I try to be sensitive to others but draw the line at the **Father/Mother God** approach. I do not see God as either male or female but I have the habit of calling God **he** in my sentences when I am not being very, very careful to be inclusive.

When I write liturgy, I will repeat **God** instead of using **he**, as in **... and God said to God's people ... .**

I do note the choice of the New Revised Standard Version of the Bible to leave masculine references to God as they are but to make the references to persons inclusive wherever possible.

For example **I will make you fishers of men** becomes **I will make you fish for people**. Even though the poetry dies a terrible death, I do welcome the change for political reasons.

The points to take away for you, the writer, and you, the editor, is that you either go with the rigid rule, choose alternative forms, or rewrite the offending sentence. This holds for formal expression. In informal forms, you can break the rule at will. In the end, in the marketplace or upon your pillow with the door shut and the lights out, you can say, **Every person should be free to make their own choices.**

As far as **s/he** goes, you already know my preference.

Words, all on their own, can topple kings and queens. Words can scar children for life. Words can create and maintain political and social forms that keep people down.

Do you know what the lion's share is?

Anything the lion wants.

What gender do you think that lion is?

A tale of two Toms and too many typos

The other day, I was admiring the postcard that I designed as a face-to-face marketing aid for my first novel. Of the 100 that I had ordered from an online printer, at least half were still in their little shipping box. The postcard really is quite nice, except for one smallish thing.

I misspelled **Grimoire** in big black display type.

A **Grimoire** is a book of spells.

A **Grimore** is a big book of boo-boos.

And just now, while writing this, I flipped the postcard over and found another instance of **Grimore**.

O wretched man that I am!

Who will deliver me from error?

When I began this **House of Verbs** book project, I fancied that I could be the exception to the rules that say –

A self-editing writer captains a ship of fools.

Old writers never die; they just choke on their typos.

A writer who edits herself has a fool for a backstopper.

After all, I was a prince among copy editors way back when, perhaps partly by my own report. I can fix copy and make it shine like grandma's pots and pans. I treat usage problems like dirty dishes. I scrub them until I can eat off of them.

I know almost all the typo-catching tricks, and I have learned a few here lately, but the first list of friend-generated typos and general glitches from my first novel totaled 14 (of which I quibbled with one). I revised all my formatted book files, uploaded them to Amazon, Barnes and Noble, and Smashwords, and declared my book clean and myself serene.

That work was from a list I got from Tom my brother-in-law and always faithful reader, who has been with me and my novel from before the beginning.

A second Tom (an old and dear friend and colleague in ministry) weighed in the other day with a two-page list of typos. Total overlap with Tom-BIL? Five. Quibbles from hapless author? One. Total typos on Tom-REV's list? A whopping 28.

Like Tom-BIL, Tom-REV gives out praise and encourages like a persistently gentle rain on a summer day.

Before you know it, you are drenched. And grateful.

Case in point. Tom-R's email bearing the bad news about typos said, *I am amazed that there are so few typos in a project this large*.

I thought to myself, *Baby, I'm amazed, too – at the number of typos that I missed.*

After looking at Tom-R's list, I am more confident than ever that the novel is clean. His list has few gaps, indicating a constant watchfulness from beginning to end. Added to Tom-B's work, the two taken together give me confidence.

In a phenomenon that I would liken to *the kindness of strangers*, I have been blessed by two close friends who believed in me enough to help me be better. If I were in my own employ, and had done work resulting in 37 missed typos, I would put me on a program and have a nasty weekly meeting, with fistfuls of printouts and red faces on both sides of the table.

The reality is that I'm OK, and I'm OK just as you are Ok. This is not a competition, and it is important, and my friends have made me shine brighter in the reader's eyes.

I could cry.

Actually, I did.

The point for you, my friend out there writing and editing and hoping and praying for a fine book and a good response, is this. Read your *quote* finished *unquote* manuscript through from end to end at least one time after you declare that the ms is whistle-clean. Pay or barter with someone you trust to read your manuscript with a cold and piercing eye. Release your book to the air and watch it fly away. Rely on the kindness of friends to give you lists of things that they notice like typos and the general run of howlers. Ask your friends to do this. They will.

In theological terms, sin boldly.

Let your zeal be your penance.

Theological note to self: Humility is a way, not a wallow.

And my one quibble with my two benefactors?

The two Toms, may they ever be blessed, flagged the same idiom – *as was* -- on p. 339 of *The Mystery Man Murders* in the trade paperback edition. They didn't like it. Both of them.

On p. 339, a character gets put in Witness Protection and gets a new name and new life. I refer to him as "(Joe Blow), *as was*".

It was a close vote, 2 to 1.

I will leave it in. After all, I am the expert.

Right?

Then I took a second look and decided to lose the comma and make it **as-was**.

Better, much better.

Winner, winner, chicken dinner.

We all win.

Capital crimes and offenses - big letters of the law

Of the many ways that we can offend one another with mistakes and miscues of grammar and usage, problems with capitalization land high on the list for some of us. The rest of us capitalize at will and seemingly without any particular reason.

If you want to know the rules and regulations, any grammar handbook will put you in a right relationship with your nouns. What I have to offer is advice on breaking those same rules and bending those rules, or making choices about those rules.

When I started as a copy editor, the Associated Press style book was a skimpy pamphlet -- like Little Egypt's dancing attire -- dressed in a scarf and a sneeze. The AP style guide was a chubbed-up loose-leaf book by the time I took Hemingway's advice and got out of the news business just in time.

What I got out in time to do was attend Seminary, with a bit of proofreading on the side.

Where once I was Down, now I was Up.

Up and Down the staircase

Newspapers use **Down Style**.

Academics use **Up Style**.

A good example of Down Style would be the headlines in most daily newspapers -- First word, caps, and proper nouns, caps, and the rest of the words lower case --

Man bites dog

A good example of Up Style would be the headlines in The New York Times, where all words except a few, and a few only, are capitalized --

All the News that is Fit to Print

If you are copy editing the work of reporters, you already know what to do and whom to follow. If you are writing for professors, the same applies. Your discipline has a style guide that you are expected to follow.

In a newspaper, a reporter will write --

The mayor of Buffalonya, in the opinion of many city hall wags, has all the personality of a human dial tone.

In Down Style, one must name a particular mayor before capitalizing --

Buffalo Mayor Joe Blowhardt gave an upbeat State of the City speech to an openly yawning crowd at city hall last night.

Notice that I leave *city hall* lower case but capitalize *State of the City*.

Welcome to *The Zone of Choice*.

More on that in a minute.

In a research paper about urban political currents, you would write --

The Mayor of Buffalonya, in the opinion of many observers at City Hall, has a distinctly flat affect. One would say that he is careful to a fault. Indeed, some liken his voice to a telephone off the hook.

In Up Style, it is enough to name the city to cap the *Mayor* (with or without the addition of a name). Same goes for *City Hall*, which is made proper by the context -- discussing the politics of a particular city.

When you find yourself in The Zone

The Zone of Choice (capped because it is a fanciful phrase; ditto for *The Zone*) is wider in Down Style. As you climb the ladder toward full-on Up Style, you will have to pick and choose your capitalized words as your choices narrow.

The halfway point between Up and Down is **Free Style**.

A word of advice.

Be consistent.

If you decide that city hall should be lower case if not paired with a particular name (such as **Buffalonya City Hall**), use the same thinking for any later constructions of this or similar sorts. If you cap City Hall, then cap Fire Department, Police Department, Mayor's Office, and City Dog Catcher.

Never mind if it looks odd and somehow cramped.

If you start down that lane, stick with your choices.

And do trust your instincts while you put your instincts under the bright light of skepticism.

Remember the watch word?

If your mother says she loves you, check it out.

Which brings up one of an almost infinite number of questions concerning when to cap and when to not.

I chose to make **mother** lower case in the watch word. There is no rule that binds me here that I cannot contradict with another expert opinion. I decided that the flow of the sentence would have stutter-stepped if I had capitalized mother.

Your mileage can and will and should vary.

The important thing is to be consistent.

Pick an expert, any expert

I have two reason for refusing to tell you all the rules and regulations about capitalizing words --

- Stealing the work of others is not nice.
- No two experts agree on all the particulars.

You can choose your experts from among the many who vie for your attention and your money. I got a 1950 Harbrace College Handbook of grammar and usage, well-used -- from Amazon the other day for less than $10, which included shipping. There are countless trade paperback-format handbooks that were printed much later.

Pick one and read it, memorize as much as you can, and go forth to sin boldly.

And consistently.

Your blog's nose is running ... catch it!

Now that I have your attention, and you are thinking that your blog just might have a head cold, we can talk about headlines, headings, and display type in general.

You are riding with an expert, if I do say so myself. From 14 years on the copy desk to countless hours spent blogging and web site construction and maintenance, to say nothing of the 300 plus blog headings in my first novel, I have been at the head of the class, dreaming up clever, accurate, compelling headlines of all stripes and types.

In my photoblogging and photo-posting to personal web sites in the past 10 years or so, I have validated time and time again just how important headlines are, even for the visual offerings. One friend raves about the headlines and cutlines far more often than he raves about the photos.

Look at it this way. If you label your blog posts without much thought, your visitors take away a negative message. As Shakespeare says, ***Nothing will come of nothing, Fool!***

Headlines (and let us just agree to use that word to describe headlines, headers, and all manner of display type, including book titles) must show up early and often if your hard work is to get a fair hearing. Maybe you have not realized this, or maybe you discount your ability to write headlines that dance and sing like faeries on Midsummer's Eve.

Break it down

The first decision to make regarding headlines is this. Is the story a hard-news story, a feature article, a public service announcement, an attempt to sell something, a satire, or some other category of writing. This is not a test. The test comes later, when visitors look at your headline and say, **Tell me more**, or, **I didn't know that**, or, **You gotta be kidding me; what do you think I am, a moron?**

At this point no one, not even your sainted mama, knows what you have written better than you do. Tell yourself what you intended to say, and check to see whether you were successful.

You are the expert.

The second decision to make is this. Given the goals that you have, what kind of headline would be best? If you write a blog post that shares a funny story from your childhood, you probably will not want to use a hard-news headline. Your better choices would be a straightforward, clever headline or a provocative headline.

For example, the headline that I chose for this discussion is of the provocative sort –

Your blog's nose is running ... catch it!

The beauty of a provocative headline lies in your visitors' inability to just back away from the crazy headline. You could no sooner **not** think about **red monkeys**.

I'm serious. Do **not** think about red monkeys.

What are you thinking about?

Just guessing, but I would say, **Red Monkeys**.

Or take the example of that little button at the bottom of a web site that says –

Don't hit this button.

That is a sore temptation, right there.

It is entirely possible that you hate this approach and feel used and manipulated. No problem, you can always write a straightforward, clever headline. Perhaps you know that your visitors would shun the former and embrace the latter.

I read a blog post a few days ago (by online writing/marketing coach Kristen Lamb) that had a headline that said –

I Miss Summer Vacation

Under the headline was a photoshopped picture of a gape-mouthed shark jumping up from a kiddy wading pool. The post was about what it was like to grow up, outside and soaking wet, in Texas. The headline did its job, aided by that precocious shark.

What might a provocative headlines do for Kristen's post? Try this –

Summer Vacation? Too much ain't enough

If the writer follows with a lead paragraph that sets a tone and explains the goals the post will satisfy, such a headline would be fine. After all, I do have it on good authority that **Too much ain't enough** is an old Texas saying.

Would that be better? Like this –

Too much ain't enough (old Texas saying)

I don't think so. That headlines moves us further from the writer's goals, not closer.

Try this –

Too much summer fun ain't enough

A bit better? I think so.

I yam what I yam

The strength of **I Miss Summer Vacation** comes from its honesty and its felt longing. A headline about missing a dead pet with a headline that says **I miss my Fluffy** would not interest me. I would bite, however, on a headline that says **I miss my dead cat**.

Why? Because you do not know what to expect from a blogger who would say something that politically incorrect. I would want to know more and would hope to be amused.

Popeye (**I yam what I yam**) knows who he is and who he is not. Popeye will be himself rather than someone else. As important as knowing your visitor is knowing yourself. The headlines will come quickly once you decide who you are, who your intended readers are, and what yours goals are for a specific blog post, story, or article.

For example –

Summer a big hit with popular blogger

... might be just fine for a profile piece, but I bet you could do better on an off day

That reminds me of one newspaper publisher whom I worked for. He decreed (and if you have not seen a pompous publisher do that, just imagine W.C. Fields saying, **Someone who hates small children and little animals can't be all bad**) ... he decreed that all reviews that ran in the newspaper would only state the obvious.

For example –

Review: Mozart played for local audience

Newspapers are not card games like poker, but if you do not have any respect for or belief in your headline writers, this is the sort of brain-dead thing you might decree, or you could decide to keep one card and ask for four new ones. That would be a bid for a type of flush. Works well if you have a crap copy desk. Doesn't work if you have a crap publisher.

The publisher, when pressed, said that since few headline writers could catch all the nuances of even a middling review, no one would get the chance to try their hand.

Do you think that the readers didn't get it when reviews suddenly began to have headlines like –

Review: Star Wars movie - The Empire Strikes Back

The publisher used a variation on **The Mushroom Theory of Management** (keep 'em in the dark and feed 'em manure) –

Keep 'em in the dark and call 'em crap.

Do not do this to those who visit your blog. They deserve to know right from the beginning what they are about to read, what your goals are, and what they might gain from going forward with you. If you ignore these questions, visitors will ignore your work.

Good mechanics are hard to find

It is probably a good thing that you do not leave execution up to a firing squad. No, you must personally pull the trigger on your headlines for your blog posts or go the absurd route of paying someone to do it for you. At the blog level, you are on your own, so you do not want to embarrass yourself. I don't file the names of writers who blog poorly. When their books come out, I am not that interested.

If you want to improve your blog post headlines, and your chapter headings and subheadings, and your book titles, there are steps to follow.

Go to a quiet place inside yourself after you decide what your goals are for the piece in question. Start playing with ideas. Allow your mind to wander. Listen for that clever inner voice that comes up with the startling ideas. Type in the best one as soon as you open your eyes. Look at the result as though you were a Martian (and if your friends assure you, frequently, that you are, so much the better). Look at the headline and story, and decide what someone else would see if this is what you decide to display.

This is how I write headlines, and it is no surprise to me that this is also how I write in general.

This is my advice. Write your headlines in the same way that you write. My way will not work for you. Yours will.

I trust my instincts when I write, based on my experience that I am generally reliable when it comes to writing down what pops into my mind. I know that I will do rounds of revising, so I trust myself from the beginning and am usually pleased with the result.

I yam what I yam. You cannot be me. No one else has ever had that as a goal, nor should you.

So who are you?

How do you write?

What kind of headlines do you see when you check your blog archives – good, bad, ugly? All of the above?

Welcome to the jungle. Don't look down. Watch your head.

How do you feel about *wordflay?*

I once won second place in a statewide headline writing contest for small dailys – one of the yearly categories of awards that the Associated Press handed out. The first-place winner was a colleague. Her strong point was thinking of a familiar phrase that fit the story and writing a simple headline that did not mix metaphors. She was dependable, and accurate. The award validated those skills.

You probably try to avoid clichés and trite phrases in your writing. Please nod your head, vigorously. This is a worthy goal for any writer. Be fresh and your readers will eat up what you place before them and ask for more. You may even try some wordplay ... an occasional pun, perhaps. If you do, you know that your readers will vary in their appreciation of such backassward antics.

When it comes to headlines, however, trade on your readers' deep cultural knowledge. Echo a favorite song, steal a book title or movie title, and pun your little heart out. Good headlines come from a slightly different place than good writing, and what is dull in the body is dazzling in the head.

For example, the best I came up with in that headline-writing contest was a six-column banner headline for a long feature article written by a newly arrived reporter who told the story of his roadtrip from the Northeast the Northwest in a rented moving van.

My headline –

From sea to sea, to see

I started with what can only be described, even by its mother, as a tired phrase that no one should use anymore, but I paired that with a new thing, **to see**, and the resulting echo was both engaging and descriptive. Punny, too.

I once spent a week on the copydesk of a metro newspaper in San Francisco that was evaluating me for a copy desk job. The best headline that I wrote, and the one that got an **attaboy** from my evaluator, was a one-column, three-line head for a three-paragraph story about an off-duty deputy who was hit by a car while he was jogging on a narrow road. The driver fled the scene; the deputy was Ok except for some bruises.

My headline --

Deputy runs
into trouble;
driver flees

The strength of this headline is that it is a hard news head that manages to also be clever but without ignoring the fact that the deputy was injured.

Notice, too, that the headline borrows, intact, a trite phrase – **runs into trouble**.

You have a second or two to hook your reader, who will move on or not, depending on your headline. It is the job of the lead sentence to continue the connection, but the first responder is the headline.

The funny thing about *ironic* and *iconic*

The funny thing about the word **ironic** is that everyone assumes the subject is **funny (but not funny haha)**. The funny thing about the word **iconic** is that everyone uses it like it was born this a.m., when in fact it is old and tired.

The thing to watch for here is unintended consequences.

I would recommend learning the definition of each of these tricky words, and I would recommend **not** using them except if and when you know what you are saying (in the case of **ironic**) and never (in the case of **iconic**). Some words were not meant to see the light of day (**iconic**) and some words were not meant to cover every situation related to everyday oddness (**ironic**).

To understand my reasoning, here are some definitions.

The meaning of *ironic*

My **Webster's II** says that irony occurs when a writer or speaker sets up a contrast between apparent and covert meanings. The irony is in the disparity.

A related sort of irony occurs in writing when the writer shares information with the reader that the characters do not have in hand, or some do and some don't. Mark Anthony's speech over Caesar's body, in Shakespeare's play, is an excellent example of dramatic irony -- Brutus is **an honorable man**, repeated far beyond what is appropriate to the situation, sets up the truth at the covert level.

My **OED** (two volumes, c. 1956, that are so big that I can only open them in bed) says that irony moves on sarcasm or ridicule.

"... the intent is the opposite of the meaning of the words used."
The Socratic teaching method, where the teacher pretends of be
ignorant of the answers of her questions, is given as an example.
Webster's II chimes in with the phrase "feigned ignorance".

The root of the word includes the Greek *eiron*, which means
dissembler.

The meaning of *iconic*

Out of the blue but having nothing to do with Superman, we
all of a sudden are labeling everything and everyone special as
iconic. If you stop and think about it, that is the opposite of what
the word means. An *icon* is something so widely used that
everyone knows its meaning at a glance and particularly when
the icon is small. That is why the symbols in computer operating
systems and software in general are called *icons.*

Banal, and small, not big and special.

Icons in religions offer a window into the eternal.

The distance between these two meanings can serve as a
warning for us.

My recommendation is to pick on another word when you
want to describe someone or something as the equivalent of a
bull-bitch tom-wallager (as John Steinbeck did in his novel
Sweet Thursday).

Calling something or someone *iconic* does not convey any
meaning worth bothering with; *iconic* has that in common with
the words *very* and *major.* What is the difference between a
major author and an *iconic author*, or between saying *I am
mad* and *I am very mad* and *I am very, very mad?*

You are better off saying what you mean, and if you don't
mean anything but a general comment about someone's
greatness, silence would serve your goals as well.

Of drama queens and kings

What better example of irony than a play of the Bard?

From the first moment that a character speaks an aside to the
audience, you see the process at work.

The confiding character, say a villain such as the halting but
dangerous Richard in the history play **Richard III**, offers the
audience a window into his darkness that the other characters

only sense, often just before being dispatched by Richard's paid assassins.

Fresh back from opening night at Buffalo's Shakespeare in Delaware Park, a free and outdoor venue, I continue to muse over the hisses and laughter that Richard evoked from us as he turned aside and gave us fresh insider information as the horrific story unfolded –

Now is the winter of our discontent
Made glorious summer by this son of York.

Richard shows us by his demonic offer of relationship just what he thinks of such a sonny day.

I also think of the short stories of the American writer O. Henry. In elementary school, I read **The Gift of the Magi**, where the husband buys hair combs for his wife by selling his pocket watch and the wife sells her hair to buy a Christmas gift – a watch fob chain -- for her husband.

That's irony that even a child can understand.

The special case of *that's ironic*

This phrase is so vague that you might say it is *very vague in a major way*.

Almost always, when a person says *that's ironic* the meaning is something like *that is odd*, *that is quirky*, or *that is funny but not funny haha*. For the one time in a hundred that someone uses *ironic* correctly in this construction, no one else, odds are, will know it. Except you.

So avoid it.

If you know your way around irony and you know that your intended readers do, too, go ahead and call things ironic. Otherwise, you would do as well to call such things *iconic examples of things that are odd/quirky/funny (but not funny haha)*.

Ironic is an iconic example of a word that is more sinned against than sinning. If you choose to sin, do so boldly.

Of fathers and daughters

My wife and I visited her brother and his family -- wife and daughter -- a while back in Washington D.C. While we all were in the car, full and satisfied from a Korean meal with lots and lots of tasty meats, I mentioned that I was writing a blog post about the words *ironic* and *iconic*.

Oh, Tom said, *Katie and I were arguing about the definition of* irony *just the other day*.

Fathers and daughters are prone to such things, I believe.

Oh, I said, *and what did you decide?*

Neither of the principals was willing to say.

Irony is like that. *Iconic* is not.

When the ear is critical, half-awake

Something that has changed for me, at least a little, is my attitude toward blemishes in the writing and speaking of self and others. That may sound like an elitist statement to you, but consider this fun fact to know and share.

I am my own worst critic.

Well, I used-to was, but after I went off on a Kindle author for selling a book with massive formatting problems, the honorific of **Worst Critic** hung in the balance until I read his scathing email and issued a contrite response.

That was a hard lesson, but I am learning from it, as we speak. I now consider myself to be fully into the never-ending process of recovery from the heartbreaking dis-ease (diss ease) of **Grammaticuss Narcissicuss.**

Being in recovery, the 12-Step experts say, is a never-ending process that shadows life itself. The cure is in the care that one takes one day at a time. For me, this means noticing but not necessarily acting on the never-ending feedback from my **Inner Editor**. He sits at the right wing of my consciousness, light-saber pencil in hand, ready to made a big, fat check mark beside any lapse in perfect expression that he hears or sees or witnesses as I imagine this or that, and write it down.

This self-critical port sniffer has one voice -- loud, snide, and self-righteous. As is true with the other parts of my personality, he offers a blessing and he offers a curse.

The blessing?

I am an excellent editor and off-the-cuff speaker. I seldom make great-big mistakes in my expressions. This has led to an income of gratifying size compared to effort, and I get lots of positive attention from readers, writers, and listeners.

The curse?

Waking or sleeping, the Inner Editor never sleeps. He makes no distinction between self and others, and he truly is one who never met a person he liked very much. His contributions are like a snowball in the face, and the nasty surprise is that he builds his snowballs around pebbles. The shock of the coldness is followed with the sting of the stone.

Could I walk away from my Inner Editor?

That is a question for you, too, and I will not answer that for either of us just yet.

Listening to the morning news

I am a big fan of National Public Radio news shows, particularly the morning segments. I wake to a radio alarm clock that is cranked up all the way to break through the earplugs that help me sleep the night away. As I wake and sleep and wake again, I listen to the news and features on NPR.

I notice the blemishes, and there are always blemishes.

Not a lot, mind you, but noticeable by their low frequency.

I would like to say that I am a big fan, but the truth is – I am a huge fan. Radio is an amazing and underfed medium, and NPR has maintained a level of excellence that satisfies, almost, my Inner Editor and the rest of me as well.

Perhaps you have an Inner Editor and have witnessed a lifetime of blessings and curses coming from that portion of personality.

Perhaps you have no idea of what I am speaking (in which case bless you for hanging on for this long).

However, I do believe that each person has an **Inner Something** that notices blemishes and shouts in the inner ear more frequently than you would like. If we factor in differences in nurture and socio-economic strata, we still will find that most of us -- with a stray sociopath in the water trying to manipulate us into fishing him out of the drink and making him captain of the lifeboat -- are sitting on the benches and pulling the oars like good little boys and girls while a cocky coxswain shouts well-timed abuse over our bowed little heads.

One of my mentors called this guy **The Zapper**.

When *perfect* is not good enough

When too much, rather than being not enough, as that Texas saying would have it (**too much ain't enough**), is just too damned much and is causing problems for you, what do you do?

Do you stifle that Inner Editor?

Do you placate that Inner Editor?

Or do you notice without judging that Inner Editor?

I have tried all three of these styles of personality maintenance and to tell the truth I still do. The big difference is that I do not get stuck anymore in one style. Stifling only makes him more shrill and more disruptive. Placating him means that a maniacal monotone is in charge of the inner orchestra.

So I notice and move on.

And I repeat this as necessary.

I am still working out the implications concerning my life as a writer and preacher and editor.

Stay tuned.

Hey, don't point that probe at me!

I suspect that it is time to talk about being suspicious.

By this, I do not mean that you should work on sticking out in a negative way.

What I do mean is that you need to suspect every word that you use of having a hidden agenda.

For example, here is a headline from the far past –

Agents probe Nixon's brother

Can you see the problem? No?

Imagine two G-men and a cattle prod, with a hapless guy assuming the touch-your-toes position.

That's what I'm talking about.

You would not want your readers to have that reaction if you used the word *probe*. Or if you did want your readers to have that reaction, then you want to be in charge from that direction.

Here is another example –

Forty million Americans use the condom.

Allow this sentence to produce an image in your mind. Can you see a line stretching into the distance, waiting to use that one condom? Here the unsavory joins the absurd to give you not one but two red flags of warning.

Certain words -- such as *suck*, *screw*, and *frick* -- demand careful use. Other words become monstrous only in narrow ranges, so be there when they try to go off the Rez.

Another subtle problem can come from the images that accompany your words. I once redid the Local News page to move a cute picture of a dog away from a news story about a child who was badly injured in a dog attack. The stand-alone photo sat directly above the news story, with a headline of the same width as the photo. The only indication that there was no relationship was a 1-point rule around the photo and cutline.

Look as well as listen, and do not stop being suspicious.

Puns are good, clean fun when you have a reasonable degree of control, but when the puns are unintended, embarrassment or worse can follow.

For example –

Her real name was Nancy, but all who knew her called her Gay.

Rewrite this before the stuff hits the fan. And do not assume that capitalizing Gay will be any sort of defense. You may not think that it is fair to be held to such a standard, but you will be, so be suspicious.

If a friends or colleagues have a problem with something that you wrote, listen to them, carefully, even if you think they are crazy, blind, and stupid to say what they are saying. You can take the advice or not, but do not fail to stop, listen, and review. If you are not certain, ask another friend or two for their opinions, but not in such a way that you signal to them what the **right** answer is. You are not trying to be right here. You are trying to be careful and respectful, and in control of your words. Sometimes you will need help.

Acronyms and the words they become

Watch your acronyms.
For example –

FUBAR

FUBAR can mean **Fouled Up Beyond All Repair**, but do not kid yourself. Many of your readers will know what the **F** actually stands for. You may choose to use the acronym anyway, but maybe not in a sermon.

The choice is yours to make, so you need to be informed.

Same goes for **SNAFU (situation normal all fouled up)**. Most of your readers will know the original, salty wording.

Yet another example is **PDQ**. Who among us would say that it means **Pretty Darn Quick**?

Darn it!

Another problem comes when an acronym enters the language as a word in its own right. What was once a clever abbreviation for a situation far from normal has become a **snafu**, a noun that means the same thing. If you do not know the history of the acronym, you will not be able to assess the word that it has become. You will not be in control of the undertones and overtones of the word.

I like the acronym **JFGI (just f-ing Google it)**, but I do not use it in my sermons. Same goes for **WTF**.

If your mother says she loves you

What we are talking about is a variation of the aforementioned copy editor's rule that says **if your mother says she loves you ... check it out!** If you find that you do not want to build in such cynicism to every breath that you draw as a writer, then pay some cynic to do this for you. I would rather be my own cynic, since I cannot afford to pay someone else to do this. Besides, I do not think there are many out there who could match my level of suspicion.

Suspicion, mind you, is not the same thing as paranoia. You can suspect all words and watch them closely, and not be paranoid. You would have to suspect the words of plotting to make you look bad before you could be called both suspicious and paranoid.

However, there is no sin in adding a dollop of paranoia to your lurking watchfulness over the words that you use. You can think like a paranoid person without being one. That would be a valuable skill, since you are paranoid only if no one is out to get you.

Read your writing like your grandma would. Or the Church Lady. Or any person likely to take offense. Then decide if you wish to offend or not. It helps to know who your readers are and what they will tolerate. In my case, I need to decide what a minister in public can write and speak. I have decided that I have more leeway in what I write as citizen Jon Rieley-Goddard, but not much. That is not as unique as you might think. Most of us know where the warning pass is and who stands there, ready to judge and to punish lapses in discernment.

You want to pick and choose the times that you fight for what you believe to be your right.

I wasn't thinking is not much of a defense.

Online is forever

One of the biggest reasons to be careful and thoughtful about the words that you use is the fact that anything you put online will be there forever. To assume anything else would be naïve. Recent timeline changes on Facebook are an example of a policy decision that modifies your choices without your having any control over the application of new standards. You can opt to hide anything from your timeline, but Facebook searches and displays all your posts prior to your review. You only have prior control over what you post to Facebook in the future.

The point is to be relentlessly careful and thoughtful.

If you choose to be provocative, be certain of your rationale.

Be the persona you intend, not some addlepated persona that emerges from a chaos of inattention.

Do be bold. There are too many boring writers already.

Your right to say what you wish far outstrips your desire to be held in good repute by those who know you and those who encounter you. I believe that I have the right to shout the F-word from any high place I desire, but I know that I do not have the financial resources to win that argument in certain professional quarters.

After this, therefore, because of that

I once used a four-letter word to make a point strongly in a post on a private blog shared among a handful of trusted colleagues. When we decided to go public and invite others to join the conversation, I chose to take down that post, but the damage was done. Another colleague had shared the content of the private blog with a committee that had power over all of us. As in the Facebook example, the choices of others can change your sense of privacy as well as fitness.

The trick is to anticipate the choices that others will make.

Which is impossible.

So pay attention. Learn from what you see.

It is a lot like online security. You learn of new phishing exploits and scams after the fact, but you pay attention and learn more and more to think like the most scummy spammer that you can imagine. You begin to notice certain patterns.

That is your best defense.

Careful, thoughtful, vital

My professional status abridges my right to shout anything I want from any place I choose, This reality, however, does not remove me from the ranks of writers who have something vital to say. I can make my points without using any word stronger than *bleep,* and you can, too.

If you show what you mean rather than say what you mean, you will be vital and interesting. The words are still your best friends, as they always were. That has not changed.

The words, however, will not stop being little tricksters.

Watch for the tricks and be the one who decides which ones will see the light of day.

The richness of language is its beauty, and you are a lover of that beauty.

Be like a lover. Stare at each word and burn it into your brain lest the blessing of beauty become a curse of murky thinking and sorry execution.

When Shakespeare said something like **off with their heads**, he knew that some trickster character was likely to pun on maidenheads. One assumes that where there was a Will, there was also a suspicious writer lurking in the way.

Go and do/be likewise.

Do be do be do.

Writers go through phases over phrases

You need to be in charge of your phrases.

You want to be idiomatic.

You do not want to appear idiotic.

Writers go through phases in connection with their use of phrases. Be one who fosters a permanent curiosity about where phrases come from and what they originally meant (since meaning, like sand, shifts with the winds and seasons).

Build on the solid rock of **LookItUp**.

A dictionary of phrases would be a good thing to have on hand. For two reasons. First, you will not easily (or ever, in many cases) find phrases listed as entries in your everyday dictionary. Certainly not by the first word or as an entry of the phrase intact. Phrases will usually be down in the body of the definition, or not. Second, a phrase-based dictionary goes into the history of each entry. I find this sort of thing to be interesting and tend to remember details. If you don't, the best defense is to Google your phrases to make sure you got the spelling right. And the meaning, too.

For example –

... in a pig's eye ...

How would you ever know, if you had not looked it up, just what a pig's eye has to do with anything? My Webster's II mentions **pig in a poke** and gives a definition (an offer that conceals important information). No mention of **in a pig's eye**.

One citation I saw by Googling says that pigs have small eyes, lending something small-minded to the meaning of the phrase – an expression of disbelief (v. http://www.phrases.org.uk).

Another example –

... not by a long shot vs. *... not by a long chalk*

There are a few questions that this example raises. Is one phrase better than the other? Is one right and the other wrong? Where did these phrases come from?

One Google source (The Free Dictionary) says that **not by a long shot** is informal and **not by a long chalk** is old-fashioned.

I would say that either would serve and that both are trite and overworked. Well, that may be unfair, since I am the one who brought up the two as examples. The point here is that you can use any word or phrase that you wish; just be sure of your understand of those words and phrases. I like to use overworked phrases as a base for wordplay, since everyone will be familiar with the original and just might chuckle or groan over the damage that I do-do.

Out of site, out of mine; or, whirled peas

Be sure that you quote others correctly, especially Shakespeare, Twain and the Bible. Writers assume that they know their favorite quotes by heart from their favorite sources. These three are my favorites writers that I assume I know by heart.

If you are going by what you assume that you have always heard, look it up. That is how **world peace** becomes **whirled peas**. Tricks of memory and hearing can turn simple idioms into complex, idiosyncratic absurdities. Music lyrics pose this problem. If you pull a quote or idiomatic phrase or snatch of song from memory, take a minute and Google it to be sure you have remembered right.

I was in my 40s, which is by far old enough to know better, when I learned that I was being both inaccurate and misleading when I said that **power corrupts.** The full quotation says that **power tends to corrupt, and absolute power corrupts absolutely.**

The problem is that by leaving out the second half of the quotation, you would be able to claim that power at any level is negative, an assertion that my community organizing trainers were vehement in opposing. Power is what groups of people can generate, so learn how to organize people and money for power, they said, or settle for living out other peoples' values rather than your own.

The entire quotation, from Lord Acton, is this –

"Power tends to corrupt, and absolute power corrupts absolutely. Great men are almost always bad men."

(v. http://www.phrases.org.uk/meanings/absolute-power-corrupts-absolutely.html)

A writer who says **site** when everyone knows the proper word is **sight** will not be taken seriously in many places outside of kindergarten. **Not by a long sight**. At best, you will be praised as one who uses English as a second language surprisingly well (with apologies to those who actually do this so well).

If you assume that the biblical verse **May the Lord watch between thee and me while we are absent one from another** is a blessing, you would be better-served to look up the context (two men – one young and provoked, and one old and devious -- peeing on opposing sides of a fire hydrant to define their territories). Same goes for **your people will be my people**. This wedding liturgy staple draws upon the love of a daughter (Ruth) for her mother-in-law (Naomi). We often ignore such things when we like the sound of the words and do not wish to be bothered by the origin or context.

Three stages of a writer's life

Like children, writers go through phases.

The **infantile** phase fits a writer who could care less about the origins or even the spelling of a phrase. He would not care about the difference between **idiom** and **idiot**, and would be likely to call me a wanker or worse for caring. Since none of us would cop to being infantile, since there is no one here but us chickens, we can just move on to the next stage – adolescence.

An **adolescent** writer feels equal parts of irritation and admiration toward those of older years who understand language, like a sullen teen pretending to ignore a pompous parent.

Adolescent writers sense that there is a world of meaning out there. Writers move on from the adolescent phase when they decide that they want to be one of those who understand language at the deeper levels and begin to do things that move them upward.

The final phase is maturity.

The **mature** writer knows much and is eager to learn more, and to share not only the fun facts but also the deep joy of playing in the fields of the lord's language.

Maturity in general comes through mixing effort and patience with a pinch of time. Although I cannot hasten maturity, I can assist. In my experience, those writers who read a lot also understand language more deeply than those writers who don't have the time or inclination to do much reading. It helps to read books such as this one, and it helps to look up words and phrases that are new to you. However, these are baby steps compared to reading, reading, and more reading.

By reading, I mean reading with an eye toward the craft of the writer. How does she set up her story? How does she treat her characters? What is her attitude toward language and toward the reader? What would you change if you were her editor? What tools can you borrow for your own writing?

Reading will expose you to what you want to know better. Reading for writers is like muscle memory for musicians. Things will just sound right, or wrong.

A writer who does not read much sees little. Small eyes do not take in much. Readers notice.

Show your readers what big eyes you have.

An idiotic exercise?

The writer's task is to anticipate those places in his work where ignorance will rear its ugly head.

Impossible, right?

I will grant you that catching your own mistakes borne of ignorance is at the least a matter of significant difficulty.

But just short of impossible.

When I was a copy editor, and the pressures of press deadlines were not that sharp, in the early hours of the evening after most of the reporters had gone home, I would look up any word that I did not know at least by sight (which, no brag just fact, was rare), words that I suspected were misspelled (usually because they did not look right to me), words or phrases that I assumed that I knew (this is a good place to scratch first, always), and trite phrases (to be sure of spelling and aptness).

In other words, I put myself on a permanent program of improvement so my boss would never feel a need to.

The proper or preferred pronunciation of words is a weak spot for me, so I spend time puzzling out how words should sound as well as puzzling out what words should be asked to say. To know a fun fact but to be afraid to share it out loud for fear of pronouncing a word incorrectly is a vexing thing that is amenable to correction.

A mark of maturity is knowing who you are and what you do poorly. After all, anything worth doing is worth doing poorly.

The challenge is to keep moving.

You will get there if it don't get dark.

In the end, you are the one who will keep your mistakes and your ignorance, those mad dogs, from biting you on the butt.

Jon Rieley-Goddard works and lives in Buffalo, New York, with his wife, Cathy, and their two cats, Bella, and Slava. He is a writer, photographer, and minister.

Before embracing the call of the Word, Jon was man of many words -- a copy editor on daily newspapers for 14 years.

The Mystery Man Murders stands as the first novel in the series titled *Grimoire - the Bros Grim Breakfast Serial - a story in pieces*.

The Double Daily Double Murders is the second book in the series.

The Happy Family Murders is the third book in the series.

Did you find a typo or other *oops*? Email **boldface@baldybooks.com** with the details.

For the latest news on the *Grimoire* series, visit http://JonRieleyGoddard.com